750

46414

D0783588

CHAINS

CHAINS

Baron Moss

Bachman & Turner:
London

Bachman & Turner
5 Plough Place
Fetter Lane
London EC4A ILD

© Baron Moss 1978

All rights reserved. No part of this publication
may be reproduced, stored in a retrieval system
or transmitted in any form or by any means, electronic,
mechanical, photocopying, recording or otherwise, without
the prior permission of the publishers, Bachman & Turner.

ISBN 0 85974 071 4

First published 1978

Typeset by Inforum, Portsmouth.
Printed and bound in England by Chapel River Press, Andover.

This one is for my old man
and, as he would have said,
about bloody time!

The Prisoner

"Who the hell is he?"

Through the spy-hole in the door the two men looked at the crumpled figure lying on his side on the floor of the cell. In the harsh light they could see his face was cut and bruised. The neck of his shirt was torn.

"The files are on the desk. We've been watching him on and off for years. But we never thought he was into anything this big."

"Why on earth did he do it?"

"That's what we want you to find out, Doctor."

"Thanks. It looks as if you've already been trying."

"Just a little."

"Any success?"

"Not much. Nothing we didn't already know really."

"Are you sure there is more?"

"There must be. Look Doctor, we know what he did. That takes guts. Initiative. Technical know-how, and a bloody strong motivation. We want to know what that motivation is. He might have done it all by himself but that's not likely. So we want to know who else is involved."

"How much time have I got?"

"A week. Maybe less. Nobody knows we've got him here yet. But we'll have to tell them soon. And when they know, we're going to be under strong pressure to do something. And quickly. After all, you can't blow up most of the world's political leaders in one big bang and get away with it, can you now?"

"What's the latest news?"

"Seventy five dead. Over two hundred injured. The whole place a shambles."

"Terrible. Terrible. And no indication why?"

7

"Oh, indications, yes. Bits and pieces. But what we want is the whole story."

"You'll be lucky. Well, better let him rest up tomorrow. I'll read those files and we'll start the day after."

"Thanks Doctor. That's fine. We'll look after him tomorrow. Make sure he's feeling fine, and after that he's all yours. Don't forget what we want . . ."

"What's that?"

"The whole story."

PART ONE

One Step Forward

1933 — 1948

Joe

"Dad! Dad! They're here!"

The door burst open and Joe's curly head darted round, his big brown eyes glistening with excitement. "The cart's here Dad, come on!" And then he disappeared.

"Ay, ay! Such excitement!" Samuel Gold smiled at his ten-year-old son's enthusiasm and looked across the room to where his wife was standing by the window.

"They're here Roshka?" he asked.

"They're here."

She did not turn round and her voice sounded tired. She stood there, nervously fingering the old lace curtains.

That's how it was. You live, you work, you save. You have children and bring them up. You collect together a few things to make up a home and then they pack up the whole twenty years in cases and bundles, load them all on to a cart, and move.

Easy for them. What does it mean to them, a home? How much did they . . .

"You want to take the curtains with you?"

Feeling her husband's hand on her shoulder she turned her head up to him and smiled.

"Don't be silly Shmul. Still . . ." She ran her hand along the worn lace-work of the hem, still stiff from the last starching. "They were good curtains. You remember when we bought them?"

He slipped his arms round her ample waist and leaned his chin against the fine black hair that was drawn tightly round to a bun at the back of her head. His eyes followed the pattern of the lace. Did he remember? Weren't they the first lace curtain they had ever bought? "Pure French lace sir," the assistant at the big store had said, looking down his nose at the rather odd couple with their East End accents.

"Is this the best?" Shmul had asked.

That's what he always looked for. The best.

"Remember Shmul, it's got to be the best, you told him."

"And what did he say to me, that snotty-nose?" They laughed as they remembered together.

"We have better sir," she sucked her cheeks in to make her face thin as she mimicked the shop-assistant of fifteen years ago, with his high-class accent and his disdainful manner, "but I'm afraid it's very expensive . . ."

Her eyes sparkled like a young girl's, in anticipation of her husband's reply, remembering how it had rung round the store, startled the assistant, caused the nearby shoppers to look up and smile and made her stomach turn somersaults in an agony of shame and pride.

"Don't be afraid, my boy, I told him, I'm not going to eat you. Here's my money. I want the best you got!"

"Remember. Roshinka, the way he looked. He never seen so much money, the poor *schlemiel.*"

"It was a lot of money, though, even for those days."

"Ah, but it was good stuff . . . look, the best. Still good." He pulled the curtain across and held it out so that they could both see the lace-work pattern, a horn of plenty, spilling out fruits and flowers, with cherubs floating above on each side, their snow-white bottoms now faded, and only here and there an occasional sign of careful sewing together of broken threads. Good stuff.

"Ay, Shmul, Shmul," she sighed, and looked down through the window where Saunder's cart had just drawn up outside the shop. "With you it's always got to be the best. Nothing is good enough. You're not satisfied we got a good home, we worked hard, bought nice curtains, nice things . . ." She turned to look at the heavy, leather-upholstered chairs, their curved legs ending in eagles' talons, each grasping its balled foot; the gleaming mahogany sideboard with oval mirrors and turret shelves, on which the silver candlesticks had stood every day except Friday, when she had taken them down and placed them at the head of the table, on the spotless tablecloth, one on each side of the plaited *cholla* loaf, lit the candles and, joining her raised hands at the fingertips in the way her mother had taught her, praised God for the coming of the Sabbath.

Now, everything was packed and ready to go.

But still she clung to the impossible chance and, patting the lace curtain back into its customary folds as her husband let it drop

11

back, she said, without daring to look at him, "You not satisfied with all this? Got to start moving somewhere better? Who knows what it's like there? Who knows . . ."

He cut her short.

"What's the matter with you? You starting again? Nothing's any good for her . . ." In a second his mood had changed. Too late she realised that she had set him off on one of his uncontrollable fits of temper that had become an almost daily part of their lives for the last five years. His face had become flushed with anger and the veins at his temple throbbed as he launched into a tirade against her.

"Whatever you do for her is no good. How many years I worked? Twenty years! Twenty years, night and day, in that damn, bleddy shop . . ." He stamped his foot violently on the floor, making the whole room shake and causing the electric light bulb in the shop below to dance and swing on the thin wire that joined it to the ceiling.

"What for? For her! Working and saving . . . twenty years for nothing. What's the good of giving her anything better? Does she know anything better . . .?" With each tormented twist another nerve-end seemed to snap.

His wife stood helpless, pressed against the window, her eyes closed, fighting back the tears. There was nothing she could do with these sudden rages, except to try to avoid them and to stop the children upsetting him.

They didn't understand. Just as she had not understood at first. Now she had grown used to it as you grow used to living at the foot of a volcano, planting your seeds each year in its good fertile soil, looking up suddenly at the warning rumble, the angry glow, wondering if this time it would be the end.

So she waited for the slight lessening of the pitch that always marked the turning point. Only keep the children away from him when he was like this. Especially little Joe, with his *chutzpa*, the cheek of a dozen monkeys, sometimes seeming to provoke his father deliberately, always wanting to have the last word.

When Shmul had one of his tempers trying to put in your own words was like throwing petrol onto the fire.

Her heart jumped as she heard Joe running up the stairs, three at a time, shouting "Come on Dad, they're ready!" She started towards the door to stop him but it was too late. Before she could get half way across the room he was in.

Standing there with his thin little legs spread wide, his hands on his hips, his usually sallow face now aglow with excitement, Joe

12

looked from one to the other, sensing the tension, catching his mother's warning look.

Careful, Joe. Careful.

"Come on you two," he said. "No time for your silly rows now. The cart's here and they're ready to move."

He took two steps towards his father and took hold of his waistcoat and pulled at it eagerly. "Come on misery, it was your idea to move, wasn't it? If you don't hurry up it'll be too late and we'll have to start unpacking everything and you'll have to stay in this 'damn bleddy shop' all your life."

He stamped on the living room floor as he had seen his father do so many times over these last years when the little corner shop, once the symbol of his success, had become the millstone holding him back from bigger things.

He tugged again at the waistcoat, looking straight at his father, ready to meet his eyes if he should lower his head. Ready, too, to duck out of the way and run like mad if necessary. His mother raised her hand to her breast to hold down the fluttering heart that threatened to choke her. She wanted to fling herself between her husband and the boy, but daren't move.

The little fool, the *lobus*, he'd get such a hiding . . .

Her husband took in a deep breath, seeming to fill every part of his body with air, and dropped his bloodshot eyes to the little hand that tugged at his waistcoat. As he did so his hand grasped the boy's, his grip tightening on his son's fingers as he searched the boy's face, seeing there a defiance in the mouth, so like his own, that he was forced to smile.

With a great sigh the father transferred his grip from the boy's aching hand to his shoulder.

"All right, you *momser,* you. We're coming."

The mother's eyes closed as she silently suppressed a sigh of relief. The boy grinned from ear to ear.

It had worked!

Suddenly the grip on his shoulder relaxed and a heavy push sent him sprawling towards the door.

"*Nu,* what are you waiting for? Why aren't you downstairs helping?

"And you Mrs. Gold," he shouted over his shoulder as he strode through the door, "if you want to take those curtains better pack them up now — we're moving!"

The moving of the Golds was quite an event for Sandle Street.

For twenty years they had occupied the rooms above their corner bakery shop, supplying the surrounding neighbourhood with fresh warm bread straight from the basement bakehouse.

In winter the local kids loved to stand on the pavement outside the shop, their feet warmed by the ovens below, their eyes fascinated by the fairy-tale assortment of fancy cakes and marzipan figures in the window. For this was Shmul's speciality. The icing tool was his brush, the cake his canvas. He would sit for hours in the little room behind the shop putting the finishing touches to a wedding cake, which, displayed in the shop window for the week before the wedding, was as essential as putting up the banns or the announcement in the 'Social and Personal' column of the *Jewish Chronicle*.

The sickly-sweet smell of fresh-baked bread, seeping up through the floorboards, had woken husband and wife every working day since the business had expanded enough for them to employ a night baker. It had mingled with the smell of new-born babies at each of Roshka's three confinements and had succumbed only to the all-embracing smells of her kitchen. The *chulndt,* simmering over Friday night so that she didn't have to light the stove on the Sabbath, the *lockshun* soup, the *blintses* and, yes, even the *strudel* and cheesecake. ("I don't care what you say, Shmul, I'm not having shop cakes in my house, even if they are from my own shop.")

Now it was finished. Anyway for the Golds.

Another baker was taking over the shop, but not the old-fashioned bakehouse. The Sandle Street shop would merely be one of his branches, supplied from the modern central bakery in Whitechapel.

For Rose, as her neighbours called her, and Samuel Gold, as it was written down on his Naturalisation Certificate, it was the end of the old life and the beginning of the new. For the neighbourhood, too, that Sunday morning foreshadowed the end of an epoch and the ushering in of a new age when a shop was no longer a social centre where the local craftsman made and displayed his work, where you picked up a loaf of bread to test its crispness between your fingers, smelt the fresh yeast and felt its warmth against your cheeks.

Soon their bread would come in vans, already cut in unvarying slices and wrapped in greaseproof paper flaunting the slogan, 'Untouched by human hand!' When Shmul had first heard of this he had turned to his informant in amazement, stretching out his hands still white with flour, the criss-cross lines on his upturned

14

palms like footpaths in a snowy landscape.

"Not touched by human hands? That's *good*? That's something to be proud of? Is something wrong with human hands then? Look ..." He stretched across to pick up a golden brown loaf, the diagonal cuts along the crust shining a lighter shade, the white, softest underpart giving way to his fingers.

"Look at this," he said, "This is what you call bread. When they make this without human hands I'll sell my shop."

Now he had sold his shop. An opportunity had arisen that he wasn't going to miss.

For five years he had been supplying cakes and confectionery to Hyman Bender, the caterer. It had always annoyed him to have to put his handiwork into Bender's little corrugated paper pastry trays, but the orders had been substantial, the money had been good and he had found it useful, for weekend weddings and receptions, to be able to dispose of the odd pastries left over from the previous week in the shop.

But always, at the back of his mind, as he sat late into the night finishing off batches of pastries, cutting glacé cherries into quarters, one for the centre of each fondant-covered cube, he thought of the day when he would go up to old Bender and say, "*Nu* Hymie, you're getting on. It's time you retired and had a rest. How much you want for all this?"

He imagined himself casually waving his arm to include the large, mirror-walled restaurant that was crowded each day with East End businessmen, the clean, congested kitchens, and, above all, the ornate carved staircase, flanked by potted palms that led to the great ballroom and reception rooms on the first floor.

"The Arcadia Ballroom" (Proprietor: H. Bender, certified by the Chief Rabbi and the *Beth Din*) had become the hallmark of respectability for every Jewish wedding in East London, and the guarantee of success for the hundreds of functions sponsored by local organisations, ranging from the Annual Dance of the Jewish Lads Brigade to the Christmas Party of the Convent of the Sacred Heart, whose hiring contract always included the use of Mr. Bender's shiny top hat for the Master of Ceremonies.

But it had not come about the way Shmul had planned it. Old Bender, pillar of the local synagogue, had died of a heart attack just six weeks ago, following on a heated argument with the other members of the *shool* committee about whether an appeal for funds for the synagogue extension should be made from the pulpit on the Sabbath. He had left a widow and three married daughters who had their own lives to lead in Stamford Hill and Golders

Green and who were not the slightest bit interested in the East End and its catering facilities.

After the funeral, having buried all the old man's faults and exaggerated his many virtues, the three sons-in-law took Shmul to one side and offered him the business. Cutting short his protests that this was not the time nor place for such things they assured him that there was no time like the present. Did he expect them to spend their valuable time coming down to the East End in the next few months to discuss it? They all knew he was the best friend of their dear father-in-law, (*oleh basholem*, may he rest in peace), and for their part they were not interested in the money so long as their dear mother-in-law had enough to spend the rest of her life in comfort, she should live to a hundred and twenty years!

It was settled then and there, but Shmul didn't tell his wife until a week later, when the *shiva*, the seven days of mourning, was over and he had had time to realise what it all meant and make his plans accordingly. Like a schoolboy preparing for a test he ran through all the questions she would ask him ("What do *you* know about ballrooms? Where are you going to get the money? Where are we going to live . . ?") and rehearsed his answers in advance. But some of the answers weren't so easy to find. What *did* he know about ballrooms? Listen, if that old *schlemiel* Bender, *oleh basholem*, could run a ballroom, so could he! And hadn't he saved for years for this, working and slaving in that damn, bleddy shop . . . Ay, wait, wait already! Don't work yourself up just thinking about the argument. Wait till she starts.

But she didn't start. There was no argument. The opposition had been hesitant and shortlived, her cautious reasoning overcome by pride in her husband's ambition and confidence that he would always get what he wanted.

The best. He always had to have the best.

So now she followed him downstairs to see that everything was put into the cart, leaving behind her lace curtains through which a lone sunbeam slipped down to caress the faded buttocks of the cherubin.

* * * *

As they walked through the empty shop they could see that the work had already commenced. Much of the heavier furniture had been moved down to the ground floor yesterday in readiness for Saunders' men who wanted to get the job over quickly and get back to their Sunday dinner.

They were only doing it as a favour really. A favour to their guv'nor, Alf Saunders, the greengrocer, neighbour to the Golds for every one of their twenty years in Sandle Street, and as a favour to Sam Gold himself, reckoned by most Gentiles in that half-Jewish, half-Gentile neighbourhood to be "one of the good Jews."

The friendship between the cocky, cockney Saunders and the quick-tempered, open-hearted Jew dated back to the early days of the 1914-18 war, when, thrown together by similar problems, they had found that they were the same kind of people, differing only in background, religion and accent, although who was nearer to the 'King's English' of the time it would be difficult to say.

Alf had at first made fun of the heavy Russian-Yiddish accent, but when he saw his neighbour at work, saw the pride he took in turning out a good loaf of bread or a handsomely decorated cake, and began to share with him the problems of war-time dangers, bringing his wife and three children down to their bakehouse to shelter from the Zeppelin raids, he developed a respect for the Jew which was soon shared by the whole neighbourhood.

"Gold's all right," they would say, "not bad for a Jew."

And now they knew that he was going, they gathered at the street corner and stood on their doorsteps to watch the cart being loaded.

"Got a few good things there, ain't they?"

"Trust a Jew-boy. They look after themselves all right."

"Course they do. Still, he's not a bad 'un."

"Oh, he's not bad. Mind you, they've done themselves proud. Must 'ave made tons o' money out o' that shop. They say he's bought up them ballrooms down the Mile End Road."

"What, the Arcadia? No wonder he's called Gold. Look at that sideboard. Must be worth a few quid . . ."

Little Joe ran up and down giving orders to everyone. "Here's the next thing, this cupboard. Mind the door, be careful . . ." until one of the men gave him a friendly clout on the back of the head, saying, "Shut yer mouth, young Joe, or I'll put yer old man onto yer."

After that Joe stood on his dignity and showed off in front of the other kids by feeding sugar lumps to the two big cart-horses, stretching out his hand to them cautiously in much the same way as he had to his father earlier that morning, ready to fly if they opened their mouths too wide.

Joe's two elder sisters, Sadie and Hetty, quietly helped their

17

mother to get all the linen and bedclothes squeezed into the cart. They worked steadily, except for an occasional push for Joe whenever he got in their way, and a shy, reserved smile for the men as they lifted their bundles onto the cart.

This whole business of moving was embarrassing to them. Laying bare their household possessions to the whole neighbourhood, their tables and chairs, their beds, even their sheets, they felt to be somehow indecent and each time they handed up one of their bundles they turned quickly back into the doorway of the shop, heads down, not talking to anybody.

But soon all was ready.

The shop was emptied, except for a few precious parcels, including a black tin box, that Shmul wanted to have with him in the car he had hired to take the family and which, at that moment, drove round the corner and stopped behind the cart.

It was a big black Daimler of the type always used for Jewish weddings and funerals and it caused quite a stir among the crowd now gathered on the pavements. It was much too big, specially as Joe had already perched himself on the driver's seat of the cart and wouldn't come down, and when Rose saw it she looked up at her husband and said with just a trace of sarcasm, "The best?"

"The best," he replied, without a flicker of a smile, and reached for his overcoat which was lying across the marble top of the shop counter.

He swept a few stray breadcrumbs off the counter onto the floor and struggled into his coat, assisted by his wife.

Shmul looked around the "damn bleddy shop", the empty shelves, the glass showcases, the big coloured calendar from the firm of flour millers.

He went up to the calendar and tore off the date.

"See this Roshinka," he said, handing it to his wife, "keep it for a remembrance. It's a big day."

Rose looked at the date through her tears.

It was the 29th of January, 1933.

The following day, as Samuel Gold was getting down to his new business Adolph Hitler was appointed Chancellor of Germany, the Reichstag was dissolved and thousands of Storm Troopers and Hitler Youth jubilantly paraded through the Wilhelmplatz singing the Horst Wessel song.

A Storm Trooper was shot dead by the Communists in a street battle.

18

The shot was not heard as far away as the Mile End Road.

* * * *

"Where's Joe? Not in yet?"

As Shmul came into the living room he looked around at the family. His wife was sewing at the table, and as she screwed up her eyes to thread a needle he saw how closely she resembled her mother, who had died only a year ago.

The girls were listening to a play on the radio. Sadie in the armchair, her legs curled up underneath her, Hetty on the floor, close to the set. At their father's question Sadie put her fingers to her lips and Hetty, grimacing in annoyance, put one ear right up against the loudspeaker, placing a hand over the other to keep out all interruptions.

"Don't shoosh me, my girl!" Shmul immediately bristled up, and at the tone of his voice his wife put down her sewing and threw a warning look at her daughters.

"Joe's gone to the pictures," she said.

"That I know already. But he should be back by now. He went off straight after tea. It's already nine o'clock and he ought to be home. Where's he gone?"

"I should know where he's gone?" His wife smiled. "My children don't tell me anything. Only 'Give me money, Mum, I'm going to the pictures,' Who with, what pictures, what you going to see, such things they don't tell me. It's none of my business." She nodded her head slowly and looked up over the rims of her glasses at her two girls. Fine girls, good girls, both of them, but somehow not her girls any longer.

Sadie, at eighteen, was now working in the restaurant. It had been decided that she would go into the business as soon as they had moved, and now, after three years, she knew all there was to know and was very popular with the lunch-time customers, sho called her 'the little *balaboosta*', the lady of the house, a title which Sadie preferred to translate into the more formal manageress.

Hetty, who would be fifteen next week, was still at school and would be sitting for her Matriculation the following summer. She was very different in temperament from her sister, although both girls had that Eastern Jewish beauty which glows from almond shaped eyes of deepest brown, set in peach-soft skins framed with thick black hair.

The older sister was already acquiring a womanly plumpness. She used very little make-up and wore her hair long, in a plait, that she curled round the top of her head revealing the gentle hollow at the back of her neck. Her eyebrows were carefully but not drastically plucked and were the subject of most searching scrutiny in her bedroom mirror every night. The almost imperceptible upwards-pencilled end of each brow emphasised still more the oriental appearance which, in a less business like, bustling person may have seemed exotic, but in Sadie seemed not out of place.

She needed no rouge, for alone of the three children she had inherited her mother's fresh, rosy cheeks, and only on her lips did she apply, and this with infinite care, the dark carmine shades which suited her so well. She dressed neatly, as becomes a young businesswoman, and, every day, insisted on a fresh, spotlessly white overall for her work in the restaurant. Even though she would not serve a customer herself, or move one knife or fork to a new position on the white starched tablecloths, she refused to enter the restaurant without her fresh overall. "It sets the tone, Dad," she explained patiently to her father. "Anyway," she added, in a take-it-or-leave-it-manner, "if you want me to be in the restaurant that's my conditions. If you don't want it I'll go and work somewhere else."

"Conditions, *noch*! What's come over these children today? You work for them all your life . . feed them . . bring them up . ."

But Sadie got her fresh, white overalls and the restaurant got 'tone'.

Despite that, the customers didn't seem to mind, and Shmul almost admitted he was pleased when an old friend nudged him, as Sadie went past their table, and said, "A fine girl, your Sadie. A real *balaboosta*. Spotless clean she keeps everything. A *machaya*, a pleasure to look at her."

With Hetty it was different. True, she was still a schoolgirl, but she seemed to take her school so seriously. When she came home for tea she would sit down at the table with a book propped up in front of her, replying only in monosyllables to her mother's questions. Shakespeare, Beethoven, Shelley, were names her parents had never heard of, and she found little interest in their conversations. The ballroom, the ladies guild meetings at the synagogue, Cousin Ada's baby — who cared about such things? And that ridiculous accent of theirs. After all, they had been in the country now for thirty years, it was time they could speak the language properly! Mother couldn't write a word of English and Dad couldn't do more than sign his name. Probably wouldn't even have learned that if he hadn't had to for his Naturalisation.

It was positively embarrassing, when one brought one's non-Jewish friends in, to hear the way one's mother talked. As for father. You couldn't tell him anything! Just try to correct his pronounciation and you'd get such a look . . .

"Don't you start teaching me, my girl! I don't want no lessons from little *shnips* like you! You're going to school to learn, so better learn how to talk to your father and mother."

"But, father . . ."

"No buts! I don't want to know! Finished your homework already? Then go help to do the washing up and let your mother sit down and rest a little. Such children . . . such lessons they get at school. Her mother and father should slave for her all day and night so that she can come along and teach them how to blow their noses!"

Since moving to Mile End Road the two girls had no need to share a bedroom and this, coupled with the fact that Sadie had 'gone out into the world' while Hetty was still at school, had caused them to drift apart. Sadie was now an adult, living a life which, while not entirely independent of her parents, put her on an almost equal footing because they were partially dependent upon her. Outside of the business her main interest centred around David Fine, the handsome young secretary of the Zionist Youth Organisation to which she belonged.

They saw a lot of each other, both inside and outside the club, and when she was not with David she was thinking about him and thus life for Sadie was fine.

Hetty despised boys. So fas as she could judge from her own unfortunate experiences their sole interest was to get their hands up under her skirt. Three times that had happened, twice with Jewish boys and once with a Gentile. They were all the same and in each case, once in the pictures, once in Victoria Park and once at a Christmas party, the boy had received a resounding smack on the face and Hetty had strode away straightening her skirt. The Gentile had called her 'a lousy little Jew-girl'; one of the Jewish boys had called her a 'stuck-up *shikser*' and the other was so astonished he couldn't think of anything to call her.

One boy that both sisters were agreed upon was their brother Joe. He was a menace.

He had been bad enough before, but since his *barmitzvah* in the summer when he had stood up in the synagogue to sing his portion of the law, followed by the big reception his father had given for him in the ballroom, there was no holding him.

21

He was interested in everything — for five minutes! He would run off to the public library and come back with an armful of books, H.G. Wells, Agatha Christie, Rider Haggard, H.G. Henty, fling himself into an armchair and read through them solidly ignoring all conversation, visitors or meals until his father took a hand.

Saturday afternoons he would tell his mother he was going for a walk with a friend — which was true. But the friend had Joe's football boots in a parcel that had been left at school the day before and the walk they took was to Mile End Station where the School Junior XI was assembling before departing for the weekend match. If his parents had found out he was travelling by train on the Sabbath — and playing football — *Ay!*

Then he bought a mouse. A tame one, golden brown. He kept it in a drawer in his bedroom and, during the Passover festival, fed it on *Matzos*. The mouse survived the *Matzos* but not the discovery by Joe's mother when she went to put some clean shirts in the drawer.

So the mouse went . . . to be followed by tadpoles.

"Mum, can I have a bowl or something?"

"Sure, what for?"

"To put water in, Mum."

"Natural! What am I, *meshigah*? But what's the water for, boy-chick?"

"Tadpoles, Mum. At school they got lots of tadpoles and they want us all to take some home to watch them grow."

"What is this — tadpoles? It's a plant? An animal? What is it?"

"Little fish, Mum. Ever so small. Can't make a mess or anything 'cos they stay in the bowl. You got a bowl?"

"Wait a minute, Joe," here his mother turned to him, seriously, "These tadpoles, they're *kosher*?"

Undaunted, Joe confirmed that they were hundred per cent *kosher*, the bowl was produced and next day the tadpoles were moved in.

Father didn't lower himself to look at such things. ("A zoo now, they want to make of the house! Mice, fish . . . next thing they'll be bringing an elephant . . .") Sadie smiled condescendingly and thought she would tell David about them. Hetty approved of the study of biology and contributed a sea-shell, collected on their last holiday, towards the tadpoles' home comforts, and the mother affected interest when her husband was not present and indifference when he was. One afternoon when she had the house to herself she sat in front of the bowl for twenty minutes watching the tiny black dots wriggle themselves from one side of the bowl to the other. "Tedpoles, *noch*," she whispered to herself "It's a wonderful world . . ."

How wonderful it was, she only found out when the tadpoles sprouted legs and jumped out of the bowl onto the polished surface of her sideboard where they had the place of honour. From the sideboard to the drawing-room floor was but one more step in the great forward march of evolution that took the tiny frogs from kitchen to bedroom, from bathroom to lavatory and even downstairs to the ballroom.

But that was going too far!

"What is happening here? It's not enough they turn my house into a zoo, but frogs I got to have in the ballroom? Where are we, the Mile End Road or Hackney Marshes? Perhaps I should open up a special restaurant for frogs, eh? Phone up, Sadie, phone up the *Beth Din* to get a special certificate . . . Golds Restaurant, kosher for frogs . . ." Shmul stormed about the flat looking for the boy. But he had taken a lesson from his froggy friends and disappeared.

That was all months ago and tonight there was anxiety in Shmul's voice as he enquired of his son's whereabouts. It was late. Joe should have been home an hour ago. With all his faults he was not the sort to worry his parents like this. He could have met with an accident, the Mile End Road was always full of traffic. If he had gone to the Empire that was all right, it was on the same side of the road as the restaurant, but if it was the La Bohemè, or the Palladium, he'd have to cross the road, and for the Troxy, the new luxury cinema in the Commercial Road, he'd have to go a long way . . .

The door-bell rang.

Mother and father looked up at each other across the table. "Hetty", Shmul said, "run down and open the door."

"Oh Dad," the girl protested, "I'm listening to . . ."

"HETTY! OPEN — QUICK — THE DOOR!"

Each word snapped out separately like the lash of a whip. The last word, accompanied by a quick jerk of her father's head towards the drawing room door which led down to the street door by a narrow flight of stairs, left no room for arguments.

In a fit of temper Hetty switched off the wireless and flounced out of the room. The sudden silence, broken only by retreating footsteps petulantly stamping downstairs, seemed to bring a chill into the room, taking the parents back to their own childhood in Tsarist Russia, and as the mother felt the cold fingers of memory grasping at her stomach, she cried out, "Shmul, you don't think . . ."

"It's all right Roshka . . . he's coming."

A wave of relief passed over her as she heard her son climbing the stairs, climbing unusually slowly for him. His hand rested on the doorknob, half-turned it, then stopped.

The door opened and he came in.

"Joey, my boy! What happened?"

Joe stood holding the door, blood streaming from a cut in his forehead, one eye horribly bruised, his jacket torn at the shoulders. His face was distorted by the effort to keep himself under control but at the sound of his mother's voice it all snapped and he took three faltering steps into the room, sank to his knees, buried his face in his father's lap and wept without control and without end.

"Joey, my son, my boy! Tell me what happened."

His mother was on her knees beside him, circling him with her arm, smoothing back the hair that stuck, clotted with blood, to his forehead.

Shmul put his hand on the boy's shoulder, felt the bare warm skin through the great tear in the shirt and raised his eyes to meet his wife's. Gently he eased his hand under Joe's chin and lifted the boy's face up to the light. The tears mixed with blood in red streams that ran down his cheek. The bruise now seemed to cover the whole of one side of his young face, completely closing the eye. His father bent down to kiss him first on his lips, then on his cheek. When he raised his face his own lips were smeared with his son's blood.

"Don't cry now, boychick, don't cry," he said as the tears started to well up into his own eyes.

"Come on my *Barmitzvah* boy, you're a man now, not a little boy any longer. Tell me, Joe, who did this to you?"

The boy struggled for breath through his tears and pain.

He shook his head from side to side and clutched the lapels of his father's coat as he shouted "They did it — they did it! To me and Barney Cohen — me and Barney. They did it."

Quietly, almost inaudibly, because he knew the answer and was afraid to hear it, knowing it would tumble his world to pieces, his father asked, "Who, son? Who's they?"

In another burst of crying the boy flung himself into his father's arms.

"The Blackshirts," he sobbed, "the Blackshirts."

* * * *

"Don't be silly, Gold, you're talking like a Communist!"

"Who's a Communist?" Schmul glared across the table at Finestein, warden of the synagogue. "You seen what they did to my boy, those bastard Blackshirts? And Cohen's boy? And you sit there and say we can't do anything about it? Fine Jew you are. A fine leader of the community. You make me sick."

"Don't start working yourself up, Gold," interposed the quiet voice of Sam Drayton, one of the younger members of the synagogue committee which had gathered in the committee room that evening to discuss what action it should take about the latest fascist announcement — a march through the streets of East London the following Sunday, October 4th.

"You know I've been up to see your Joey," Sam continued, "and I feel just as bad as you do about all this. We're all worried about these hooligans, who wouldn't be? And it doesn't do any good," he said, turning now to Finestein, "calling each other names, especially as it seems the Communists are our only friends at the moment."

"Communists our friends? That'll be the day." Finestein laughed as he thought of the way the Communists had brought the workers out on strike at his little tailoring factory only three months ago. "I tell you they're only trouble-makers. Sure they fight the Blackshirts. Why? Because they love us? A *nachtige toog*! Like night is day, they love us! Because they want to stir up trouble, that's why. I know them, take it from me." He leaned back in his chair and looked round the table at the ten other members of the committee.

Next to him were the other wardens; Goldman the oil shop-keeper, with his usual two-day growth of grey stubble, and Harris, the furniture manufacturer. The first, one of the original founders of the synagogue, elected for his piety and his long associations with the community, the second, for his generous donations towards the synagogue funds. Next to them sat Gold, also a founder member of the synagogue and one of the most enthusiastic organisers they had ever had, to say nothing of the value of the Arcadia ballroom given free of charge, for all synagogue functions.

Then young Drayton, the solicitor, who had followed in his father's footsteps by taking over his flourishing legal practice,

25

and also his membership of the *shool* committee. Drayton, whose father's name had been Dreher, was the only British-born member of the committee and had been elected that year as the result of the younger members of the synagogue running a campaign for 'new blood'. The other committee members were all between forty-five and seventy-five, having arrived in Britain from Russia, Poland, Lithuania and other parts of Eastern Europe at the turn of the century.

Typical of these was Myer Greenfield, a fifty-one year old Pole sitting next to Drayton. He had arrived in London, penniless, without any knowledge of the English language, thirty-five years ago and now owned sixteen dress shops in different parts of the metropolis.

Hyman Shechter, seated on his left, was fat, rosy-cheeked and completely bald. For that reason perhaps he had never been seen without his bowler hat on. He occupied an important position in the community as a *Kosher* butcher, and his shop was as full of laughs and jokes as it always seemed empty of meat. Every customer was greeted by name and held a mysterious whispered consultation beneath the brim of the bowler followed by further whispered instructions from Shechter to his assistant. Nobody knew what anybody else was getting — or paying — and rich and poor alike, everybody preferred it that way, especially Hyman Shechter who, although no East End Robin Hood, was enabled thus to add a shilling to the rich man's chicken and take off, perhaps sixpence, from the poor man's *kishka*.

At this moment the brim of the bowler hat sheltered a whispered aside to the skull-capped head of Rev. Eisenstein, the *chazan* or cantor. Obviously the story was not fit for the ears of the rest of the committee for the *chazan's* mouth curled up in a smile and his twinkling eyes went up, just as they did on Sabbath mornings in the synagogue, when in full voice he lifted up his eyes to God, pausing on the way for a surreptitious survey of the ladies' gallery.

"Mr. Drayton is right, this is no time for calling names," came the quiet voice of the last remaining member of the committee. "Also Mr. Shechter," and here the voice took on the tone of authority, "It's no time for your jokes." It was '*the Rov,*' Rabbi Aaron Hirschfield, sad-eyed, grey-bearded leader of the community. His arms rested before him on the table, his long thin fingers gently tapping the polished surface.

"My friends," he went on, starting in the same way that he started his sermons, or when he spoke at weddings or funerals, "this is a serious matter for us. Next Sunday these . . ." he looked up and, in searching for the word his eyes met Gold's, ". . . these swine, hooligans, Blackshirts, Fascists, call them what you like, are going to march through Whitechapel, they say. What for? Because its the quickest way to their meeting in Victoria Park? No, because they want trouble. They are the trouble-makers."

Without looking up he put his hand on Finestein's arm, as one would when explaining something to a child. His finger tapped up and down on Finestein's wrist to emphasise his points as he went on. "That's the first thing we must realise. They are the ones who want to provoke trouble. They want blood. What for? I'll tell you what for. They've got nothing else to give. That's what for. What is a Fascist, eh? It's something new? We didn't see them in Russia?" He raised his hands and looked round the table. "He's nothing new. He's nothing more than a man. Yes, like us. He's not satisfied, he's got trouble perhaps. No work, bad wages, competition in business, who knows? There's enough trouble these days for everyone to have a good share. *Nu*? So what then? So comes a Mosley, a Hitler, a Franco, makes no difference, and says to them 'You got trouble? It's the Jews to blame'. They go to the poor people and they say 'See that Jew Finestein, he's got plenty of money, they're all the same these Jews . . . capitalists'. Then, Finestein," here he leaned over towards his neighbour, "they go perhaps to the business people and say to them, 'You got trouble? It's those Jew Communists that are to blame'. Jew Capitalists, Jew Communists, what matters who you blame so long as it's the Jews. One minute," he put his hand once again on Finestein's arm to check an interruption, "let me finish, please.

"That doesn't mean the Communists are right. They fight the Fascists, sure. They're the only ones that do, sure. Why do they fight the Fascists? For their own reasons, not our reasons. I was talking last night with Abe Stern . . ." They all looked up at this and Harris said "Stern, the Communist?"

"Yes, Stern the Communist. He came round to see me."

"What did he want? He's got a nerve."

"Sure he's got a nerve. It takes a nerve for a Jew, a Communist, to get up on a soap box, in Bethnal Green every week in the middle of all the Fascists and say that the Fascists are no good. Yes, he's got a nerve. So he plucked up his courage," here Rabbi Hirshfield smiled at his joke, "and came to see the Rabbi. What for? To tell me that the Communists are going to stop Mosley next Sunday and . . ." he paused here and looked up, his sad eyes questioning each one of them in turn, "to ask me to call on my

27

congregation to support them."

"So we should!" "Rubbish!" "Join the Communists? I'd sooner be dead!" "You may well be!" A babel of voices broke out after the Rabbi's announcement and it took several minutes before the meeting was restored to order, while, all the time the Rabbi stared at the table in front of him.

"*Nu*, Rabbi, and what did you say?" asked Goldman, the oil shop-keeper, nearest to him in age, experience and knowledge of the Torah.

"I listened to him Goldman, and he told me about Fascism. Some things I knew already, some things I didn't know. And he told me about the Communists and why they fight the Fascists — and also why they fight the capitalists, because they believe that one is part of the other. And some of it made sense to me and some of it didn't. And he told me what they're going to do on Sunday and I tell you my friends there will be terrible things on Sunday, there will be fighting and smashing of heads and breaking and tearing apart on Sunday in the East End." He paused and his head sank on his chest, "But I don't think the Fascists will march through Whitechapel."

"And you Rabbi," insisted Goldman, "you told him what?"

With head still sunk on his chest and eyes fixed on his fingers now lying flat on the table, the Rabbi sighed and said "I told him no."

"You're wrong Rabbi," cried Drayton. "Why did you say no?"

The Rabbi looked up at him, and leaning across the table, reached out a hand towards him.

"Why did I say it? Because I'm a Jew, and I'm living here on sufferance that's why. I've been thrown out of one country and I don't want it to happen again, that's why. And if people spit on me I'm not going to make a fuss and draw attention to it. And if they call me names I'm going to ignore them and take no notice. And if they want to march I'm not going to stop them. I'm not going to make a whole business about it so that the Government should say 'These Jews are nothing but trouble, let's get rid of them,' and if they . . ."

"And if they get hold of your son, Rabbi?" Gold interrupted the Rabbi's impassioned flow, "and open up his forehead with brass knuckles, and knock in his face with a rubber pipe, and tear his clothes off his back, and kick him in the testicles and pull out his hair . . . a boy of thirteen, a *Barmitzvah* boy, Rabbi, then what will you do? Why didn't you tell all that to my Joey last week

28

when you came up to see him, eh? Why didn't you make for him another *Barmitzvah* speech like you made him in *shool*? 'My dear *Barmitzvah*, today, according to Jewish law you have become a man.' That's how it always starts, eh Rabbi? But go on, carry on now with your *Barmitzvah* speech. 'Today you have become a man, so when they spit on you, be quiet, when they call you names, lie still, when they march, stay at home, when they beat you up, ignore them, when they smash your shop window, take no notice and when they kill you?" He paused, and into the silence that filled the little room he threw his last two words. "You die!"

When he finished nobody had anything more to say. The Rabbi's fingers no longer tapped the table. Gold rose to his feet, breathing heavily, his face red but now calm and controlled.

"I also had a talk with Stern last night Rabbi," he said, "I told him what I think of the Russians. My whole family was killed in their damn bleddy revolution. He said it wasn't the Communists and maybe it wasn't. I don't know, I don't care. But I hate Russia for what it did to me and my family before the revolution and I'll always hate Russia, Communists or no Communists. But if you think I'm going to sit here like a *schlemiel* and let it happen here what they did to us Jews in Russia, or what they are doing now in Germany, you must be *meshuga,* stark raving mad, all of you."

"What did you tell him, Shmul?"

"What did I tell him?" said Gold as he made his way to the door, "I told him he could have any help he wanted from me to fight these Blackshirt bastards, and" as he aimed his parting shot Shmul looked round at the committee with a scornful smile on his face, "I gave him the Arcadia Ballroom free of charge next Sunday night for a victory celebration."

* * * *

It was a bright, sunny morning, very mild for October, despite the wind that swept the leaves along the gutters outside the grim sooty walls of the London Hospital.

Joe looked up at the hospital's big clock and he hurried along the broad pavement of Whitechapel Road, hoping he wouldn't be too late, wondering what his parent would say when they found he had slipped out of the house.

Nearly half past eleven and already there was an air of battle over the East End. Loudspeakers had been touring the borough since early that morning calling the people out to Gardiner's

29

Corner at one o'clock.

The Fascists' demonstration was to start from here at two o'clock. They planned to march from Gardiner's Corner, the nerve centre of the Jewish East End, through the Commercial Road, with its sprawl of side streets and alley ways of Jewish tenements, sweat-shops, businesses and slums, almost until they reached the docks and then turn North again to Victoria Park where the swans picked their way anxiously through the shallows of the lake aware only of the approach of winter.

Already crowds of people were on their way westwards along the Whitechapel Road to Gardiner's Corner.

From every wall the whitewashed messages called out THEY SHALL NOT PASS, and at the junction of New Road, four foot long letters scrawled right across the road MOSLEY MEANS MASS MURDER! Joe stood on the curb and put his head on one side to read the slogan. His eye was completely better now but he still had a long red scar on his forehead.

"Come on there son. You don't want to be hanging around here. You get off home." Joe looked up into the eyes of the policeman.

"I was only looking at that" Joe protested, "nothing wrong with that, is there?"

"Never mind that. I don't want any sauce from you. You just get off home."

For once Joe thought it better not to answer back and hurried across the New Road in the direction of Aldgate.

As he reached the other side of the road he heard shouts behind him and looked back to see a Black Maria drive up to the corner and several helmeted policemen step out and take up positions across the road. Suddenly the place was full of police and Joe pulled himself up the metal railings locked across the front door of a sweet-shop to see what was going on.

Over the helmets of the police he could see a Union Jack waving in the wind behind a banner which he couldn't make out. They were coming up the road, whoever they were, towards the police cordon, now reinforced and stretching two-deep right across the Whitechapel Road. The clink of spurs and the clatter of horses' hooves brought Joe's head round again. Coming towards him, from Aldgate were a group of mounted police, bunched together, standing up in their stirrups to see over the heads of the line of police ahead of them.

Now the Union Jack had reached the cordon. Joe could read the words on the banner: British Legion. The medals on the chests of the leaders glinted in the pale sunshine as they argued with the police. While they were arguing the mounted police passed through the cordon towards the marchers, members of the Jewish Ex-Service Men's Assocation, who were now breaking their ranks to gather round their leaders and listen to the argument.

"Break it up there . . . break it up."

The horses nosed gently into the crowd.

With delicate mincing steps, the highly trained beasts pushed their way into the people, their tails brushing the marchers' faces, their hooves clanging down perilously close to the freshly polished boots, their glossy flanks swinging round to manoeuvre the body of the marchers away from their leaders.

Crowds were now gathering on all sides. At the fringes of the cordon the police were getting pushed around by the crowd on the pavement.

Another black van drew up with more reinforcements.

There was a sudden swelling of noise in the centre of the crowd.

Joe saw a horse rear up on its hind legs. The banner was pulled down by the police. The reinforcements began to clear the crowds from the pavement. Amid boos and cat-calls Joe saw them rip the cloth to pieces and one red-faced policeman broke the poles across his knee and flung the pieces in the gutter.

"Get down off there!"

A hand pulled Joe down to the pavement and Joe looked into the eyes of a young policeman. "You better get off home young 'un," said the policeman, "otherwise you might get hurt round here today," and, lifting his eyes apprehensively over Joe's head towards the crowd in the middle of New Road, he pivoted the boy round and gave him a playful push on the bottom.

Without a backward glance Joe started off towards Aldgate in a run. Crowds were now gathering on the streets. Groups stood together talking and gesticulating at the street corners. Women with worried expressions leaned out of the windows, shouting an occasional remark to neighbours or friends on the pavements.

Everybody was making towards Gardiner's Corner.

In the distance Joe could hear a loudspeaker touring the back streets ". . . everybody out to Gardiner's Corner . . . one o'clock . . . Mosley must not march . . . the Communist Party calls on the people of . . ."

"Trouble makers!"

Joe looked up sharply at the voice at his elbow.

A middle-aged Jew, hands pushed deep into the pockets of his heavy overcoat, turned and spat into the gutter.

His companion, slightly built, thin and sallow, twisted the grey stubble around his lips into a grimace and replied, "Without them there'd be no trouble?"

The other didn't reply. He stood on the curb frowning, then half-turned to look towards Aldgate and raised his eyes to the first floor windows above the tea-shop outside which they were standing.

"Maybe there would, maybe there wouldn't. But take it from me, wherever you find trouble, you find *them.*" He took his hand from his pocket and gestured with his thumb over his shoulder to the windows on the first floor where peeling painted letters proclaimed them to be the offices of the Communist Party.

Joe followed the man's gesture and then dropped his eyes to the narrow doorway beside the tea shop.

It was open.

A wooden plate on the door was printed with the words "COMMUNIST PARTY — Whitechapel Branch". A *mezuzah,* the tiny symbolic scroll encased in metal which every religious Jew has on his doorpost, was still there, relic of the previous tenants.

Joe stood in the doorway, looking up the dark flight of stairs that led up to the first floor. Thin, narrow stairs, covered with worn linoleum with scratched metal strips along the treads. Grey, plaster walls, cracked in places and rubbed shiny by a procession of proletarian elbows. At the top a yellow bulb glowed weakly at the end of a wire.

"Excuse me, kid. In or out, but don't block the door."

A big heavily built man with a muffler round his neck and a brown paper parcel under his arm brushed past Joe and quickly mounted the stairs, the steel tips on his boots bringing sparks from the metal strips.

As the broad shoulders stood silhouetted for a second against the landing light and disappeared, Joe made up his mind, and stepped across the threshold. He put his hand to his lips and automatically reached up his fingers to transfer the kiss to the *mezuzuah* in the traditional manner, but stopped half-way.

He smiled, almost apologetically, at the little metal case nailed to the doorpost, shrugged his shoulders and went up the stairs two at a time.

* * * *

By one o'clock Gardiner's Corner was packed with people. No traffic could pass along the wide roads. As working class London converged onto Whitechapel by bus, tram, train, and foot, the crowds became one solid human barricade stretching right across the road and pavements, their faces turned towards Leman Street at the far end of which the Fascists were assembling.

But they couldn't see the Fascists for police.

Six thousand foot police, brought in from all over London, and an entire mounted division, were concentrated in the quarter of a square mile between Leman Street and Whitechapel Road.

With linked arms they tried to keep back the people but it was impossible.

"Don't talk daft! 'Ow can I get back?" replied one exasperated man to the policeman who, gently at first, but now getting red in the face, had been trying to keep his section of the street clear.

"Now just keep on the pavement. Keep the road clear, that's all."

"Clear for who? Who's side you on?"

"Never mind about that. Just step back a bit. Keep back."

But they couldn't step back if they wanted to. Behind them the pavement was packed tight with people. And still more were pouring into the street from the exits of the Tube stations, from the bus stops and the pavements.

With their backs to the crowd now, the police linked arms and, edging backwards, levered the front rank of the crowd out of the gutter and onto the pavement, straining with shoulders and buttocks against the solid human mass.

Sweat poured from their brows. Screams came from behind them as the crush became unbearable. One policeman's helmet was knocked off into the road. Another stumbled and fell backwards into the arms of a buxom Jewish housewife.

"Oy, Sarah!" came a voice from the crowd behind her, "you wait until I tell your Abie. Making love to a policeman in broad daylight!"

"My hero he is, didn't you know?" she replied, laughing over her shoulder, "he's come to save me from the Blackshirts!"

"More likely save the bloody Blackshirts from you . . . look out! Buffalo Bill is coming to the rescue!"

With a clatter of hooves a group of mounted police cantered up the road towards the gap in the line of police where the crowd was already streaming through.

The good-humoured banter turned to boos and screams as one horse reared up and slipped on the curb-stone. In regaining its footing its shiny flanks pushed into the faces of those at the edge of the crowd who, in turn, attempted to push the rearing beast away with their hands.

One man leaned forward and landed a hefty punch on the horse's leg, another grabbed at the rider's stirrup. Two more mounted police closed in, batons out now. A roar went up from the crowd.

Someone fell. A young man was dragged out of the crowd and along the street his arms pinned behind his back.

Now the police had linked arms again and, with the help of the mounted police were trying to regain their lost ground.

It was impossible to lift an arm, people were packed so tight. Only the taller ones could see what was going on.

Suddenly there was a great crack of breaking glass as a shop window gave in to the pressure of the people being pushed backwards. Women screamed.

A mounted policeman pushed his horse through the crowd. The cordon gave way and the people surged onto the roadway. Leman Street was blocked completely.

A silver-braided officer turned sharply on his horse and rode back quickly to the temporary police "battle headquarters" off Tower Hill where London's Commissioner of Police was receiving wireless messages from police cars all over the area.

A double line of police had cordoned ofn the whole area and inside the safety zone the Fascists assembled. A charabanc drew up. Two windows were broken and as the black-shirted men filed out several faces were bleeding, hit by the showers of glass.

Sir Oswald Mosley, their leader, had not yet arrived, but they were lining up in military formation. At their head two black pennants were fluttering in the breeze, on each one the silver insignia of the lightning flash in the circle.

Most of them were dressed in severe, military style. Unjacketed, black shirts tucked into black trousers with shiny black belts and boots, their only decorations were the silver 'flash in the pan' armbands and the bright brass buckles of their belts. The latter were not solely decorative, but, together with brass knuckle-dusters, key rings and razors provided the armoury that had become so well known in the East End of London over recent years.

Leman Street and Commercial Road were now blocked to the Fascists. Would they have to cancel their march or was there an alternative?

On the other side of Leman Street immediately opposite Royal

Mint Street where the Fascists were lined up, was Cable Street. A long, rather narrow street, running parallel to Commercial Road until they came together just before Salmon Street, this seemed the only alternative to humiliating withdrawal.

The police observer plane, which had been hovering over the area since mid-day reported a few people filtering down towards Cable Street from Commercial Road and a small crowd at the entrance where it joined Leman Street. Otherwise it was deserted, and if the Blackshirts were diverted down Cable Street they could by-pass the crowds, join up with Commercial Road later on and carry on with their march as advertised.

The police cordon around the assembled Fascists parted to allow a black car to go through. It was Mosley. A well-aimed brick crashed through the side window but he was unhurt and lifted his arm in the fascist salute as he stepped out of the car.

Tall and well-built, with thick black hair and a heavy black moustache, he went straight into discussion with a group of his own leaders, bending his head to hear their reports, his sharp eyes taking in the situation, glancing from the ranks of his blackshirted followers to the encircling cordon of police, then straightening up to survey the growing crowds beyond.

He shook his head angrily several times, evidently in sharp disagreement with his lieutenants and then strode over to the knot of silver-braided police officers who were standing by a police van at the corner of the street.

When he returned to his colleagues he was angry and frowning. They turned to him, the leader, the promising young politician who had promised them so many things so quickly, who had given them uniforms, badges, drums and banners. They felt the power and personality of the man as his angry glare swept over them.

As he took in a deep breath, seeming to grow even more in stature, his mouth twisted into a sneer and, to the disappointment of those around him who expected a tirade against the police, the Jews and the Communists, he shrugged his shoulders and said: "Cable Street".

* * * *

"Cable Street," said Abe Stern as he replaced the telephone receiver on its hook.

For a second the curiously assorted group of Communists in the small, first-floor room were silent. Nobody glanced at the big map of the Borough of Stepney that was pinned to the wall. They needed no map, because they knew the area as well as they knew each other.

This was their Cable Street, their Leman Street, their White-chapel. They were born in its crowded tenements. They had played marbles along its gutters on their way to school, had fought and squabbled in its squalid side streets and courted in its unlit alleys.

And now in their minds they were each seeing the corner of Cable Street and Leman Street, the grey, shabby buildings, the little shops, the clutter and clank of railway trucks shunting backwards and forwards in the goods yard and the constant overhanging smoke and acrid smell that gave way only to the more insidious mists and fogs that sidled up from the river where the tugs fussed and farted about and the cliques of barges drifted aimlessly with the tides.

"So Leman Street's blocked, eh?"

"Yes," Stern replied, "Bert says that you couldn't get a needle through Leman Street now and the police have given up trying to keep it clear.

"He saw Mosley drive up . . ."

All heads jerked up at the name.

". . . and somebody slung a brick in his window. Bert's been watching 'em with a pair of binoculars from his bedroom window and he reckons they've decided on Cable Street."

"Not much else they could do, unless they pack it up altogether."

"That's what we've got to make 'em do."

"Well, we're ready for 'em in Cable Street. If the lads have got any sense they'll have that lorry on its side by now. Sam . . ." Stern turned to a tall, square faced man who was standing by the window, "You'd better get down there on the bike and see how things are going. See if there's a YCLer you can take on your pillion to send back straight away with the news, eh?"

Sam Bent, a stevedore at the London Docks, pulled a white muffler out of his pocket and tied it round his neck, looking round at his comrades as he pulled the knot and turned up the collar of his jacket.

"O.K.", he said quietly and picked his way through the chairs towards the door. As he passed them he put his hand on the stooped shoulders of a bald-headed Jewish tailor and then, with a grin, ruffled the short red hair of a young Irish railwayman. He winked at 'Ma Bernstein', terror of the rent-collectors and landlords in one of Stepney's biggest blocks of tenements, and, as he reached the door, nodded briefly to Stern.

"See you," he said, and went out.

There was silence in the room for a moment then Ma Bernstein asked Stern, "You sure they got everything ready in Cable Street?"

"They're ready," Stern replied. "We arranged for the lorry, some mattresses, boxes. There's railings there, if they need them. There's bricks, There's people. It's not a wide road. We'll stop them all right."

"And if they can't get down Cable Street?"

"Well, it's either The Highway, which will be a big defeat for Mosley because it's right down by the river and like going round the back way instead of going right through the East End, or they'll have to call it off and ..."

Suddenly the door burst open and a bespectacled young face poked into the room.

"Sorry comrades. Where's Sam gone with that kid?"

"What kid? Oh, Sam. He's gone down to Cable Street. He's sending the kid back soon with the news. Why?"

"Christ!"

"Why? What's up?"

"He's the Gold kid. He's not even a YCLer. He just blew in and said he wanted to find out about the Communists and we were sorting things out and told him to sit down outside for a minute. Next we know Sam's grabbed him and they've gone off on his bike. Cable Street ... Christ!"

"Who d' you say he was?"

"The Gold kid. You know, the one that got done up by the Blackshirts. Gold from the Arcadia."

"And he wanted to find out about us?"

"Yes. Said he wanted to know what we stood for. How we worked and all that ..."

"Well," said Ma Bernstein, edging her buxom frame more comfortably in the protesting wickerwork armchair, "he's certainly picked the best way to find out."

* * * *

When Joe got to Cable Street the battle had just begun.

It had taken only a few minutes on Sam's motor bike, cutting through the back streets to a point about a hundred yards 'behind the lines'.

"Christ," exclaimed Sam, as he stopped the bike, "looks like they've started already. Come on kid, let's shove this bike away quick and see what's doing."

As they both dismounted and pushed the motorbike up on the curb and into a dark little alleyway between two shops the distant murmuring erupted into an angry roar and Sam quickly darted out into the street.

With Joe behind him, he ran with long strides along the pavement, keeping close to the sides of the houses.

Suddenly he stopped, turning back for Joe.

"In here."

Joe found himself in the doorway of a tenement block, at the bottom of a flight of narrow stone steps leading upwards into brown-tiled darkness.

"Listen kid . . ."

Joe looked into Sam's face, seeing him clearly for the first time. The grey eyes looked tired, his lips drawn tightly together, his smooth shiny cheeks showing signs of a hasty shave.

" . . . You stay here, see. I don't think they're going to get through but you'll be able to see how things go from here. If we stop 'em here and they turn off down the Highway you'll have to nip back to the premises and let 'em know, but don't move till I come back and tell you . . ."

The shrilling of police whistles brought both their heads sharply round towards the corner of the street, only twenty yards away.

"If they do get through . . ." the stevedore's quiet eyes met the dark eager eyes of the boy, frightened, excited, determined. "Well, you bunk up the top of these stairs and stay there, see?"

The boy nodded.

If they do get through . . . he thought of the night he and Barney had been coming back from the pictures.

A big, strong hand gripped his. "See you, comrade," and Sam was gone.

Pressing himself against the railings Joe watched him quickly make his way towards the crowds now filling the narrow entrance to Cable Street.

An old lorry rumbled up the street. As it reached the 'front line' the driver jumped out and beckoned to the crowd. With a roar they swarmed round the lorry and upturned it.

Some planks of wood and mattresses, dragged from a nearby timber-yard where they had been stored in preparation, quickly extended the lorry into a barricade stretching right across the street.

From the other side of the street an ant-line of men and women streamed out of a decrepit boarded-up shop with pieces of old furniture, chairs, brass bedsteads and table-tops and piled them onto the barricade.

"Lousy rotten Fascists!"

A woman's scream from the tenements above him made Joe look up to see three women leaning from the top-storey window, throwing milk bottles at the police on the other side of the improvised barrier.

A new wave of booing signalled the approach of a group of mounted police, batons drawn and held aloft, but this time they were met by handfuls of glass marbles scattered along the roadway beneath the horses' hooves. Their delicate riding school stepping turned to clumsy side-slipping and stamping of hooves as the frightened beasts, eyes wide with panic, nostrils dilating, tried to keep their balance.

Leaning forward now, with batons lowered, the police made an effort to control their mounts, but the fear of the animals flowed into the riders. Trained like circus animals, both horses and riders were lost against this new ringmaster cracking the whip.

A policeman's helmeted head had appeared over the barricade at the far side of the street. Unnoticed by the crowd who were busily occupied strengthening the main section which was being attacked by the police, this brave soul clambered over the old furniture and dropped onto the pavement on the other side.

Then he stopped, clearly at a loss to know what to do.

Before he could make up his mind he was seen by a burly docker who called out to his mates, "Look what's crawled out of the cheese!"

In a moment they had surrounded him and as the docker faced the young policeman, neither knew where to begin. They both knew that, if this were on the other side of the barricade, the police would have frog-marched the docker to the nearest Black Maria and rushed him off to prison.

But the dockers? What could they do with this policeman? Despite their detailed organisation they had not allowed for 'prisoners-of-war'!

The young policeman sweated as the stock phrases turned round and round in his head . . . 'Now, come along, you'd better come quietly . . . Break it up there . . . Move along . . . Don't let's have any nonsense from you . . .' but none of them seemed quite suited to this occasion.

Alone, surrounded by angry workers, separated from his colleagues by a mountain of mattresses and old furniture this amputated arm of the law suddenly found himself wondering what he was doing there at all.

"What we going to do with him, Bert?" asked one docker.

"Better sling him back on the other side . . ."

"Don't be daft. There's enough bloody police over there without sending 'em another one."

"What then? *We* can't keep him."

"Don't see why not. We could shut him up somewhere."

But now more police were trying to scale the barricade. Some were dragged over, others were knocked back. Helmets went flying as batons clashed against railings. Joe wondered what had happened to the Blackshirts. The fight seemed to be between the people and the police with the police getting the worst of it.

Pelted with milk bottles, rubbish and water from the top-floor tenements, cursed and crushed by the crowds that filled every inch of the road from Gardiner's Corner to Cable Street, with marbles beneath them and barricades in front of them the police gave up.

Sir Philip Game, the Commissioner of Police, told the Fascists that their march was off. They formed ranks, lifted their arms in the Fascist salute to their leader and dispersed.

The battle of Cable Street was over.

They did not pass.

As he watched the crowds breaking up, Joe felt an arm round his shoulder. He looked up to see Sam, his face dirty, his jacket ripped at the lapel, his grey eyes no longer tired but smiling.

"Well kid," he said, "we stopped 'em, didn't we?"

"We sure did . . . or at least, you did."

"All of us did, kiddo, all of us. Come on, time we got back."

They pulled the motor-bike out of the alley and together pushed it into the road. As Joe settled himself on the pillion he put his hands onto the man's broad shoulders in front of him. The engine roared and the bike turned out of Cable Street. Joe lifted himself up and shouted into Sam's ear "Comrade" — he didn't know Sam's name — "Comrade?"

"What is it kid?"

"D'you think I could join the Y.C.L.?"

"Mean to say you're not in the League?"

"That's right. But today . . . all this . . . I want to do something . . . it's all over now, but . . . could I join?"

"All over kid? It's just beginning . . ." and the bike swung into the Whitechapel Road, slowing down to thread a way through the crowds that stretched right down to Gardiner's Corner and beyond.

Margaret

The ten o'clock hooter, signalling the end of the afternoon shift, woke Margaret up with a start.

She hadn't been properly asleep, but somewhere in that no-man's land between sleeping and waking where furtive thoughts pick their way through the barbed wire entanglements of everyday life.

At the age of eleven, life to Margaret meant the crowded classroom of the elementary school, the even more crowded kitchen downstairs which seemed forever full of smelly pit-clothes strung across the front of the mantlepiece to dry before the roaring fire, and her mother either washing, ironing or cooking. With two sons and a husband down the pit, all on different shifts, the home seemed more a lodging house, always somebody coming in, black with coal, hungry . . . weary . . . dirty.

The fire was always roaring, with a basin of water on for somebody's bath, or a kettle for somebody's tea, or a saucepan for somebody's supper.

But when her father was on 'afternoons', down the pit from two o'clock till ten, then, at least, Margaret could be sure of a little privacy from the time she ran up the narrow flight of stairs that led straight off the kitchen to the bedroom, where her little brass bedstead stood under the window, separated by a gap of less than two feet from her parents' big double-bed which almost filled the rest of the room.

The only other piece of furniture in the bedroom was an old-fashioned chest of drawers pushed up to the door so that it could never be opened properly and you had to sidle round it to get into the room.

At night, before going off to sleep, Margaret liked to see if she could make out all the familiar little articles that her mother always arranged so neatly on top of their chest of drawers.

The oval mirror, framed with plaster flowers, sent back a pale message to the moon. The wedding photograph, the little round tin of hair curlers, the long shiny box that was always kept locked, a bottle of cough medicine with its lopsided cork, a painted china statuette of a horse and foal which one of the boys had won at the fair three years ago.

All were in their usual place tonight and Margaret, reassured, turned her back to the room and curled up in an effort to get to sleep before her father got back.

The two boys were on 'nights' this week and had left for the pit a little while ago.

Downstairs she could hear her mother getting the tin bath out for her father's return.

What a life she has . . . always on the go, and none of *them* ever lift a finger to help. Just sit around expecting to be waited on like lords . . . especially him. Cook their meals, wash their filthy sweaty clothes, scrub the pit-muck off their backs, try and keep the place looking clean with *them* bringing in all the dirt of the pit all the time . . . don't know how she does it. She looked tired tonight when she pushed me up to bed. She must have been beautiful once. That wedding photograph showed . . .

Margaret's head darted round, trying to see the photograph on the chest of drawers.

A sudden inclination sent her scuttling over the wide expanse of her parents' bed till she held the wedding photograph in her hands and returned with it to her own bed.

Snuggling down in her warmed bed-clothes she held the photograph up with her arm outstretched to catch the dim light from the window.

There they were, more in her memory than as she could actually see them in the moon's light. He, tall and round-faced, she, a buxom country girl all dressed up in white lace, tall, even though she only came up to his shoulders, standing upright and looking proud and happy, a bouquet of lilies in her hand.

Margaret smiled to herself, comforted, as she looked at the photograph. That's how her parents were really. Not like they had been these past years, never seeming to have a word to say to each other, she providing his wants mechanically in the same way every day with nothing more than "Here's tha dinner . . . tha water's ready", and always "Ah wonder there's owt left to dig in pit, tha's got it all on tha back . . ." as she scrubbed him clean in his bath. And he accepting it all with never a word of thanks, coming in without a greeting, going out without a word.

Between the two of them now there seemed nothing shared but a weariness, an acceptance that this was the way things were and the way they would always be.

Sometimes at weekends, when he was rested, he'd liven up and at Sunday dinner he'd turn to his daughter and with a smile that reminded her of the wedding photograph would ask "Well, now, young Margaret, how's tha going on at school?"

But he never went as far as giving a helping hand and after he'd eaten his fill he would lean back on his chair and yawn, "Ee-ee, that were reet good. Ah think ah'll tek a nap . . ." Then he would heave himself up and lumber through into the front parlour where he would stretch out on the sofa for the rest of the afternoon.

His departure was a signal for the boys and with a gesture imitating his father Edgar would push back his empty plate, stretch himself, and say "Well, ah'm off down t'road. Art cooming Bill?"

Bill, two years younger than his brother and not yet quite used to the ways of men would turn at the door and say "Tara Mum. Be back for tea." And then the two of them were left alone. The women, left with the women's work. Washing up, clearing away, getting tea ready to be eaten, washed up and cleared away.

At times like these Margaret felt closest to her mother who, when the girl rose to gather the dirty dishes together would reach out a restraining arm and say "Nay, leave it rest awhile, luv, it's Sunday. Sit tha'sen down and tek it easy. All t'others are."

"Why don't they gi' thee a hand, Mum?"

"Who? The lads?"

"Them, and me Dad?"

"Ee, luv, that's asking, that is. Why don't they indeed? They're men, that's why. They do their load in t'pit. Time they've finished, they're fit for nowt, they reckon. 'Appen they're right . . ." This last with a wry smile that Margaret could not understand.

"Has th'ever been down pit, Mum?"

"Nay, lass, and never will if ah've owt to say in it. Ah've seen the way they go down and the way they coom oop. And ah've seen what it does to 'em."

"But it's 'ard for you Mum, on the go all the time."

"Aye lass", said the mother, rising with a sigh, and gathering the plates together, "it's 'ard for me, an' it's 'ard for tha' Dad and the lads, an' it'll be 'ard for thee. It's 'ard for all ordinary folk, men women and children, wherever they are. Always will be ah suppose."

Margaret was thinking about those words, lying in bed, when she heard her father's hob-nailed boots resounding up the cobbled street. Through the side alley and up the back yard they clattered, quicker than usual, she fancied. The atmosphere in the house changed, as he opened the back door and came in. Through the thin walls, up from the kitchen, filtering between the cracks came the smell and blackness of the pit.

Now the sound of water being poured into the bath, heavy boots being pulled off and thrown aside, splashing, and her father's loud laughter, followed by shouts of protest from her mother.

He wasn't beating her, was he? Nay, that he'd never do, rough as he was. Two doors down they had big rows and she's heard her Mum say Harry Hodgkin's been at it again but never her Dad.

What was up then? They were coming upstairs, her Mum still protesting "Nay Jim, don't be daft, you'll waken Maggie . . ." as the door burst open and he came in pulling her mother behind him.

He didn't turn on the light but peered into the darkness towards the child. Through her half-closed eyes she could make out the dim figures standing by the door. She breathed heavily, imitating sleep and her father appeared satisfied and turned to her mother.

"She's alreet. Fast asleep. Come on now . . ."

"Nay, Jim, not now; leave it be. It'll waken her up."

"We'll not waken 'er. Come on and stop messing about wi' me."

Suddenly, with a push he had thrown her on to the bed and stepped towards her, into the square of the moonlight that shone through the window. The child's wide-open eyes were hidden in the shadow as she stared in amazement at the whiteness of his glistening body, still wet from the bath, his head and thighs cut off by the shadows.

On the bed her mother tried to lift herself but lay back, sobbing as if in pain.

"Gi' o'er moaning, tha'll waken t'child," he whispered, and as he bent down over her mother Margaret could see his face, the eyes wide open and shining, circled with coal-dust, his wet hair falling forward over his brow.

"Stop it Jim, stop it! Tha's hurt my back."

"Gi' o'er, I'm not stopping now, tha knows . . ."

Margaret lay still, not daring to move. She could have reached out and touched her mother's long hair, which hung over the side of the bed.

In the darkness the two bodies mingled in a whispering, sobbing, grunting, panting, heaving bed-creaking whole.

"My back, Jim, my back."

"There's nowt wrong with tha back that this won't cure."

The child could stand it no longer, and, jumped up in her bed, clutching her parents' wedding photograph, screaming out through her tears, "Stop it, stop it! You're hurting her!"

Slowly her father raised himself. First his tangled hair, then his glistening forehead, and his coal-rimmed eyes came into the moon's spotlight, staring at his daughter, quivering before him on the neighbouring bed. His face was less than three feet from hers and dimly she could see the ghostly whiteness of his body tapering down to where it met her mother's, lying motionless beneath him, her clothes stained with the wetness of his body, her neck and shoulders white, her eyes wide with horror, staring at her, upside down, from the edge of the bed.

"She's dead!" Margaret screamed. "You've killed her!"

Her open mouth was stopped by a resounding slap as his arm streaked out towards her like a snake in the moonlight.

"Gi' o'er shouting and turn tha'sen round" he ordered.

Automatically the child obeyed and as she turned towards the wall she heard the bed squeak once again as her father lifted himself off it and switched on the light.

*   *   *   *

It was three years after the incident with her father, and Margaret at fourteen, and on the first day of her first job, was feeling quite grown up. Until she met Sally.

"Sal, this is the new lass. Margaret Houghton's the name. Show her where everything is and what she's to do, will you?"

Margaret could see those green eyes looking her over. Looking at her ill-fitting skirt and school-girl blouse, her coarse stockings and unfashionable shoes. Standing in front of the other girl she suddenly felt like a baby.

"Sally will tell you what to do Miss Houghton. If you do what she tells you, you can't go far wrong. Goodbye for now."

"Thank you Sir."

She half-turned to see him closing the office door behind him. He's nice.

"Not far enough for him, anyway."

"Pardon?"

"Can't go far wrong enough for him, I said. That's the first thing I'll warn you about in this place kid. Old Harry Winters. Personnel. Too bloody personal that's his trouble. What d'he say your name was?"

"Margaret. Margaret Houghton."

"Mine's Sally Marsden. This is Harry. Another one. Just as bad, too, but we know how to keep him in his place."

The boy smiled at her from his place, a large desk behind which he sat on a high stool reminding Margaret of those drawings in the Charles Dickens book she had been given for Christmas.

"Hallo."

"How do you do."

"Polite, aren't we? Still makes a change here."

She felt herself trembling a little at the other girl's taunts and turned away from her to look around the office.

The room was about the size of her front parlour at home. Cream coloured walls with one big window high up through which she could see the backs of houses with part of a sign saying 'Reckitts Blue'. Must be somewhere at the back. Calendar with a picture of flowers, clock saying twenty to ten, a row of green metal filing cabinets, a pile of newspapers on the floor, Harry's feet resting on the crossbar of the old fashioned desk, his socks striped below the trouser turnups.

"How d'you like it?"

Margaret looked up to find the girl leaning back in her chair, one elbow resting on the back, her hand patting the hair behind her ears. Blonde hair, but not yellow or golden the way you picture in your mind. Grey. Nice blouse, though. Greenish. Like her eyes.

"It's . . . it's quite nice."

"Nice? Well, it's not bad." The girl leaned forward now, reaching for the handbag at her feet.

"Smoke?"

"No thank you."

"Don't blame you. Harry?" She tossed a cigarette on to the high desk and the boy caught it.

"Ta, Sal."

"First job?"

"Yes, it is."

As she lit a match and inhaled the girl's eyes narrowed, her shoulders contracted a little, her body concentrating on that first inward breath.

"That's better. Oh it's not a bad place to start. Look at him, started here a mere youth six months ago, now he's a man of the world with the Editor begging him to write the editorials."

Harry laughed.

So did Margaret. Everything was all right. He was nice. Even green-eyes wasn't so bad.

"Don't take no notice of her. You'll be all right." He held his cigarette away from his face and puffed out smoke confidently, with his shoulders back and a smile in his eyes.

"Where do I sit?"

"Over here." The girl balanced her unfinished cigarette carefully on the rim of an ashtray on her desk and rose, smoothing the tight grey skirt down over her buttocks. She led Margaret over to a table piled high with newspapers and box-files. "Here, Harry, get rid of some of these luv."

"Sure."

Harry jumped up and started moving the papers on to the floor and Margaret was surprised to see that he was not much taller than her.

"Here y'are Madame, all ready for you."

Taking out his handkerchief the boy made an exaggerated sweep over the surface of the table, finishing with a deep bow in Margaret's direction. His heavily greased hair fell forward over his forehead.

"Thank you."

"Better get her a chair from outside, Harry."

"O.K."

He straightened up and his right hand smoothed the hair back into position. He winked at Margaret and went out. The girl went back to her desk, picked up the cigarette and inhaled. She turned and looked straight at Margaret.

"How old are you, kid?"

"Sixteen."

She smiled. "When?"

Margaret dropped her eyes, confused.

"Last . . . last month. Well, six weeks ago actually."

"Actually? Come off it, luv." She put the cigarette in her mouth, placed her hands on the desk behind her and lifted herself slightly backwards and upwards so that she was sitting on the desk. She crossed her legs, took the cigarette out again and screwed up her eyes at the smoke.

"Doesn't matter to me. P'raps you're older than you look. I'd have said just turned fifteen."

"How old are you then?" Margaret asked.

"Twenty."

She laughed at Margaret's look of surprise.

"Actually," she said, leaning across the desk and stubbing the cigarette out carefully in the ashtray, "I'm twenty tomorrow. *Exactly!*"

At that moment Harry came back carrying a chair. He stopped and stared openly at the long expanse of stockinged leg the girl was displaying as she leaned across the desk. She looked at him and unhurriedly returned to a sitting position, her skirt remaining well above her knees.

"Keep your mind on your work Harry-boy. The lady's waiting to sit down." She flicked some ash off her skirt, stood up and walked round her desk to her seat.

* * * *

The morning passed quickly for Margaret. She made tea and took it to the others working in offices on that floor. Harry helped, glad to be passing on his old job to her, and passing on all his acquired knowledge of the rest of the staff at the same time.

"It's only what they call Administration down here. All the real work's done upstairs. Editorial, reporters and all that. Down here it's just accounts and vouchers and advertising like. Management, too, like old Winters. You've met him. Ever worked on a paper before?"

"No. This is my first job."

" 'Course. I forgot. This is Accounts through here. There's old Snotty, always sniffing and sneezing he is, and Mrs. Arbutt. She's not bad. Bit of a cow sometimes but better than him. If you want any petty cash go to her, not him." He pushed open the door. "Morning Mr. Snow, Morning Mrs. Arbutt. Here's your new Catering Officer!"

Back into the corridor again. Harry closed the door while Margaret held the tray.

"Told you, didn't I?" Right snotty-nose he is. Better in here. Advertising. The fat bloke will be Jim Passmore. Jim and tonic we call 'im. When the pub's open the Advertisement Department's closed. He's all right though. She does most of the work. When he's out, that is. When he's in, he's mostly in her, or trying to. Caught 'em at it once. That was a right lark. Tell you about it sometime. Morning Miss Shelley, Mr. Passmore not in yet?"

Mr. Passmore was not in and Miss Shelley was busy with a big pair of scissors. Margaret didn't believe all that about her and Mr. Passmore. Not her. She looked much too old. And nice too. And anyway there wasn't room. He was making it all up. Harry caught her expression as they moved on.

"Don't believe me do you?"

"At her age?"

"Don't be daft, she's only thirty-five. Just right."

"But she's got grey hair."

"All cats are grey in the dark. This is old Winters in here. Old Harry. Personnel, office manager, general nosey-parker and ladies' man. Watch him, luv. He'll give you a week to settle in then *he'll* try to settle in! Watch him."

"You've got a one-track mind. He's very nice. Old enough to be my father."

"Knowing him, he might *be* your father. Can't tell with old Harry."

"Shut up. Don't be daft."

The office was empty.

"Not here. May be in with the boss. Leave it on his desk. Put the saucer on top to keep it warm. Here, not on the wood, he'll go barmy. Put it on the blotter."

Outside again, it seemed ages since she had first stood outside that office waiting for her interview. Funny. She felt quite an old hand now.

"Next one's the boss." Harry straightened his tie. "How do I look? No messing about with him. Never met him, have you? He's all right. Best thing with him is straight in and out. No talking, specially if he's got somebody with him."

This time Harry knocked on the door and waited for a call from within, then held the door open for Margaret to go through.

He was much younger than Margaret had expected. Not much hair but his forehead was very sunburned. Heavy black-rimmed glasses, eyes deep behind them, shining.

"Thank you, my dear."

London accent.

He put his hand up and removed his glasses. Funny, that made him look older. Wrinkly lines at the corners of his eyes.

"Morning sir. This is Margaret Houghton. Just started today."

"Good morning Harry ... Margaret. Down here please. Thank you."

The room was big and light and carpeted all over. Big desk too, with glass on top, papers in piles, books, picture on his desk in a frame, probably his wife. His hands were long and white and gentle.

As he raised the cup to his lips he looked up at her, his eyebrows wondering why she was still standing by the desk. Confused, Margaret turned and left the room.

"Should have said good morning or something," muttered Harry after the door was closed.

"Should I? Thought you said best say nothing."

"Well, that doesn't mean good morning or thank you. That means don't start chattering about the weather or anything. Don't matter. Like him?"

"Not bad. Who's the picture?"

"What picture?"

"On his desk. I couldn't see it 'cos it was turned away from me."

"His wife I suppose. Or daughter. Looks a bit young for him. Anyway, that's the lot."

She was still thinking that it was funny his hands were white and his forehead was brown, and that she had never seen such long, gentle fingers, when they returned to the office.

Sally looked up. "Well, how was the tour of inspection? D' you meet everybody?"

"They all seem very nice really."

"She didn't see old Jim and tonic. And Winters wasn't there either. Probably in the lav."

"Didn't miss much. Less you see of those two the better."

A phone rang on the girl's desk.

"Yes, Mr. Wingate. I'll come right in."

She replaced the phone, opened a drawer and took out a notebook and pencil.

"Duty calls. Now for a solid hour of listening to the words of wisdom of yours faithfully, for and on behalf of, Charles W. Wingate, director. I could do without him this morning. Monday's bad enough without him. Sooner you learn shorthand luv and get in there the better I'll like it."

"Could I?"

The girl looked up at her and Margaret dropped her eyes.

"I mean . . . would they want me to . . . and what about you?"

"Ah well, we'll worry about that when it comes. Right now luv, you'd better get those papers filed. Harry'll show you where." Twisting herself round so that she could see the seams in the back of her stockings the girl smoothed down her skirt again, took up her pad and went out.

* * * *

"Ayoop, here she comes. Fookin 'ell. Bloody trackless gets more fookin crowded every bloody day."

The hum of the single-decker trolley car's electric motor was the only sound to disturb the pitch-black silence as, at quarter to six, Bill Houghton stood at the corner of the street with Jim Marsh from two doors up. Bill was seventeen and for the last three months he had been working on the coal-face with Jim and another collier Sam Burton.

Fifty-fives they called it. A new face that Jim and Sam were opening out. Two of the best colliers in the pit. Bill was lucky to be working with them. He could learn more from them than all the rest of the pit put together. And earn a bit of cash, too. But didn't they shift it! The coal seemed to jump off the face as soon as they looked at it and then he had to break it up and into the tubs and away with them down the roadway to the junction. Clip 'em on the wire and then back again for the next lot.

Bill yawned.

"What's oop lad? Tha still asleep? Tha'd better waken oop afore tha gets down pit. If tha falls asleep down theer lad tha's joost as likely never to wake oop."

Asleep . . . wish he was. Back in bed before the alarm went at five. Edgar grunting in the other bed. All right for him. On afternoons. Two till bloody ten, home like a gentleman, have your supper, listen to the wireless, and bed. Wake up any time you like and the rest of the day's yours. Better still on nights, like Dad. Least you don't miss anything. Might as well be in the bloody dark down there as up here. Bloody dark it was this morning too. Bill drew his pyjama jacket round him as he peered through the window. Without turning on the light he fumbled his way to the door and quietly opened it.

Opposite, on the other side of the two foot square landing, was the door of Mum's room. Not a sound from her or Margaret.

Fingers spread out to touch the wall on either side, toes feeling the cold linoleum on each stair, he went down the steep little staircase that divided the house in two. A bedroom on each side upstairs, a parlour and a kitchen downstairs.

At the bottom he opened the kitchen door, switched on the electric light, shielding his eyes from the glare. The fire still glowed in the grate and in front of it his pit clothes warmed, hanging on a string like dead flags, smelling of dried sweat.

Could do with a pee. Not going out there . . . too bloody cold.

52

He shuffled over to the sink wedged into the alcove next to the stove and, turning on the tap with his left hand he pulled his penis out with his right hand and, raising himself on his toes, placed it on the rim of the sink. Aah-h-h.

He smiled as the yellow stream mingled with the water and swirled round the plughole. Still smiling he reached for the kettle, standing on the tiny draining board and held it under the tap.

Some bloody life, ain't it. In one hole, out the other. Turn on the tap, pour it in the kettle, drink it down, piss it out and down the drain you go.

Bill peered out of the window by the sink, into the early black morning. The light from the window fell on to the scrubby back yard, across the tiny path that ended at the upright wooden box that housed the lav.

Bloody cold.

He turned off the tap and let his penis drop back into his pyjama trousers as he placed the kettle on the stove. Slipping his pyjama top off he stepped quickly back to the sink, turned on the tap and cupped the flowing water in his hands. For a second he stood there, half naked in the cold electric light, then he dipped his face into the water and made a great show of rubbing it over his head and neck. He reached for the towel, dried himself sharply, and put on his vest. He slipped down his pyjama trousers and put on a pair of football pants, black with coal but warm and dry and stiff with sweat. Head first into the flannel shirt, feet first into the trousers that once belonged to Edgar's new blue suit. Button up as he sat down into the old chair in front of the stove and reached for his socks. Long woollen socks that he tucked his trousers into and folded over carefully then up with a jump to look at the clock on the mantelpiece alongside the rent book, the picture of Dad in uniform, the tea tin and all the other odds and ends.

Quarter past.

Time for breakfast.

On a cool corner of the stove stood the frying pan and in it two sausages and a lump of fat his mother had placed there last night before going to bed. Bill took the handle of the frying pan in his right hand and, bending his knees, picked up the wooden sink cover from the floor and placed it over the sink. Then, bending down again he lifted the gas ring from the floor and placed it on the sink cover and transferred the frying pan to the gas ring.

He reached for the box of matches on the mantelpiece, while turning on the gas tap with his other hand. With a pop the gas ring came to life and the fat began to melt round the mottled pinky-blue sausages lying like great fat slugs in the black pan.

Bloody sausages. I'm fair sick of 'em.

He turned to the table and lifted the white napkin from the bread and the dish of butter. His place was laid. A knife, a fork, a large white plate, a china mug, a bottle of milk. The pepper, the salt, the sugar pot. The bread board, the bread, the knife.

Cut myself a slice now.

Bloody sausages stink the place out.

Kettle's boiling.

The teapot was on the mantlepiece and he reached it down with the tea tin and placed them both on the stove. He poured some steaming water into the pot, swilled it round, then poured it out through a hole in the sink cover. Two spoonfuls of tea from the tin, then filled the pot and put the kettle on the floor in front of the stove.

"Come on you bastards, let's be having you."

The sausages were ready.

Sitting there at the table Billy quietly slipped away into his early-morning dream as he forked the sausages into his mouth, followed by bites of bread and gulps of tea.

He dreamed he was alone, the only one. The quiet upstairs, the black silence outside, was no longer the silence of sleep but the emptiness of the end. He was the last one. This was the last sausage on earth, the last mug of tea ever made. When he had finished it he would go out into the everlasting black, into the unknown end of the world where death lived alone and life was dead.

Only the clock still lived.

Christ . . . half past.

Knife, fork, plate and mug on to the sink cover. Down in the old chair again to pull his pit boots on. Ooh, bloody great things. Laces round the back, now the front, underneath, front again, bow round the side, that's it. Muffler round the neck, jacket on, pit helmet. Bloody cardboard, lucky they never had this sort of thing in King Arthur's time. One good swipe with a lance and you'd 'ad it.

> *All in the blue unclouded weather*
> *Thick-jewelled shone the saddle-leather,*
> *The helmet and the helmet-feather*
> *Burn'd like one burning flame together,*
> *As he rode down to Camelot.*

Right, that's it. Camelot, here I come!

"Half past Ma."

"Right Billy."

Now the 'snap' tin, with today's selection of gourmet sandwiches, bread and fooking butter like fooking yesterday and fooking tomorrow, stuffed into the capacious jacket pocket, water tin under the tap gurgling from empty bass through bubbling baritone to top-full tenor runneth over, surely goodness and mercy will follow me . . . aye and they'll be bloody late too if they don't hurry.

Last look round, all well. Unbolt the back door and out.

Bloody cold. No fooking moon. No fooking stars. Nothing. The end. Like I said.

As he passed the window the light caught him hunched up against the cold, water tin dangling on a cord from his shoulder, hands in his trousers pockets, leaning forward against the wind.

*   *   *   *

"Ayoop Billy. "As tha goin' on?"

"Ayoop Robert. Ah, Joe."

"Still sleeping Billy lad? This fookin trackless'll waken thee oop. It's nowt much of a dream car."

Wedged tight in the open doorway, hanging on to the rail as the trolley swerved round the corner pushing the weight of the packed men inside on to him, Bill looked round at the faces, jammed together pale and white in the overhanging light, like potted shrimps.

There was not much conversation. Outside an occasional street lamp flashed by and now and then the lights of the trolley danced madly along the windows of the closed shops in the narrow street. The overhead wires flashed and for a second lit up the limbo through which they rode, shaken from side to side, pressed hip to thigh, blowing steam into each other's nostrils, measuring the pit dirt in each other's eyes.

With a jerk the trolley pulled up at the pit.

"Anyone for Bookinam Palace?"

"Fookinam bloody palace more like it."

Spilling out on to the roadway, joking, cursing, greeting each other they streamed through the pit gates, some stopped to talk to friends just coming off the night shift, others made straight for the lamp house.

Nearly three thousand men worked at the pit, drawn from villages and little towns around, walking, cycling, wedged into trolleys, spat out three times a day into the pit yard and sucked down hungrily into its greedy black jaws. Already the great beast was throwing up the remains of its last meal, digested, sucked dry, coated with the blackness of its belly, smeared with the slime of its saliva, choked by the foul air of its intestinal passages.

They emerged from their hole like trolls, small and black and strangely shining in the light of their own lamps, and stood there for a moment breathing in . . . just breathing in.

"Ayoop son. 'Lo Jim."

It was Dad. Coal-dust stuck to the ends of each hair on his grey moustache and the night's stubble prickled his chin like a fungus.

"This lad o'mine gettin any coal yet?"

"Ah we'll mek a collier on him . . . when he wakens oop."

No word of praise was expected or given. No word more passed between father and son. All was understood, unspoken. They had to hurry, the pit was getting restless. Above them it groaned and glowed as the great wheels turned and boots clanged across the metal gangway that led to the lamphouse.

Hear the numbers being shouted out before you as you join the queue. Hear the click of lamps being tested. Twist on, twist back off. Hear the swing of those doors approaching. Shout your own number.

"One-two-nine-owt-seven."

Breathe in, suck in, now's your last chance. Through the doors and the cage was just coming up. Quickly now, the pit was waiting, drooling at the wheels as the great greased cables slid slowly to a stop.

As the bars were drawn away the men sprang out like greyhounds from the trap, straightening up as they went, not stopping for a greeting or a passing word, out into the air.

In you go. Head down, mind your lamp. Turn to face the door. In come the others. Turn backs to you. Then more. Squeeze tight. Back of Jim's neck, his shirt frayed with some white lining showing through the rough grey edges, threads separated, mingling with the hair on his neck.

The bars clanged. No light now save the light of their own lamps. No sound now save the holding of breath as they waited for the drop.

Then it came. Silently and slowly at first, but then faster and faster, with only the walls of the shaft roaring past you. No noise of machinery, of motors or cables, or controls of any sort. Just drop, sheer drop.

And then the smell. As always, about half-way down. A smell

almost of burning but not as strong as that. A hot smell. Singeing? A sweetish hot smell. Burned chocolate. But acid too. Fetid. Burned shit.

Suddenly thinking of his breakfast, frying in the pan, he felt sick. Sick with the smell, sick with the thought of the work ahead of him, sick at the unending drop, sick as he had felt on his first morning at the pit, and every morning since. And just as suddenly the cage slowed down, lights appeared outside and they had arrived, half a mile below the surface of the earth, at the pit bottom.

He followed Jim quickly through the large, lofty, well-lit passage-way which opened into a concrete-walled, vault-like area crossed by rails on which a line of coal-filled tubs was standing.

Over by one wall some men were talking, squatting on their heels, waiting for their mates. Others were making their way through one or other of three different passageways that led from the pit bottom. One of the squatters detached himself from the group and came towards them.

"Ayoop Jim. Tha's late. Ah, Billy boy."

"Fookin trackless" grunted Jim, and without another word led the way through one of the passages. The squatter winked at Bill, who smiled back at him and said "Ayoop Sam. As' tha goin on?"

"Oh, ah'v 'ad a nice long sleep 'ere waiting for thee and yon mate o'mine. An' we'd better be after him or he'll be waiting for oos."

Sam turned, hitched up his trousers and followed Jim, leaning slightly forward as he walked, his head lowered, his shoulders rounded, arms hanging loosely at each side. From one hand swung a round water tin, from the other a heavy lamp, still unlit. He was much younger than Jim, about thirtyish, small and thin. He moved quickly and effortlessly and had soon caught up with his mate. Bill ran, stumbled, got into his stride and was just behind as they reached the turn in the passage where the overhead electric lighting finished and they stopped to click on their lamps.

"Joost on" said Jim, looking at his heavy timekeeper. He snapped it shut and replaced it in his waistcoat pocket, to which it was attached by a chain.

It was six o'clock in the morning. Their day's work had begun.

* * * *

But it was nearly an hour before the first slab of coal was

levered from Fifty-fives coalface by Jim's skilfully directed picks. An hour of walking, stumbling, crawling, bending along nearly two miles of dark passages with uneven rocky floors and gradually decreasing headroom. And every second of that hour the air became thicker, the roof became lower.

Denton Main, like most other pits that honeycomb beneath the green grass of Britain's countryside, was designed for profit, not for comfort. Sinking the shaft, constructing the wheel-house, putting in the pit-top machinery and apparatus had involved the owners in heavy capital expenditure. Once the shaft was in the owners wanted to get the coal out — quickly. Nobody was interested in long-term plans for the most economical or efficient way to get the coal out. They just wanted as much as possible out as quickly as possible.

So roadways were started through the coal seams radiating from the pit bottom. And on each side of the roadways faces were dug into the coal stretching perhaps twenty perhaps a hundred yards. Rails were laid along the roadways and the coal was loaded into tubs and pushed along the roadways to the pit bottom by young boys and ponies.

Everywhere along the roadways the coal faces were being pushed forward as the coal was dug and hacked and grabbed from its million-year-old resting place.

Gradually the coal-faces pushed further and further away from the pit-bottom. It took longer and longer to get there. It cost more and more to get the coal out. The owners would not invest more money on machinery to transport the men through the underground passages or to cut the coal. Why should they? Their fathers and grandfathers had recouped their initial outlay many times over and now they were very comfortably off thank you and making good profits. Why spend it on modernisation?

So now, at Denton Main, the newest coal faces were miles from the pit bottom and the colliers working them had to walk for an hour or more before they reached their place of work. And with every step, every time they stumbled over a new piece of fallen rock or scraped their bowed shoulders on the low roof, they cursed the owners for their greed, the managers for their inefficiency and themselves for ever coming down the pit. As the sweat ran down their backs it watered and nourished a bitter hatred that passed from father to son. As the grains of coal pushed into each little scratch, leaving a permanent tattooing of blue marks on faces, shoulders, legs and arms, they rubbed in, too, an everlasting hostility, a mental tattoo that ranged collier against

58

coalowner, men against management, class against class.

"The bastards" muttered Jim as his lamp knocked on a fallen prop and went out.

They were now nearly three quarters of the way to the face and had just pushed through the last air-lock door which helped to control the flow of air through the complex of passageways and tunnels.

They were glad of the excuse for a rest. They squatted on their heels while Jim banged the heavy base of his lamp against the prop, clicked it back and forward, till the light came on.

"A 'tha' staying here then?"

"Ay" smiled Sam, "I'm admiring the view." Easing his buttocks he farted noisily. "That's better."

Jim sniffed and looked at Bill.

"Fookin 'ell. Better'n what?"

"Better out than in."

Jim stepped over to the air-door.

"Aye, an it'll be better out there than in 'ere, tha knows."

He held the door open and a sudden rush of air flowed past him. He let it close and the air became still and hot again.

"This'll do 'ere" said Jim. He placed his lamp carefully on the ground and leaned his water tin against it. Then he took his snap tin out of his pocket and placed it on the floor by the lamp.

He took off his jacket, his shirt, vest and trousers and rolled them all up carefully into a bundle, his big white belly folding into creases as he bent down. That done he rose and taking his bundle in one hand, he swung his lamp with the other so that he could see the stones lying one on top of the other along the wall of the roadway. Hooking his lamp to the wedge at the top of the nearest wooden prop, the big man grasped one of the wall stones and pulled it away revealing a black hole behind. He stuffed the bundle of clothes into the hole, pushed back the stone, retrieved his lamp and turned to the others.

"A 'tha fit?"

"Ay, fit to bust." Sam threw back the traditional reply over his shoulder as he too stuffed his clothes into a hiding place in the rock wall and pushed back the stone.

Bill, too, had been removing everything but his football shorts, boots and socks and soon they were all ready to move on over the last quarter of a mile to Fifty-fives face.

Now the sweat flowed freely down their bodies as the heat became more and more intense. The roof and floor, too, became more and more uneven and Jim frequently held his lamp up to look more closely at the roof and carefully kicked to the side the occasional rock that had fallen on to the rails during the night.

The back of a tub, painted white, reflected their lamps from a distance and they knew they had arrived at the face.

"Ayoop, now where is it?" Jim crouched low to accommodate his great frame to the four feet of space between roof and floor and held his lamp level with his eyes as he scanned the rocky walls. Crab-like he edged along the wall until he had found the spot, then, resting the lamp on the floor began once again to remove a heavy boulder. Reaching into the hole he pulled out pickaxe, shovels and a long crowbar. Silently the others took them up as the big man edged the boulder back into position. The last fifty yards with the extra load was stumbled in sweat and silence and, as they reached the row of tubs left there for them by the night shift, Bill sank to his knees and rested his wet forehead against the cold metal.

In the light of their lamps he watched the other two pick their way along the face that branched out at right angles from the roadway which had now come to a stop in a solid black wall of coal. This was it. The end of the road. Two miles out from the pit bottom, half a mile down, hot as hell, dripping with water, a space about forty feet long by eight feet wide and four feet high. A space where three half-naked men would spend the next six hours together in darkness, scratching madly against the wall of coal, propping little matchsticks up between roof and floor to stop half a mile of solid rock falling in on them, listening fearfully to each tell-tale creak, breaking up each chunk of coal they prised away from the seam, with pickaxe swung obliquely to avoid hitting the roof or the props, and knees bent so that their bowed backs did not scrape the roof.

"Let's 'ave a minute."

Having completed his inspection of the condition in which the night workers had left the face, Jim clambered over to the stone packed wall opposite the coal and squatted down on his haunches. Sam and Bill squatted alongside him.

For a moment all three remained silent and the quiet was as deep as the pit itself. And as black.

Sam was the first to break the silence, scratching the hairs on his chest where beads of sweat were glistening like dew drops in the light of his lamp.

"Ah'm, fookin shagged out afor I start."

"Ah. Too much fookin boozin last neet. Ah saw thee in t'poob wi' that lass. Did tha' 'ave 'er?"

"Did ah hell as like."

"Tha' didn't! By, tha should a seen him Billy boy, sniffing round 'er like she was a bitch on 'eat. Ah thought tha was in there lad. She fookin wanted it tha knows. Tha can tell in their eyes."

"Ah she fookin wanted it reet enough. An her fookin hoosband came and fookin gi' it to her."

"Fookin 'ell. Was that 'im then? That little rat-face?"

"Fookin was. Fook 'im. 'Ee, Billy," changing the subject, Sam looked over to the boy, "ah saw tha' lass last neet."

"Our Margaret?"

"Aye. All dressed to kill she was. In Barnsley. Ah just coom out the flicks and there she were, corner of the street. Ah were joost goin oop to say allo like and oop cooms this fookin car. Fookin big un it were. This bloke leans over and opens door and in she gets like. Didn't say owt and off they go."

He paused. "Tha wants to watch her lad."

Aye, watch her, Billy thought. Like I watched her yesterday, pretending to be asleep up in the bedroom. Hearing her in her own room first when she got home from work, changing to go out. Then her steps in high heeled shoes crossing the room, opening the door, crossing the landing, opening my door.

Shutting my eyes as she comes in.

Slit them open now and christ there she was right in front of the bed, those long legs, all silk stocking till the top. White thighs made whiter by thin black suspenders.

She bent down, slightly sideways, removing first one shoe then the other so as not to wake him and as she leaned forward he saw her breasts falling away from her body, overflowing the black brassiere.

She tip-toed across the room to the chest of drawers by the window. Hers was the top drawer. As she stood there searching through the drawer he noticed the awkward sag of the top of her stockings where no suspenders held them, and thought she's getting a big bottom. Big altogether for her age. Only sixteen. She pushed the drawer shut and he closed his eyes again.

Watch her? Not likely.

"Nay. I'll not watch her. She'll 'ave to look after 'ersen. She's old enough tha knows."

"By! She's only a child, lad. Once these young lasses start running around wi' men in big cars tha' knows, they get big ideas."

"An big bellies too more'n likely" grunted Jim. He took the watch out of his waistcoat and held it into the light. "Fookin 'ell.

We'd better get some big ideas too, or it'll be a fookin long time afor you're pickin up young girls in a big car."

As they scrambled up Sam's face came close to Bill's in the circle of light thrown out by his lamp.

"Think on, lad" he said. "Think on what ah've told thee. Ah'll say no more. Joost watch'er."

* * * *

So that's it, Margaret thought to herself.

That's all there is to it.

He seems satisfied enough.

She studied him, lying slightly away from her now, one arm stretched out towards her, his hand just under the hollow of her neck, the other hand resting on his stomach, one finger absently scratching the curly black hairs.

Isn't it small now. Funny, like a little old lady.

Got a bit of a belly on him though. Strange how you don't notice that when he's dressed. Still he's got a lovely broad chest. Those ribs come up almost square the way he's lying there. White. Very white skin, like a baby. Just a few little hairs round his nipples, black as well, but the hair underneath his arms is brown. Funny that.

Sally had been right.

It wasn't anything special. It's been far more exciting just playing around sometimes. This was all over so quickly.

She watched the slow automatic movements of his finger and half-smiled to herself.

Funny little thing. It had been so big. Now it was so small. He had certainly been in a hurry. Couldn't control himself at all, couldn't stop ... couldn't talk ... couldn't open his eyes. Just going away there like a madman. Like some animal.

Men!

Christ, don't they fancy themselves. All dressed up, sitting there behind their big desks. Do this Miss Houghton, do that Miss Houghton. *I* know what to do. Just got to lift my skirt half an inch over my knees and they're away.

Do anything you like with them.

Sally was right.

You can do anything you like with them, she'd said. She was a girl was Sally. Knew all about it. Took a while to get to know her, but that time when she'd seen young Harry trying to kiss me she'd been really marvellous. She took me out for a cup of tea in that café and said "What's all this with young Harry?"

"He wanted to kiss me"

"And didn't you want him to?"

"No. Of course not"

"Of course not? Well, why didn't you stop him?"

"How could I? He's stronger than me"

"Don't you know how to stop men messing around with you?"

Margaret shook her head.

"Hmm. Do you know how to *start* 'em?"

"What d'you mean?"

"D'you know anything? About men I mean. Love, kissing, messing about. Sex"

"Well . . . I . . ."

"Come off it Maggie lass. Let's have it. This is the first time you've been kissed. You don't know what it's all about. You've never seen a man with his trousers off have you?"

Margaret thought of her mother and father. The way she'd cried out, the light of the moon on his body.

But she shook her head.

"Look luv. Now Harry's tasted blood he won't be able to keep his hands off you. What're you going to do about it?"

"I don't know Sally. What should I do?"

"D'you like him?"

"Harry? He's all right. I like him. But . . ."

"But not like that, eh? What about the others? Any of them try anything yet?"

"What others? Who d'you mean?"

"All the other twopenny-ha'penny Romeos wandering around the office. Old Harry for instance."

She thought of the way he'd stood behind her when she was standing at the filing cabinet. He'd asked her for that Williams file. Came up behind her while she was looking for it. Right at the back it was, she'd had to pull the drawer right out. Forced her back on him. His front moved against her. And in the corridor the way he turned sideways to pass her. Sometimes he put a hand on her shoulder, came up from behind when she was typing and leant over to look at the letter. All that.

"Not really."

"Not really. I see. What about Jim? Or our dear Mr. Wingate?"

"Oh no! He wouldn't. He doesn't even look at me."

"Don't be so sure. Our Mr. Wingate doesn't miss much."

Sally had been right there, too. But even Sally wouldn't have dreamed that I'd be lying here in "our dear Mr. Wingate's" bed, with him lying there beside me all naked and quiet and satisfied. Our dear dignified Mr. Wingate, so calm, so efficient, so poised and civilised in his office, even Sally could never imagine him the way I'd got him five minutes ago. And I can do it any time. I know I can. I've got him now.

It's so easy too.

Sally had been right about that.

"Look luv, it's simple. When you go to the seaside you put on a bathing costume and you sit around on the beach, right? You're showing all your legs right up to the top, and half your body too. The men walk by and they'll look you over all right but they don't get worked up 'cos they're used to it on the beach. Everybody's doing it. It's all legs there."

"So?"

"So in the office you walk around in a blouse and skirt. You're all covered up from your knees to your neck. If your skirt comes up about your knees their eyes pop out. If they get a chance to look down your blouse and see a bit of your bra it makes their day. They're mad! They could see more on any beach in the country."

"But I don't see what all this . . ."

"Don't you? Look silly. If it makes 'em happy to see a bit of leg why not make 'em happy?"

"But it's wrong."

"If it's not wrong on the beach it can't be wrong here, can it?"

"But won't it make them . . . well, want more?"

"Now you're learning! Of course it will. Give 'em an inch they'll want a yard. Show 'em a bit of leg and they'll want to explore. Of course they'll want more. And the more you give 'em the more they'll want. Comes to that, the less you give 'em the more they want, too. But then you've got 'em, Maggie."

"Got them?"

"Of course. Then you've got them just where you want them. Then you tell *them* what to do. Take young Harry. He'll do anything for me. Anything. I just sit on his desk now and then and cross my knees when I'm having a fag. Doesn't hurt me but his hands shake like a leaf when he's giving me a light. He doesn't know what to look at first, the fag he's supposed to be lighting, or up my legs or down my blouse. Poor kid. I'm his dream girl. Bet he tosses himself off every night dreaming about me."

"But is it fair?"

"Fair luv? All's fair in love and war Maggie . . . and this is war."

*   *   *   *

"Penny for them."

Margaret started. His eyes were open now, smiling at her.

"What?"

"Penny for them. Your thoughts. You were miles away. What were you thinking about?"

"War."

A small frown creased his brow. He propped himself up on his elbow, drawing his hand away from under her neck. His belly sagged towards the sheet.

"War?" And I thought you were thinking about something important. Like us." He smiled at her again and reached over to stroke her hair.

"Don't worry about war love, there isn't going to be one. You heard what Chamberlain said didn't you? Peace with honour. He's been over there and talked it over with Hitler and it's all right. He's a good man. There won't be any war, don't worry. . ."

The fool. Did he really think I was thinking about their little war? Bloody men make you sick. So full of their own importance, so busy running the world that they can't see what's going on under their noses.

Penny for them! That's a nerve. Wonder what he'd do if he really knew what I thought. Wonder what *he* thinks? Don't believe all that stuff about his wife not understanding him. Bet she understands him all right. She looks shrewd enough. Bit of a cow probably. Wonder what she's like in bed. This bed. Bit of a lark sleeping in her bed while she's away with the kids. Wonder if she'll ever find out. Perhaps the neighbours had noticed? But the house was out of the way and it had been dark as the car came up the drive. Anyway, that's his worry.

She looked round the comfortable bedroom with its regency striped wallpaper, fitted carpet and heavy brocade curtains, and thought of her own bedroom at home which she still shared with her mother. She looked at the silk counterpane so quickly dragged aside and now crumpled at the corner of the bed with one of his white feet resting on it like some prize exhibit. She looked at the varicose vein that marbled the whiteness just above his knee and the heavy solid body and thought of her father again as she had seen him that night with her mother. Six years ago. Since then he'd never entered the bedroom again except once. Once only, and that was the following night when he'd tramped up the stairs and found her sitting up in bed with her arm round her mother, staring at him.

He looked at her for a full minute, then at his wife, then at Margaret's empty bed, opened his mouth to speak, changed his mind, turned and left the room. He slept downstairs that night and the following day arranged to go on permanent night shift and Margaret moved into her mother's bed.

That first victory in the battle against men stimulated no further actions in the mind of the eleven-year-old girl who just breathed a sigh of relief that it was all over. But it sidled into her unconscious, there to stay, coiled up in sleep sometimes, at other times slithering round the corners of her brain, its bitter tongue darting out to prick her memory. And now and then it reared itself up and writhed and swayed and spat poison and hate into her blood. Hate for her father and for all men. They were all the same. The more she saw that they were all the same, the more she hated them, and resented their assumed superiority, and wanted power over them so that she could hurt them.

Now she had that power.

Now she could do what she wanted.

But what did she want? What did she want with this one, lying there so smugly, deciding the fate of the world while his finger explored the depths of his belly-button?

"You see," he was saying, "we've got to be careful of the Russians. All very well for them to get up in the League of Nations and talk about supporting Czechoslovakia. After all, what does Czechoslovakia matter anyway?"

What indeed?

What did it all matter?

The only thing that mattered was that she could do what she liked with him. But he did talk such a lot.

"They want to get us into a pact against Hitler. To stop war, they say. But Chamberlain's already stopped war . . ."

Stop this, stop that. Talk, talk, talk. I'll soon stop you.

"Anyway we'll be better off if Hitler gets Czechoslovakia. That'll take him nearer the Russians and he's bound to have a go at them sooner or later. Let them kill each other off, that's what I say . . ."

As he talked on, Margaret turned towards him and reached out her hand. With the tip of her little finger she touched the tip of the little old lady.

He stopped talking.

"You men are all talk. If you go on talking about war you'll likely talk yourself into one."

"Nay, it's not only men Maggie. Tonight it's a woman talking. Good talker, too. Tha wants to come and listen."

"Ah don't. Ah've better things t'do than stand in t'square listening to a lot of Communists. If there's t'be a war at all it'll be their doing."

"Nay Maggie, we're not all daft tha knows." For the first time her brother Bill entered the discussion that had sprung up over the remains of the supper things. Still seated round the table were Bill and Edgar, Margaret and Bill's friend Herbert who had called round to take Bill down to the meeting.

Herbert Spencer was five years older than Bill and was one of a group of colliers who worked the new coal-cutting machine on Forty-fives face to which Bill had recently been transferred. It was the first machine down Denton Main and one of the first in the whole coal field. Most of the miners were suspicious of it, especially the old ones.

They were afraid that the way it undercut the coal and brought it down would bring the roof down too. They were afraid of the wider effect of the vibration, they were afraid that the noise it made would make it impossible for them to hear the warning creaks of the wooden props before a fall. They were afraid that the machine would do their job and they'd be out on the streets again.

Herbert Spencer was not one of these.

"Nay, lads," he'd told them at the Union lodge meeting, called to discuss the new machine, "machinery has got to come. Pits'll die wi'out machinery. If we don't master t'machine, it'll master us."

Spencer had won the way and a group of younger men had been working with the machine for three months now. And could it eat up that coal! Like a hungry beast its teeth tore into the coal face and like ancient priests serving some fierce god the colliers worked frenziedly amid the clouds of coal dust and continuous clatter. Not everybody could stand the strain and after a month young Freeston had had enough and dropped out. That was how Bill came in.

Bill and Herbert had become friends and Herbert was often round at the Houghton's, specially at Sunday tea.

Some thought he came for the food, because Herbert was a great eater. Others said he just came for the audience, for he loved to expound on the causes and cure of all man's sufferings. One or two, however, suggested that he really came because of Margaret, for it was on her that he turned his gaze while putting away the ham pie, and it was to her that he directed much of his oratory.

But Margaret wasn't having any. At eighteen, Margaret was choosy, where men were concerned. And well she might be.

She had inherited her mother's country freshness and buxom figure, but combined it with her father's height and carriage so that, although she was a big girl she did not look heavy and her long, well-shaped legs gave her a slim and graceful appearance. Her face was open and intelligent, with very little make-up except a splash of lipstick on her mouth, and a dark shadow on her eyelids that drew attention to her great black eyes.

"One day" her mother used to tell her when she was a child, "tha' Dad coom back from pit wi' two bits of coal. Two tiny round bits of shining black coal. And we put 'em joost 'ere," and she would bend her head down until her nose touched the little girl's nose and their eyes looked deep into each others, and place a finger gently on each eyelid. "And that's how you got such lovely big black eyes." And they would both burst out laughing and hug each other.

Like coal they were. So dark that it was difficult to distinguish the pupil from the iris. But shining with the inner light of the coal that gleams in the dark; deep as the seam that runs for miles under the green hills; strange with all the history of the world locked in its silent layers; delicate with the gentle fossils of fern and foliage. All this.

But hard too. Hard as the coal.

And with it, her own personal hardness which began that night with that moonlit body which became all their bodies. The fear of one man which became a contempt for all men as she used each body to satisfy her desire for revenge on the one body she couldn't touch.

She thought of Wingate and smiled at the way she could turn him on or off like a tap. She thought of the others and how easy it was to work them up and how satisfying it was to stop just at the right moment.

She thought of the young man she was due to meet in an hour's time in Doncaster. That very posh young man, very superior, whom she had met at a party and who had brought her home in his

68

car. Simply by putting her knees near the gear lever she had started him off. Three times he'd changed gears, brushing her knees with the back of his hands, and each time she could see him changing gear mentally and finally at the fourth time he put his hand on her knee.

She didn't move away until he took his hand off to change gear again and she changed her position slightly, moving her legs further away from him.

Nothing further happened until the car swerved round a bend and she was pulled over to him and put a hand on his thigh for support, pressing her fingers hard into his flesh.

The road straightened, she leaned back, but left her hand on his thigh.

He looked at her but she looked straight ahead at the headlights on the road. Now they were entering the village.

"Better drop me here" she'd said, lifting her hand from his leg and pointing to the approaching street corner. She had hopped out of the car quickly when it drew up. Not even a goodnight kiss. But as he asked when he could meet her again she knew she'd got him.

She smiled again thinking how for the last three days the boy must have been planning tonight, telling himself how easy she'd been, feeling her hand on his thigh, working out what he was going to do.

Like hell! She wouldn't go. She'd go down to the square with Billy and Herbert. She just didn't feel like little boys tonight.

"All right, Billy" she said, turning to her brother, "I know you're not daft. But what good d'you think it'll do?"

"People have got to know what it's all about lass. Somebody's got to tell 'em."

"Why can't they read the papers?"

"That's the trouble" exploded Herbert. "They lap up all the lies they read and they think they know what's going on, an' all the time it's just bloody lies."

"Nay" replied Margaret, beginning to enjoy making her brother's friend annoyed. "If it's owt you don't agree with, it's lies. It's only the truth if you say it."

"Look lass . . ."

Herbert was away. He leaned forward towards her across the table, his clean shaven face reddening along the cheeks so that the high cheek bones themselves stood out white. He cleared a space in front of him by pushing the cups and plates to one side and his hands were rough and strong but scrubbed so hard that even the ingrained coal along his finger nails looked clean. His cuffs were white under the blue serge suit which seemed too big for him and he leaned forward to make his point, and as his neck came out of the enveloping jacket she thought of the tortoise she had kept as a pet and smiled.

He's a tough one, she thought.

Bit of a titch, though. Not big like our Billy and our Edgar. But he knows what he wants even if he doesn't know what he's talking about. He puts it across. He's sure, that's what I like. He's sure.

". . . ahm sure. Sure as hell that if people really knew that was going on they'd have this lot out and start to run the country proper."

He paused for breath and went on quickly, tapping the white tablecloth with one finger.

"Give you an example."

That favourite phrase of his. He was always giving people examples.

"Remember that strike five years ago? 1934. Right?" He looked round the room for confirmation. They nodded. Who wouldn't remember?

"Five weeks we were out. Right?"

His grey eyes looked straight across the table into Margaret's. "What for? 'Cos we was bloody starving, right?" This time there was no need to look around for confirmation, they all remembered.

Starving. Bread and dripping.

"How much did your Dad bring home every week then, Maggie?"

"Nay, he didn't tell me. How much Ma?"

Sitting in the rocking chair by the stove her mother put down her knitting and looked out of the window where the evening sun was reddening the bricks on the wall of the lav.

"Not enough to put food in our mouths. Not proper food. Not enough to feed him properly either. An' he had to go down pit wi'it."

"Ah'll tell you how much," Herbert's fingers clenched into a fist and, as he went on, he struck the table four times.

"Forty-four-bloody-bob. Forty-four bob. That's what it worked out every week in Yorkshire. And you know how much them bloody coalowners made that year?"

"More'n that I dare say."

"You're right Billy. More'n that. More'n four million bloody

70

pounds." Again the fist pounded the table four times. "And last year" he continued, now well into his stride, "they made nearly fourteen million. Now then," he suddenly sat back upright in his chair and lifted one hand, his index finger pointing up towards the ceiling, his head jerking round bird-like, to make sure his audience were giving their full attention. "Now then" he repeated "remember what the bloody papers had to say about us then?"

There was silence in the room broken only by the ticking of the alarm clock on the mantlepiece. The point was made, but Herbert believed in hammering it home.

"Did they say owt about your kids not having enough food Mrs. Houghton?"

The mother smiled and shook her head.

"Did they say owt about the lads that were killed down pit, Billy? Over a thousand that year, just bloody murdered, three of 'em in our own pit?"

"Blood on the coal" muttered Billy, his eyes fixed on the salt cellar in the middle of the table.

"What *did* they say then Margaret?" Now he was leaning right across the table, his eyes piercing into hers. "If they didn't say what it was all about, what *did* they say?"

Fascinated, Margaret shook her head.

"I'll tell thee. Communist agitators, that's what they said. Trouble makers."

"And wasn't that right?"

"Course it wasn't. Communist agitators! The Communists were bloody starving too, weren't they? What were they agitating for? A Communist Prime Minister? Sending the King to Siberia? They was agitating for two bloody bob, that's what. Another two bob a day."

"Ah, but could gaffers afford it?" Now Edgar entered the discussion for the first time. Two years older than Billy, Edgar was bigger and more solid looking, more blunted at the edges than his younger brother.

Herbert turned to him.

"Question is Edgar, could *you* afford it?"

"Eh? What's tha mean?"

"Could *you* afford it. Could you live on less mate? Could your Ma give you enough food? How long could you go on starvin' boy? That's the question."

"But if the gaffers couldn't afford to pay you any extra, what could you do?"

"Look Edgar. If an industry can only run by keeping its workers on starvation level there's only one thing you can do."

"What's that?"

"Get rid of the boogers who're running it and put someone else in."

"Who?"

"Herbert, of course!" Margaret jumped up, laughing, and picked up the teapot. "I'm making some more tea. Any of you starving workers want some?"

"Nay lass," said Herbert, annoyed at the sudden interruption that had spoiled his peroration, "It's nowt to laugh at."

"That's just the trouble with your lot. You never see owt to laugh at. That's what you should be agitating for, more laughs as well as more money. More happiness, that's what people want. We're fed up with stay-in strikes and stay-out strikes, and stay-down strikes and stay-up strikes. Why don't you organize a stay-happy strike?" Margaret smiled to herself as she filled the teapot. "By!" she exclaimed, "you want to get some women running your party, you'd get a bit of sense in you then."

"But we have lass, we have," replied Herbert, quick to seize his chance. "That's what ah was telling thee before. This speaker tonight is a woman. Reet good lass, too, from Leeds. Tha' wants to come and hear her."

"Do I?" Margaret stirred the tea in the pot, replaced the lid and brought the pot to the table. She looked at Herbert with a smile playing around the corner of her lips.

"All right then," she said, "Ah'll coom."

*   *   *   *

As they walked down the main street towards the square it seemed as if the whole town was taking advantage of the fine summer's evening. A group of miners stood outside the Denton Arms. Further up two more miners squatted against the wall on their heels, chewing tobacco. Young girls in summer dresses giggled and stopped to look in the shop windows, young men dressed in their Sunday best watched them from the other side of the street and laughed noisily among themselves.

Herbert called out to a group of them as they passed.

"Ayoop! A'tha going to meeting? Tha's going wrong way lad."

"Nay Herbert," replied one of the boys, "we've got our own meeting, sithee," and, laughing loudly the group crossed over to

join up with a giggle of girls on the other side of the road. "Tha'
wants to coom wi'oos, Herbert," the boy called out, "there's
nowt much doing down there."

And there wasn't.

The meeting had been started a good half hour but there were
not more than half a dozen men standing around in front of the
red painted wooden platform which stood to one side of an
asphalt covered square in the centre of a group of low buildings
and shops. Along one side of the square ran the main street and
green-painted metal poles carried the trolley-car wires along at
the level of the open first floor windows where women were
relaxing, arms folded, the supper things cleared away and all the
passing world to enjoy. The other three sides of the square were
bordered by narrow pavements which, at each corner, led off into
little streets from which men would appear from time to time,
screw up their eyes at the sun, listen to the speaker's words
floating towards them as they looked to see who was about, and
then move off down the street.

One or two stayed, leaning against the walls of the buildings, to
see who this woman was who was standing behind the platform
with Frank Mason. They all knew Frank, tall, burly, red-faced,
president of the Denton Main lodge of the Miners Union, and
secretary of the local Communist Party branch. But the woman?
She was a new one.

Not often you see a woman at meetings. Mostly stay at home.
Plenty to do there without bothering about meetings.

This one wasn't bad with her mop of red hair. Tall, too, but a
bit scraggy. 'Bout time that lad stopped talking then we could
hear what the woman had to say.

"Who's he?" Margaret asked Herbert as they walked across
the square and stood midway between the group around the
platform and the group leaning on the wall opposite.

"That's Eddie Sanders. Engineer. From Sheffield. Good lad."

"Aye, he looks it."

Herbert glanced quickly at Margaret, a slight frown on his
forehead, but she appeared engrossed in the speaker. As this was
why he had brought her down here he couldn't grumble, and he
shrugged his shoulders and turned back to the speaker.

At her other shoulder Bill leaned towards her and said,
"Knows his stuff does that lad. They reckon he's on the Yorkshire
Committee of the Party. Only six months ago he led a strike at
Sevens and Lake's where he works. Two thousand on 'em there he
had out, and he got 'em all three ha'pence an hour more in their

wage packet."

"Did he?"

"Him and the union, Billy," put in Herbert, "him and the union. Don't forget that Margaret. No man does owt by hissen."

"No? How d'he do it, Billy?"

"Ah don't know much about it, Mag, only what ah've heard at meetings like, but they say he's right good at negotiations and all that. With the bosses tha knows. Right tough wi' em. Takes no bloody nonsense and the men are all wi' 'im. Bosses know that and that strengthens 'is 'and. It's like old Frank Mason there, he's good when it comes to talking to t'office and laying down the law. And old Herbert here, he's not afraid to speak his mind to t' gaffers down pit. But this lad's better."

"He's better looking, too," Margaret thought, and gave her attention to the speaker.

"And so comrades, women have come to be regarded as nothing much more than pieces of property in modern society. To the rich man she is a plaything, a pretty toy to be kept in the bedroom or dressed up and paraded around in front of one's friends and acquaintances like a race horse or a new car. To the working man she is a slave who has to work all day in the kitchen, cooking his food, washing his clothes, keeping his home clean and his bed warm. If he had to pay someone to do all this for him it'd cost him a few quid a week and it'd cause a bit of a scandal. Like this he's only got to marry her and he gets it all for nothing and he's respectable into the bargain."

He's right. They think they own us. All they've got to do is marry us and put a ring on our finger and . . .

". . . in fact I begin to wonder if the wedding ring doesn't originate from the sort of ring that farmers put in the noses of their cattle so that they can put a rope in it and lead them around!"

Right! Like bloody cows.

"But comrades, this enslavement of woman has got to stop. For too long, men who would fight against any injustice to their fellow workers, would come out on strike, go without proper food maybe for weeks to improve the conditions of fellow trade unionists, have been prepared to condemn a vast section of the working-class, *their own wives,* to conditions of near-slavery and exploitation that they would never dream of putting up with themselves in the factory of down the pit."

Vast section of the working class? Their wives? I suppose you could call 'em that.

"We Communists, as you know, have always fought to improve the conditions of the workers . . ."

There he goes. Always patting themselves on the back.

". . . In the Soviet Union . . ."

Knew he'd bring Russia in. It's always Russia. They never do anything wrong there.

". . . where the first Socialist State is established, private property has been abolished. And that goes for women, too . . ."

What?

"I don't mean," the young man smiled at his mistake, standing upright on the platform and putting up a hand to push back the light brown hair from his forehead, "that they've abolished women! We Communists have been accused of lots of things, but nobody's ever accused us of wanting to abolish women. Strictly in confidence . . ." and he leaned forward with his elbows on the ledge of the platform and his eyes, ranging round the scattered audience came to rest on Margaret, ". . . we're in favour of them. Very much so."

He's nice. At least he's got a sense of humour. More'n most of 'em have. Nice eyes, too.

"No, I mean that in Russia they've abolished the idea that a woman is a bit of man's private property. Under Socialism women are the equal of men. They have equal rights, equal opportunities for jobs and education and an equal chance to get to the top in any trade or profession. They are paid an equal rate for the job and enjoy full equality of status with men in every sphere . . ."

But they still have to have the babies.

"We know, of course, that women are not the same as men physically. We men may think ourselves clever but not one of us can give birth to a baby . . ."

Second time he's said what I've been thinking.

"But seriously, imagine the effect of liberating millions of women from the slavery of the kitchen, and seeing them play an equal part with men in industry, in the professions, in the cultural social and political life of this country . . ."

"That's what you were saying before, Maggie, isn't it lass?"

Margaret, annoyed at this interruption by Herbert nodded but did not reply.

"Imagine, too," he was saying, "the effect of millions of voices added to those who demanded that the Government agree to the proposals for a Mutual Assistance Pact that the Russians made last May . . ."

Mutual what?

"What would *they* have said, when the Government finally got round to agreeing to talking to the Russians and sent to Moscow not the Prime Minister, not the Foreign Minister, not *any* minister, but a Foreign Office clerk, a full-time Civil Servant by the name of Mr. William Strang?"

Who's he? Why didn't they send anybody else? Why don't I know these things?

"What would the women have said when the Government finally got round to realising the need to plan a military defence against Hitler and sent, not the Chief of Staff, not even a field marshal or a couple of generals, but some obscure admiral they dug up, who goes by the glorious name of Sir Reginald Plunkett Ernle-Erle-Drax!

"And how did they send him? By air? Oh, no! There's no hurry, after all we're only trying to stop a war! By train? Bit difficult that one, considering we've already given Hitler most of the railway lines stretching from East to West across Europe. So we sent him on a nice long sea voyage. After all, he is an Admiral isn't he?"

As the speaker developed his ideas on the way the Chamberlain Government was taking the country into war Margaret realised how little she knew, how little she had previously cared about all this. Now, suddenly, she began to want to know. She felt just like one of those ignorant cows he had been talking about. Leaving it all to the men. It's my bloody world as much as theirs. At least they've got a woman up there. Wonder what she'll have to say for herself.

Herbert and one or two others in the audience clapped as the young man finished. Big Frank Mason steadied the platform and the woman climbed the three steps and looked at the scattered groups around the square.

"Friends," she said in a low voice, "I don't have such a good voice as Eddie Sanders. Would you all be kind enough to come a little nearer? It will save me shouting and losing my voice." She lifted both her hands from the ledge of the platform and, with a gathering-in circular movement of her arms, beckoned them all in closer. Reluctantly, but somehow unavoidably, the men leaning up against the far walls of the square came in closer to the platform. Soon, as one group converged on another and they all came together, a small crowd was gathered round the platform.

The woman, who had remained silent while this process was taking place, repeating her beckoning movements once or twice to different parts of the square, now looked down at the faces

76

below her and smiled.

"That's better," she said, "now I can see you."

She started in that low, almost musical voice with a faint trace of Wales somewhere in it and the words flowed into the crowd and carried to the edge where they seemed contained as if by the rim of a bowl. Passers-by saw the crowd by the platform and the woman talking but they could not hear what she was saying so that walked over and attached themselves to the edge of the crowd. And as the audience grew bigger so her voice seemed to carry further without getting louder and the words rippled in ever-widening circles round the upturned faces of the people.

They watched her as much as listened. Watched the continuous flowing movement of her hands, watched the sharp chin that turned, bird-like, from one side of the crowd to the other, watched those dark eyes that looked back at them, each of them, individually, for the length of a sentence or a phrase.

She spoke first of things that they knew. Of their own lives, their work, their struggles. And she took them with her because they knew that this was the way it was. This was the way they lived. This had happened to them.

They listened. They watched. They nodded.

All except Margaret.

Margaret's eyes were on Eddie Sanders who, after a few words with Big Frank Mason, had picked up a bundle of newspapers which had been lying at the foot of the platform and was now walking round the edge of the crowd offering them for sale.

Herbert, too, was watching him and as he neared their part of the crowd he turned to Margaret and said "Ah'll not be long lass, ah've got to have a word wi' Eddie. Will tha' stay here?"

"Nay" replied Margaret quickly, holding on to Herbert's arm, "ah'll coom wi' thee." And they were both stepping through the crowd of men who made way for them without turning their attention from the speaker.

"Daily Worker?"

"Tha'll not sell one to me Eddie lad, ah've got a dozen at home ah've not sold yet!"

"Herbert! How're you going on? I was hoping to see you before the meeting. We've got to sort out these education classes."

"Ay. Ah were going to get down early but ah stopped by t'bring this lass down else she wouldn't come tha' knows."

"Why not?"

The question was directed straight to her and he looked at her with very clear grey-blue eyes, his eyebrows lifted in a slightly puzzled look, puzzled that anybody should not want to go to a meeting. His skin was smooth shaven and his blond hair, a little long at the sides, was brushed back behind his ears. His collar was white and starched and he was obviously wearing his best suit, dark brown, and against it rested the copies of the papers he was trying to sell.

"Nay," replied Herbert, speaking for her, "she's just obstinate tha' knows Eddy."

"Herbert, you're talking like a coal owner not a collier. Let the lass speak for herself. Did you not want to come down?"

Margaret dropped her eyes for a moment. Then she looked up again, straight at him, eyes wide open so that a ring of white appeared above the black pupils, laughing.

"Not much."

"Then why did you?"

"Ah'd nowt else to do," she lied, thinking of the boy in the car, waiting for her.

"That's a good reason. I wish all the other people here with nowt else to do had come along to the meeting. We'd have a right good turn out."

"Nay, Eddie," Herbert put in, looking back to the crowd spreading out from the platform, "this is not bad. Best we've had here for years."

"Christ man, I should think so. We're practically at bloody war, aren't we? We should have the whole bloody town out. They'll be out right enough when the bombs start to drop."

Look at the way he burns! There's fire in him. You can see it in his eyes. So cool and clear before, but now glowing like steel suddenly white-hot in the furnace. He's different, this one.

"What d'*you* think about it?"

Once again the question was directed straight at her, the blue eyes looking into hers. Was he trying to catch her? Did he want to show her up? Was he really asking because he wanted to know what she thought?

"Nay, ah know nowt about it. Ah'm only one of these ignorant women you were on about."

"Did I say women were ignorant?"

Now she'd got him annoyed.

"No, but you reckoned we were all about the same as slaves, and that."

"And you're not?"

"I'm not." She lifted her chin and narrowed her eyes as she said it. So there, Mr. Know-all! Think you know all about women. Well you don't know about me. I'm different, too.

"That's true," he replied smiling. "You're not, that's obvious. For one thing, look at that." With a jerk of his chin he indicated the crowd gathered round the platform. "Must be getting on for a hundred now, and apart from Isabel you're the only woman here. These bloody miners," he shook his head, smiling at Herbert as he did, "they're a wonderful lot when it comes to working-class solidarity but when it comes to women they're as bad as Hitler."

"How d'you mean?" asked Margaret, puzzled at the strange comparison.

"What was it he said Herbert? 'Kinder, Küche'. . ." he paused, trying to remember the phrase. "Children, the kitchen . . . and something else, that's all women are good for according to the Nazis."

"Bed and breakfast some of 'em say oop 'ere," added Herbert.

"And what do you say we're good for?" Margaret wanted to get him going again, but Herbert interrupted.

"Nay, lass, ah've got to sort out these classes with Eddie, we've no time to discuss all that again. Coom and 'ave a drink Eddie."

They were standing outside the Queens Arms and now, in the fading light, a warm glow of light came through the frosted windows and occasionally, as someone went in or out of the public bar, a shaft of yellow light and the sound of men's voices splashed on to the pavement.

Eddie looked quickly at the meeting, winked at Margaret and said "Aye, good idea Herbert. There's probably more workers in there than out here. Make it a bitter and get one for the lass."

Suddenly she felt his arm round her shoulder as he guided her through the door, after Herbert.

"Where shall we sit?"

She looked up at him, his eyes searching the room and noticed how the lobe of his ear was red, almost transparent, with a soft down of blonde hair running round it. His eyebrows, too, were picked out in gold by the light. He was not tall, but his arm sloped down from his shoulder to hers and his hand gripped firmly round her arm as he directed her towards a table in the corner.

"How's this?"

"Fine."

"What's your name?"

"Margaret. Margaret Houghton."

"Mine's Eddie Sanders. Glad t'know you. Any relation of Billy Houghton?"

"He's my brother."

"Ah." That smile again. "That explains it. Good lad, Billy."

"He's out there."

"Is he? I didn't see him."

"Here's tha pint Eddie. And a light for thee, Maggie." Herbert returned carefully placing the three glasses on the table beside the papers, the dark brown liquid overspilling as he did so, running down the side and forming a little pool on the glass table top.

"Ta, Herbert. Mind the 'Workers', lad. I've got to sell them yet."

"Tha'll get shot of 'em quicker if they smell o'beer," Herbert replied. "Ow many's tha got?"

"'Bout a dozen."

Herbert shot a quick look round the crowded bar, smiled to himself, winked at Margaret and reached for the pile of papers.

"Gi' me them, then, and we'll get shot o'them now before we get down to business."

He tucked the papers under his left arm and, taking his glass in his right hand, threw back his head and emptied half of the contents in one swallow.

Replacing the glass on the table he turned suddenly and made for the nearest group of men at the bar. "Ayoop Henry, does tha' want to read summat good?"

Margaret, laughing, looked at Eddie and found him smiling at her. She suddenly felt better, more confident.

"He's got a nerve, has Herbert," she said, picking up her glass.

"He's a Communist."

"Are Communists the only ones with nerve then?"

"I didn't say that. But it takes a bit of nerve to be a Communist. It's like anything else. Mining for example." He raised his glass to his lips and looked at her over the rim as he slowly drank. "You have to be tough to be a collier, right?"

"Yes."

"So you'll generally find most colliers are tough. Doesn't mean to say that other people can't be tough, too."

"Engineers, for instance?"

He smiled.

"Engineers, for instance."

Now it was her turn to look at him over the rim of her glass as she raised it to her lips. He lifted his glass again.

"Women, too."

For a moment they both drank.

"You going out with Herbert?"

80

She laughed.

He raised his eyebrows questioningly.

"He's Billy's friend. He came in to fetch Billy to the meeting. I came too. I told you. I'd nothing else to do."

"No boy friends?"

He had wrapped the casual question carefully in that quiet intonation of his and placed it delicately between them, like a parcel. How to unwrap it? What did it contain? A beginning or an end? Was she exaggerating? Did it make any difference to him? Then why did he ask? Do I want him to think I've got lots of boy friends — or none? Do I care what he thinks? Hell! He'll have to take me as he finds me.

"Nobody special."

"Ever been on the moors? Walking I mean."

She shook her head. "No. Always meant to but somehow I've never got round to it."

"You should Margaret. They're wonderful."

How strange her name sounded coming from him.

"Aye, I've always heard they were."

"I go walking there whenever I can." Once more he raised his glass to his lips. "Like to come with, next time I go?"

She smiled into his eyes and sipped her drink. "When shall we go?"

Suddenly she was calm again. The questions asked. The answers given. The issue decided.

"Let's have a look at the little book." He took a pocket diary out and thumbed over the pages.

"Never do to get your girl-friends mixed up."

"Five girl-friends," he replied, not looking up. "Monday, Area Committee, Tuesday Trade Union Branch, Wednesday Shop Stewards quarterly , Thursday speaking at Brightside and Friday branch meeting. Christ! What a week! And we can't go next weekend because I've got this education class of Herbert's . . ." He quickly flicked the pages . . . "How about the following Sunday? Two weeks today? September the third?"

"Lovely, September the third. Will I meet you somewhere or will you call for me?"

"I'll call round. You're up at Paynes Road aren't you?"

"That's right. Fifty-six. How did you know?"

"We Communists, y'know. Got to know everything." He smiled again. "No, I came up with Herbert once to call on your Billy. Must be six months back. You weren't in."

Six months wasted.

"Anyway, I'll call round about half past nine. O.K.?" He looked up at her as he unscrewed the cap of his pen.

"Lovely."

"Good." He wrote in his diary and she saw her name being written down on the blank white space. It looked funny upside down. So did the date.

Sunday, September the third, nineteen thirty-nine.

"That's a date then, if they don't start a war by then."

"Don't say that."

"Here we are then!" Suddenly Herbert was back, scattering a shower of coppers over the table. "Ah've got shot of the lot for you. Now what about those education classes?"

Zena

Zena took all her clothes off and stood in front of the mirror and looked at herself.

She was fourteen.

It was the morning of September the third nineteen thirty-nine, just before eleven o'clock. The world was getting ready for the biggest war in history. Zena was getting ready for the world.

She turned sideways so that she could see the profile of her young breasts, shaking her body so that they moved up and down.

Beside her was a table and on it some sheets of white paper and a box of pastels. Without changing her position Zena took up one of the pastels and held it between her thumb and fingers, the way her mother had shown her, poised an inch away from the top of one of the sheets of paper.

She looked at herself again in the mirror and then at the empty sheet.

Her eyes narrowed as she concentrated her gaze on the line of her chin, seen slightly sideways, as it merged into her neck and shoulders. Her hand began to move and the same line appeared on the white paper. Quickly now the line grew, following the pastel down the sheet of paper. The shoulder, gently curving but with a suggestion of the hardness of the bone beneath, running into the smooth flesh of the arms, merging now, in semi-profile with the nipple, then straight down over the ribs into the bowl of the navel until it stopped at the inverted triangle of her belly.

For a second the pastel rested there on the paper while Zena looked at the same point on her body in the mirror, wondering whether to go straight on in unbroken lines following the curve between the inside of her thighs, or to go back to the place where the hip diverged from the belly and run strongly down the outside of her thigh to her knee.

The pastel hesitated and, while she was deciding, she began to scribble in a mass of curly hairs at the bottom of the triangle.

The hip bone. That was the way. Sharply protruding from the belly's curve, bone beneath skin beside flesh, all in a line, in the way she held the pastel, in the strength of her fingers as she drew the line down over the taut muscle of the thigh, on to the knee-bone and down the shin to the ankle, the high curve of the foot, and the final end of the toe.

There it was.

No more just a sheet of white paper. Not even a piece of paper with a line on it. On each side of the line now, the paper had come to life. On one side was flesh and bone and personality, on the other side was space and time and situation. Not yet all there but more and more there with every inch that the line grew.

She stood back and looked at it with half-closed eyes and without moving her head her eyes moved from the mirror to the paper and back again. Then she moved forward into position again and her hand was once again holding the pastel poised an inch above the starting point. The same second of hesitation and then quickly the pastel descended on to the paper and another line grew on the white sheet. As this line followed the curves of her side, dipping deeply into the hollow above her hip, swelling out into the hard young softness and straighter then into the longer curves of the side of her leg to her heel, so life was gathered together between the two lines and the space, the time and the situation flowed round the life thus held between them.

Quickly now and without hesitation the pastel moved between the lines and with smaller lines and dots and smudges created breasts and arms, and eyes, a nose, a chin, a navel.

Now it was all there, or enough anyway, inside the lines. Enough to be alive. Now for the space around her. A place, a time.

Standing straight in front of the table now, feet apart, she rested one hand on the paper and leaned forward over the drawing, trying to visualise the scene. A wood? The water's edge . . . the sea. Waves and a high cliff? A luxurious boudoir, heavy with drapes and a tiger rug beneath her feet. A slave market with chains round her wrists and ankles and leering men bidding for her.

Like a god she smiled as she wondered what world to create and, like a god she suddenly decided, for no good reason, to place a tree beside the girl. A young tree, tall and straight with branches spreading just above the girl's head. Behind the tree a horizontal line created a plain stretching empty as far as the eye could see. And there it was. That was that. A mystery. Did the girl come from the plain? Was the tree the beginning of a forest?

Zena put down her pastel and left the mystery unsolved. The drawing was finished. The girl was created, placed in her world.

"Zee!"

Her mother's voice, from downstairs.

"Coming, Mummy."

"Hurry up, he'll be on in a minute."

Oh yes, Chamberlain. The Prime Minister was broadcasting at eleven. Daddy said there was going to be a war. Quickly she tucked a vest into her knickers, pulled on a skirt and jumper, looked around for her slippers, found them under the bed, and stood for a moment before the mirror once more.

This time the mirror showed a young schoolgirl, tall and fair skinned, with long smooth hair pale blonde in colour and skinny legs. She turned her head from side to side, gathered her hair together with one hand and slipped an elastic band over it, holding it tightly together at the back of her neck while the end curled over her shoulder. That'll do.

As she opened the door of her room she turned back wondering whether she should take her drawing down or not, decided not, and ran downstairs two at a time and entered the lounge just as the chimes of Big Ben boomed over the radio.

Her parents were sitting together on the big settee before the empty fireplace and, as Zena entered the room they both looked up at her. Her mother lifted a long delicate finger and placed it on her lips, then patted the empty space on the settee beside her. Zena stepped carefully over the pile of newspapers scattered all over the floor and sat down next to her mother. The voice of an old man spoke to them from the box.

"I am speaking to you from the Cabinet room of number Ten Downing Street . . . this morning the British Ambassador in Berlin . . . a Final Note . . . unless we heard by eleven o'clock . . ."

She looked at the big clock on the mantelpiece and imagined the scene. A big white envelope, stern faces, clicking of heels. Our ambassador, calm and cool in evening dress, a satin sash, medals. Them in uniform, Nazi swastikas on their arms.

". . . that they were prepared at once to withdraw their troops from Poland . . ."

She remembered photographs of young girls in national costume, gay with ribbons and peasant embroidered blouses, and imagined German tanks turning round and going home.

". . . a state of war would exist between us . . ."

The tanks turn their guns on the Ambassador. They fire. A stain of blood appears on his satin sash. He falls to the floor and they all crowd round and shout at him in German.

". . . I have to tell you now that no such undertaking has been received and in consequence this country is at war . . ."

War. Upstairs in a little brown box, a gas mask. They all had one. Breathe in. Breathe out. The black rubber sides flapping.

At school last week, like black snouted pigs, they had practised for the evacuation. Labels round their necks like parcels. And every parcel had its little brown box.

"Bloody fool!"

"Jim . . ."

"Oh I can't stand that bloody old hypocrite talking away there about all he's done to avoid it, when the whole damn thing's the result of his building up Hitler for years to fight the Russians."

A low wailing sound rising sharply and then falling again came to them from outside the window. Zena felt her mother's arm round her.

Her father quickly walked across to the window scattering the pile of newspapers with his feet. He pushed up the glass pane and looked out into the garden.

Set high up on a hill overlooking Hampstead Heath he could see the grey mass of London below him with the sun glistening on the distant dome of St. Paul's Cathedral. With a sickening sigh the air-raid siren died down.

Zena looked at her mother who smiled back at her and squeezed her hand.

"Don't worry dear," she said.

"Is there going to be an air-raid Mummy?"

"Probably not dear. It may be just a practice."

"Should we get our gas masks?" remembering the practices at school last week.

"Yes, dear, that's a good idea. Run up and get them. Ours are on the floor by the dressing table."

For the first time in her life Zena felt frightened. Really frightened. It wasn't a practice, she was sure of that. This was an air-raid and they would come over in planes and drop bombs, and the gas masks wouldn't work and they'd all be dead and the Germans would win. They'd come marching up the street, across the Heath shouting and saluting and killing people. And Mummy and Daddy would be dead. Where did she say? On the floor by the dressing table? They're not there. They'll both get gassed. Oh, here they are.

Picking up the two brown cardboard boxes by the strings she turned and went into her own room. As she crossed the floor she looked at the drawing of herself again on the table by the mirror.

Suddenly she picked up the pastel and on the straight line of the horizon she smudged a trail of smoke drifting across the sky. Above it, high up, she marked five dots, flying, in formation towards the girl. Then she moved the pupils of the girl's eyes to the extreme corners so that she appeared to be looking back over her shoulder, listening, afraid.

Downstairs, her mother had joined her father at the window and they both stood there, he with his arm around her shoulder, anxiously scanning the sky.

"We should have sent her away with the school," her mother said.

"Don't worry, love" he replied "there isn't going to be anything. And I'll know tomorrow whether the firm is going to evacuate. If it does we can all be together. There's no point in Zee being in Somerset and us being up North is there?"

His voice was comforting and his arm round her waist was reassuring. The sky was clear and the birds in the garden didn't know there was a war on.

"I don't think there's going to be anything," he said, turning away from the window. "Probably another smart move to take our minds off the fact that all this is his fault!" He turned back to her, holding out his arms. "How about a cup of coffee, eh?"

She smiled back and walked into his open arms, clasping him round the waist. "I love you, Jim. I really do."

"Still?"

"Still." She smiled to herself and added "In spite of everything."

"Or because of everything?" he asked.

Entering the room with the three gas masks in their boxes Zena looked for a moment at her parents, standing by the window, until her mother noticed her.

"Hullo Zee," she said, releasing herself and putting up a hand to her hair. "I was just joing to make some coffee. Want some?"

"Funny way to make coffee!" The girl's jests served to hide the embarrassment she experienced whenever she found her parents embracing. She liked to think of them being in love, but when she saw them loving each other it made her slightly uneasy, brought home to her the sources of her own origin, made her feel less of a person. She ceased to be one of three, a member of the family, but something extra, something smaller and somehow incidental, something outside the group which consisted only of the two of them. She could join in their talking, she could go out with them to concerts, to the cinema; she could eat meals with them, wash up, help clean the house. In all this part of their lives she could join as an equal member of the group. But in this she could not join. This was something only for them and she was kept outside.

"You help Daddy to clear up this mess," said her mother, indicating the papers on the floor, "and I'll make the coffee."

"But what about the air-raid? Shouldn't we take shelter?"

"Doesn't appear to be anything much," said her father, looking out of the window again. "There'll be plenty of time to take shelter if we hear the guns. Come and look," he held out his hand to her, "there's not a thing in the sky."

She joined him at the window and looked out over London.

"Will they come that way?"

"Should do. That's South-West, and I suppose they'll come over the North Sea and up the Thames. That's over there." He raised his arm and pointed a little to their left. "But you never know. They may come over the Channel and up over Kent. That way over there. Who knows? They may never come at all." He dropped his arm and put his hand on her shoulder.

Feeling a little better Zena sought reassurance for the other problems which were troubling her. "Daddy," she said, starting to pick up some of the newspapers which were scattered about, "we will win the war, won't we?"

He sat down on the floor facing her and reached for the newspapers next to him. "I'm sure we will, love."

"Will it take long?"

"That I don't know, Zee. I hope not."

She was silent for a while as she piled the papers on top of each other, headline on headline, column upon column, page upon page.

"Daddy," she went on, looking up into his face, "what's it all about?"

He smiled. "It's all in there love," he said, adding his pile of papers to hers and thumping the top of the pile with his fist, "pages and pages of it."

"But you say you can never believe anything you read in the papers."

"True. That's right enough."

"Then why do you read them?"

He laughed.

"That's a good one. Well, after a while, one learns how to pick out a bit here and a bit there. You learn what sort of lies each paper tells. This one, for instance," he picked up the paper on top of the pile and looked at the head of the page. "The *Daily Mail*. Not long ago they were telling us what a great chap Hitler was and what nice people the British fascists are. This one ..." he picked up the next on the pile ... "the *Daily Sketch*. Well, only this summer Lord Kemsley who owns it went over to see Goebbels, Hitler's propaganda minister and offered him space in his newspapers to print the Nazi point of view. This one ... ha! the dear old *Daily Express*. Earlier this year they were saying 'No war this year!' You see, love, you've got to realise that papers aren't just abstract things, pieces of paper which magically drop through your letter box each day, bringing you the word of God or something like that. Papers are people. They are owned by people, mostly very rich people. They are written by people. Every time you pick up the *Daily Express* you are getting a personal message from a very rich man called Lord Beaverbrook. When you compare what he says with what actually happens, after a while you can soon weigh up how much is likely to be true and how much false. See?"

"Yes, but what I don't see is why he should tell you anything that isn't true."

"Well simply because it's what they want you to believe."

"But Daddy," she went on, "how do we find out the truth then?"

"Ah, the truth." With a sigh he put his hand on his knees and got to his feet and walked over to the window, where he stood for a while looking out. "Well, Zee, I've come to the sad conclusion that there is no such thing as the truth. There are only points of view. Take this business of strikes we were talking about the other day," he went on. "The people who own the factories, and the people who own the newspapers too, are mostly interested in making money. After all, that's what they're in business for. One of their biggest expenses is the wages of their workers. They can only get more money by getting their workers to produce more goods for the same money, or to take less money for producing the same quantity of goods ... cars, or what have you. That's their point of view, and from that point of view anything the workers do to get more money is wrong. The workers on the other hand want to get more money, too. They want to live better, perhaps even afford one of the cars they spend their lives making. So from their point of view anything they can do to get more money out of their employers is right. They're both right. What you've got to do is to decide which side you're on, love. It's as simple as that."

He smiled at her as if to say "and that's not true either."

"Which side are you on Daddy?"

"Me?" He looked back at the sky again. "It depends what we're talking about. On an issue like this strike I think the factory workers are right."

"Are you a Communist then?"

"No love, because on other issues I find myself disagreeing with them."

"What sort of things?" she asked.

"Oh, things like the Russians signing the Non-Agression pact with Hitler. The Communists say it's a great move for world peace but I doubt if world war would have started without it. Yet you see love," he crossed the room to pick up one of the papers, "what the Russians say is true from their point of view. They reckon they could only promise to come to Poland's aid if the Poles would agree to the Russian army crossing Poland towards Germany. That makes sense. But the Poles wouldn't agree. They wouldn't accept any military assistance from Russia. And our people apparently refused to persuade the Poles so the whole thing fizzled out. Now the Germans are marching through Poland. And we're at war."

"Who was wrong then?"

"They were all wrong, love. All of them. The Poles were wrong to refuse Russian help. We were wrong to go along with the Poles. And the Russians were wrong to sign up with Hitler." He threw the paper on to the pile by the settee. "It wasn't necessary. The Russians were wrong, and it's time the comrades admitted it."

"And it's time for elevenses." Standing in the doorway with the tray held in front of her, her mother looked round the room. "I thought you were clearing up. What have you been doing?"

"Looking for the truth," said Jim, bustling around quickly, tidying up as he went.

They drank their coffee without talking, each thinking of what war might bring.

"Daddy," said Zena, "if I come up North with you and Mummy, can I go to Art School instead of an ordinary school?"

"I should think so Zee. We'll see, eh?"

Suddenly the low wailing noise started again, climbing quickly into a steady high-pitched moan.

"All clear, Jim!"

Putting down her coffee she put her hand on her husband's knee beside her. He smiled and put his hand on hers.

Over the rim of her cup Zena looked at the two hands, the fingers clasping, on her father's knee.

"Good," she said.

* * * *

As the new model stepped, naked, out of the changing room and walked over towards the dais, Lewis turned to Zena and said "Bit scraggy, isn't she?"

Zena smiled back, without taking her eyes off the model.

Scraggy. That's just like him. Can't be serious about anything. She was thin, true. Specially round the ribs and shoulders. But her breasts were full and rounded with enormous pale nipples.

As the model took her place on the platform old Sandford, the 'Life' master, busied himself around her, putting her into the required pose.

Why can't he let her just walk around? Then you'd get the flex and play of the muscles. Still, I suppose he knows what he's doing. That's not bad. Getting her to lean her bottom on the high stool pushes the flesh out interestingly there, and with her arms back it throws the breasts forward, hanging full and heavy. How can I get that heaviness? That soft weight of what's inside. Milk, I suppose. Glands, Tissue. Flesh. Soft, like mine.

Yet mine are hard. Firm, rather. Not hard, firm. That's what Lewis had said that evening three months ago when he'd come up behind her and put his arms round her. They'd both been working late finishing a still life. Everybody had gone except old Sandford who was pottering about in the Life Room getting it ready for the evening students.

Sitting astride on the donkey stool Zena had been trying unsuccessfully to capture the reflection of the bowl in the rounded bottle. Odd, that. A curved surface, like the fruit bowl, becomes straight, looking at it from her position. Yet drawing it straight is not right.

"It's not straight." Lewis's voice behind her was the first indication of his presence. He often stood there, silently watching her work, now and then putting in a word of criticism, a hint on technique.

She respected his advice because she admired his work. His drawing was sure and confident. He would look and look for a minute or two and then his hand would dart all round the sheet, making imperceptible dots and marks on the paper. The foundation, he'd call it. Rather like those drawing puzzles in the children's magazines where you had to join up a maze of jumbled dots, following the numbers, and as you joined one to the other so the picture took shape before you.

With Lewis, though, the dots and lines were his own private code. And when the "foundation" was laid, he would stand back again and look for another few minutes in silence. Then with absolute confidence he would translate the code into solid three-dimensional objects. A nude body, a bottle, the folds of a robe were all one to him.

Lewis was twenty-one, the oldest full-time pupil at the School of Art. He was not tall and his broad figure made him look shorter than he really was. His hair was thick and straight and yellowish in colour. That dark yellow that almost verges on to green. Zena had decided that if she painted him she would paint his hair green. It would be psychologically right for him, she thought. Green hair.

For there was something of the satyr in his face. It was a rough, country, almost peasant face. Coarse in texture, but hinting at something fine and sharp beneath like an unfinished piece of sculpture. And he spoke like that too, in a rough, country voice straight from the Cumberland fells which his parents farmed. But what he said was always to the point, always considered, rounded off, complete in itself. It was as if, in speech too, he sketched out a silent "foundation" in his mind before filling it in with words and sentences.

So when Zena heard that rough voice behind her saying "It's not straight" the pencil stopped in her hand.

"What d'you mean Lewis? It looks straight."

"But it's not straight, is it?"

"Doesn't that depend on how you're looking at it? My pencil's straight and if I hold my pencil up to the reflection in the bottle then the line of the bowl runs along the line of the pencil." She held her pencil up at arm's length before her, to show him, closing her left eye and looking with her right eye along the length of her outstretched arm to the reflection in the bottle.

"Is the bottle flat?" he asked.

"Of course not."

"Does it even look flat?"

"No-o-o."

"Then how can a line, drawn across the bottle, be a straight line?"

Zena began to see it. Yet there was still a doubt. "But Lewis," she said, "suppose you're on top of a hill and down there in front of you a road runs straight down the hill, up the next hill and over the top. You know it's a straight road, dead straight, because you've just come up it in a car and you haven't had to turn the steering wheel all the way. It's dead straight, but it goes up and down. Isn't it the same? Wouldn't you draw that road as a straight line?"

"Try it!"

"What d'you mean 'try it'? How?"

He sat down behind her astride the donkey stool, like a couple on a motor bike. He reached forward over her shoulder and as he began to draw on the top of her sheet of paper she felt his body pressed against her back, his cheek against her ear, his arm against her shoulder, his knees against the back of her thighs.

"There's your hill, in the distance. This space is your valley and you're on the top of the hill here. Right. Draw your road." He put the pencil into her hand which was resting on her thigh and as she raised her hand his remained on her thigh.

She began to tremble with excitement, wondering what was going to happen next. Her hand outstretched to the drawing board was shaking and the line that was intended to be the road started off faintly at the top of the distant hills.

Then she felt his other hand on her hip. He suddenly seemed to be all round her.

"There," she said, jerking herself forward on the stool so that a few inches of space separated her body from his. "There's your road."

"But where's your valley?"

Without the contact of his body Zena concentrated once more on the sketch. It was true. There was the straight horizontal line Lewis had drawn for the distant hill, and there was the shaky but straight vertical line she had drawn from it to indicate the road. But there was no valley, no dips in the line where the road should dip, no depth, no road. Just a line.

"I'll show you," said Lewis with a sudden eagerness and she felt a hand on each elbow. "Put your hands behind your back." He took her arms and put them behind her back, her hands resting, palms outward, on the stool between them. Quickly he moved forward, sitting close up against her again, imprisoning her hands between his legs. She gasped. She could have snatched her hands away but didn't want to. She didn't even want to move her fingers lest she discover what she knew to be beneath the rough corduroy which was pressing down on her upturned palms. She could not move forward along the stool because there was no more room. She was trapped. Wonderfully trapped.

She smiled to herself as she heard old Sandford moving an easel across the floor of the Life Room, separated from them by only a sliding door partition. A call would bring him in, even the clatter of a donkey stool being pushed over. But what it would take to make her call out, to make her jump up and push the stool over, was all a jumble in her mind of the warning voices of her childhood, gossipings in the cloakrooms of her schooldays, headlines from the newspapers.

Not this, certainly. Not this closeness, with his front pressed up against her back, his legs against hers. She wondered if this was the way it felt, the closeness between her father and mother. The closeness she could never share.

"Now look." Amazingly he had the pencil in his hand and, with his arm right across her shoulders had placed it against the top left hand corner of her sheet of paper. "Look down," he said, "watch my fingers."

She followed his instructions and bent her head to look down at the knitted hollow between her breasts and beyond them the thighs divided below the skirt and the wooden seat of the donkey stool between them. Suddenly his other hand gently touched her side and with an odd mixture of amusement and excitement she watched his two fingers begin to move like little legs, climbing up the knitted slope of her breast.

So gentle were the tiny steps that she felt nothing but the excitement of seeing his fingers on her breast and knowing that it was happening.

Fascinated she watched the fingers continue their march, now stepping it out down into the hollow of her bosom. Suddenly she felt she had to giggle, remembering a childhood game which repeated itself in her mind.

"Walkey round the garden . . ."

Her mother holding her hand.

" . . . like a Teddy Bear . . ."

Her mother's fingers, like his, marching up her arm.

" . . . one step . . . two steps . . ."

The ecstatic convulsive climax of anticipation, laughing and giggling and hugging together as she reached the armpit.

" . . . tickly under there!"

But now his fingers were approaching the second hill-top and they seemed to drag a little, tired at the long uphill march. No longer so light and gently she could feel each step pressing into her breast. But his other hand moving too, tracing the contours of the march across the paper like the needle of a seismograth recording the tremors of her pounding heart.

"See?"

She nodded, unable to trust her voice to speak, lest it should betray her excitement and spoil the game he was playing. Or was he seriously trying to teach her how to draw?

For a moment of panic she wondered if she had been wrong about him. But it was too late. The lesson was now in full swing.

"That's one way of doing it." Lewis's voice was soft in her ear, but so calm and matter-of-fact. She listened for a pitch of excitement but could detect nothing as he went on.

"Here's another way. Watch."

Starting again up the side of her ribs, his hand once again commenced the uphill journey. But this time pressing heavily with the palm, upwards along her breast until it was completely enclosed, engulfed, encompassed. She watched, head bent, not breathing, her teeth biting into her lips as he paused, contracting his fingers to squeeze and then release her before moving into the dip and then up again.

"Watch the line."

She heard his whisper and without quite grasping its meaning, nevertheless, almost automatically raised her eyes to the second line he was drawing.

It was a straight line. At first thick, then almost disappearing into a fine delicate thread, then thickening quickly and now, as his palm rose, gathering upwards, lifting and pressing, so that the line tapered finely into nothing.

Suddenly the pencil dropped from his hand and, as she heard it drop on to the floor she felt his fingers grasping her breast, his lips kissing her neck, his other hand on her knee reaching up under her skirt and she panicked. Without knowing quite what she was doing she snatched her hands free from the weight of his body and kicked back at his legs. With a cry of pain he released her and the next thing she knew Lewis was sitting on the floor clasping his leg and moaning, she was standing up by the side of the donkey stool and old Sandford was standing in the open doorway looking slightly puzzled and saying "Is there anything wrong?"

Finding her voice, she replied "No, Mr. Sandford. Only Lewis has hurt his leg."

"Oh. The bad one?"

Of course. She had forgotten. Lewis's gammy leg. The reason he wasn't called up and fighting. She ran to him and bent down, whispering "Lewis, I'm sorry. Is it . . ."

He looked up at her, his eyes seemingly floating in pools of pain. His face was pale and he looked suddenly old. He opened his mouth to speak and his eyes closed and he fainted away.

* * * *

Two months passed before Lewis came back to school. Zena had written two little letters in the first month, asking how he was and giving some news of the happenings at the school. But she had received only one brief note in reply, saying he was getting on all right. It covered only one side of a small sheet of writing paper with his large scrawly handwriting and was so formal and cold in style that Zena felt absolutely nothing as she dropped the letter into a wastepaper basket and carried on with a drawing.

It was coming on. Even without Lewis's criticisms her drawing was developing quickly. She was at it day after day, eight hours a day, and then often back again in the evening to night school. Subconsciously too, she had taken in the lesson that Lewis had ended so disastrously, and made her pencil give life to the straightened line with fine graduations in the pressure, slight variations in the slope of the lead. Old Sandford was pleased.

So were her parents. Looking at Zena's bulging portfolio of sketches and studies her mother smiled wistfully and thought of the two delicately handled water-colours which were the only things she had ever actually finished. Could she have been like this?

She heard her husband come in the front door and closed the portfolio. As he opened the door to the living room she could see he was cross.

"What's the matter dear?"

"Honestly, Suie, it makes you sick."

She rose, concerned, and went to him. "What does, Jim, what is it?"

He put his cheek to hers in imitation of a kiss and threw his newspaper on to the table.

"Russia's only been in the war a couple of days and already the rats are beginning to crawl out of their holes. It's sickening."

"Russia? Rats? What on earth are you talking about?" The incongruity of the whole thing brought a smile to her lips as she sat down next to him at the table.

"It's no laughing matter."

With an air of exaggerated patience she composed her face and said "All right, it's not funny. Then will you please tell me what it's all about, if it's so serious."

He took up the paper and looked for the paragraph that had upset him. "Just listen to this: 'If we see that Germany is winning the war we ought to help Russia, and if Russia is winning we ought to help Germany, and in that way let them kill as many as possible.' Well?" he looked up at her, "What d'you think of that?"

"That's a terrible thing to say. Russia are our allies now. Who said it?"

He looked back at the paper. "Some bloody fool American. Senator Harry S. Truman."

"Oh," she smiled, "an American. That explains it, they're always telling other people how to fight wars. Who is this man anyway. He's not important is he?"

"Truman? Never heard of him. Honestly, though, it makes you sick. They sit out there on their backsides while we fight the bloody war for them and they've got the nerve to tell us how to do it. Wouldn't be surprised if they come in when it's all over so they can say they won it for us."

"Errol Flynn to the rescue!" she joked, hoping to change his mood.

"Ah well, " he sighed, "I suppose we can be thankful he's just some two penny-ha'penny Senator from Missouri and not anybody of any consequence. I wouldn't like to imagine the fate of the world if he ever got to a position of importance."

* * * *

"You know Suie," he said later, when they had finished their tea, "I'm not very keen on all this."

"All what, love?"

"Well, this Bruce chap. And Zena. He's a lot older than her."

"It could be good for her Jim, getting about with somebody older than herself. Broaden her outlook."

"Hmm-mm. Don't think much of his outlook."

"Oh I don't know. He seemed a sensible sort of man. Just because he doesn't agree with you that doesn't mean he's no good does it?"

She smiled at him as she gathered up the tea things, not even sure herself whether she meant that remark to be a gentle joke or to be serious. Jim had become so intolerant lately. Other people's ideas exasperated him. He had no patience. Every discussion became an argument. Perhaps the strain of the job was telling on him. Even when he was away from the laboratory it was still going through his mind. And now that it was all top secret and he couldn't talk about it at home the strain of bottling it all up inside him was beginning to tell.

But apart from the job it wasn't as if the war had brought them any great hardship or suffering. In fact, their life in the little North country town was restful and pleasant. They heard the planes fly over. Sometimes theirs, mostly ours. More and more the bombers were taking the war into the heart of Germany. But apart from a short visit to their home in London the nearest they had got to an air-raid was the attack on the airfield, ten miles away.

No, it must be the strain of his work. He was beginning to look old. Not so much in actual physical appearance, although his hair was grey enough, but in the way he did things. The way he looked at everything, peered almost, even with his glasses, as though normal vision was not enough and he wanted to see below the surface. The way he sat down, lowering himself gently on to the chair. That was his piles, though. They seemed to be with him continuously now. Could that be the cause of it all . . . the strain, the impatience, the tiredness?

Poor Jim. Yet when he smiled sometimes, and reached out his hand to her he was just the same as ever. A person can change so much and yet not change at all.

His stillness puzzled her. It was so unlike him to sit looking into space. She put down the tray and went over to him.

"Penny for them."

"Only a penny?"

"Well, three ha'pence." She smiled as they played the usual game of words, knowing it gave him just those few second to collect himself together, to decide which of his thoughts he would reveal to her.

"I was thinking about Zee. And wondering whether I am becoming the sort of interfering old father that I swore I'd never become. I was wondering whether this Bruce is really no good for her or if it is just me getting old and possessive and not being able to realise that my little girl is no longer a little girl . . ." he paused " . . . and that I'm no longer a young man. Christ, Suie!" he looked up at her and grasped her hand, "he must be at least thirty. What does that make me?"

He was frightened. Actually frightened, like a little boy. Poor little Jim. She smoothed his hand and spoke to him in a very matter-of-fact way.

"You're forty-one my boy, you know that. And I'm thirty-nine. Nearly forty. And it's not Bruce that makes you forty-one. You'd be that if he'd never been born. But he has been born, and he's met Zee and they seem to like each other and I don't suppose it'll do any harm." She looked at him, trying to see from the expression in his eyes if she was getting through to him, and added "And I don't suppose for one moment that anything will come of it."

"Oh? Why not?"

"Well, for one thing he is so much older than her. Later on a difference of twelve years may not seem important, but at eighteen . . ." she shook her head, ". . . it's flattering but it won't last. Anyway, not with him."

"Why not?"

"There's not enough there for Zee. She'll eat him up."

"What d'you mean?"

"Well he's all right. Interesting enough for round here. He's an artist and I gather from Zee a pretty good one. The fact that he teaches at the school has probably helped. Young girls often fall for their teachers. I did once."

"You never told me."

"It wasn't important. Neither will this be. He's not . . ." she searched for the word, ". . . big enough for Zee. She's alive, vital, full of it. Drawing and painting have been everything she wanted. Now she's beginning to want something else. Perhaps it's her painting that wants something. Maybe that's why she's attracted to Bruce. But he's not going to be enough. At least I wouldn't have thought so. Not enough intellectually. And not enough physically either."

He looked up at her sharply.

"What makes you say that? Has Zee said anything?"

"No, silly. But I get the feeling, somehow, that there's not much there, physically. Or do I mean sexually?"

"You don't think he's queer, do you?"

"I don't know Jim," she replied. He looked away. "I never thought," he said. "Poor Zee."

She got up and took up the tray once again. "Poor Bruce, I'd have said."

"Poor Bruce? Yes, I suppose so. But poor Zee, too, if you're right."

"Well, if I *am* right, it can't do her any harm."

* * * *

The last rays of the setting sun rested for a moment on the corner of the screen in Bruce's top floor studio as Zee felt behind her back to undo the button of her brassiere. As she slipped her arms through the straps and dropped the brassiere on to the chair with the rest of her clothes she felt a shiver run through her body which had no connection with the disappearance of the sun or the temperature of the room. Beyond the screen she could hear Bruce walking about, preparing his easel, and she lifted her trembling hands to steady them on her trembling breasts. Beneath the smooth skin she could feel her heart jumping about like a caged animal, sending the blood tingling to her nipples and down through her body. Her fingers followed the flow down across her navel until she held herself to herself and knew that now there was no turning back. Now she would go to him.

She stepped out slowly from behind the screen and looked at him.

For a full minute he did not notice her appearance, being too occupied in fixing a large canvas on to the easel in front of him. Zee stood there, quite silent and still, holding her breath, waiting for him to see her.

Suddenly he looked up.

Their eyes met and then she watched his gaze slide gradually down. She felt her breasts rise as she breathed in deeply, straining towards him like two greyhounds she had within her on a leash.

"Oh good," he said, "you're ready."

His voice broke the tension, and feeling suddenly light-hearted she twirled around on one heel, lifting her arms as she did so. "Yes, sir, I'm ready," she replied as she faced him again. "Where do you want me?"

The left side of his mouth went up in that wry smile of his which she knew so well and understood so little. As always it was accompanied by a sadness in his eyes so that the whole effect was not so much a smile as a sigh.

"Would you sit on that chair Zena."

He had pointed to a chair just behind her and gone back to adjusting his canvas. And it was as if she had become naked inside as well as outside. There was nothing. Only a heart pounding away in the empty sack of her skin and a horrible sick feeling with the knowledge that there was nothing to sick, only emptiness.

100

Mechanically, almost automatically, she eased herself into the wooden chair. It was hard and cold on the backs of her thighs and the carved back was uncomfortable so that she leaned forward, her arms resting on the wooden arms of the chair.

"Are you warm enough?" His voice came from behind the easel. He didn't even look at her.

"Yes, thanks."

She shivered.

What was happening? Why hadn't he come to her? Didn't he even like her?

She looked down at her body and her breasts seemed to be hanging limply like paps and two rolls of fat ran around her middle. She leaned back and breathed in, pulling in her stomach and pushing out her chest.

"Don't do that Zena, just relax. Be natural."

She looked up and saw him watching her now and the warmth flowed into her again. She leaned half out of the chair and rubbed the back of her thigh where the slats of the chair had made red marks in her flesh.

"Your chair is not very comfortable," she said, pouting.

"Isn't it? Here. Try this." He turned and picked up a cushion from the divan behind him and threw it to her. It landed on her lap and she grasped it and held it to her, opening her legs slightly, biting her lower lip with her teeth. The softness of the cushion between her thighs was his first contact with her. She watched him, wide-eyed, as she held the cushion to herself. Would he see? Would be understand?

He smiled again. That same smile.

She leaned right out of the chair towards him, resting the whole weight of her body on one arm of the chair while she placed the cushion on the seat. She sank back into the chair stretching out her legs, lifting her arms up until each hand held a corner of the high back of the chair and she was almost reclining full-length, obliquely.

"How's this?" she asked, moving her hips, as if to settle herself more comfortably, as he looked at her.

"Oh no. Much too flat. Anyway you couldn't keep that pose up for more than a few minutes. You'd be slipping on the floor. Look, just sit up. I'll show you."

He came towards her, smiling.

This was it. This was how she had imagined it when he had first asked her to pose three days ago and every night since then when she had thought about it lying in her bed. He would pretend not to be interested. She would pretend to pose in some way or another. He would pretend to want to put her in the right pose. He would come up to her, take her arm perhaps, to begin with, and place it, oh somewhere ... put his hands on her body, as if to turn it sideways, then suddenly turn it towards him, holding her tightly, pulling her towards him ... this was how it was going to be.

"Look, push yourself back in the chair," he said quietly.

He was still pretending.

Her eyes were wide open and staring at him, watching the way he was studying her body. Oh quickly, now, quickly; must she go on playing this silly game?

"Back a little."

Apparently she must. All right. A little pressure with her feet and she slides back on the cushion till her back touches the back of the chair. Now what?

"Now move your legs over a bit."

"Like this?"

"Not so far. Look."

He held her knees in his hands. Now? Now! Gently he moved her legs a little with his hands.

He stood back. The contact was broken. He studied her again. Her still-wide eyes waited for his to reach them. As they did there was no answering gaze. Just that same smile.

"That's fine," he said, "let's start."

He turned and went back to his easel. Through a mist of tears Zena could see him jerking his head backwards and forwards, first to look at her for a second then to concentrate on the drawing on the canvas. Occasionally he would say something in that quiet voice of his but his voice was only the background to her thoughts.

Perhaps he really had wanted to paint her. Obviously he was more interested in painting her than making love to her.

Perhaps all those signs of his interest in her at school were in fact no more than interest in her work. Those times when he leaned across her to draw on the corner of her sheet of paper the way Lewis had done. Perhaps, unlike Lewis, he was really trying to teach her something.

But to ask her to pose for him. Surely that meant something. When Lewis had asked her she had known exactly what he meant, and had said no. But him? Perhaps after? But no, it was no good now. Maybe he has to pluck up courage to do it. Should she give him a lead ...

Hell! Why should she? She didn't even want it now. Everything had gone from her body now. It was just a body. It meant nothing at all to be sitting naked while he looked at her and drew her. He might not be there. She might not be there, for that matter. She wondered if this was the way models felt. It was quite ridiculous that he should want to draw her body. With a roll of fat round the middle. And goose pimples all up her thighs and arms. She was cold.

"Bruce," she said, "I'm getting cold."

"Wait a minute," he replied, not looking up but concentrating fiercely on his canvas. "I'll fix up the other fire." He glanced up at her. "Don't move yet. I won't be a second," and back went his eyes to his drawing.

He stepped back, looked long at the canvas with his head on one side, glanced at her, then back again, and with a grunt threw down his charcoal and came over to her.

"How's it coming?" she asked, stretching her legs quite naturally this time, without a thought of attracting him.

"Not bad. Not bad."

He crossed behind her chair and brought out the little portable fire that had been behind the screen and carried it round in front of her. "Not enough practice," he went on, "that's my trouble."

"But you're drawing all the time at school."

"Not like this Zena. A bit here, a bit there. Going from one to the other. But never on my own like this. Quietly, on my own, with my own model, in my own time, with no interruptions. This is the way."

He sat on the floor at her feet and as she rubbed a little warmth back into her thighs she smiled at the sudden thought of the complete lack of sex in the situation. Had anybody told her that she could sit like this, naked, with a man at her feet, just chatting and feeling nothing, she would have thought them mad. Where had it all gone? They were the same people. Those were the same hands that had held, for a moment, these same knees. But where was the heat within her? Could it be turned on and off like the electric fire? Could she turn it on, or would it have to be him? Or another man. How? Just by looking at her? And yet that look may not mean anything, as Bruce's obviously hadn't. Had he done it with other girls?

"Do you find it so difficult to get models then?" she asked.

"Oh yes, hellishly difficult up here. They're so narrow-minded in these little provincial towns. If you ask anybody to pose for you they immediately think you want to seduce them. Even the professionals at the school won't come and pose for me up here.

They think I'm after them and that makes it difficult at school and so I don't ask them."

"And aren't you?"

"Aren't I what?"

"After them."

"Good God, no!"

The sudden vehemence surprised her. She looked at him but he avoided her eyes and started to get up. Then, standing above he looked down into her eyes and the corner of his mouth came up again as he said, very quietly, "You see Zena, I'm not made that way."

She laughed. "What do you mean? We're all made that way, aren't we?"

The smile had gone and all that was left was the sad silent sigh in his eyes. "Apparently not. Some of us are made differently. And I'm one of 'em." He looked at her hard for a moment, then turned and walked back to the easel.

She felt sick again.

She looked at herself, at the fires, at the walls of the room, anywhere but at him.

And then she laughed.

He looked up at her sharply. "What's so funny?"

"Me," she said, looking into his eyes now and feeling strangely superior.

"What's funny about you?"

"Well, I've been so worried, since you started drawing me."

"Worried? About me? Me seducing you?"

"No. You *not* seducing me. I thought there was something wrong with me."

He smiled again. "And it's nice to know that there's something wrong with me and not you, eh?"

She hesitated and looked down. "I suppose so."

"Are you so sure it's you that's normal?"

"What do you mean?"

"Well, what makes a thing normal . . . the number of people that do it?"

She thought for a moment. "Yes, that's right."

"So here in England, it's normal for a man to love a woman and marry her and have a family and that makes him a normal man, right?"

She nodded.

"And in Africa maybe it's normal for a man to have half a dozen wives, right?"

104

"Yes, but I don't see. . . ."

"Wait a minute Zena. So what's normal in one part of the world may be abnormal elsewhere, eh? Now, a long time ago in Greece it was quite normal for men to love young boys, nobody thought it strange, in fact they made quite a thing of it. Ever read anything about those days?"

"Not much," she replied, "but I've heard about it."

"Nowadays, in Greece, they don't think so highly of it. I don't think they're as bad as we are here, but they don't make a religion out of it. Times have changed."

"So?"

"So what is considered normal has changed too. All I'm trying to say is that, what is normal has got nothing to do with what is natural or even what is moral, what is right and what is wrong. I'm as natural as you are. You like making love to the opposite sex. I like making love to my own sex. That's all. After all, it's not normal to be beautiful, is it? Most people are not beautiful, they're quite ordinary looking. That's normal. But we don't penalise beautiful people. We worship them, put them on pedestals, take photographs of them . . . even paint them." He smiled at her again as he said that. Now the old sideways smile but a straight open smile as if it were now all made clear and revealed and there was nothing more to hide.

She blushed and smiled back at him. "Bruce," she started, but did not go on.

"Yes?"

"Is it . . . is it hard . . . being a . . ."

"Homosexual? Well, it can be. If you meet someone and fall in love with them it's very hard sometimes. But that's only happened to me once and a long time ago. Otherwise it's just like anybody else. You see a boy perhaps and you think to yourself 'He's nice' but you don't have the opportunity to meet him or talk to him and that's that. That happens to you too, doesn't it?"

She nodded, trying to understand.

"Me, I shall probably be the equivalent of a spinster. I'm just the same as any other person of thirty, man or woman, who hasn't found anybody to love them. I live. I enjoy myself. I paint. I don't spend all my spare time in public lavatories trying to pick up young boys any more than you spend all your time on street corners picking up men. There are homosexual sex maniacs just as there are heterosexual sex maniacs. But most of us just go on living a very ordinary life."

"So you don't resent the law then?"

"Resent it? Of course I do. Hell, who are these people who get highly moral about who I can make love to in one moment and go off and sleep with somebody else's wife the next? And I resent all these well-meaning people who are so sorry for us, too. All this business about being 'sick'! I'm not sick. I'm not diseased in mind or body. I just happen to have been born in a country and in an age where my type of love-making isn't in vogue. Too bad. But I'm as healthy as they are. I'm as natural as they are. The only thing that's not natural about homosexuality is that is doesn't help to propagate the human race. But most so-called civilized people are busy putting most unnatural little rubber things all round their sexual organs when they make love, in a desperate effort to prevent propagation, so what's so different about me? I imagine I'm no more frustrated than most of that lot."

He looked up at her again and grinned. "I've been doing a lot of talking and not much painting," he said. "You must think I asked you up here with an ulterior motive."

"I did before," she replied with an answering grin, "but I don't now."

"Good," he jumped up. "Now let's get on with the painting."

* * * *

The boys in Air Force uniform were the first visitors to the exhibition since lunch time.

Zena had almost given up in despair when they walked in. Sitting at the table by the entrance with a neat pile of catalogues on one side of her and a little cash box on the other, she had had absolutely nothing to do but fiddle with the poster pinned to the front of the table. EXHIBITION OF PAINTING BY PUPILS OF THE SCHOOL OF ART. CATALOGUE SIXPENCE. ADMISSION FREE. She had read the catalogue five times and now even the novelty of seeing her own name in print had worn off.

AFTER THE RAID. Zena Clare. 20 gns.

Twenty guineas, that was a laugh. The exhibition had been open for two days and not a picture had been sold. Practically nobody had been in to see the paintings let alone buy them. Except yesterday when the mayor opened the exhibition and the local bigwigs were there, walking round the room looking at the paintings like tourists in a strange land. "That's nice . . . I like that one . . . what's that called? . . . Hm-mm . . . charming . . . those flowers are good . . . that's the castle, I can recognize that . . . nice bright colours . . . bit morbid isn't it? . . . what on earth? . . ."

She hadn't heard any comments on her own painting as she had
been too far away when people had stopped to look at it. She had
tried to understand the looks on their faces but it was impossible.
They were a complete blank. A long, empty look, a glance at the
catalogue to see what it was called, then on to the next one.

Even when she had seen them comment to each other there had
been no animation. If she had been there, instead of her painting,
saying to them what the painting was trying to say, then they
wouldn't have been like that. They'd have reacted in some way.
Argued with her, agreed with her, even laughed at her, but at
least said something. Like this they passed by as if they were
mourners at the funeral of some distant relative whom they had
never met.

There must be something wrong with it. After all their faces do
light up when they see Bruce's flower paintings. And those
landscapes of Kate's get a reaction, even if it's only recognition of
the scene.

But that was yesterday. Since then there had been hardly a
trickle and this afternoon it had dried up altogether.

So her heart beat faster as the two Air Force boys walked
through the door.

One of them was very tall and heavily built. His blue forage
cap sat straight up on the top of his head, unlike most of the boys
who wore them over on one side. It looked ridiculously small on
so large a man, and if it were not for the matching blue uniform he
might have just come away from a party, still wearing his funny
hat. To complete the illusion he had the sort of face that people
put on for carnivals. Big red nose resting on a coarse bushy
moustache, bulbous sleepy-looking eyes and bright red sticking-
out ears. But the overall impression was not coarse but calm,
easy. He moved with a smoothness that was strange in one so
large, but put Zena in mind immediately of the sea-lions she had
seen in the London Zoo.

So engrossed was she with the big man that she hadn't noticed
his companion until she heard a coin rattle on to the table and a
voice say "Catalogue, please."

She turned to the smaller man and, seeing him by himself, not
alongside the other, realised that he wasn't small but, if anything,
a little above normal height. But in everything else he seemed the
opposite of his friend. His hat perched impossibly on a wild mass
of black hair like a bird on a bush. A flickering in the almond-
shaped eyes, a quickness in the movements of his fingers and in the

way he spoke just those two words "Catalogue, please."

She looked at the half-a-crown that he had thrown on to the table and, picking it up she placed it on a catalogue and handed them both over to him with a smile.

"It's free for the Forces," she said.

He raised his eyebrows and in a voice edged with sarcasm said, "Well, ain't we lucky, eh?" and turned to his friend.

"Well, Smudger, what did I always tell you? The best things in life are free. And now look, I'm right again. Free. It's all yours. The world of art and culture lies before you — and it's free . . . free to the Forces." The intonation of that last phrase mocked the way she had said it, and he waved towards the paintings as he continued. "Enjoy yourself, lad! See the paintings, it's free! And tonight you can have a free ride in an aeroplane and drop some free bombs on somebody else's art gallery."

She didn't like him. All this showing off and waving his arms up and down annoyed her, specially that last wisecrack.

"Turn it up Joe." The high-pitched voice, coming from such a big man, was another surprise to her, and she looked round to make sure it was him, and he grinned at her like a walrus beneath his moustache. "Don't take any notice of him. He's a bit off." He tapped his head. "They don't let him out very much and when they do I've got to look after him. But he's quite harmless."

For a moment she took him seriously and looked so alarmed that they burst out laughing.

"Come on Smudger, we'd better look at the paintings. You're frightening the lady."

She took out a book and pretended to read as they started round the gallery, but they were obviously in a gay mood and wanted a bit of fun with her as much as they wanted to see the paintings.

"Hey miss, what's this?" They were both standing in front of one of Mr. Anson's abstracts. Mr. Anson was an evening class student and spent his time painting geometric patterns in pastel shades. Sometimes they finished up as quite pleasant designs, other times they just didn't work out at all. But every time, when he considered the painting finished, he would spend several minutes gazing at it earnestly in silence, then paint the title in bold capital letters in the top right hand corner, followed by the date. The other students said this was to make sure he remembered which way up it should be, but Mr. Anson just smiled, carefully cleaned his brushes, packed up his paints neatly in an attaché case and went home to his wife.

The painting that had caused the big man to call out to her was called "Wednesday Afternoon."

"What's this got to do with Wednesday afternoon?" he asked her. The smaller one was looking appreciatively at her legs, and, as she uncrossed them, got up and brushed her skirt down, she watched him watching her and thought to herself 'You may have come in here just to look at me, but now you're here you're going to have a look at the paintings whether you like it or not.'

"Don't you think it's gay and happy?" She directed her question at the big one, but his friend answered, still looking at her. "Sure it's gay and happy! In the middle of a war, millions of people getting killed all over the world and he's gay and happy ... on a Wednesday afternoon. What Wednesday was this, before the war started?"

"You had a little joke with me just before," Zena replied, "and you had a jolly good laugh didn't you? Did you forget there was a war on? Did you forget that millions of people were getting killed all over the world?"

Their eyes held each other as the challenge was met, and the tightness in his expression relaxed into a grin. All the lines of his face turned upwards, emphasising the almond shape of his deep brown eyes.

"She's got you there Joe," said his friend.

Their eyes still held until his smile was answered in the corners of her eyes and then her lips as she heard him say "Got me? Yes, she's certainly got me all right." Suddenly he turned to the painting again. "So it's gay. It's happy. But why 'Wednesday Afternoon'? Answer that one."

She walked over to the painting and stood there between the two men and it suddenly came to her why Mr. Anson had given it that title.

"Wednesday is half day closing in this town."

Now she saw it. Little Mr. Anson. Busy all the week in his shop, imprisoned behind a pane of plate glass, condemned to a life sentence of service with a smile and customers being always right. Mr. Anson with his tidy geometric mind, with everything in its right place, had stood in front of this painting when he had finished it, had felt the sense of freedom and happiness that the chance interplay of colours had created and had seen it. Seen it long before her and the other students, seen it before these two boys, and had spelled it out in neat capital letters in the top right hand corner.

She looked up at the big man's face but he still hadn't got it and was looking puzzled. She turned again to the brown eyes she knew were waiting for her, and he was nodding as he smiled. Not a straight up and down nod but slightly sideways, a nod that should have been accompanied by a shrug and seemed not to be saying "Yes" but "Yes?"

"She's certainly got all the answers, this one, eh Joe?"

"She certainly has Smudger," he answered, the smile ripening into a real grin that turned his face into that of a saucy child. "And that's not all she's got. So come on," he held his hand out to her and somehow, without knowing why or how, she felt her hand in his, being led along, "let's look at the pictures."

* * * *

Three hours later, as she listened to Joe discussing the war with her father, saw him sitting comfortably in the armchair by the fire as if he had been one of the family for years, she wondered how it had all happened.

In the gallery she remembered only her hand in his and now he led her round and talked and joked about the paintings. How sick she had felt inside as they approached her own painting. How warm and big and happy when he'd said to his friend: "Now this one at least is about something real. They're real people Smudger, aren't they? Whoever this girl is," looking at the catalogue, "she knows people, doesn't she? Zena Clare, know anything about her?"

She nodded, hardly trusting herself to speak lest she should cry. "Mm-mm. It's me."

"You!" The look of amazement on his face made her laugh. "You did that?"

She nodded again. "All my own work."

"But that's *good*." At the last word she felt his hand almost crushing her own in emphasis. She opened her eyes wide and looked up at him in mock modesty. "Is that so amazing?"

He smiled apologetically. "I'm sorry. Of course not. I just didn't realise I was walking round with . . . you know . . ." he hesitated, looked at her seriously now. A long look it was, not as if he were looking for anything but rather as if he had just found what he had been looking for.

He smiled broadly and, taking off his Air Force cap with one hand he held the other hand out towards her.

"Zena Clare, I'm proud to meet you. My name's Joe Gold. And this is my mate Herb Smith. We call him Smudger."

Thd big man reached up to take his cap off too, following Joe's lead, and holding out his hand.

"Pleased to meet you miss. Real good that," nodding at the painting on the wall. "I like it."

After that everything seemed to happen so quickly. They had talked about her painting, and then painting in general and then what else she was doing. Somehow she had invited him home to see some more of her work, or had he insisted on seeing some more? And he had gone off with his friend promising to come back and collect her when the gallery closed at five.

When he came back, just before five, he was alone. And she hadn't even asked about his friend. Smudger. And he'd taken her arm and walked with her, talking excitedly about paintings he had seen in the National Gallery in London at a recent exhibition of war artists, asking her questions all the time until they had arrived at her house. And he'd been so nice to her mother. Charm. Yes, whatever it was he could certainly turn it on when he wanted to. He just seemed to open up like a flower turning to the sun. Not so much when he wanted to, or when he felt like it, but when the situation created it. When the sun shone.

And her mother lapped it up of course. It was years since anybody had been so nice to her and before they even started to look at Zena's paintings and drawings they were drinking tea, and talking about London, and Joe had agreed to stay to supper.

For one brief moment, when he had left the room to wash, her mother had smiled at her as she gathered the teacups on to the tray and said, "He's nice." That was all.

Then he'd come back and they went upstairs to her room and pulled all her drawings out and Joe had sat on the floor looking at one and then another, sometimes saying nothing, sometimes just "that's good." Once or twice he'd shake his head up and down in that odd sideways manner and sigh "Ayayay." What excited Zena was the unerring way he picked out the ones she liked best for his praise, passing over the ones she didn't like in silence. Except one. A drawing of herself in the nude which she had done soon after that first time she had posed for Bruce. Perhaps there was too much in that drawing of what she had hoped for from Bruce. The face, the breasts, the twist of the body. It was all too obvious. She should have thrown it away long ago.

He studied it for a while and, without looking up said "This you?"

"Yes. It's not very good. It's not really worth keeping."

"It may not be good technically but it's you." He looked up at her quickly and saw her blush and looked back at the drawing.

"Be a pity to throw it away. If you don't want to keep it I'd like it."

"You can . . ." she stopped herself quickly, suddenly seeing the drawing pinned up in the barracks above his head and Smudger and all the others crowded round, laughing and whistling.

"No," she said, "it's . . . not very good. I'd rather not."

He smiled up at her.

"I don't want it as a pin-up you know. Second-hand sex never had any attraction for me. If it'll make you feel any better I promise you I won't show it to anybody in the camp. I'd like to have it at home though. I'd put it up in my room alongside Van Gogh, Modigliani and Diego Rivera."

"Who?"

"Don't tell me you've never heard of Rivera?"

She shook her head.

"Ayayay! The greatest mural painter since Michaelangelo . . . better even, in content. Do you know *any* of the Mexican revolutionary painters? Orozco, Siqueiros?"

She shook her head again.

"God help us and save us!" he exclaimed, clapping his hands to his head in mock anguish, "what do they teach you here?" And without waiting for an answer he was off on an excited, enthusiastic appraisal of what she was later to find out was one of his favourite subjects, Art and the People, both with capital letters.

But it was all new to her and wonderfully thrilling to be with somebody who was so excited about painting, and she listened, fascinated, until her mother's voice called her down to supper.

As they hurriedly collected the drawings together he held up the nude and said to her, "Can I have it then?"

When she shrugged her shoulders and replied, as if it were of no importance, "Of course, if you want it," she knew she was giving him more than a drawing. She felt that he knew that as well. But all he said was "Good," and they went down to supper.

*　　*　　*　　*

The biggest surprise for Zena, in a day of big surprises, came at the end of supper, when in reply to a question from her father about the way the men in the forces would vote if there was an election, Joe replied, "Me? I'm a Communist. Most of the lads are pretty left. A few will vote Communist where there's a candidate, the rest'll vote solid Labour I'd say."

Until then the conversation had gone with a swing. Joe was obviously well-read and could talk easily, even enthusiastically, about books, poetry, music and painting. There were big gaps in his appreciation but he brushed them aside as of little importance and talked about new writers, artists and composers that they knew little or nothing about. Yet all this without making them feel that they were provincial, or old-fashioned, but rather enjoying his youthful enthusiasm.

Zena could almost see her father getting younger. He hadn't enjoyed a discussion like this for ages. Not really since they'd moved up from London at the beginning of the war. She hadn't noticed her father growing older until, seeing him growing younger, she remembered what he used to be like.

And then the word "Communist" brought back the atmosphere of their home in London and the people they used to have popping in all the time, the continuous talks and long discussions into the night. The odd words that used to filter up to her bedroom as she lay awake in the dark. "Communist . . . Stalin . . . Trotskyist . . . Trials . . . Spain . . . Fascism . . . Hitler . . . War."

Yes, it had all ended with the war, and now that the war was coming to an end, was it all going to start again? Since their move from London her parents had hardly ever discussed such things. At least not when she had been around. It was as if, between them, there was no point in discussion. And with her, there had never been the need. She had her painting. There was the war. Everything else seemed unimportant.

But now this young man began to make her feel that these things they were talking about were suddenly terribly important. That the war wasn't just a simple question of listening to Mr. Churchill's broadcasts, watching the bombers fly over Germany, reading how the Russians had liberated another town overnight. The war was politics. It wasn't just a question of beating Hitler, but how you beat him. What sort of position you left yourself in after you'd beaten him, what sort of position your allies were in after it was all over. Allies? The Russians were so popular now with the Red Army advancing on Berlin that Zena had forgotten how unpopular they'd been at the beginning of the war.

"All right," Joe was saying, "Churchill wants to win the war. I'll give him that. And if he needs to co-operate with the Russians to win the war he'll co-operate with them whether he likes them or not. I'll give him that too. But co-operate in such a way that he gets the maximum advantage out of it so he ends up strong and they end up weak. Why d' you think they took so long opening the second front in Europe?"

He had this disconcerting way of suddenly finishing off with a question flung right at you. It wasn't clear whether he wanted an answer or just time to have a breather and collect his thoughts. But the question hung there and he was looking at her. She fished desperately round in her mind trying to remember about the second front and the arguments there had been about it and heard herself say, "Well, we weren't ready for it."

"But we promised Stalin there'd be a second front in 1942. It didn't come till 1944. Did it take all that time to get ready?"

Her father interrupted. "But don't forget Joe, we weren't exactly doing nothing all that time. Churchill decided to go up into Europe through Italy."

Joe snorted, contemptuously, and said "Huh! The famous 'soft underbelly'! If ever there was an example of Churchill's hopelessness as a military strategist this is it. Soft underbelly! Tell all the boys that died at Cassino how soft it was! All you've got to do is look at a map. Who else but Churchill would want to crawl all the way up Italy into Europe, over the Apennines and then over the Alps, before you get to Germany? Christ! If they'd sat down for a year to find the hardest and longest way into Germany they couldn't have done better."

"But the Germans weren't only in Germany remember," interrupted her father. "We'd just cleared them out of Africa, and Sicily and then Italy was the natural follow-through. And then there was Greece."

Joe looked up sharply at him. "Greece. Oh I won't forget Greece. I was there. We've just come back from there, me and my mates, and d'you know who we've been fighting in Greece? The Germans? Not likely. The Greeks. It's not even the Greek fascists mind you. But the guerillas. The same people who had been fighting the Germans all the time."

Her father leaned forward towards him. "You were in Greece?"

"That's right. Only got back here a couple of weeks ago."

"Tell me, what actually happened?"

"Well, it was simple enough. Most of the Greeks were behind ELAS which was the left-wing resistance army."

"The Communists." This time it was her mother who interrupted.

Joe shrugged his shoulders. "All right, the Communists. The point is they were the ones who had the *people's* support all over

114

Greece. Everybody admits that. Even Churchill. So when we land in Greece and, with the help of these ELAS boys clear out the Germans, the question is who is going to be the Government of Greece? If there'd been an election ELAS would have won, or rather EAM which is their political party. And that would have meant Greece would have gone Communist. And their dear old King George who was here in London all the time, would have been on the dole. And what's more important all our business interests in Greece would have gone, and perhaps more important still, Russia would have had an outlet in the Mediterranean. So . . ." Joe lifted both his hands, palms outwards, in a gesture of resignation, "out come the tanks, up go the bombers and Democracy was brought to the Greeks, who, if my memory serves me right, were the people who invented it in the first place."

"Why didn't the Russians protest, or do anything?"

Joe looked at her mother, who had asked the question, and then looked down, "I don't know," he replied, "perhaps they did. You don't hear everything."

"They didn't," said her father. "And for a very simple reason. When Churchill and Eden went to Moscow last October they did a deal with the Russians. We could do what we wanted in Greece and the Russians could do what they wanted in Bulgaria and Rumania. And this is the result of it."

"But do you mean Jim," asked her mother, "that the Russians would just sit down and say nothing while Communists were getting shot and imprisoned in Greece?"

"They had an agreement with Churchill. When are we going to realise that all the Russians are concerned about is themselves? If they have to do a deal with Hitler they will, as we saw in 1939. If they have to do a deal with Churchill they will, so long as it gives them their security. If it means temporary inconvenience or embarrassment to Communists in other countries that's just too bad. Even if it means a potentially Communist country going back into the hands of the capitalists they're not concerned provided Russia's O.K."

"A bird in hand is worth two in the bush?"

"That's right Zee, more or less. They reckon that only by superhuman endeavour were they able to establish the first socialist power in the world and anything, everything, must be sacrificed to ensure that the socialist state survives. And most communists throughout the world think the same I imagine." Her father looked at Joe. "So far as they're concerned, the important thing is to make sure that the only Socialist state survives and grows strong. Whether it's Russia or China or Madagascar is not important. Nationalism or patriotism as such means nothing. They're patriotic not to any one country but to an idea. That idea happens to have established itself first in Russia. So Russia can do no wrong. Right my boy?"

This time the boot was on the other foot, and Joe found himself confronted with three faces waiting for an answer.

He leaned forward in the armchair and looked slowly from one to the other, a slow smile gathering at the corners of his mouth. For a moment his eyes rested on Zena and the smile broke into a grin. He turned to her father.

"You have a very beautiful daughter, Mr. Clare, right?"

Zena blushed as Joe looked back at her, still smiling. Her mother raised her eyebrows and turned a puzzled look at her husband who, recognising this as an opening gambit and not as a diversion, kept his eyes fixed on Joe and nodded agreement.

"Right," Joe went on, and turned to Zena's mother. "Remember all the pain and problems of having her as a baby, Mrs. Clare? The pain first, the sheer pains of birth and then the nights of disturbed sleep, the business of changing napkins, the worry every time she became ill? I don't know about Zena, but me, I was an awful baby. Measles, whooping cough, scarlet fever, I had the lot. But my mum stayed up at nights and gave me chicken soup and pulled me through. Daresay you did the same, eh?"

Her mother smiled and said, "All except for the chicken soup."

"Well, she's probably all the better for that." Again he looked back at Zena. "She looks a bit of an angel now," he went on, "but she probably wasn't always like that. Maybe now and then she did something wrong. You knew it was wrong. Perhaps she even knew it was wrong and inside the family you'd argue it out, the three of you. You might even give her a wallop or stop her pocket money. But Christ, if anybody else started to wallop her, or do her any harm, you'd be there in a flash, protecting your little girl, wouldn't you?"

"A good argument, my boy," her father said, a gleam of excitement in his eyes, sitting forward on the edge of his chair, "but it doesn't follow. When Zee did anything wrong we told her off, and were able to put her right. Who tells Russia off, you? Harry Pollitt? I don't believe it. And then if anybody tried to hurt Zee it wasn't for anything she'd done wrong, but when people attack the Soviet Union it's because of the bad things they do.

Because of all the people in Russian prisons, because they want to dominate other countries and shove Communism down their throats."

"But you're arguing against yourself. You said just before that the Russians weren't concerned with other countries. When the Russians don't help the Greek communists you pour scorn on them. On the other hand you blame them for pushing communism down everybody's throats. You can't have it both ways! As for people attacking Russia because of the prison camps and lack of freedom and all that, well that makes me laugh. Take Britain. How many people have we had in prison in India alone since we took over the white man's burden? I reckon Nehru must have spent half his life in and out of British prisons. And God knows how many Africans spent their lives in camps the British people haven't even heard of. You think just because you can get up in Hyde Park and say what you like you're living in a perfect democracy, but you know very well that if at any time what you're saying and what you're doing has the slightest chance of endangering the state you'll be put away. Look at what happened during the General Strike when there really was some possibility of the workers taking over the country and running things themselves. First thing the Government did was put the twelve Communist leaders in prison. Just like that. Oh yes, we put people in prison too. And we've been running other people's countries by the force of our arms for years. No, what the capitalists object to is not prison camps or lack of freedom but Socialism. And when we stick up for Russia it is not prison camps, not intolerance we're defending, but Socialism."

Joe stopped for a moment, breathless. He went on quietly. "We'll sort out the prison camps. We'll sort out the lack of freedom and all the other things. But we'll do it our way. We'll do it in a way that will strengthen socialism, that will take away the bad and leave the good stronger. Not the way they want, by getting rid of the whole lot, and putting back the land owners, the aristocracy and the capitalists. We'll do it our way."

He looked up and caught Zena looking at him and his mood changed again.

"Hey! Weren't we going to the pictures?"

He hadn't forgotten, after all. She looked at her watch. "Well," she hesitated. Did he really want to go' He seemed to be enjoying all this talking so much, and Dad was enjoying it too. "It's getting rather late. We've missed the beginning of the first film."

She left it open. For him to decide.

He looked at her, trying to get what she wanted out of her eyes and, finding it there, jumped to his feet.

"That doesn't matter. Don't forget I haven't been to the pictures for months. This is civilisation! Culture! Progress!"

"What is?" asked her father, somewhat peeved at the sudden break-up of the discussion.

"Bob Hope and Bing Crosby! My favourite Americans."

"Brh-rh!"

Her father shook his head in mock disgust and started to fill his pipe.

"Goodnight Mrs. Clare and thanks a lot for a wonderful meal. It was just like being at home."

"Except for the chicken soup?"

Their eyes met.

"Except for the chicken soup."

"Goodnight Joe, it was nice to have you with us. Come again.'

"Thanks. I'd love to. So long Mr. Clare. I enjoyed our discussion."

"Night Mum, 'night Dad."

When they were gone her mother walked slowly back to the living room. She stood in the doorway and looked at her husband who was slowly puffing away at his pipe, gazing into the distance. He turned his head round and looked at her for a moment, then took his pipe out of his mouth and said "Well?"

"Well?" she echoed.

"This is where we came in."

"Is it?"

"Perhaps not." He thought for a while, gazing back into time again. "Perhaps it's where we go out."

Eddie

Slowly the corpse shambled towards him.

Eddie wanted to run. Or to hold out a hand to steady the shuffling creature that jerked forwards one painful step at a time, like a puppet with tangled strings.

"Christ, Eddie, look at them."

What were they? Were they really dead or was it possible there was some in-between state where the dead still go through the motions of living, like old actors playing a part they have long forgotten, with the footlights glistening in their far-away eyes?

They had seen heaps of creatures like this by the entrance just as they had driven into the camp and, though sickened, the two soldiers had come to accept death as part of their life. They were corpses and they had seen corpses all the way through France and Germany. French dead, German dead, their own dead. They all looked the same. Death had demobilised them and their war was over.

But here, these dead were walking towards them. Walking? Shambling, shuffling, stumbling, eyes staring from the sockets of skulls, skeleton fingers hanging on to each other for support, the rags that covered them tearing as they collapsed and sank to the ground. The holes that could no longer be called mouths twisting into open shapes to emit animal sounds that had not been heard on the earth for ten thousand years.

"They're after the food, mate."

His friend's voice reminded Eddie of the sack of potatoes he was carrying on his shoulder. He remembered his orders to deliver the potatoes to the camp kitchen, remembered how they had driven up from Regimental Headquarters at Celle through the bright April sunshine. Like a man trying to fight his way out of a nightmare he remembered there was a real world, with houses and people, and sunshine and food.

The leading corpses were within a few yards of them now and he could hear their desperate breathing alternating with horrible little birdlike cries. One of them who must have been a girl, or a woman, or a crone, because her rags hung round her legs like a skirt, fell forward exhausted on to her knees and, as she fell, lifted her bones in a sort of prayer and screamed as she was pushed face downward into the ground by a ragged unseeing skeleton who stumbled, arms outstretched, right over her without changing the crazy expression on his face, without looking down, without uttering a sound.

Suddenly the smell of them came upon the two soldiers. A sour, decaying stench of human excrement. Not excrement made by humans but humans who had become excrement. With the smell, and the closeness of the corpses, and their empty eyes and their stretching finger-bones, came fear.

Fear of disease. Of contamination. Fear of death. They looked at each other, dropped their sacks on to the ground and backed away.

In horror Eddie watched the first corpses desperately fling themselves with what strength they could muster, on to the sacks of potatoes. In a moment the sacks were covered with a jerking, writhing squealing mass of rags and bones. Some of them, exhausted by the effort, overcome with the thought of the food in the sacks, lay crying on the ground kicking spasmodically in a fruitless effort to propel themselves over the earth towards the sacks. Others crawled over them, bone rubbing against bone, trying to push a way into the heap of struggling creatures fighting for the potatoes.

Gradually the pushing and jerking subsided and the high-pitched squeals and cries slid into sighs followed by silence as here and there a body extracted itself and crawled away, half naked, half animal, half alive.

As the heap of skeletons dispersed, each silently, unspeaking, the weaker ones who had not managed to get near the sacks crawled over to examine the remains. Without a sound they turned the torn and empty sacks over and over, felt the ground with their fingers like blind creatures, examining each little piece of earth, each pebble to see if it was food, and just as silently, without a sound, without hope, without expression, turned and went back the way they had come. In a little while they had all disappeared, gone like ghosts the way they had come, with only the torn pieces of sacking on the ground and a few marks where

120

somebody's bones had been pressed into the earth.

"Christ."

Eddie looked at Stan.

Neither of them could speak.

After a while Stan turned, put his arm on Eddie's shoulder and said "Come on mate, we'd best join the others."

They turned and walked together, silently, in the direction of one of the big barrack-like buildings.

"The bastards."

At last Eddie spoke and those two words were all he could say at first.

Stan looked at him and replied. "Aye, they're bastards all right. But that's war, ain't it."

"War? Christ, Stan, this isn't bloody war, it's barbarism. This is the way those bastards think. They're the bloody master race. Everybody else, well ..." he waved his hand at the surrounding collection of huts, the barbed wire fences, "... they get this."

"But these places are only for Jews and suchlike ain't they?"

Eddie stopped and faced the other man. "Only for Jews and suchlike! Christ! You bloody simple sod. The Jews are only a fraction of the people they'd have put away if they could. The Nazis reckon they're the bloody master race man, get it? Everybody's inferior to them. Everybody, see? The Jews are only the thin end of the wedge. Everybody'll agree to putting those away. They're only Jews. 'Give us a hand' they say, 'to put these Jews in their place.' And so silly bleeding sods like you give 'em a hand. After all, they're only Jews ... and suchlike. They pick the Jews up by the arms and you take the feet. And together you carry 'em over to the pit. One, two, three and you throw 'em in. But you can't let go, mate. You're stuck. And before you know where you are, you're in the bloody pit with them. And those bastards are standing up at the edge looking down at you and laughing their guts out. Honestly, I don't know who's worse sometimes, you or them. If it wasn't for people like you with your 'only Jews and suchlike' they'd never have got where they are. 'Suchlike!' That's *you* mate, fucking suchlike."

His friend looked at him. He'd heard it all before from Eddie all the way through France and Germany. He was a good lad. But he did go on. When you thought about it, what he said made a lot of sense. Sometimes. About these Jews and suchlike. Suchlike. Don't know much about them. Never really knew any Jews. What he'd heard tell of them wasn't good. Still ... all this ... those bloody walking skeletons. Those potatoes.

"You may be right Eddie boy, but if we don't get back to the others we'll both be in the bleeding pit. Come on."

Quickly now, the tension of their earlier experience broken by Eddie's outburst, they made their way to the other side of the long black building. They could hear the sound of the bulldozer in operation and sharp orders ricocheting along the walls of the huts.

Belsen.

Who'd ever heard of it? thought Eddie as he made his way, still feeling sick, round the side of the huts to the open space beyond, where he and Stan had been ordered to "help clear the place up."

The concentration camp of Bergen-Belsen was one of the network of camps established by the Nazis in Germany, and later added to in Czechoslovakia and Poland as their armies overran Europe and spilled into Russia. Belsen had become a "sick" camp, to which the chronic sick, the dying and the dead, were brought packed in cattle trucks, from many of the other camps all over Europe. Hundreds died on the journey to the camp. They died standing up in the trucks, their open mouths sagging into the shoulders of the corpses crammed up against them. They died in the stench of their own excrement, trampled between their toes on the floor of the truck in which they had travelled for days without food or drink. They died in a state of decomposition, already green and rotting before the last breath left them.

They died in trucks, they died in lorries, they died on their feet, shuffling in ghost armies along the roads.

Died? They were killed.

Killed by every German who drove a train or a lorry, by every German who watched them shuffle along the road, by every German who saw the smoke of the incinerators rising into the sky. Killed by every German who provided food and equipment for the camps, who provided billets and entertainment for the guards in the neighbouring villages. Killed by every German who told about it on his leave and every German wife and mother and child and aunt and uncle and friend who listened.

And knew.

They must have known, thought Eddie.

Don't let anybody kid you that they didn't know.

It was all too big to be carried out in secret. Vast camps like these. Hundreds of thousands of people being brought in all the time. None going out. It wasn't as if they even wanted to keep it a secret. They boasted about it. This was their programme. This was their policy. The extermination of the Jews.

And suchlike.

Where would it all have ended?

As the two soldiers turned the corner into the open space Eddie's question was answered.

Rising before them was a great mound of dead bodies. Twisted and bent and stuck together, like a vast heap of macaroni, legs sticking out all over the place, green rotting skin stretched tight across white staring bones, a hand with fingers outstretched, a face, an eye, a mouth. This was where it would have ended. This was where it had ended for hundreds and hundreds of thousands.

It was impossible to tell man from woman on the ghastly heatp. Here and there the delicacy of a limb, the size of the features, showed that children had joined their parents in a mass exodus from life such as had never before been experienced in the world's history.

There must have been a thousand dead and naked bodies congealed together but it could have been ten thousand or a hundred thousand.

A movement in the midst of the tangle of twisted limbs caught his eye. A face had moved. Two eyes had looked at him, the mouth opened to cry. Somebody was still alive in all that mass of death!

Eddie started towards the heap, his eyes fixed on that one face, appealing, looking, crying out. An arm stretched out towards him and it seemed that the fingers moved but he could not tell if the arm belonged to the face, and even as he ran towards it he lost the face for a moment and stopped, staring at the spot where those eyes had cried out to him. Another face, another pair of eyes, stared at him, black eyeballs fixed madly in liquid sockets sunk so deep into the skull that Eddie was suddenly reminded of those potato masks he had made as a child with eyes and teeth cut out and candles flickering through the holes to frighten little girls.

Desperately his eyes searched the pile. The top of a head, diseased and covered with sores, a back, every bone of the spine standing out separately, a leg with shining silvery smears as if snails had been crawling over it, a stomach pregnant with starvation, balloon-white and shiny, down to the triangle of curly black hairs.

Where was she? Or he . . . or it? He took another step towards the human junk heap and felt a hand on his shoulder.

"Keep away from there lad."

He turned to see the Sergeant who was directing the operations of the bulldozer.

"But there's something alive in there Sarge. I saw her."

"There's nobody alive there, boy." The voice was kind and soft, coming incongruously from a face that was tightly drawn in hard lines.

"But I saw something move. Her eyes. Her mouth opened."

"Rigor mortis. There's nothing alive there. Not what we call alive. Only the lice, and they're getting out as fast as they can."

Eddie turned and took a step nearer the heap.

"That'll do, lad. Don't get any nearer and don't touch anything."

The hand was on his shoulder. Hard and firm. He turned his head and looked into the Sergeant's eyes.

"Typhus," said the sergeant.

"Come on, boy," he went on, increasing the pressure on his shoulder in such a way that Eddie eased away from the heap. "I want you down the side there." He pointed to the other side of the pile of bodies where a great pit had been dug. Two men were standing there, waiting, looking down into the pit.

"We've got to bury this lot," the Sergeant waved at the bodies, "and quick. Otherwise the whole place will stink to high heaven and we won't be able to control the typhus. So we're going to push 'em in, see, with the machine. It's a rotten job, but it's got to be done. They won't feel anything. Not any more.

"Those bastards over there," he went on, indicating the waiting men, "are SS guards. Worked here at the camp. They're going to pick up the odd ones that escape the bulldozer and throw 'em in. Right?"

Eddie nodded. SS guards.

"I want you to keep the bastards at it." The sergeant paused for a moment and they both looked across the pit at the two men and it was as if the pit was purgatory itself and there waiting on the other side were the devils, ready to cast the souls into damnation.

"All right lad, get moving."

In a daze Eddie walked along the edge of the pit towards the two SS men. On one side of him rose the human rubbish heap, on the other side the ground fell away from his feet and the layers of black earth lay open in a gigantic grave.

It was all too big. Sickness and hate and a terrible weariness flooded into his head as each step took him nearer the two guards. What sort of creatures were these? He had heard the theories that all the concentration camp guards were violent criminals, recruited from the goals of Germany, or sex maniacs and perverts. Yet these two looked ordinary enough.

They looked up as he approached. One was slightly taller than the other and his head was nearly bald. Wisps of grey hair ran from his temples above his ears and round to the back of his head. His face was sallow and fat around the jowls. His eyes were grey and, for a moment, they met Eddie's stare with equal hate, then dropped to the ground and he said something to the smaller man standing alongside him.

Unlike the fat man this one was nervous and his long fingers were continuously on the move, rubbing his hands together, pulling at the edge of his uniform, brushing the blonde hair from his forehead. Everything about him was sharp and pointed and nervously moving until the muttered word from his companion. Then he put his hands into his pockets and fixed his eyes on to the ground.

Eddie looked at them. Those two quite ordinary men had something inside them that made it possible for them to create this vast heap of death. They must have seen these people actually dying and done nothing to help them. Worse than that they probably laughed at them, kicked them, spat in their faces and left them lying on the ground. No, this was more than that, even. People don't do that sort of thing to dogs, or any stray creatures they see dying in the road. Not casually. This can only be done deliberately. As a plan. People have to be convinced that this is part of something bigger. That these bodies are like germs which must be destroyed for the good of humanity. No, not humanity, because these corpses had been part of humanity themselves. For the race. That's it, the race. Not the human race. The master race. That's what they thought they were. Two members of the master race. Christ! They look just like a couple of lads back in the factory. The little one could be old Foxy Lambert. Same nose and foxy look. Same nervous movements. Can't keep still for a minute. And the other one could be Bert Taylor with that bald head and fat face.

Could it be Bert there? At the edge of the pit, under different circumstances? Could old Foxy kick a dying man out of his way and spit on him? Could either of them imagine themselves to be part of the master race?

He looked at the pile of dead, and one leg, all skin and bone, sticking out of a heap at a ridiculous angle suddenly made him think of India. Delhi. Walking along the street one morning he had tripped over such a bony leg. And it hadn't moved. He had looked into the shadow of the doorway and seen the hunched up body wrapped in its miserable rags and wondered if it was alive or

125

dead. And he had gone on his way, because one got used to those turbanned skeletons lying in the gutters, used to the naked little pot-bellied children with match-stick legs and old men's eyes, used to walking past them. And the officers in his Regiment and government men, the top brass in their big cars on their way to play polo or soldiers, or bridge or politics, they wouldn't even see the starving crowds that slept on the pavements all night and begged in the gutters all day. They rode by like a race apart. The master race.

Of course it was different. We hadn't created the poverty and starvation in India. Not as a matter of deliberate policy anyway. We had just been there for a hundred years and done nothing about it. As a matter of deliberate policy? Those Indians who had wanted to do something about it we'd thrown in gaol. But the gaols weren't concentration camps. Or were they? Could we, like the Germans now, disclaim all knowledge of the misery and suffering that had been caused?

The bulldozer started up. Its great jaws were closed as, with clenched teeth, it slowly edged into the clot of corpses. For a moment nothing happened. The caterpillar tracks bit deep into the mud, the engine took on a higher pitch.

Eddie, the two S.S. men, the other soldiers dotted round the edge of the huge pit, fixed their eyes on the unmoving mass of bodies which stuck together in one great body, a monster with a hundred legs, a thousand arms, a million staring eyes.

Suddenly the monster moved. It gave way to the relentless pressure of the bulldozer and broke apart, one section seeming now to crawl towards the pit. As bodies parted which had been joined in death it seemed that arms stretched out to each other. A pair of legs, belonging to nobody, in falling to the ground one after the other, seemed to run towards the pit. A man, as his body was pulled upwards, swung his arm loosely in a farewell wave. Like an umbilical cord a white torso still linked the moving section with the bulk of the heap, arms caught in the former, its legs firmly twisted into the latter. As the bulldozer pushed further forwards the body seemed to stretch, held horizontal above the gap between the corpses, two empty breasts hanging towards the ground the only reminder that this was a human being and not just a piece of elastic.

Why didn't they go and dislodge the body? Eddie started to shout, but his voice could not be heard above the roar of the bulldozer and, from his seat, the driver could not see the twisted body now stretched to breaking point.

Then it broke.

No noise, no scream, no tearing of flesh or cracking of bone. The woman's white body, already rotten and tinged with gangrene, split in two and one part stuck out of the main heap while the other hung limply by the side of the now steadily moving pile of bodies that the bulldozer had pushed to the edge of the pit.

As the bodies reached the pit they seemed to tumble in, almost gladly going to their great grave. Some dropped down feet first, others, starting horizontal, turned gracefully as they fell and dived headfirst on to the bodies below. Some went in alone, others clung together. As the mass of corpses was broken up the breeze brought the smell of a thousand deaths to Eddie's nostrils and he could stand no more.

He turned and sicked up all he had in his stomach. And as he stood, relieved, with head bowed, looking down at the vomit between his feet, he felt the eyes of the two SS men on him.

He looked up and saw them staring at him, the fat one with a cynical smile at the edges of his lips, the foxy man grinning with his sharp little eyes.

Eddie loosened his rifle from his shoulder and pointed it towards them. Their eyes met his, no longer smiling. He started walking, feeling the rifle strong and powerful in his hands. He raised the barrel, pointing it directly at the chest of the big one, each step taking him nearer to them, along the edge of the pit now filling with broken bodies.

Above the noise of the bulldozer, above the smell of the bodies and the sight of empty eye sockets, above the taste of the sick in his mouth, above all these now was the feel of the gun in his hands and the knowing what he had to do.

He stopped.

All he could see now were the eyes of the fat man whose smile dissolved into horror as he realised what the soldier was going to do.

Eddie slid his finger on to the trigger. This was right. This was the only thing to do.

Suddenly the bulldozer stopped.

A voice rang out across the pit.

"Sanders!"

His finger trembled on the trigger. His eyes closed and another wave of sickness rushed through him and seemed to drain all the feeling out of him, down from his head through his shoulders into his groin. He felt suddenly weak and dripping with sweat, his legs shaking.

He lowered the rifle and turned his head. "Sarge?"

"Get those two bastards over here, clearing up these bodies."

"Sarge."

Eddie turned back to the SS men and saw that they too were covered with sweat. He motioned them on with his rifle. "All right you bastards," he shouted, "get moving."

*   *   *   *

The war in Europe ended in April 1945. Hitler and Mussolini were dead, the former burning in his Berlin headquarters to the sound of Russian guns, the latter hanging upside down in a square in Milan to the screams and jeers of the Italian populace. And the victorious Churchill turned to the exultant British public asking not for blood, sweat, tears and toil, but for their votes in the General Election.

Eddie, on leave, decided to devote his time to working for one of the Communist Party candidates, Bert Head, who was standing for the industrial constituency of Blackton in Yorkshire, not far from Eddie's home town.

"HEAD FOR SOCIALISM!" That's not a bad slogan, Eddie thought, as he stood outside the Party Committee Rooms. They looked pretty deserted inside. Eddie tried the door. It was open, and he went in. At the end of the room a girl was seated on a desk, her head bent over a box of index cards, checking them off against a constituency list, her hair falling across her face.

Eddie looked at the girl with the hair. It was dark red, but so dark it was more black with a red sheen than anything. And masses of it, rising from her forehead in waves, then flowing backwards and down round her face, in which those eyes of equal blackness now looked up at him with that expression that he knew from somewhere, way back.

"Don't I know you?"

"Could be," she smiled. "Your face is familiar. Where?"

Christ, he thought, she's all right. Who'd ever expect to find anything like her in the Party Committee rooms! The old Party must have changed. Vive la Guerre! She's certainly got everything she ought to have under that sweater. Nice to snuggle down between those when it was over and feel her heart beating right under your ear. And legs, too! From the way she was sitting on the edge of that desk she obviously didn't mind showing them off either. Get those wrapped round you Eddie boy and they can keep their bloody war and their elections and everything.

"You come from round here?"

"Further north," she replied. "Bagley, near Doncaster."

Bagley. It was coming. That red black hair. Coal. Bill whatshisname . . . a meeting . . .

"That rings a bell. What's your name?"

"Margaret. Margaret Houghton."

"Houghton. That's it! Bill Houghton. That's your brother isn't it?"

Bill Houghton. That meeting. Selling Daily Workers. Herbert Spencer. The pub. Christ! This was the girl he'd arranged to meet the day that war broke out and he hadn't gone, because of the war, and he hadn't seen her since.

"That's right. You knew Bill?"

"Used to. My name's Sanders. Eddie Sanders. Met you once, with Bill, and a little bloke called Spencer. There was a meeting up at Bagley, remember? In the square. And we had a drink in the pub and . . ."

"And?" She looked up, still smiling and it was clear she didn't remember. Or was she playing it that way? She was no fool, this one. No kid, either. Must have been nearly twenty then so she'll be about twenty five now. No wedding ring anyway.

And?

She was waiting.

He might as well remind her about that as well. Christ, with four days of his leave still to go she could be the answer to a soldier's prayer. Might as well make himself comfortable.

He took off his black beret and, loosening the tunic of his khaki battledress he looked around the Election Committee Rooms for somewhere to sit.

There was a chair behind the desk but he didn't want to sit there, with a desk between him and those legs. Opposite the desk, ranged along by the shop window there was a row of chairs, piled high with leaflets. More leaflets and some rolled-up posters were stacked against the neighbouring wall on which a big map of the constituency was pinned and parts of this had been coloured in with red and blue and green crayon. Eddie's eyes flitted from one side of the room to the other. In other days it had been a shop and the other walls were lined with shelves. Where once tins of food, or balls of wool, had been stored there now lay stacks of *Daily Workers,* collecting boxes, canvassing cards, more and more leaflets, an odd collection of books and, pinned to the wall behind the desk a poster with a picture of a smiling man with glasses and the legend, "HEAD FOR BLACKTON".

His eyes had come full circle and returned to hers, still looking at him.

"You know Bert Head?" he asked, picking up a pile of leaflets from one of the chairs and putting them on the floor.

"Only since the election," she replied, moving herself slightly higher on to the desk as he sat down on the chair, his eyes at the same height as her knees. "You?"

"Christ yes. Ever since he came into the Party. Knew him a bit when he was in the Labour Party too. He was one of their best blokes you know. Councillor and all that. Up and coming. But when he came into the Party I worked with him a lot. On the City Committee. Then on the District Committee."

"You were on the District Committee?"

Eddie felt rather pleased at the way she'd asked that. With a certain surprise, almost respect, in her voice. He put his hand into his tunic pocket and brought out a packet of cigarettes.

"Three years. Till I got called up. Smoke?" He held out the packet towards her and watched for her to get down off the desk. She uncrossed her legs and, with hands resting on the edge of the desk on each side, lowered herself the couple of inches till her foot, toe pointed downwards, touched the floor. Her skirt was held by friction and the weight of her body and her legs slipped through it those few inches revealing for a moment a strip of stockinged thigh above the knee. Then her foot took the pressure of her body and she pushed herself away from the desk and the skirt fell back into position as she came towards him and took the cigarette.

He looked up at her and knew she had been watching him. He took a cigarette from the packet, struck a match and held it so that she would have to bend towards him. Her V-necked sweater fell forward but, sitting down, he could not see very much except a graceful, powerful neck disappearing into the bow of her collar bones. Anyway she was watching him. He wondered how much she thought he could see.

"Thanks," she said, straightening up. She stood in front of him for a moment, inhaling, and pulled the edge of her sweater down, tightening the wool across her breasts. Then she turned and walked back to the desk and as she walked slowly away from him Eddie had a first chance to take her all in without feeling she was looking at him.

She's certainly putting on a show, he thought. Wonder if this is specially for me or if it's just the way she is. Bagley. Christ she must have set Bagley on fire if she was like this there. But he didn't remember her like this. Pretty, yes. A little bit tough, but then they were all tough in the mining villages. Was she going to hitch herself up on that desk again? That'd be interesting.

She turned as she reached the desk and leaned her back against it, one leg slightly in front of the other, her arms folded across her bosom.

"You were telling me," she said. It was more a statement than a question.

"Was I?"

"About Bagley. And a meeting. And a pub." She blew a ring of smoke upwards and as the smoke cleared round her face he saw she was smiling that same smile and knew that she had remembered all the time.

"That was a long time ago," he said.

"Nearly six years," she replied, looking at him now.

"You remember?"

"I remember two weeks after that meeting."

She remembered.

"I'm sorry about that. Still, there was a war on — just."

"You could have written."

Christ, was she really that cross? After six years? Or was she putting it on?

"The moors are still there," he said, trying to shift the conversation into more positive channels.

"I know. I've seen them."

She turned her body so that she could reach over the desk and flick the cigarette ash into an ashtray. "I've seen lots of things in the last six years," she said. She seemed suddenly restless and walked along the shelves tidying the pile of leaflets.

He watched her for a while in silence and then said quietly "So have I, Margaret."

The sound of her name on his lips brought her to a halt and she looked at him and then walked over and sat on a chair at the end of the row.

"Germany?"

"Oh, Far East mainly. At first. Burma and India and round there. Then Africa for a bit. Then back here getting ready for the invasion. Then France and Germany."

"Sounds like a Cook's Tour." She turned up just the corner of her mouth in a wry smile that didn't even go as far as her dimples.

"Whoever cooked that one up wants shooting."

"More shooting? I thought all the shooting was finished."

"Christ, girl, you don't think they're going to leave things as they are do you? Germany's beaten. Hitler's dead. Fascism's finished. The Red Army's in Berlin and half Europe is going Communist. Is that what they wanted when they started this bloody mess six years ago?"

"They?"

"Chamberlain, Churchill, the Tories, the bosses, the people who own this country. They took years building up Hitler and now they've had to take years pulling him down. And after all that they're worse off than when they started. D'you think they're going to just sit down and accept it? Use your Marxism, comrade."

He leaned forward and stubbed the cigarette end out under the heel of his army boot. He looked up to see her smiling again.

"Yes, comrade," she said, mock-serious.

"When did you join the Party?"

"Couple of years ago."

"Why?"

"Oh, lots of reasons. Perhaps it was Churchill on the radio telling us about the wonderful Russians." The dimples flashed. "Perhaps it was Stalingrad. Perhaps it was old Herbert the way he used to keep bashing away at me. I used to make fun of him but I took it all in you know." She paused. "Perhaps it was you . . ."

"Me?"

"That was a pretty good speech you made at that meeting. Don't suppose you remember what it was all about."

"I don't, that's a fact. About the war I suppose."

"About a war that's been going on for thousands of years. A war of liberation."

"Eh? What one's that?"

"The liberation of women." She made a dramatic gesture with her arm, half in fun, half serious, then jumped up and went to the desk and picked up a packet of cigarettes. "Here," she said, coming back to him, "have one of mine."

"Thanks."

This time there was something about her manner, the way she walked, the way she had spoken, the way she offered him the cigarette that diverted his attention from her legs and her body and he didn't even notice that, in sitting down with only one empty chair between them she had crossed her legs in such a way as to reveal the rounded thigh muscles running up from the knee. He was more interested now in what she was saying.

"Yes, the liberation of women. You were very eloquent about

132

that, and, for me, up in Bagley, a miner's daughter, that was quite an eye-opener. Before that I'd been fighting my own private war against all men." She turned her head away from him to blow out a cloud of smoke and she was smiling again as she looked back at him and went on. "I was doing pretty well, too. Then I went to your meeting and for the first time I realised I didn't have to fight all by myself. And something else. I didn't have to fight all men. There were some who were on my side."

"Your side?"

"Well, that's not quite right. What I mean is that there were some — *are* some men — who don't think women are inferior beings fit only for 'cooking and fooking' . . ."

He looked up sharply as the word came from her lips. It was the first time he had ever heard it from a girl, or a woman. She appeared not to notice his reaction and went on.

"Mind you, there are some reactionary buggers in the Party, too. Every time you go to a meeting in some comrades' houses it's still the little woman who slips out quietly to make the tea while her dear comrade husband is busy laying down the law. Catch me doing that! If they want tea they can make it themselves."

He couldn't help smiling at the picture she had conjured up in his memory of the meetings in comrades' homes.

"What're you laughing at?" she asked.

"I wasn't laughing. I was just thinking how right you were. In some ways, anyway. We've got a long way to go, even in the party. Tradition dies hard.

"You know Margaret," he went on, reaching over to the desk to flick the ash from his cigarette into the ashtray, and then facing her, "people come into our Party for all sorts of reasons. Some because they want equality of the sexes, some because they want equality for all races, some because they want equality for all classes of people. That's good, because that's what the Party's for and it's good that people recognize this and come in. And it's good because they bring this enthusiasm for their particular cause into the party and all these enthusiasms stimulate the sort of discussion and action that the party thrives on. But it's important to realise that all this is still only a part of the Party's total policy. We're out to change the whole system from Capitalism to Socialism. We'll take these bloody slums out of the hands of the landlords who've been making a fortune out of people's poverty and misery for years. We're going to take these factories out of the hands of the bosses who've been running them purely for their own profit and not for the benefit of the people that work in them. We're going to change the country and we're going to change the world. And when we do it women will be equal to men and black will be equal to white and there won't be upper classes and lower classes . . ."

Something about the little smile that played about her lips made him stop. Was she laughing at him? Was she just leading him on with all this equality-for-women stuff? After all, if she had been in for two years, she must know all this as well as he did. What was she thinking?

"Isn't that right then?" he asked.

Her smile broadened and the dimples deepened into grooves in her round pink cheeks. "Oh, it's right enough," she said, "but one thing always worries me in this wonderful world of yours — sorry," she corrected herself, " — of ours . . ."

"What's that?" he asked quickly, anxious that there seemed some doubt in her mind, eager to get to grips with it, confident that he could find the answer.

"Well," she said, the smile now filling her whole face, "once we're all equal, who's going to make the tea?"

The cow! She's been having me on all the time. Still it's nice to meet someone with a sense of humour about the Party. Thought at first she was going to be one of those intense ones. All Marx and no larks as we used to say in the Y.C.L. She's all right. I'll play it her way. With her I'd play it any way.

He reached over, stubbed out his cigarette in the ashtray and returned her smile with a grin. "All right," he said, "I can take a hint. You show me where the kettle is and I'll make the tea."

"But," he added, lifting a warning finger, "you wash up."

* * * *

She didn't.

Neither did Eddie make tea. No sooner had he put the kettle on than things began to get busy in the Committee Room. Albert Head, the candidate, came in with Ray Saltmarsh, his agent, and Mick Boyle one of the full-time Communist Party workers from the District Office at Leeds. Eddie knew them all and was soon immersed in an animated discussion on the progress of the campaign and didn't even notice the kettle boiling away. Margaret did. She got up and went over to the little gas ring, turned off the gas and returned to the discussion.

For the next few days Eddie immersed himself in the election, canvassing for votes from door to door, distributing leaflets to the workers streaming out of the great steel works, speaking at meetings at factory gates, in schoolrooms and at street corners. Margaret watched him, felt his enthusiasm, became caught up herself in the fever of activity rapidly mounting to the climax of polling day.

They talked nothing but elections, were hardly ever alone together, spent lunch times swapping the morning's experiences of public reactions with the candidate and others, and the evenings at meetings, after which they returned, with the others, to the committee rooms to check all the canvassers' returns, add up their totals of promised voters, plan the next day's activities.

One evening after Ray Saltmarsh had counted the canvassers' returns for the day and added them to the previous day's total, Bert Head took off his glasses, wiped them with his handkerchief, laughed and looked over to Mick Boyle. "Eh, that's not at all bad y'know," he said. "If we're not careful Mick, we may get elected."

"Why not?"

It was Margaret who spoke and her words echoed the thoughts that many of them had been thinking over the past few days.

"We've been getting a wonderful response," she continued. People are with us. They really do want a change now and they know we can give it to them. I know none of us thought we would get Bert in when we first started but now it's different. We were out of touch with the people before. But they're way ahead of us. Honestly, it's a pleasure to knock on a door and say you're canvassing for the Communist Party."

There was silence for a moment when she had finished and then Mick Boyle spoke. He was a heavily built man, clean shaven, his almost shiny face topped by short straight hair that was dark with greying flecks at the temples and round the ears. He smoked constantly and it was through a haze of tobacco smoke that his voice emerged, tinged with a distant flavour of Dublin.

"It's certainly true, Maggie, that we've been getting a good response, but there's a world of difference between five thousand Communist promises and five thousand Communist votes. People are very nice you know. Anything for a quiet life, they think. If a Communist comes to the door tell him you'll vote Communist, if a Labour man comes tell him you'll vote Labour. Communist, Socialist, many of them don't know the difference. True, they won't vote Tory. They know what that means round these parts, and they'll never vote Tory. But don't expect too much Maggie. This is the first General Election you've experienced lass. It's exciting and it's good to see people take the Party seriously, more seriously than we do sometimes. Seriously enough to give it their vote despite the fact they know we're not putting up enough candidates to form a Government even if we all got in. Which we won't."

There was a silence as he stubbed out his cigarette on the cluttered ashtray and then Ray Saltmarsh said, "We'll get a bloody good vote though."

"That's just it," said Boyle. "Ray's right you know. You'll get a bloody good vote. Look, how many party members have you got in Blackton? A hundred? Hundred and fifty?"

Ray nodded and said "About that."

"How many Daily Workers d'you sell at weekends? Normally I mean, not elections. Another hundred? Not as much?"

"Not as much."

"Call it a hundred. and And in the factories?"

"About ten quire."

"Call it three hundred. A hundred at weekends that's four hundred, a hundred and fifty party members that's five hundred and fifty people in this constituency who you'd have reckoned support the party one way or another before the election. Now you've already got more than two thousand people here who have promised to vote for Bert. Two thousand and you've only just canvassed half the streets. Christ, it shows how much support there is for the party if only we'll just go out and look for it instead of playing the part of working class martyrs with our backs to the wall half the time."

"But Mick," Eddie interrupted, "you said yourself that a lot of them say they'll vote for us just to be nice."

"Right, but being nice is not being antagonistic. They're not nice to the Tories you know. They tell 'em straight they've never voted Tory in their lives and aren't going to start now. All right. Cut it in half. Make it a thousand who really mean it. A thousand in only half the constituency. Christ Sam, there's maybe a couple of thousand potential recruits here for you mate. How about it?"

Sam Whelan, secretary of the Blackton Branch looked up at him over his rimless spectacles. Engineer, fiftyish, always so neat and dapper that he looked more like a bank clerk than a shop steward at one of England's largest factories, Sam smiled and took a pinch of snuff from the little silver box he had been taking out of his waistcoat pocket while Boyle was talking.

"Voting's one thing Mick," he said, "joining's another."

"But . . ."

"Wait a minute now." Sam held up his finger to stop Boyle's interruption. As leader of one of the Party's most important branches, member of the District Committee, the Steel Advisory Committee and various other Party committees for many years, Sam knew his strength and was not going to be interrupted. These youngsters might hang on to every word of the London Irishman but not him. He'd seen them come and go. Sent up from King Street full of enthusiasm, going to change the world overnight. After a while they settle down and realise it takes a little longer. Then they get restless and hanker for the big city again. They miss their big demonstrations, their high-powered discussions at Party Centre working out targets for us to achieve. Two thousand new recruits? That's a laugh!

"I'm not saying there's not the support, tha' knows. I'd not be bloody shop steward if there wasn't. When the Party takes power in this country there'll be millions supporting us, not thousands. I think your two thousand's an underestimate, not an overestimate. There's still those who won't tell you they're going to vote Communist because they're frightened to. Memories are not short round here, tha' knows. They remember the slump. They remember men being laid off. They remember men being victimised, and they'll not tell you or anyone else which way they're voting. But Christ man when the times comes I know whose side they're on." Sam paused and looked round, his eyes red with all the cigarette smoke and slightly enlarged behind his spectacles. "But that's not joining."

"Why not Sam? Why won't they join?"

"Well it's simple lass," Sam turned to Margaret to reply to her question. "What do they see us Party members doing? They see us standing in the rain of a morning selling the Daily Workers as they go into the factory. They see us standing on a platform on the corner of the street in the bitter cold shouting our heads off, they see us spending our Sunday mornings walking round the estates knocking at people's doors with petitions and they think to themselves 'They're not going to catch me doing all that.' They may admire us for all the work we put in and they may even think it all for a good cause but they don't want to get involved. And sometimes," Sam finished up, taking from his top pocket an immense watch that was hanging by a chain from his lapel, and studying the face as if it was a new and strange object he had not seen before, "sometimes I don't blame 'em either."

He pulled himself up with a grunt and looked all round the Committee Room.

"A'tha coming lass?"

Margaret darted a quick glance at Eddie, smiled at Sam and jumped up quickly.

"Right," she said, "I'm fit."

"Christ!" said Eddie, looking at his watch. "Half twelve. I'm off too. I'll walk down with you."

They all got up and after locking the shop door they parted, Margaret, Sam and Eddie going up the road towards the factory, lying like some silent beast in its own mess of slums, and the others going back towards the City centre.

In the three weeks of the election campaign, while Margaret was working full-time for the Party, running the Committee Rooms, she was staying with Sam and his wife in their back-to-back house that stood so near to the factory that you could hear its heart beating as you lay in bed at night, see its eyes watching you as you went out into the privy in the back yard, feel its hot breath on your face as you stepped out of the door.

As they reached the corner of their street that ran right into the very jaws of the beast, the factory gate, Sam stopped for a moment.

"I'll leave the door on the latch for you lass. Goodnight Eddie lad. See you tomorrow?"

"Sure Sam. Tomorrow."

"Goodnight Sam," said Margaret. "I'll not be a few minutes."

"Nay lass, be as long as tha' likes. Longer the better otherwise t'owd lady will be thinking ah've been out with you all night."

"Well you have Sam. No denying it."

"Ay."

There was a sadness in the way he turned and walked down the street like a child being sent to bed thinking of all the wonderful things the grownups would be doing without him.

"He's sweet," Margaret said, leaning back against the brick wall of the corner and watching the little man disappear into the dark like the end of a Chaplin film.

"You're not bad yourself."

A smile plucked at the corners of her lips and she turned her face slowly towards his.

"Cigarette?" he said, putting his hand up to his tunic pocket. She shook her head.

"You smoked too much tonight."

"You smoke too much altogether."

Her eyebrows lifted.

"Who says so?"

"I do."

"I won't have any man telling me what to do and what not to do. Give us a smoke." She reached a hand up to his tunic pocket and undid the buttons. He put his hand over hers and grasped it tightly, feeling her fingers relax.

"Won't you?" he asked.

"Won't I what?" As she lifted her other hand towards his pocket he grasped that too and held both her hands now in his, pushing them slowly down to her side, bringing his body close to hers, smelling her hair, feeling her closeness through his tunic.

"Let any man tell you what to do."

"Any man?"

"Me."

"Think I need telling?"

He kissed her quickly, suddenly. And then again slowly, softly. He freed her hands which slid upwards round his neck as his hands pulled her body towards him. Her mouth opened to his kiss but she didn't seem to fall away under him as other girls had. His tongue met hers coming out to him and he could feel her hands now on the back of his head, now on his shoulders, pulling him into her as her tongue went deeper into the corners of his mouth.

Taken by surprise by her initiative he suddenly found the pressure relaxed, the tongue gone, the kiss ended, and realised this was the first time in his life that *he* hadn't decided when the kiss was going to end.

"That was nice," she said, simply.

"More?"

He bent closer to her, determined to regain the initiative, but she put her fingers to his lips, gently. Firmly. Slightly shaking her head she disturbed the tiny sparkles in her eyes which flashed momentarily as she smiled.

"No. I must go now."

He tried to nuzzle his way through her fingers to her lips, but felt the strength holding him away. She kissed the tip of his nose through the bars as if he was a prisoner and repeated "I must go."

He stood away from her and she straightened her dress.

"Margaret," he said.

"Yes?"

"You know there are two more days to polling day and after that I've only two more day's leave."

"Is that all? It's gone so quickly."

"Margaret will you come away with me for those last two days?"

Now. He'd said it. He asked her as he'd been planning to ask her for the last week. How would she react? If that kiss meant anything she liked him at least. Enjoyed him would be a better way of putting it. But this was different. Would she be offended? Would she think he was pushing it? After all he'd only known her a few days and most of that time they'd been working. The odd glance now and then had been the only sign. A secret smile once, through the smoke and haze of the Committee Room. Not even a touch, or holding hands until tonight. Not even a kiss until now. What would she say?

"Where?" she asked.

"You mean you'll come?"

"That depends. Where?"

"Where? Anywhere!"

He threw his arms out wide, looking up at the dark night, the yellow street light sliding along the black walls.

"London! Paris! Rome! San Francisco! China! Timbuctoo! . . . Pontefract!"

"Pontefract! Why on earth?"

"I stayed there once in a strange house opposite the castle in a bedroom as big as a barn and a lav like a ballroom with steps up to the seat which was on a dais like a throne."

"No thanks. No point in going away with you if you're going to spend all day in the lavatory having delusions of grandeur."

"Where then? Anywhere you like Margaret. I don't care. So long as it's just us."

"You promised to take me to the moors once."

"The moors. Would you like that?"

"It could be fun."

"It could be heaven."

She looked at him seriously and for a moment traced the line of his chin with the tip of her finger and brought it to rest on his mouth. He made a kiss with his lips and she pressed her fingers to them, looking at him all the while in the way that had nothing to do with seeing.

"I must go," she said.

"Goodnight love."

"See you in the morning."

He watched her walk away down the street, saw her standing by the door looking back at him, draped for a moment in a flash of yellow light as she opened the door.

A flash of yellow light.

High above the city the bomb exploded, and the little man who had given the order, and who was now on his way back from Europe to Washington, expressed his satisfaction.

"This is the greatest thing in history," he said.

The name of the little man was Harry S. Truman and earlier that year he had become President of the United States, on the death of Franklin Delano Roosevelt.

The name of the city was Hiroshima and within a few minutes of the flash eight thousand Japanese men, women and children were dead.

The Japanese got the message and, four days later, offered to surrender. This meant that the Russians, already poised for attack, would not over-run Japan as they had Germany and the whole of Eastern Europe. The war was over.

*   *   *   *

Germany
March 12th 1946

My dear magnificent Maggie!

I've just read your letter and I'm on top of the world. Who cares about getting married? I thought you'd prefer it that way, for your Mum's sake more than anything, but you know darling I don't believe in all the old mumbo jumbo any more than you do.

So long as we're together I don't care if we've been blessed by the Pope or Uncle Joe or anyone. And in three short months (less, by the time you get this letter!) I'll be out and we'll be together again — for good.

Wonderful thought.

Of course we can go and live in London. One thing about modern war is that they need highly trained men to run their war machines and the dear old Government has spent a lot of time and money training me to work all their little electric gadgets and believe it or not I'm now a highly-qualified bloke and I should be able to get a good job when I get back.

Mag, Mag, it'll be wonderful being with you again and knowing we have the whole of the rest of our lives together *without any interruptions.*

It's as if happiness, like everything else during that lousy war, was being rationed, and if you turned the pages of your ration book after the page marked 'fats' and 'sugar' you would find one marked 'happiness'. It would be all split up into little squares like the other pages and there would be five squares cut out for Blackton and two for the moors and they'd cut out seven for that week in London and that'd be that.

But now, Mag love, that will all be over and nobody will ration our love, nobody will tell us how much we can be together.

You say you are going down to London to look for a job and perhaps get things ready for us. That'll be grand because I gather it's not so easy to find anywhere to live down there these days.

I'll have to go back home first to collect my things together and say goodbye to the folks. How about coming up with me to meet the family? You'll go for Mum (even though she does make the tea when we have meetings). She might even teach you to make a cup of tea! By the way, can you cook?

All right, I've read your letter and I know you do not intend to be an unpaid housekeeper and a slave in my kitchen and a whore in my bed — and all that! But I can't cook either and we've got to eat and two can't live cheaper than one if we live in restaurants. How do we work this one out? I've got an idea. You be a slave in my kitchen and I'll be a whore in your bed! Fair enough?

I gather they're planning a big trial of war criminals here later on this year. I really don't know why they bother. It's all so bloody obvious. They'll make a big song and dance about a few of the top boys that are left (like Goering and Hess), shove a lot of them away in cold storage till everybody's forgotten about them and then quietly let them out. The really big ones like Krupps, the ones with the money and power, will get away Scot free.

After all, if they're going to build the Germans up again to fight the Russians they've got to have somebody left to do it for them. And who better than Krupps and the rest?

There seems no doubt, judging from Churchill's speech at Fulton last week, that they're going to have another go. He tried it in 1920 and he'll go on trying till he totters into his grave. If he wasn't such a menace he'd be laughable but the trouble is people like him can lead the whole world into another war. All this business about Communist tyranny and iron curtains across Europe. Christ, he was glad enough when that iron curtain was closing in on the Germans while he was climbing up Mussolini's soft underbelly.

Memories are short love, aren't they?

But the same applies to the Party I suppose. How the hell we could have thought Churchill would ever change is beyond me. That daft 'Crimea Policy' of ours. All pals together. Churchill, Stalin and Truman going forward to create a better world. God help us, we were about as naive as they make them. I must say the people were way out ahead of the party then and certainly showed Churchill what they thought of him. The poor old boy must have had quite a shock when Labour got in with such a terrific majority.

It was great to hear that the Party won Mile End in the L.C.C. elections. When Piratin won Stepney in the General Election I thought it might be a bit of a fluke. You know, riding in on the crest of the wave. But when they followed it up with ten seats on the Council and now two on the County Council it looks as if all the Party's years of work in Stepney is bearing fruit. I bet having people like Abe Stern and even Ma Bernstein on the Council will shake them up!

Or is it Joe Stalin that's doing it? In the army it's been 'Joe for King!' for the last couple of years and though it's said in fun there's a serious thought behind it always.

The frightening thing is the way it can be turned on and off overnight almost. At the beginning of the war the Russians were the biggest bastards under the sun. Poor little Finland and all that. Then when Russia came in on our side they couldn't find anything good enough to say about them. Now the war is over this Fulton speech of Churchill's looks like they're going to swing the other way again. And once the newspapers get the message, and the B.B.C. and the film boys and the churches, I just wonder how long it will take 'Uncle Joe' to become 'that tyrant Stalin' and then how long before 'the Nazi beasts' become 'our German allies'? Five years? Give it ten! We all thought this new United Nations organisation would sort things out but now I'm not so sure.

Am I being a miserable so-and-so Mag? Sorry! Those next ten years are going to be glorious ones for us, love, anyway. And the next ten, and the next, and all the years after!

Look, what about children?

That's one thing I can't do as well as you. Yes, I can make the tea, cook, wash up, clean the house as much as you can and agreed we share all that. But kids? I'm licked! And if we have them are they going to grow up bastards without their Mum and Dad being married?

Think about all this Mag and write to me. Write quickly because I miss you so much and that week in London is so long ago now and the six months before I'm demobbed is so far off.

I miss you, love.

I love you, miss!

Sit down *now* and write to me, please!

All my love,

Ed.

*   *   *   *

"I'll have to bring Krupps in," thought Eddie as he walked along the tree-lined road, the low summer sun taking a last peep into the bedroom windows before retiring itself for the night. "That's a good way to explain what's behind this Berlin Blockade business."

It was a long road and now, half way up, the houses fell away on one side and green gates opened into a park, sloping away in tree-lined paths that separated wide expanses of grass and beds of black earth in which ranks of scarlet salvias paraded like guardsmen before the admiring crowds of blue and white lobelia and alyssum.

Bit different from Blackton, he thought, as he watched two young lovers step gently across the fallen shadows of the trees. Never thought I'd be taking a class in a neighbourhood like this. Fine houses. Trees. Neat gardens in front. Garages. Cars. Yet Bill and Amy Westfield are as good a couple of comrades as you'd find anywhere. Solid. Work hard too. Bill as Branch Secretary. Amy in the Women's Group. Good solid middle class comrades. Funny that. There was Bill now, messing about in the garden again. But why not? To hear some of the comrades talk you'd think it was a crime to be clipping your hedge when you could be out knocking on people's doors selling them pamphlets. Yet there he was chatting away to his neighbour across the hedge. Bet he's talking about Berlin.

"Evening Bill."

The big man turned round. He was wearing an old pair of grey flannel trousers and a faded yellow sports shirt which, open at the neck, revealed a mass of curly red hair on his broad chest. His face was tanned and his eyes shone with genuine pleasure to see Eddie.

"Hullo Eddie. Nice to see you again. How've you been?"

"Fine Bill, fine. You?"

"Wonderful. In the pink."

"You certainly look it. And Amy? The kids?"

"Oh, couldn't be better. Well, they should be. Just spent three years' bonuses on a holiday for them."

"Where d'you go?"

"Venice, Eddie. I was just telling Mr. Tracy here." He pointed across the hedge towards his neighbour who, resting, held the long handle of a hoe against his chest and nodded at Eddie.

"Evening."

Eddie nodded back. "Must be a wonderful place," he said.

"Fantastic, Eddie. Absolutely fantastic." Bill smiled. "I was just saying to Mr. Tracy here that we thought it would be a good idea to see some of the wonders of the world while they're still here. We were talking about this Berlin business. What d'you think about it Eddie?"

Good old Bill. Berlin via Venice. Revolution via roses. Politics over the garden fence.

"Well," he replied, moving a little nearer to the hedge so that Bill's neighbour could hear better, "I spent a good bit of my life recently pushing the Germans back to Berlin all the way through France and Germany. And the Russians did the same from their side. The Russians got there first and so far as I'm concerned they can have it. I've been in some of the concentration camps and I've talked to some of the Germans who tell you they didn't know anything about it and if anybody thinks I'm going to war with the Russians over Berlin or the Germans they've got another think coming."

Not quite the Party line, thought Eddie, but he gets it across. Simple, straightforward. People understand this way of talking.

Mr. Tracy was nodding, in sympathy with Eddie's remarks. Leave Bill to follow it up later with the full line, the detailed analysis, the cold war, the Americans, two camps and all that. The point was made. No war for the Germans.

"You're right there," Mr. Tracy was saying. "I've done my bit. They won't get me back in a hurry fighting for the Germans."

They. That's it. You're on common ground now. You've both done your bit. You're on one side, and 'they' are on the other side. The old class line-up already becoming clear.

". . . Mind you," he went on, "I don't trust these Russians. They're out to dominate the world, just like Hitler was."

"Oh, I wouldn't say that" said Eddie quickly. "You don't want to believe everything they tell you about the Russians . . . ('they' again. Having established the 'they', build up on it. 'They' want you to go back to war . . . 'they' are telling us about the Russians . . . if one's wrong the other must be . . . it follows, doesn't it?) . . . after all, d'you remember what they told us about the Russians before the war, what a lot of villains they were, how they couldn't fight, their tanks were made of cardboard, they had no boots, they were all starving, they were all so oppressed by the Communists that they'd rise up and revolt as soon as they got the chance? Remember? Well they soon changed their tune when Russians came in on our side didn't they?"

"True enough," Bill's neighbour nodded again and suddenly began hoeing the rose-bed cutting down the tiny weeds that were springing up around the stems of the bushes. "Never know what to believe these days, do you," he said, looking over his shoulder, without stopping.

It wasn't a question. It required no answer and Eddie looked at Bill who smiled back at him.

"Well, you've done your bit of weeding Eddie" said Bill, "now you'd better come inside; they're waiting."

"Right, mate," Eddie replied with a grin, "I'll leave you to plant the seed."

The front door was open and Eddie went through into the hall, followed by Bill. They were met by Amy, a tall robust woman of about forty, in a bright print summer dress, taking a quick glance at herself in the hall mirror on her way out.

"Hello, Eddie, how are you?"

"Fine Amy. You?"

"In a mad rush. I'm supposed to be over at Lorna's at eight but the kids were hell tonight. I've only just got 'em settled in. You'll probably have them coming down in the middle of your class."

"Do 'em good."

"I doubt it," she grimaced. "Nothing will do them good. Not even you, Eddie. How's Margaret? Will she be at Lorna's?"

"Is that this Women's Committee?"

Amy nodded, searching in her bag for something.

"Yes, she's there. Left the same time as me."

"Bill dear," she turned to her husband, still searching in her bag. "Have you got the car keys? I thought I had them in my bag."

"They're in the car. I left them there when I got back. Thought you'd need them."

"Oh darling!" She stared at him reproachfully as she pushed everything back into her bag and snapped the catch.

"Go on, you'll be late."

"I *am* late. 'Bye darling. 'Bye Eddie."

She pushed out through the front door and Bill looked at Eddie and shrugged his shoulders. "Mad," he said with a smile.

"Aren't they all?" Eddie smiled back.

"Wait till you've been married as long as we have Eddie. Fifteen years. Then you'll realise there is madness and madness."

Married? Funny how conventional the conventional people in the party are, thought Eddie. Bill knows we're not married, so does Amy. Yet they always talk as if we were. It takes more than a Party card to change human nature.

Eddie looked at his watch. It was just gone eight o'clock. "Lead on, Bill," he said, and followed him into the front room.

* * * *

There were six people seated around the room and they stopped talking when Bill and Eddie came in.

Eddie counted them automatically, registered the fact that they were all new faces, and followed Bill to an armchair before which there stood a small coffee table.

Eddie sat down in the armchair. Bill sat on a straightbacked chair next to it, took off his wrist watch and put it on the table and started talking.

"Well comrades. This is the first of a series of discussion classes we're running in this branch for new members of the Party.

"Most of you have been in the Party now for a few months and we thought it would be a good idea to get you together and give you some idea of the basic ideas the Party stands for, its theory, its strategy and tactics . . ."

Eddie listened to the good old words rolling out . . . 'basic . . . theory . . . strategy . . . tactics . . .' and took the opportunity to look round the room and study the new members. It was a comfortable room, typical of middle class homes of surburban London. This was what they called the lounge and it always had a three-piece suite like this, perhaps a few straight-backed chairs, a coffee table, and a nest of occasional tables. A plain fitted carpet and pelmetted curtains to match. This one had a bookcase, which was not usual. The people in the room were not usual either. At least four of them were not the types usually seen reclining in the uncut moquette armchairs of suburbia.

The first, sitting on the edge of his chair and taking in every word of Bill's opening remarks, was a young man, probably under twenty. He was clean and shiny and had put on his best suit to come to his first class. On his lap was a note book and his short fingers grasped a pencil. Eddie could see the black lines around his finger nails which the boy had not been able to scrub away. On top of the open page of his pad Eddie could make out the words "EDUCATION CLASSES" and underneath that he had already added "Strategy and Tactics."

Next to him an older man sat back in an armchair and as Eddie looked at him their eyes met and then the man looked away and gave his attention to Bill. Workers' eyes, thought Eddie. Like Blackton. He had no notebook, no pencil, but his eyes had already taken more notes than the young man's pencil. Good to have someone like him here. Experience. Better if it comes from the class than me.

The girl next to him was different again. Working class? Well, yes, but could pass for something else. Serious looking. Plain but pretty. In fact everything about her was neither one thing nor the other. She had a figure under that dress. The dress itself was a bright cheerful print. But she wore it in such a way that the print wasn't bright and the figure wasn't there. About thirty? Teacher?

No doubt about the next one. He'd come in uniform. Railway porter. He'd be not much more than twenty. He wasn't quite comfortable on that chair. Not really listening to Bill. More interested in the room. Looking at everything quickly like a bird in a strange garden making up its mind about the scraps of bread on the bird-table.

Next to him an older man sitting quietly and confidently in his chair looking at his own boots stretched out in front of him and listening with a slow smile as Bill spoke.

Finally a dark boy with glasses, about the same age as the first lad and just as keenly attending to Bill's words. Corduroy trousers this one. Open-necked shirt revealing a rather fine, almost effeminately graceful neck. Black wavy hair and glowing eyes completing the somewhat poetic impression. Student probably. Maybe Jewish.

". . . understand the class structure of Society," Bill was saying. "And who could do this better than Comrade Eddie Sanders who is with us here tonight. Eddie has a long and wide experience of the Party both up in Yorkshire and here in London. He is a member of our own Borough Committee and the London District Committee and is also secretary of the local branch of the Electrical Trades Union . . ."

Eddie noticed the young man on his left scribbling away madly. Saw his own name go down on the pad, followed by the words

". . . Yorks . . . Lond . . . E.T.U. . . ." and then, as the boy stopped writing, Eddie realised that Bill had stopped talking, that the introduction was over and the floor was his.

The young man, with pencil poised and nothing to write, looked up at him expectantly.

"Well comrades," he began, unscrewing the cap of his fountain pen and placing it upon the white sheet of paper on the table, "first of all I think it would be useful to get clear on what we're trying to do tonight and the way we're going to do it."

He paused.

The young man was scribbling away.

What on earth can he be scribbling about? He hadn't said anything yet.

"This is going to be the first of a series of six classes, one every week for the next six weeks, in which we are going to examine some of the basic theories of our Party . . ."

Suddenly he could imagine that pencil inscribing those words "basic theory" on to that white page to be followed by pages and pages of words yet unspoken.

"Now the method we're going to use is called 'controlled discussion.' (Oh Christ man, don't write down 'controlled discussion' in your little notebook. What good will that do you?) All that means is that you do all the work and all I do is listen. In other words we're going to learn from each other. We're all different," he looked around the class, "we've all had different lives and different experiences. We're going to learn from each other's experiences and by discussing them see if the theory and practice of the Party measures up, and if it points the way forward.

"The control part is where I come in and my job is to bring in to this room other people's experiences; the experience of the Party if you like, and the experience of the working class, not only in this country, but abroad, and not only in our lifetime but going back over the years. The method of control is simply like having a chairman to keep the discussion on the right lines. By that I don't mean what is called 'the party line' but to stop us wandering all over the place so that we don't finish up the evening having had a good old chat about lots of different things and having reached no real conclusions. I wouldn't want our comrade here to have a notebook full of our pearls of wisdom and not know what the hell it's all about when he reads it."

The pencil stopped in mid-sentence.

The young man looked up at him, now knowing whether to

smile or not.

Eddie smiled at him and said, "I might add comrades, that it's not a bad idea to have a little notebook and make a note or two. It's not so much reading them through afterwards and learning them by heart. After all, we're not having any exams or anything, but writing down a point that has become clear in the course of discussion helps to keep it clear in your mind. And then there will be the odd fact, a bit of information here and there, that you might find useful in your discussions at work. Don't worry about it for tonight though. Tonight we're only getting to know each other and exchanging a few ideas. But try to remember for next week, eh? Right." The boy was smiling at him and now sat back comfortably in his chair. His pencil lay motionless on the notebook ... "We'll begin, shall we?"

"One of the words you'll hear a lot in the Party is this word 'class'. Class war, working class, middle class. Yet we often find that comrades aren't entirely clear about the meaning of this word. Some of us aren't even always clear what class we're in! Now what about you, comrade? What class would you say you're in?"

His eyes rested on the older man next to the boy with the notebook. Their eyes met again and this time he looked surprised at first, then slightly amused.

"Me?"

Eddie nodded.

"Working class I am. Always have been."

"And you comrade?" His eyes turned to the girl next to him She looked startled and put her head slightly to one side, like a bird, as behind the lenses of her glasses, her eyes searched for the answer. When she spoke her voice had a northern accent. Not Yorkshire. Nottingham perhaps, or round there.

"I suppose I'm working class. At least I work for my living. So did my parents." Suddenly, after the first edge of nervousness had worn off, she spoke confidently, looking straight at him. "Yes, I'm working class. Definitely."

"Right. Now what about you comrade?"

The older man took his eyes off his shoes long enough to look at Eddie and confirm that the question had been directed at him, then his smile broadened as he said in a soft, apologetic voice, "Well, I'm afraid I must confess to be middle class." He looked up, not at Eddie, but at the girl who had spoken before him. "Not that I've never done any work. On the contrary. But I've always worked for myself. Had my own business. Employed others to do the work. Definitely middle class I would say." He turned his eyes to Eddie and his eyebrows went up, furrowing his forehead. "Wouldn't you?"

"We'll come to that in a minute comrade," Eddie replied and turned to the dark boy sitting next to Bill. "And you comrade?"

The boy frowned, and did not speak for a moment and then said "I don't know." He looked down at the floor, then up at Eddie. His eyes were big and a slight upward tilting of his eyebrows as they came towards the nose drew two sharp vertical lines into the smooth whiteness of his forehead like a road on a map that suddenly stops. "I'm not sure what a class is, you see. I don't work, at least not for my living. I'm a student. My dad runs his own business like . . . this comrade." The word did not come to him easily. Comrade. He had hesitated, not knowing how to refer to him. It could have been 'this gentleman' or 'our friend here' but in the moment of hesitation Eddie's method of address came to him. Comrade.

"Mind you," he went on, "he worked hard all his life. It's only these last ten years he's had his own business. And he's worked harder since he's been his own boss than when he was working for somebody else. Would you call him working class? And if he's not, what am I? Is it hereditary?"

"Well," said Eddie, "there are a few questions there for us to answer. Anybody care to have a go? Our comrade's father has worked hard all his life. For most of it he worked for other people. Then he got his own business and he works just as hard. Or harder. But he probably employs other people to work for him as well now, eh?"

He looked at the boy for confirmation, and saw him nod his head.

"Right. What class was he in before? Has he changed now? If so, what is the change?"

Eddie looked round the room. The young lad next to him bit his pencil. The man with "Blackton" eyes looked puzzled. The girl put her hands into her lap and smoothed her dress. The railwayman took a cigarette from a pack in his pocket. The older man studied his boots still stretched out before him and the dark boy, still worried, looked from Eddie to Bill and back to Eddie.

Nobody said anything.

"Right," said Eddie when he felt the silence had gone on long enough, "let's get a little more information. What's your name, conrade?" This to the dark boy.

"Michael. Michael Levy."

"Look Michael, d'you mind if we get a bit more information about your father?"

The boy smiled and shrugged his shoulders.

"Sure," he said, "ask away."

"Well, what sort of business is he in?"

"Furniture. He's got a furniture factory in Hackney. Makes bedroom suites mostly. Awful stuff."

"O.K. Before he went into business on his own account what was he?"

"He was a cabinet maker. A craftsman really. He worked in one of the big places in the East End. My mum says he used to be very clever with veneers."

"And how did he get his own business? Did he save up the money? Look Michael, if you don't want to tell us any of this you don't have to. We can get at the problem another way, but it's always better to use actual examples we know."

The boy smiled again.

"I don't mind," he said, and went on to answer the question. "Part of it he saved up. Part of it he borrowed. Most of it came to him from my mother's father, who died just over ten years ago and left some money. He used it to buy a little factory, got the bank to lend him some more for the machinery and raw materials and that was that."

"Good Michael, thanks." Eddie turned to the others. "Now what was the difference between Michael's father before and after he got his own business?"

"Well ..." the man with Blackton eyes faltered on the brink and then took the plunge "... first he worked for a boss and then he became a boss himself."

"Yes," said Eddie 'that's true. What was he doing all the time before and after?"

"Working?"

"Yes, but not just working, what was the result of his work?"

"Well, furniture I suppose. He was producing furniture."

"Right comrade," said Eddie, feeling the thing beginning to move and switching quickly now to the girl. "Now how was he producing this furniture? With his bare hands?"

"No, with tools, I suppose."

"With tools, that's right. Anything else?"

She looked puzzled for a moment.

"Machinery?"

"Good. Machinery. What else, comrade?" Now the railwayman's turn. The thing was definitely moving. They were sitting up. Their brains were ticking. They were wondering what he was getting at with these questions, so simple that they all knew the answers. They were looking for the catch. But there wasn't any. It was wonderful when they found out how simple it all was.

"Well," said the railwayman, "he'd need wood and nails and glue and all that. Raw materials."

"Now we're getting there. And you comrade," Eddie looked at the man who was no longer studying his shoes, "you run your own business, too. What did he need above all, where all this machinery and raw materials were available?"

"Well, a factory I suppose. Is that what you mean?"

"I don't mean anything comrade. You're the ones that are sorting all this out. I'm just asking the questions. And if any of you want to ask any questions don't wait for me, just jump in. And if you don't agree with the answers just say so. So what have we got so far? We've agreed that both before and after taking over his own business Michael's father was engaged in production, right?"

He looked around. They all nodded.

"And to carry out this production he needed tools, machinery, raw materials, and a factory to put them all in, right?"

They nodded again.

"Now our comrade here . . ." he looked at the 'Blackton' man, ". . . what's your name, comrade?"

"Wain. Sam Wain."

"Sam told us that the difference was that in the first place Michael's father worked for a boss and then be became his own boss. Now what did you mean by that Sam?"

The man thought for a bit and then said, "Well first of all, like, he was working for somebody else. It was the other bloke's factory, the boss, like. It was him who owned all this machinery and the wood and stuff and he just paid Mike's father to make it into furniture . . ."

Eddie nodded, encouraging him to go on.

"Well then, like Mike here says. When his dad got his own business he owned his own factory and machinery and all." He paused and thought for a moment and then looked up at Eddie. "That's the difference I reckon."

"Good Sam, good." Eddie turned to the others and summed up. "Now Sam says the basic difference between Michael's father before and after he owned his own business was that first he was working with another man's tools, machinery and raw materials in another man's factory and afterwards it all belonged to him. The difference was in his relationship to all those things, right?"

He looked at the girl who nodded at him and he asked her "Can you think of a word or a phrase that we could use to describe all these things? The machinery, the factory, the raw materials?"

"D'you mean his capital?"

Eddie miled. She's way ahead. But we've got to take it slower. Make sure they're all with you. "Well, it is capital, yes, but let's see if we can get something simpler than that first. Take it back to what Sam said Mike's father was engaged in before and after. D'you remember Sam?"

"Production, wasn't it? Production of furniture?"

"That's right, and all these things are?"

He looked into the girl's eyes wondering if it would come.

She pulled her eyebrows together.

"Aids to production?"

"Aids? Yes, that's right, but they're more than aids aren't they? They don't just help you to produce. You can't produce without them."

He looked at her. She looked back and then looked down, puzzled. It didn't matter. It was just a word. It would have been good to come from her, or any of them. But it didn't matter. It was just a word.

"Means?"

That was the word. It had come from the older man, with the still outstretched legs. He was smiling confidently still as he threw in the missing word.

"Means," said Eddie. "That's it. The means of production. All these things that are so necessary to produce things, the factories, the raw materials, wood, steel, coal, cloth, the power that drives the machines, the machines themselves, we call all these the means of production. Clear?"

He looked round the class. They nodded, eagerly now. They had taken a step. Taken it together. Taken it themselves. Such a tiny step that they didn't themselves realise it. And having done it themselves it had been easy and they would remember it. He could have just told them all this in a few seconds. But they had done it themselves. They were on the way. Nw. If he put it to them now, would they get it? Why not? They were practically there. Try.

"So we might say," Eddie started slowly, looking at each of them carefully as he went on, "that you can tell one class from another by it's relationship to the means of production. Right?

154

That means that it's not a question of how much money you get each week but *how* you get it which decides whether you are working class or ..." He looked at the girl again. "What's the opposite?"

"Middle — no, upper class?"

"No comrade, what was that word you usd before to describe the means of production, that we said we'd come back to?"

She tried to remember.

Her brow creased, her eyes turned inwards to look for the lost word, her cheeks flushed. She couldn't remember.

"Was it 'capital'?"

This time it was the dark boy, Michael.

"That's it. And the class, the group of people, who own all the capital, the means of production, is called?"

"Capitalists?"

"Right. There it is. In capitalist society there are two classes. Working class and Capitalist class ..."

"Why just in capitalist society?" The interruption came from the young note-taker and was his first contribution to the discussion. He went on, "Wasn't it always like that? Rich and poor, I mean. Some people owning everything and the rest having to work for them?"

Good boy, thought Eddie. Just right. Now we'll take 'em right back to the beginning. Engels. Origin of the Family.

"That's a good question comrade. What's your name?"

"Jim Braithwaite."

"Well im, let's have a look at that. Let's go back a bit. Let's have a look at the sort of society that existed in England before capitalism. Anybody remember their history?"

And so he took them back, step by step, century by century, society by society. Back to feudalism, back further to slave societies and further to the ancient communal societies. Guiding them, prompting them, he pulled from each of them recollections of their early schoolroom lessons, added to it from his own store of Marxist reading, and having established how society began, and what it was, brought them forward again, step by step, this time with a new understanding of history unfolding, growing from one form of society to another. He showed them how man developed with the invention of tools, the discovery of metal, the use of fire, the spread of agriculture, the specialisation of labour, and as they found the answers to his questions so a new picture of man arose in their minds. Man in control of his future. Man pulling himself up from the swamps, man struggling against the shackles of slavery, against the tyrannies of feudalism, man organising the overthrow of capitalism. And as they traced the rise of man so the old names of history began to fit into the new pattern and make sense. Spartacus and the slave revolt, Wat Tyler and the Peasant's Revolt, Cromwell and the English Revolution, Robespierre and the French Revolution, Lenin and the Russian Revolution. They all began to fit into a pattern.

This was as much as could be done in the first class. Establish the pattern of history. A pattern in which the six martyrs of Tolpuddle meant more than the six wives of Henry the Eighth and in which nobody cared whether Edward the Eighth laid his tired head on some obscure American lady's fashionable breast because more important things were happening at that moment in Spain where a Fascist General, Franco, was leading an insurrection against a popularly elected government and starting a civil war that would rend the whole fabric of the world in two for half a century.

As they broke up, talked to each other for a while, said their goodnights and left, Eddie could see that it had come to them, this new way of looking at life. He had told them nothing new, revealed no hidden mysteries. Merely guided them to look with new eyes at the stock of information stored up on the shelves of their minds, helped them to take it out, dust it and rearrange it so that there was suddenly more room on the shelves and a desire to go out and get more information, read more books, talk to more people, understand more what had been going on behind the pages of history books and the headlines of newspapers.

"Not a bad bunch, eh?" It was Bill.

"Not bad at all. They were all chipping in quite nicely towards the end." Eddie paused for a while and then went on. "Always amazes me what people have got in them once you give them a chance to sort it out. That railwayman for example. Quiet as a mouse to start with. Shy or something. But Christ, when he came in on the housing question he had it all. The business of landlords and property and the homeless. Who is he?"

"Charlie Smale. He ought to have all that pat. He's one of the squatters. The Party put him and his family in Leicester Lodge. He was there for a week with a dozen other families, remember? Barricades up. Sandbags. Police all round. The Party getting food into them. God, that was quite a show."

"Oh he was there was he? No wonder. Did he get a house or anything?"

"They all did. Council requisitioned some empty houses just

156

the other side of the park. Bit dilapidated, mind you, but somewhere to live. Before that they were all split up. Him in lodgings. His wife and kids in some 'half-way house' somewhere. Oh yes, he's learned what it's all about. That's why he's in the Party."

Eddie shook his head. "I don't know," he said. The more I do these beginners classes, the more I come to think it's me learning from them, not them from me."

"Bit of both I suppose Eddie," replied Bill. "How about a cup of coffee?"

Eddie looked at his watch. Half past ten. "Christ!" Then he added "No thanks Bill. Don't want to be late tonight. I'm selling 'Workers' tomorrow outside the factory. Up with the lark."

"And to bed with a Wren."

Eddie smiled at the old war-time joke and thought of the little blonde girl in W.R.N.S. uniform he'd met at that dance.

"I nearly did once," he said, standing up.

"And?"

"It was those black silk stockings. I'd just got back from the East. Hadn't seen anything like that for ages."

"Very fetching."

"Very. Those black silk stockings worked you up — but those black woollen knickers let you down. Very off-putting."

Bill shook his head with a smile.

"Black-outs they called them, didn't they?"

"Wouldn't be surprised."

"Eddie, what's going to happen with this Berlin business?"

"Christ knows. It certainly looks as if the Americans want a showdown."

"Will they go to war on it?"

"They're mad enough for anything."

"But hell, who wants to go to war for Germany?"

"That's not the question, Bill. What the Americans want is that Germany should go to war for them."

"What, now?"

"Not now, but later, when they've been built up again. So now they've got to protect the West Germans, build up their confidence, strengthen their economy, so that when the time comes the Germans will be prepared to march East again."

"The bastards."

"Precisely. That's why a thing like this blockade is so useful to the Americans. It enables them to paint the Russians as awkward sods and the Germans as poor starving people that can only live by the Americans flying food to them."

"Sounds like Amy." Bill went to the door as the sound of voices broke into their discussion. Amy came into the room, followed by Margaret, whose eyes went traight to Eddie, smiled, and then transferred to Bill.

"Hullo Bill," she said. "All right?"

"Fine Margaret, fine. And you?"

"Wonderful. We had a wonderful meeting. How was your class?" This last to Eddie.

"Very good. Very good."

"How many?"

"Six. But good."

"Bill!" Amy exploded, "you didn't put the kettle on. We came back expecting a lovely cup of coffee and here you are sitting here yakking."

"I asked him," Bill protested, "but he wouldn't have any."

Eddie went over to Margaret and grasped her arm just above the elbow. The bare flesh was cool to his touch and with the back of his hand he could feel where the straps of her brassiere cut into her side beneath the thin summer dress.

"My fault Amy," he said. "Bill asked me but I have to go. Up early in the morning outside the factory."

"But just a cup of coffee!"

"Thank you Amy but I really must go. If I don't wake up at six the world's workers are going to be without their daily dose of enlightenment and that will never do."

"The world's workers." Margaret laughed. "All two of them!"

"It was three this morning," Eddie said, pushing Margaret towards the door.

"My! Fifty percent increase." Margaret's brown eyes laughed into Eddie's, but she went willingly towards the door, guided by the pressure on her arm.

"Four tomorrow" Eddie lifted his finger in imitation of the famous gesture of Lenin, and went on "forty next week, four thousand next year."

They laughed and went out into the summer night with the moon throwing black shadows across the grass in the park.

"Have you really got to go out again in the morning?" Margaret asked.

"Really," said Eddie. "And we've got seven hours before then and I'd rather spend them in bed with you than talking to Bill and Amy."

"Funny couple."

"Funny? Why?"

"I wonder if they're happy?"

"Why shouldn't they be? They look happy enough. Nice house, all the trimmings. A car. Good job."

"I don't know. Things Amy says sometimes."

"Such as?"

"Oh, just things."

"You're nuts."

"Thank you. But I sometimes wonder."

"What, whether you're nuts?"

"Fool. No, I wonder about all this Party activity they do. Always rushing around. Meetings, classes, discussions. Always a house full of comrades."

"Is that bad?"

"With us, no. It's our life. But Amy? I sometimes wonder what it's like when everybody's gone and their little semi-detached house is empty and there's just the two of them downstairs and the children asleep upstairs and nobody discussing anything. Just themselves. I wonder what they talk about? Or if they talk at all?"

"Funny couple," Amy was saying just at that moment, as she emptied the last of the ashtrays on to a copy of the Daily Worker.

"What's funny about them?" asked Bill, coming up behind her and slipping his hands under her armpits and on to her full breasts.

She smiled with pleasure and placed her hands on his. "Well, all this rushing around. Meetings and selling Workers and trade unions and women's groups twenty four hours a day. It's just not natural!"

"I know what is."

He increased the pressure of his hands.

"Stop it Bill," she said, keeping her hands on his so that he couldn't take them away. "You're an old married man and you should know better."

"I do know something better." Now he was squeezing her hard and she gasped and dropped her hands down behind her feeling for him as he took the lobe of her ear in his open lips.

"That's better," he said as she found him and squeezed gently, the way she knew he liked it.

"You're just a dirty old man," she said, throwing back her head until it rested on his shoulder and his lips went from her ear, along the line of her jaw, to her neck.

"That's right," he replied, his eyes following the long line of her neck down to the foothills of her breasts, held between his hands. "You like dirty old men?"

"Mm-mm," she said, "I love 'em. But not till I've got ready." She raised her hands once again to his, this time meeting with no resistance as she took his hands off her breasts, and turned round to face him.

They stood, looking at each other for a while, just as they had looked at each other for the first time sixteen years ago, saying and seeing nothing. And because they saw nothing but each other's eyes they didn't see the wrinkling skin around the eyes, the flabbiness around the chin, the greying hair around her ears, the baldness of his head.

He leaned forward and kissed her.

"Funny couple," she said.

"Who," he asked, "Eddie and Margaret?"

She released his hands, smiled at him, and went towards the door.

"No, silly," she replied. "Us."

*   *   *   *

"Who's that on the platform?"

Eddie stood on tiptoe to look over the heads of the great crowd towards the man who had just clambered on to the top of the loudspeaker van.

"That's Claud Berridge."

"Who's he?" asked Margaret.

"A.E.U. man. Chairman of the London District Committee."

"Of the Party?"

"Yes."

It was dusk on the evening of the last day of October 1948. Since early afternoon people had been filling this rather odd-shaped square square known as Clerkenwell Green in Central London, much to the surprise of the two or three local inhabitants who went about their business in the village-like backwater that this area usually became on a Sunday afternoon.

It was many years since this spot had, in fact, been a village green. Now only a few smoke-grimed plane trees lifted their leafless branches to the wintry sky, remembering better days.

It had the strange quality of a square in a remote provincial township in France, an atmosphere which was heightened by a rather pompous building on its west side, occupied by an insurance company, with such grand pillars and porticos that it might have been the Town Hall. The public lavatories, set in an island in the centre of the square, added to the continental atmosphere. Two separate entrances, one for "Men" and the other, not for women but "Ladies", led down into an underground world from which the occasional Orpheus returned, buttoning up his flies, without a backward glance.

Stone steps led up to this little island and provided a vantage point for many spectators at the meeting who clung to the railings regardless of whether they were men or ladies and were able to see over the heads of the crowd gathered before the rather ramshackle building on the north side of the 'green' which was dignified by the name "Marx House."

"Funny," said Margaret, clinging with both arms to Eddie's arm, "we've been here nearly three years, and I've never been to Marx House."

"Nothing much to see," replied Eddie, looking about the crowd to see if there was anybody he knew, "only the library and a few souvenirs of Lenin."

"Lenin?"

"He workd here. He produced *Iskra* here before the Revolution. That was the paper of the Russian Party."

Suddenly spotlights illuminated the great banner that hung from the windows of Marx House and Eddie realised how dark it had become. He looked around. The square was full. Must be ten thousand, perhaps fifteen. Lucky it wasn't raining. Quite warm actually. Funny banner that. A bit arty. A great big sun rising. Is thas supposed to be the new Daily Worker? They were all singing the "Red Flag". Joining in, Eddie felt big and warm and strong as their voices lifted to the words.

> We'll raise the Scarlet Standard high
> Beneath its shade we live and die
> Though cowards flinch
> And traitors sneer
> We'll keep the red flag flying here.

He felt Margaret hugging his arm.

Now what? Wish those loudspeakers would work. Something about 'our great French comrade, Marcel Cachin . . . join in . . . the Marseillaise . . .' and they were singing again. This time the rousing cheerful song of the French revolution. Yet how wistful that little bit where the tune falls away and he always forgot the words. Sounds like most of the crowd forgot that bit too, but soon they were off to the tumbrils with

161

Osarmes, sitwayong!
Formay vo buttayong,
Marshong, Marshong . . .

Wonder what old Cachin thought of our accents? Now what was Claud saying? Who? Harry Pollitt! Good old Harry.

A great cheer greeted the Communist Party leader as he walked confidently to the microphones. All round the square now people were leaning out of windows wondering if their little island had been transported to a foreign land, floating on a sea of upturned faces, washed by wave upon wave of cheers.

"This is our proudest day," he was saying in that strong Lancashire voice. "Not only for those who are assembled here, but for those all over the country whose pennies, whose sacrifices and devotion have made this day possible . . ." As the stocky little man went on talking about the early days when the Daily Worker had been launched, and the struggles to keep it going, and the great new building that was situated only a few minutes away where the first copies of the new paper were at that moment being printed, Eddie thought of the workers who rushed past him into the factory every morning. "Worker. Buy the Daily Worker. Read the news the others won't print." Five last week. He'd got up to a sale of five on Friday, standing there in the freezing cold from quarter past six till just gone seven. Nearly eight hundred workers passed him through that factory gate. Five of them bought a copy of the Worker.

Still, the five would get it out of their pockets at lunch time, in the canteen, and they'd read it while all the others were reading the Daily Mirrors and Expresses. They'd take part in the daily discussions and they'd say "Ah, but it says in the Worker . . ." and perhaps fifty or a hundred people would know. And these would carry it on and perhaps when they met their mates at the pub they'd say "A bloke at work was telling me that the Daily Worker says . . ."

And the five becomes five hundred.

But it was hard work.

That night, however, nothing was hard. It was cheers, cheers all the way. That night was the end of the line, at the top of the hill, what they had all been working for. True the view at the top was of more and more hills stretching away into the distance. But they'd got there. Nearly a quarter of a million pounds in share capital had been subscribed by working people, some as individuals, as Trade Unions, as Co-operatives, to finance a new Daily Worker, buy it a new building, a new rotary press, new equipment of all kinds. Tonight they were getting somewhere. As Pollitt was followed by the aged Marcel Cachin, who brought greetings from the French Communists, and he in turn was followed by Bert Papworth, a cockney bus driver with a voice like a rusty saw, excitement grew in the crowds who were waiting for the Editor of the paper.

Suddenly lights sprang up all over the little square and a circle of flaming torches surrounded the expectant crowd as a man was seen climbing on to the loudspeaker van. As he got to the top he straightened up and waved a newspaper over his head. It was Bill Rust, the Editor, and that must be the first copy of the new paper.

The crowd went mad with delight. Even the people framed in the upstairs windows of their houses were caught up in the excitement of an event which they knew nothing about. Eddie looked at the people around him. Faces upturned towards the man on the loudspeaker van, a glow that was more than a reflection of the flickering torches, as if each had their own flame within them. Next to him an elderly lady caught his glance and smiled back at him. "He's a good man," she confided, "Bill Rust. A good man."

A good man. Everybody felt that. Everybody felt everybody was good that night and as Rust finished speaking the crowd surged round him, carried him on their shoulders in a strange disciplined ecstasy out of the little square on to the broad highway of Farringdon Road where the brand new building stood with lights shining from every window.

Soon the road was blocked. Packed solid with cheering crowds, barring the way to trolley buses and traffic as far as the eye could see. Even the police that night were cheerful as they gradually cleared a way for the traffic to pass through and edged the crowds back on to the pavements.

The torches were dying out. The ecstasy ebbed away, the great rotary press had taken over from the crowds and its steady roar filled them with satisfaction as they made way for the first vans taking the papers to the railway termini.

"Cup of coffee?" Eddie asked Margaret as they flowed with the stream of people northwards up the Farringdon Road.

"Mm-mm. Good idea." Margaret was still holding his arm and she was warm and flushed and contented looking, Eddie thought. "But where can you get coffee round here on a Sunday night?"

"There's a place up here." He turned her to the left as they came to the crossroads and they walked up towards Grays Inn Road. "We get a cup of coffee here sometimes after District Committee Meetings."

"Ah, now I'm going to see where you carry on your gay life," Margaret laughed.

"Gay life!" Eddie laughed back. "Here it is. Come in and see how gay it is."

He pushed open the door of the cafe and held it for Margaret to go through. They stepped into the light of a long fluorescent tube that ran the length of a marble-topped counter. Halfway along the counter was a glass case which presumably at busier periods contained sandwiches and buns. Now it was empty. Beside it was a great silver urn, curved and carved with ornamental flowers, reflecting their approach, upside down, squat and square around the ornamental equator of its distorted world. Behind the silvered monstrosity, squat and square too, but not in reflection, a little dark man interrupted his conversation with a man at a nearby table, to turn his head and look at them.

"Evening" he said, without smiling, or moving at all. Only his head moved on his neck. It came round from its position facing the man at the table until it faced them. His body leaned against the counter, as fixed as the urn and the empty glass case.

"Evening." Eddie returned the greeting. "Two coffees?" It was more a question, asking if two coffees actually existed, rather than a request for two cups of coffee.

"Two coffees." The reply was a re-statement of the problem. Not a confirmation that the coffees would be forthcoming. Eddie and Margaret made their way to a marble-topped table opposite the counter, while the dark man, still motionless, let the two words float between himself and the urn, waiting, perhaps, like a high priest for some sign from the shining idol on the counter that two coffees would be miraculously delivered.

Eddie, watching Margaret undo her coat and look around, thought suddenly of that first time he had met her in the pub. She turned to him, still flushed and smiled when she saw him looking at her. "Funny place," she said, "very gay."

"Very."

"It was good, wasn't it?"

"The meeting?"

"The meeting, the torches, the march, the new building, the singing. Everything."

"It's a big day."

"You know what I thought, just after the meeting?"

"About me? What?"

"You looked replete, full up, content. The old Cheshire cat look, like you used to when we made love and it was right."

164

The smile left her face and she brought her eyebrows together in a frown.

"And now?"

"Just now you looked as if you wanted to again."

"Wanted what?"

"To be right."

She didn't reply for a moment, but pushed with her finger a crumb that remained on the table.

"Two coffees." It was the little man and the two coffees had indeed miraculously materialised and were now steaming before them.

"Thanks" said Eddie, not looking up.

"Want sugar?"

"Please."

"Sugar." A glass sugar dispenser stood before them, between the two cups, and, as if he had never moved, the little man was back behind the urn.

Without adding any sugar Margaret automatically stirred her cup of coffee and said, without looking at Eddie. "Of course I want it to be right again. You know that. But don't be impatient. It's not been that long."

"Three months."

"Is it?" she asked.

"Three months."

"Is it so important to you? You know we said it wasn't so important. There are other things."

"Sure," he replied, "it's not important when it's going right. It's only when it's not right that it becomes important." He shrugged and smiled, more to himself than to her, picking up the sugar dispenser and holding it upside down over his coffee.

"Trouble with these things," he went on, as they both watched the sugar pouring into the coffee, "you never know when you've had enough." He paused, and looked up at her. "Like me."

"Sometimes," she said, "when you think you've had enough, you taste your coffee and it's still bitter."

They looked at each other, not quite sure what they had meant, but each knowing how the other felt.

Eddie lifted his coffee in a mock toast.

"Here's to other things," he said.

She smiled and lifted her cup.

"To everything," she said, "including other things."

The door opened and a dark thin young man stood framed against the light.

For a second his eyes went straight to Margaret's and then, as Eddie turned to see who it was, they recognised each other.

"Aha! Look who's here. Come in Zee, come in. We have friends in the camp." The young man reached into the blackness and, like a magician, drew into the doorway a girl in a duffle coat, small and graceful and with a delicacy that contrasted with the shapeless garment she wore.

Walking behind her, with his hands on her shoulders, the young man guided her down past the counter towards their table. The top of her blonde straight hair reached his chin.

Eddie didn't get up but turned round fully in his chair to face them and they stopped. "Zee," said the dark one, "this is Eddie Sanders. District Committee member, speaker, educationalist, bright spark of the electrician's union, propagandist and . . ." he leaned down and with his mouth to her ear, concluded in a stage whisper, " . . . is one of our provincial comrades from oop North."

He straightened up and looked at Margaret. "The lady I do not know. Eddie, meet my wife, Zena. We call her Zee."

Eddie got up and offered his hand.

"Hullo Zena," he said. "Nice to meet you. This is Margaret."

Margaret smiled and then looked over the girl's head at the dark thin face with wiry black hair brushed straight back from the high forehead.

"This is Joe Gold, Margaret. I think I told you about him. Works at Party Centre. Joe this is Margaret. She comes from 'oop North' too."

"May we join you?" asked Joe.

"Sure, make yourself at home," Eddie replied, bringing up a chair for Zena from the neighbouring table.

"Zee! You must meet Ernie the urn-keeper!" As he was pulling up a chair for himself Joe suddenly darted over towards the counter. "Look! See this wonderful urn, isn't it marvellous?" He reached behind the silver monstrosity and pulled out the little dark man. "And here is the keeper of the urn. Urny!" He laughed largely at his own joke and the laugh was infectious and they all joined in. Even Ernie smiled and said "Two coffees?"

Joe released him and sat down. "That's right Urny. Two coffees. Can you ever get anything else in this gastronomical doss-house of yours?"

The question, wanting no answer, got none. "Two coffees" said the little man and went back behind his urn.

"Great meeting, eh?" Joe said, taking it for granted that the others had been there.

"Great," Eddie confirmed. "Any of your doing?"

"No, no. The DW boys did this on their own. With the help of the London District, of course, as you know." He bowed with exaggerated deference towards Eddie.

"I didn't know much about it actually," said Eddie, "I've been away on a course."

"Party?"

Eddie shook his head. "No, work. Technical."

"You mean to say the powerful and mighty General Electric Company have decided they can extract even more surplus value out of you by educating you?"

"That's it," Eddie smiled, stirring his coffee again.

"Ayayay! The contradictions of capitalism!"

"End of lesson one." This last remark came from Zena who had been sitting quietly by her husband, undoing the buttons of her duffle coat, smiling to herself a little.

They all laughed.

With the lights of the flaming torches still shining in their eyes they talked about the meeting. They drank their coffee and fed themselves on the latest Communist victories in China over five thousand miles away where, even as they were talking, six hundred million people, lifting themselves painfully from an eternity on their knees, would soon be looking with curious eyes on the world outside.

And everywhere, in this world outside, were Communists like these four, in little cafés late at night, in great factories, in colleges and institutions, laboratories, coalmines, lonely farmhouses and crowded cinemas. Talking, planning, eating, drinking, making love. Dons and dustmen, Ministers of State and unemployed, each felt they grasped the future with a firmer grip as the Communist armies moved into Nanking and beyond. Each took the victory to be his own. "We're winning," they laughed as they huddled against the cold wind whistling through the Harlem tenements. "We're winning" they smiled, sipping their coffee in Clerkenwell. "We're winning" they whispered in Malaya, as the flames of their burning villages leapt high into the night and they slipped away into the jungle. In the palaces of the remlin in Russia, and in the prisons of Johannesburg in South Africa, they looked at the world and talked like these four were talking that night. Some said it in whispers, some broadcast it over the radio, but all were united, as were these four, by the belief that it was true.

That history was being written and they were writing it.
And that the future was theirs.

PART TWO

Two Steps Backward

1953 — 1956

"Who was it?"

Joe came back into the room. For a moment he said nothing. In his hand he turned two pennies over, feeling the hardness of them grating on each other as he looked at Zena sitting there with her fat belly blown up like a balloon and still two months to go.

"Who was on the phone Joe?"

"It was Hetty," he said. "About the old man. He's going." He slipped one of the coins back in his pocket and flicked the other into the air watching the way it spun.

"He wants to see me."

"Oh, Joe."

He looked up at her sharply.

"What?"

Those bloody great blue eyes. She wasn't beautiful. But yet she had such beauty about her. The eyes said nothing, but the eyebrows, the lines round them, the pull of the skin round the nose to the corner of her mouth. All this said it, not the eyes. They're just the same great pale blue nothings. You could jump right in them and not feel a thing.

"I'm sorry."

He shrugged.

"What for?"

"For him. For your mother," she paused, then went on, "for us, in a way."

Now his hand was back in his pocket turning the coins over again.

"Why us?"

With an effort she heaved her body out of the armchair and walked over to the electric fire. Waddled almost, with the weight of the child. With legs wide apart and one hand on the mantlepiece to steady herself she leaned down and switched off one of the glowing elements.

"Too hot," she said, straightening up, flushed with the effort, one hand on her back to ease a sudden sharpness.

There it was again. A particular, separate beauty, flashed on like a torch in the dark, quite isolated from the rest of her. The sudden red flush in her cheeks burned for a moment against the pale yellow of her hair like a fire in a field of wheat.

Joe smiled as he went over to her. That delicate, almost fragile face, on that round balloon of a belly. It was like those cut-out books one had as a child where, as you turn the pages, you put a clown's head on to a policeman's body with a ballet dancer's legs.

As he reached her he patted her belly and said, "Come on fatty, why us?"

She held his hand on her, half smiling, half searching for what she meant.

"Well for one thing because of this little Trotskyite in here. It would have been nice to present your father with a grandson, even if he was only half Jewish."

"He'd never have acknowledged it."

"He would. After all those girls Sadie and Hetty have given him he'd acknowledge any boy even if he was half Mohammedan."

Joe smiled. "Maybe."

"And anyway, after all the worry we've caused him it would have been nice to give him a bit of happiness."

"We caused *him* worry? That's a laugh. He's the one that wouldn't see *you*. He's the one that turned *me* out because I wanted to marry a Gentile, because I wanted to be a Communist, because I wanted to live my own life. Christ, girl, he's the one that caused all the worry, not us."

"I know love, I know. But from his point of view we went against everything he'd been brought up to think was right. You can't change these people. It's like you and Joe Stalin. Whatever *he* does is right, and you won't budge. You're just as obstinate as he is is."

Joe's hand stiffened and he withdrew it, turning away from her. "It's not the same at all," he said.

"There you are, you're already getting offended. In a minute you'll be telling me off just like you said your old man used to tell you off."

Joe looked at her angrily. What do you do with a girl like this who knows your pulse before it beats and carries your blood in

171

her belly like a banner in the wind?

"Sorry, Zee. You're right."

That's what you do.

They stood next to each other in front of the fire, not speaking, not touching. Just experiencing each other the way animals do sometimes. Like two deer at the edge of a wood.

"Hetty says he wants to see you?"

Joe looked at his watch.

"Yes," he replied, "I'd better get going."

"Should I come?"

"I've been thinking about that. Not now. No. I'll see what it's like there. Perhaps tomorrow."

"I'm burning," she said, lowering herself into the chair and fidgeting from side to side until she was comfortable. "Will you be late?"

"Christ knows. Depends what happens."

"Is Sadie there?"

"Oh they're all there. A right gathering of the clans. Sadie with her darling David and Hetty with her cynical Sam." Joe turned and walked over to the table and started looking through a pile of books and pamphlets. "Oh, I can take them" he went on, "they're just people like you and me, or anyone else. I don't like them much, they don't like me. That's fair enough. It's the old girl I can't take."

"Did Hetty say how she's taking it?"

"I didn't ask. But I know. Remember once I took you to the Yiddish Theatre in Commercial Road?"

"And I couldn't understand a word?"

"The words, no. But the atmosphere. The words don't count. The world has been going on for millions of years. Suddenly somebody invents words and for a tiny space of time, a few thousand years, everybody starts making up words and throwing them at each other like stones, and you'd think there was no other way of communicating with people than with words. Words are for little things like business and governments, writers and poets. Big things like love and hate and happiness and misery don't need words."

"Oh Joe, that's going a bit far."

"Maybe it is. But you remember that Yiddish play? You couldn't understand a word. But you remember how unhappy that mother was when her daughter went away?"

"You said it was ham."

"Sure it was ham. One hundred percent pure Jewish kosher

172

ham. That's how she'll be tonight."

"Joe. You don't mean she'll be acting it up?"

"It won't be acting love. It will be the real thing. Real true-life ham. We call it ham because we're so bloody sophisticated with our books and our plays and our slick sexy films that actual life is ham to us. She won't be acting the part of the Yiddishe Momma, she will *be* the Yiddishe Momma. And tonight it's tragedy on the programme. Tonight we're going to get tragedy that will make the Greek chorus look like the Keystone Cops."

"Joe, you call Sam cynical, but you're much worse than him."

Joe turned towards her. "I'm not being cynical Zee. This is the way it's going to be. This is not a play, this is real life. This was happening before plays were ever thought of. This is what people were trying to capture when they first started writing plays. But it's typical bloody writer's vanity to say the world is a stage. The stage is just a poor imitation of life."

Joe turned back to the books on the table.

"Seen those Congress pamphlets anywhere?"

"What Congress?"

"What Congress? Christ Zee! How many Congresses have there been recently? The Nineteenth Congress of the Communist Party of the Soviet Union." He spelled it out for her, separating each word with a veneer of sarcasm.

"Oh, I think they're in the bedroom. Weren't you reading one of them in bed last night?"

Without reply Joe walked through the door into the narrow hall and opened the opposite door into their bedroom. Switching on the light he went straight to the stool by his side of the double bed and picked up one of three pamphlets that were lying there. On his way through the hall again he picked up a macintosh and scarf that had been lying on a chair by the telephone and started to put them on as he went through the door of the living room.

"Zee, will you do something for me?"

"What?"

"Phone up Margaret Houghton and tell her I won't be at this meeting tonight. Tell her ... well tell her what's happened and say they should carry on and sort out what they want me to do and I'll see her later in the week and she can tell me about it. O.K.?"

"Who's Margaret Houghton? What was the meeting about?"

"Oh she's working on this International Women's Day event in March. They've got a meeting tonight to sort out the theme and they asked me to help them with their propaganda material. She's Eddie Sanders' wife. You'll find the number in our little book under Sanders. O.K.?"

Now the scarf was wrapped round his neck and he was doing up his raincoat.

"O.K.," she said, adding, "How come her name's Houghton if she's married to Eddie Sanders?"

"Christ knows. I don't know if they're married or living together or what. I've never really bothered to find out. Only met her once. You remember, you were with me. That night when the new D.W. building was opened. Afterwards, in that café."

Zee thought back.

"That was a long time ago," she said.

"Four years."

"I think I remember. Dark girl. North Country."

"That's right."

"He was nice. Tall and blonde, wasn't he? Very polite and . . . serious. Very sincere."

"Very sincere, that's Eddie. And serious as they make 'em. No jokes about the Party with him. Or the Trade Union. E.T.U. bloke he is. We're putting him up for the Executive."

"Of the Party?"

"No, E.T.U."

"Who's we?"

"We? The Party, of course."

"How can 'we' put him up for the E.T.U. Executive?"

"Christ, we've got enough people in the E.T.U. to put anyone on the Executive. We're very strong in the E.T.U. girl. All this guff about the party being so small and having no influence is all right for the News of the World but tell that to the bosses in the electrical industry. And this country runs on electricity, Zee. Just get your finger on the switch and you can stop the lot, just like this."

Suddenly the room was in darkness.

"Fool," said Zena, with a giggle. As her eyes grew accustomed to the lesser light of the electric fire she saw him coming towards her. He stood by her chair, stroking her hair for a while then, dropping to his knees he put his head to her belly as though listening. With one hand he tapped the roundness.

"Anyone home?"

She giggled again.

"There's someone there all right. Kicking like mad he was last night."

"Can't hear a thing. Maybe he's gone to the pictures." He lifted his head looking into her eyes, smile for smile. "Don't

174

believe there's anything there at all. Just an excuse because you're getting fat. I wish . . ." he looked at her, not saying what needed no saying.

She put her hand to his cheek, feeling the stubble around his chin.

"So do I love," she said. "Be patient."

"Huh," he repeated, "be patient."

She straightened the scarf round his neck, pulling up the collar of his macintosh.

"It'll do you good."

"Thanks for nothing. Anytime I want to be done good I'll let you know. Meanwhile, fatty, it looks like you're the one who was done good. Good and proper." He put his lips to her bulging form, feeling the rough cloth of her dress and the taughtness of her stretched skin beneath, and got to his feet.

"Ah well," he sighed, "better get going."

"What you reading?"

Joe stuffed the pamphlet into his mac pocket.

"Khrushchev. Speech to the Nineteenth Congress."

"Who's he? I've never heard of him before."

"Neither have I. Whole lot of new people brought in to this new Praesidium arrangement of Uncle Joe's. Christ knows what it's all in aid of."

"Maybe they're building up a team to take over when he dies."

"Who, Stalin? Maybe. Must say he didn't say much at the Congress. Left it all to Malenkov."

He stood by the door now, with his fingers on the switch. "Want the light on?"

"No," she said, turning her face to the fire, "leave if off. It's nice just with the light of the fire. Joe . . ." she hesitated, and did not go on.

"Yes?"

"Is it all right there? In Russia I mean." She paused again, and then continued. "I mean this business about the Jews. Do you think there's any antisemitism there?"

"Antisemitism? In Russia? Don't be daft, it's illegal."

"I know that," she replied, "but why have they shut down the Jewish theatre, and their papers and all that? And what happened to those two Jewish writers who were over here during the war?"

"I don't know. But you don't want to believe everything they write in the capitalist press."

"I don't Joe, you know that. I want to believe you. But tell me something I can believe."

175

In the silence of the darkness that separated them, she could hear the muffled sound of the pennies he was turning over in his pocket.

"Well, there probably wasn't any demand for a separate theatre. Maybe nobody read those papers. After all the Jews are free there, there's no persecution. They've probably assimilated themselves into normal life. Why go to a corny little Yiddish theatre when they can go to the Bolshoi? Zee, you know how the Party fights antisemitism, you know how any form of racial intolerance is condemned. How could the Party put up with any anti-Jewish activity in Russia, of all places? It doesn't make sense, does it?"

"I suppose not. There must be some other answer. I just wish I knew what it was."

"So do I love. I'm going to need it tonight."

"Tonight?" She looked up, puzzled for the moment, forgetting where he was going, trying to place what meeting he was speaking at that night. Then she remembered.

"You don't think they'll start arguing tonight, do you?"

"Dear David is always ready for a row, and Sam's not averse to a bit of a barney now and then."

"And you?" She smiled in the dark.

"Me? Quiet as a lamb."

"Some lamb. You're nothing more than a trouble-making Communist agitator, as David would say."

"And you're a running dog of imperialism."

"And a servile lackey of the West?"

"That's it." Joe turned in the doorway, before going and blew her a kiss.

"Night, lackey."

"Bye, running dog."

"Phone that girl."

"I will. Don't be late."

"O.K."

The door closed and she was left with the dark glow of the fire casting long shadows of unanswered questions.

He wasn't sure any more. Not about this anyway. Of everything else, maybe. But not this. She was suddenly frightened. For Joe not to be sure, this was a new thing, and fear played with panic at the edge of her mind where she saw a world collapsing like a house of party cards. Yet it was not a wholly unpleasant panic. She wasn't alone any more. Not in this anyway. So the whole world would collapse. It wouldn't matter too much

176

if she wasn't alone. If Joe were with her. But if Joe's world ceased to be her world, what then? Especially now. When she was fat and ugly. Be patient. That was a laugh. How could he want her anyway, as she was? Anybody else? Not Joe, He was too tied up with the Party. Funny, he's out most evenings. Meetings, classes, discussions. Back late three or four times a week but she never worried about other women. International women! She must make that phone call.

She heaved herself up again and made her way to the door, allowing herself, in her loneliness, the luxury of hobbling across the room like an old woman bowed down with a great weight, and laughing a little to herself as she did it. In the hallway she sat down by the telephone with a sigh and looked at their little book of phone numbers. Sanders. She dialled and listened to the buzz.

"Twothreesixnine." The voice sounded hard and metallic as if a clever little bird was sitting in the earpiece parroting a number it had learned that morning.

Suddenly she felt sick.

"Twothreesixnine," the voice repeated. "Hallo?"

"Hallo," Zena replied.

"Who's that?"

"Oh . . . this is Zena Gold here. Can I speak to Mrs . . ." God! What was her name? It wasn't Mrs. anything . . . but what was it? What had Joe said? Desperate, searching, stumbling, she gripped the receiver with both hands, lost somewhere on the wire, hanging in space without being able to move.

"This is Margaret Houghton here . . ." The voice was still there, still metallic and hard, but there. She grasped at it with relief. Margaret Houghton. Of course.

"Hallo," she said again. Silly, but it was something. A word. Till it all came back.

"I'm Joe Gold's wife," she went on. "He asked me to phone you."

"Yes?"

"I'm afraid he can't come to the meeting tonight. His father is ill. Very ill . . ." It didn't sound a good enough reason and yet she didn't want to say it, ". . . he's dying . . ."

"Oh. I'm sorry."

"We only heard a half-hour ago and Joe's rushed over there. He asked me to phone you and let you know." She was being silly. Prattling on. She'd said what she had to say, why didn't she hang up instead of repeating herself like this. What was there about that voice at the other end that she wanted to know about?

"It was nice of you to phone," said the voice. "I'll tell the others. I'll speak to him later on in the week and tell him what happens tonight. It was to get his advice on the propaganda material actually. None of us here are much good at that and it was suggested that Joe would like to help . . ."

Now *she* was going on and on.

"I'm sure he would," said Zena.

"Tell him I'm sorry. And thank you for phoning."

"That's all right. Goodbye."

"Goodnight."

It was only when she had difficulty putting the receiver back on the hook that Zena noticed how she was trembling. She was suddenly exhausted. Faint. Sick. It just wasn't possible to lift herself out of the chair, yet she wanted to get far away from the telephone. Far away.

A sharp little kick in her womb brought a smile to her lips. He was growing fast. She clasped both hands round her belly imagining how it would be when she was actually holding the baby. Soon now. Soon. Another kick. He's strong.

Effortlessly now, she rose and went into the living room, her belly becoming a balloon, not a boulder, the child somehow walking beside her, the telephone call forgotten, the collapse of the world forgotten. In the wonder of a new world being born she neither knew nor cared if an old world was dying.

As she entered the living room she turned on the light. Walking over to the table she picked up a drawing pad and the pencil that was lying on it. She sank into the armchair by the fire once again and adjusted the drawing pad to rest between her belly and the arm of the chair. She started to draw.

The baby kicked her once again, gently, as if turning in its sleep.

"Keep still," she whispered, "I'm trying to draw you."

.   *   *   *   *

"Better go right up Joe. Mother's there."

She looked old. Little Sister Sadie. What was she? Not more than thirty-five. Not that. Looked nearer fifty.

"How is he?"

She shrugged her shoulders and turned away. He followed her through the soft carpeted hall to the foot of the stairs. It must be nearly a year since he'd seen her. That awful evening when he'd taken Zee round to their place for dinner. Sadie wasn't so bad, but that pompous sod of a husband. Dear David.

Quietly a door opened and David came out into the hall. He looked old, too. And fatter. Still slick. Still well-groomed, but noticeably older and — very tired.

David held out his hand.

"Hullo Joe," he said, "I'm glad you came."

Glad I came! Joe felt the old resentment flare up in him again. Anybody would think it was his father up there. *He's* glad *I* came!

But he said nothing. In the soft grip of his brother-in-law's hand Joe felt he actually meant it. He really was glad. Relieved anyway. At least a son was here to share the responsibility. Or perhaps it was his sense of what was right. The son should be there. A son-in-law wasn't the same. Even a son-in-law like David.

"Hallo David," he said, holding the other's hand for a second, then releasing it. "How's things?"

The same shrug. But not a turning away like Sadie. Instead a hopeless smile that seemed to say 'Now he asks me how's things . . . who cares . . . things aren't important . . . they don't even exist. Things already . . .'

All he said was, "Better go up."

Joe turned his back on them both and went up. They followed him with their eyes for a moment then looked at each other, shrugged and went back into the lounge.

The same red staircarpet, the same glinting brocade curtain on the landing, even the same sudden roughness of that concealed join in the polished banister rail. And that stair rod still loose after five years.

They had got new wallpaper though. Cream, with an embossed design like a scroll and shields and a little touch of gold picking up the glimmer of the brocade. Always a little touch of gold. That was the old man.

The same smell too. That was her. Not a personal, physical smell but an atmosphere that she created out of *lockshun* soup and *gefilte* fish and furniture polish and talcum powder and those big curly chrysanthemums that cost a fortune and lasted for weeks.

On the landing, outside their room, was a new ingredient. A new smell of medicine and doctors and disinfectant. It was no longer the same as it had always been in the days before the big row. As he stood before their door, his hand on the glass door knob, he remembered the way that same door had slammed in his face, how he'd reached for the same door-knob to go in and argue with the old man, hesitated, decided not to, and ran downstairs

179

and out of the house, not even saying a word to his mother who sat weeping in the hall, her head buried in her arms on the table, shaking the tall vase of golden chrysanthemums.

He opened the door quietly and went in.

She looked up at him.

In the low light, thrown downwards by the dressing table lamp which had been draped with a silk scarf, he saw her sitting by the foot of the bed. The lamp was behind her but there was sufficient light to see that there was no surprise on her face when she saw him. She looked at him as if he wasn't there. Or worse, as if she wasn't there. He could have been Hetty bringing up a cup of tea, or Sadie who she sees nearly every day of the week, not a son she hasn't seen for nearly five years.

Five years. What were five years compared to the fifty years that were sliding quietly away from her now between the sheets?

Her eyes went from her son to her husband and she got up and moved to the head of the bed. It was only then that Joe realised how old she had become.

She was small, almost tiny, in her stockinged feet. Her hair was untidy and the ends hung grey and brittle around her ears. Her mouth dropped disapprovingly because she had not bothered to put her false teeth in and the rest of her face sagged downwards over her chin.

But it was the size of her that shocked Joe. So small. And he remembered her so big, and plump and shiny. She was just a little old woman now.

"Mum," he said, going towards her.

With her eyes still on her husband she raised a finger to her lips. "Sh-sh-sh."

She bent over him, quietly stroking the face that lay so deep in the shadows that it appeared as no more than an impression on the whiteness of the pillow.

"Shmul," she whispered, "Joey's here."

There was no response from the shadow on the pillow. Joe leaned forward over the bed, trying to make out the features of his father's face in the darkness and he suddenly panicked. He was dead! He'd been dead for hours and she was just sitting up with him pretending he was still here but he was dead!

Then the shadow on the pillow moved. In the dark a speck of liquid glittered as an eye opened. The other eye in shadow, this one took on its own personality, widening its whiteness into life, being rather than seeing, peering out of deep-sunk bones, as the face fell into focus.

180

"It's Joey, Shmul," his mother said again. "He's come to see you."

The eye fixed on him and a voice which Joe didn't recognise at all came from the shape on the pillow.

"My Joey?"

"Hullo Dad," Joe said. "It's me."

He wanted to cry. He hadn't cried since that night the Fascists beat him up nearly twenty years ago but, like that night, he wanted to run to the old man and hold him and cry his eyes out.

His father was moving now, turning his head to his wife, putting a hand out of the sheets. "Roshka" he said, "help me up. I want to talk to Joey. Help me up."

"*Shah, shah, shah,*" she soothed him and turned to Joe standing on the other side of the bed. "Help me get him up a bit."

There were tears now in her eyes as she spoke to her son for the first time in five years. Joe kneeled on the bed and reached an arm under the sheets and round under the old man's shoulders.

God he was thin. Beneath the pyjamas he could feel the sharpness of the shoulder blade. It was nothing to lift him and ease him up a little on the pillow so that he was sitting up.

"Good boy," he said, between deep breaths, and patted the side of the bed. "Sit down, eh?"

Joe walked round the bed and sat by his father.

"Roshka." The voice seemed to be gaining a little strength now. It was almost recognisable as his father's voice as he spoke again to his wife. "Go downstairs for a bit, eh? Have a rest. A cup of tea, eh? I'm all right now."

"Sure Shmul, sure. I'll go down for a while. Have a cup of tea. A little sit down." Gently tucking in the sheets which were already tucked in at the foot of the bed and smoothing away the impression where her son had knelt on the bed, she left them both together.

"She's a good woman. Your mother."

What could he reply to that?

"Sure Dad, sure."

"Good woman . . ."

Joe looked into his father's eyes which were staring, red-rimmed, at the lamp behind him. His face was prickly as a cactus with silver stubble on a desert dry skin.

Funny, how he always had such loud pyjamas. The solid citizen living it up in his dreams.

"Joe."

"Yes, Dad."

"Joe, in that drawer ... the top drawer ..." Now his eyes directed him to the chest of drawers by the dressing table. "There's my *tephilim*." Christ! He wasn't going to start saying prayers was he? "And a *sidur*." The eyes closed. "In the drawer, Joey."

Joe got up and went to the chest of drawers and opened the top drawer. There, on top of a pile of white shirts, was the red velvet bag embroidered with a Star of David in gold thread that always contained his father's phylacteries, the *tephilim*. Next to it was a Singer's Prayer Book, the *Sidur*, and on top of this two *capels*, little black skull caps. His mother must have put them there in readiness. He hadn't asked for the *capels*. Better take them over though, he must have forgotten.

He went back to the bed where his father, with a bit of a struggle, had got his arms out from under the sheets and was trying to roll up the sleeve of his left arm.

He wants to put the *tephilim* on. Without being asked Joe rolled up the old man's sleeve until the skinny bicep was exposed. So white. Like a child.

"The *capel*, Joe."

He put one of the skull caps on his father's head.

"You too. A *capel*."

He put the other skull cap on his head and opened the velvet bag. Which was which? There were two phylacteries. One was to go on the head, the other on the arm. Could he remember how they went? It was so long. The one for the head had a big loop. The other was smaller, adjustable, he remembered. There were two little black boxes, each attached to black leather thongs. One to be looped round the head, the other round the arm. Unravelling the leather thongs, Joe began to feel involved in a strange game in which he had forgotten the rules.

"The arm first."

"Sure Dad, I know." For some reason he felt it important to assure his father that he still knew all about it. That he hadn't forgotten, despite the fact that he'd married a non-Jewish girl, a *shikser*.

This one was for the head. It had a big loop. Then this was for the arm. How did it go? On the muscle, that's right. Wasn't there something about that? One on the muscle for strength, and one on the forehead for brain. Something like that.

He slipped his father's arm through the loop and fixed the phylactery on the flabby bicep, then wound the black thong seven times round the forearm. Hope that's right. Seven times. Must be.

Now let the old man hold the rest of the thong while he fixed the one on the head, then finish up winding the other one round his fingers. That's it.

He smiled to himself as he placed the end of the leather arm strap in his father's hand and closed the fingers round it.

"You hold that Dad."

Bet he thought he wouldn't remember. Christ, he'd done all this so many times when he was a kid. Every day before breakfast. What a farce. All such a bloody waste of time. So useless.

Now it was coming in useful.

He took the other phylactery from the bag and carefully and gently like an Archbishop at a Coronation, placed it on his father's head so that the black box rested on his forehead, the loop went round his head, and the straps hung down behind.

Now back to the other one.

Taking his father's hand in his own he took up the end of the thong that was resting in his palm. This was where he could go wrong. Bring it across the back of the hand and once round the forefinger. Then round the three middle fingers? Hell, the old man won't notice anyway. What's the difference? It's all a lot of hocus-pocus.

Holding his father's hand in his own as he completed the winding of the thongs, he thought how long was it — sixteen years? — since the old boy was winding the thongs round *his* fingers? Telling him how to do it, when to do it, but never why. Wonder if he ever knew why or if he just did all these things because, in turn, *his* old man had told him to? Even if there was a reason why, it would be all mumbo-jumbo. Wind the thong round your arm seven times, count your beads, say your prayers, contemplate your navel, bow down to your idol, shave your head, kiss my foot, kiss my arse . . .

"The *sidur*, Joey."

"What? Oh. Here it is Dad."

Joe picked up the little prayer book.

"Where do you want?"

"The *Shema*, Joey, the *Shema*."

The voice was weaker, noticeably weaker, and Joe, looking over the edge of the prayer book as he flicked the pages, saw the eyes of the old man narrow. Was he going? The *Shema*. Why was this particular prayer the big thing always at the end? 'Hear, oh Israel, the Lord thy God, the Lord is One.' One what? Typical bloody mumbo-jumbo. Ah, here it is. The *Shema*.

Joe looked at the familiar shape and pattern of the prayer, the way it was set out on the page with the big phrase set out there, along the top. Then a little phrase in smaller type underneath it. Then the body of the prayer. Head, neck, body.

"Here it is Dad."

Holding out his hand, his father grasped the book, but it fell away.

Joe rescued it and found the place again.

"Hold it with me Joe. Come. Sit next to me."

Joe sat by the pillow, his shoulder against his father's shoulder, his left hand holding the book next to his father's right hand, the smell of medicine and sickness flowing round him, the words of the prayer dancing on the page before him. The old man was dying. This was the last thing he would do for him. Wasn't it the only thing he had ever done for him? There must have been other things. When he was a kid. Like fetching him things, running an errand, going to *shool* on *shobus*. But they were all things he'd been asked to do, or told to do. Was there anything he'd ever done for the old man of his own free will, because he wanted to, without being asked, without being told?

"Read it Joey. Read it with me."

Automatically, not reading, but reciting by heart, out of the past, the words came to Joe's lips while in his mind he desperately sought for the memory of something he had done, some time, any time, for his father.

"*Shema Yisroel, Adonai Elohaynu, Adonai Echod.*"

With his own voice he could hear his father's, weak, hesitant, wavering, his hand trembling on the prayer book.

Was the old man afraid to die? Now, at this moment, after he'd stormed through life demanding 'only the best', was he afraid that he would no longer be able to command 'the best'? Poor old boy. Was this all his religion could give him, at the end? Fear of the unknown? What can I give him? Hope . . . confidence . . . God?

That's about all I can give him now. No good arguing, talking, persuading. The time for that is past. Now, in these few minutes I can only give him back the God that he tried to give me.

Seeing now what he had to do, Joe lifted his voice to the next phrase.

"*Boruch shaym k'vod mulchuso le'olom voed.*" Blessed be the name of His Glorious Kingdom for ever and ever.

"*Ve'ohuvto es Adonai Elohecho . . .*" And thou shalt love the Lord thy God . . . strongly now Joe recited, the whole thing coming back to him from his childhood, the intonation, the reverence, the glory of a God he had never known, passing through him like a procession seen by a tourist in a foreign land.

"*Bechol levovcho . . .*" with all thy heart.

Now he was almost singing it, like the cantor in the synagogue.

"*Bechol nufshecho . . .*" with all thy soul.

And the old man's voice was lifting with his, his fingers no longer trembling on the prayer book.

"*Oobechol Meodecho . . .*" and with all thy might.

Together, their voices rose and fell in the ancient traditional intonation. Shoulder pressed to shoulder, arm to arm, finger touching finger on the spine of the prayer book.

Outside the room, her head leaning against the door, Rose Gold listened, her happiness tinged with fear. Her boy was back. They were all together again. But for how long? So long as she could hear them, on the other side of the door, it was all right. Joey had a good voice. So strong, like a cantor. And Shmul, too.

Suddenly the voices stopped. The prayer ended. No. Not now. Not so soon . . .

Desperately she threw herself against the door, arms outstretched to block the way. But impossible. With a terrible shudder she felt it pass through her, dragging with it a little piece of every part of her body, so that she contracted and became smaller and sank down like an emptied sack.

For a while she knelt there on the floor, leaning against the door, her forehead resting on the glass door knob. Then she lifted her head, grasped the handle and pulled herself up. Silently she opened the door and there facing her was her husband, but so much younger . . . tall and handsome as he had been thirty years ago in the early years of their marriage, his hair black and curly, his arms stretched out to hold her.

"Shmul," she cried, "don't go away from me."

Stumbling forward she fell sobbing into the arms of her son.

*   *   *   *

'A car is a great thing," said Joe. "Outside there it's pouring with rain. In here it's all soft and warm and I'm being transported back to my wife and home in the lap of luxury on the wings of Mercury. Very nice."

"Mercedes, actually," said Sam.

"Eh?"

"The car. Mercedes. You like it?"

"Not any longer. You surprise me Sam."

"Why?"

"Mercedes. A mobile gas chamber."

"Joe, now you surprise me. How long do you go on hating the Germans?"

"I don't hate Germans. I just hate anybody who made gas chambers, and concentration camps. Don't you?"

"Sure I do Joe, But how do you know Mercedes were involved in that sort of thing?"

"Do me a favour Sam. What do you think they were making during the war, washing machines?"

"I don't know. Tanks maybe ... who knows?"

"Aha. Tanks are all right. You think they could have built Auschwitz without tanks?"

"Joe, that was ten years ago. Sometime you have to forgive and forget."

"That's generous of you Sam. On behalf of six million Jews you have decided to forgive and forget. They'd be grateful."

Sam didn't reply. Only the powerful windscreen wipers continued to clear two paths for them through the insistent rain. It was Joe who spoke first.

"Anyway. Forget it Sam. I'm a bit upset. The old man. Then Mum. Then all this business with the *Shiva*. I'm sorry. It's a nice car."

The *Shiva* was going to be a problem. Seven days of mourning, sitting on low stools at the house while friends and relatives came to pay their respects.

"You'll have to sit *Shiva*, Joe, for her sake," they'd said. "You must. For her."

As if she cared about anything now. But she'd want him to sit *Shiva* all right. If only for him. They wanted it for her. She wanted it for him. Did anybody ever do things any more because they were the right things to do?

"That's O.K. Joe. Forget it. How's the newspaper business?"

Cynical Sam. Always the bright boy. Every word a needle to be stuck into you just because he has a grudge against some clay model.

"Thriving Sam, never a dull moment."

"Find it more interesting than the other job?"

The other job. The unspeakable. What would he know about such things? Go explain. In the six months since Joe had been working in the Daily Worker Features department he had become completely immersed in the daily problems of analysing, directing, understanding and explaining the national and international events hourly, immediately, as they happened. No

186

time here to wait for meetings of the Political Committee. No time even to see what Harry thought about it or await the reactions of other parties. The readers couldn't wait for that. The Express will be there in the morning bashing out some lie or other. Our boys in the factories must have an answer.

"It's different," he replied, looking sideways at Sam.

"In what way?"

Does he really want to know or is he just talking? He's not a bad bloke really. Not much older than me. At least he works for a living, even if it is only in advertising. Not fat like dear David. Somehow more my generation. Why not?

"Well it's more ... urgent, I suppose. Take this Railway strike. When I was working at King Street ... that's the Party headquarters ... and something like this blew up, you'd go and have a chat with the Industrial Department. Get a bit of the background. They'd more than likely know what was going on but if they didn't they'd get some of our Rail blokes in and talk it over with them. Then we'd sort it out and decide what was needed. Perhaps a leaflet, perhaps some meetings. More often than not nothing at all. Leave it to the boys on the spot or the people in the District Party office. We'd just get all the facts. Discuss it. Get the policy right. Advise. Provide our boys with the background material. On the Worker it's different. No time for all that. A thing like this blows up, you've got to get out and find out all about it straight away. Talk to the men on the job. Phone the other side for a statement. Sort it out with the Editor and maybe our own Industrial man and you're away. Bash out a story, get it O.K'd and bob's your uncle, the masses are reading all about it the next day."

"And the strike spreads?"

The old needle.

"Ever been on strike Sam?"

"Can't say I have." Sam smiled and snatched a sidelong glance at his brother-in-law. "Mustn't let the dear clients realise they can sell their lovely products without advertising. That'd never do."

Joe didn't laugh.

"Say you were one of the world's workers, Sam ..."

"Perish the thought."

"... and conditions were bad where you were working ..."

"Mayfair isn't what it used to be."

"... wages cut, safety rules neglected, something like that ..."

"No olives with the Martinis?"

". . . and the Express came out next day and said conditions were good. Would you believe it?"

"Never believe anything in the papers, Joe, except the ads."

"No, seriously, Sam, would you?"

"Seriously? No, I suppose not, if I knew myself they were bad."

"Then suppose it was the other way round and conditions were O.K. . . ."

"Don't tell me *you* think conditions could ever be O.K?"

". . . and the Worker came out and said conditions were bad. Would you believe that?"

"Obviously not, if I knew they were good. But you might persuade workers in other parts of the country, who didn't know the conditions, to come out in sympathy."

"But we've just agreed in the first place that you wouldn't be out if the conditions weren't bad so there'd be nothing for anybody to sympathise with. And secondly Sam workers don't operate like that. To get workers out in sympathy you've got to send delegates along from the strikers to talk to them, get resolutions passed at meetings. Christ, workers on a weekly wage packet aren't going to give that up because they like the colour of your eyes. You try it."

"Have you?"

"Sometimes. In a way. It just won't work. You want to read what Lenin said about propaganda."

"He certainly managed to sell his product, I'll give him that. And to a mass market."

Now it was Joe's turn to smile.

"All the propaganda in the world, he said, will never persuade the worker if it's against his own experience.

"You can't sell a bad product."

"That's right."

"Good lad, that Lenin, he'll go far. Any time he needs a job ask him to come and see me."

Joe laughed this time.

"What'll you do, put him on the Conservative Party account?"

Sam didn't answer. As they came up to the traffic lights he slowed down. "Silly cow," he muttered as the car in front of him stopped in the middle of the two lanes, allowing no space for him to pull up alongside. "Some people want the whole bloody road," he said, as much to himself as to Joe.

"Sounds like a slogan your clients turned down," said Joe.

"Still, maybe we could use it. Make a good cartoon."

Sam moved off as the lights changed, bending forward to change gear, accelerating quickly to pass the car in front, glaring at the driver as he did so.

"Silly cow," he muttered again. "Good cartoon?" he returned to Joe's last remark. "You mean big fat tycoon in immense Rolls taking up all the road, blocking the way of the little worker in his Austin Seven?"

"Austin Seven? No, bloody great ten-ton lorry."

"Pardon me. And the caption?"

"Something simple, like 'Move over!'"

"And if he won't?"

"He would if it was a tank though, wouldn't he?"

Sam thought for a while and with one hand on the wheel, felt in his pocket for a cigarette and matches.

"Lenin say that, too?"

"Something like that. He called it the Dictatorship of the Proletariat."

"Not a good name. Doesn't sing, as we say." He fumbled in the carton and put a cigarette in his mouth. Joe reached over and took the box of matches out of Sam's lap, struck one and held it up to him.

"Thanks. Needs to be short and snappy, come easy to the tongue. Not too many syllables."

"I like Ike?"

"That was a good one. It got Eisenhower in anyway."

"I gather than was an agency campaign, too?"

"Right. You're not far from here are you Joe?"

Joe looked out into the rain. "Keep right on. You'll come to a set of traffic lights in about a mile. Turn right there."

They were both quiet.

Wonder if she phoned Margaret Houghton? International Women, there's a product for you. Sounds like the White Slave trade. Would Sam talk to me about the Tory Party campaign? Make an interesting article. Could but try.

"So why didn't you use a short snappy slogan?"

"Well it's different here. There was an issue to fight on."

"Nationalisation?"

"Freedom, we prefer to call it."

"Of course, whatever the other side is for is against Freedom."

"Good word, Freedom. You see in the States both parties were the same, no issues between them . . ."

"They were both against Freedom?"

189

"Or for it. Depending who you were. But both had exactly the same policy."

"So why an election? Why don't they combine?"

"Bad for democracy. People must have a choice. Even if both detergents are exactly the same you must maintain the illusion of choice by giving them different names."

"That what you do?"

"Precisely. We have a big detergent client who had about fifteen percent of the market. We advised him to put another detergent on the market. No, not another detergent. Same detergent, different name, different packet. Another agency, the new product. Another sales team goes into the grocers' shops. The new one pinches a bit of the old one's share of the market, and a bit of every other detergent's share, and our client ends up with about twenty percent of the whole market instead of fifteen percent. When you consider that the market is worth a few million pounds a year that extra five percent is worth having. Get it?"

"I get it. Right at these lights here Sam."

The car swerved, skidding slightly on the wet surface.

"You enjoy this advertising business?"

"Enjoy it? Yes. It's got a certain excitement. A certain glamour. You feel you're doing something, creating something. You have a feeling of . . . of power almost."

"Power? Over who?"

"Round here?"

"Yes."

The car swerved again.

"You go right up. It's a long road. We're on the corner right at the end."

"Power. First over the clients. In a way. It's interesting. These big boys, lots of money, big factories, mighty organisations, all turning out products nobody asked for and they've got to sell 'em. Some of these Sales Managers go mad if they can't sell their quotas. So they come to us. We're the experts, see. We tell 'em how to sell. So we have a certain feeling of superiority over these characters. This it?"

"Over the other side, Sam. That's fine."

The car stopped.

"Come in for a minute Sam?"

"Thanks but I'd better not. It's very late. Zena will be sleeping won't she?"

Joe looked at his watch. Two o'clock. He'd left home at eight

190

o'clock. Six hours that he could never have again. And the old man dead.

"I suppose she will be now. I told her to go bed, when I phoned."

They sat for a moment, the rain beating on to the roof of the car.

"But don't they have more power over you?" Joe asked.

"Who?"

"Your clients."

"Oh yes. In a way. But they've got to advertise. Or go to the wall. They can't stop while their competitors are advertising, or they'll lose out. So if they don't like us they've got to go to another agency. But the real power you feel is the power to change people's minds."

They were facing each other now in the front of the car, lit only by the reflection of the headlamps through the dripping windscreen and the occasional glow of Sam's cigarette.

"You may smile, Joe, but this is really important. You should know this. We spend millions of pounds every year changing people's habits, making them drink cocoa, eat bacon, wash their teeth."

"I was smiling" Joe replied "because you seem to think that without advertising people wouldn't eat, drink or wash their teeth. The Russians have been smoking for years and not a penny has been spent on cigarette advertising since the revolution. They eat more bacon there than you'd ever dream of, but they don't have a Bacon Information Council, or whatever you call it. Wait a minute . . ." Joe lifted a hand to hold back Sam's interruption. "I know you change people's minds within certain limits. I know you make them eat bacon and that's good for the bacon people, and you make them wonder where the yellow went and that's good for the toothpaste people, and you give the housewife a sense of achievement when she picks Daz instead of Shmaz, but Sam, this is such small stuff. It's peanuts compared to what we're doing."

Sam looked puzzled.

"How d'you mean?" he asked.

"Look Sam," Joe leaned forward towards his brother-in-law, "How much is spent on advertising every year?"

"On everything?"

"The lot. Press, posters, television, printing, P.R. Everything."

"Perhaps five hundred million. Maybe a bit less."

"Sam, you're not giving 'em value for money. Five hundred million and all you do is make a few poor sods drink cocoa every night instead of *Horlicks*. But Sam," the hand now was on his brother-in-law's knee and in the drops of rain-reflected light his eyes gleamed with excitement, "look what we're doing. We're changing the world, and we're doing it for nothing! Changing habits? We're not just getting them to change from one detergent to another, we're changing human nature itself. All these researches and statistics you spend fortunes on about income groups in society and classes of readership for newspapers, Sam, we're changing society, we're doing away with those classes. You're wasting your time boy, you're wasting your client's money!"

Sam took a last draw on the stub of cigarette and, winding down his window, threw it out into the rain. "Joe," he said, "I admire your enthusiasm, but if you were working for any of my clients you'd have been sacked ages ago. My detergent people are hard headed businessmen. They want facts, not theories. They want that extra five percent of the market, and we give it to them. You may think that's a small achievement but Joe, my boy, it's big compared with what you've done. At the end of the war you had two Members of Parliament, right?"

Joe nodded, knowing what was coming.

Sam continued. "Now you've got . . .?"

"None," said Joe, "but . . ."

"Wait a minute Joe, I haven't finished. At the end of the war your Party membership was what, about fifty thousand?"

"About that."

"And now?"

"About the same," Joe lied, remembering his disappointment when he had heard it was down to just over forty thousand.

"Listen Joe, when you can produce a five percent change-over to Communism then you can talk about changing the world. Even one percent would be something. Meanwhile the change is in the other direction. You're losing votes boy, you're losing members." Sam fumbled in his pocket for his cigarettes. "And if the Russians carry on the way they are doing," he added, finding the carton and pulling out the cigarette, "You're going to lose a lot more, specially Jewish members."

At last. Joe had been waiting for this all the evening. But Sam apparently did not want to pursue it.

"Not now Joe." The cigarette was lit and Sam leaned across and patted him on the knee. "If we carry on much longer we're both going to lose our wives."

Joe hesitated, hating to cut off in the middle of an argument, specially at a stage where he was at a disadvantage, but relieved nevertheless that he didn't have to go into all this strange Jewish business that was going on in Russia.

"You're right Sam," he said. "It's late." He swung himself round and opened the door, and stepped out into the rain. Holding the door open he leaned into the car. "Thanks for the lift Sam," he said, "we'll continue some other time."

"Sure," said Sam, starting up the engine. "Better get that five percent first, then you've got something to talk about." But he said it with a smile to which Joe responded.

"Night Sam, and thanks a lot."

"Night."

Joe walked round the back of the car towards his front door.

"Hey, Joe!"

He turned back and went towards Sam, who had wound down his side window and was leaning out.

"Yeh?"

"Joe, when you make yourself that drink of cocoa before you go to bed, make it Morton's will you? They're my clients."

He laughed, and Joe laughed back. He's all right.

"For you Sam, anything. Even Morton's."

*   *   *   *

Dark. Thin. Jewish looking.

That was all Margaret could remember about him as she walked up the front steps of the Daily Worker building and faced the tubby little man behind the glass pane.

"Yes?" he asked.

"Joe Gold," she replied.

"He expecting you?"

"Yes."

"What name?"

"Margaret Houghton."

On the wall a bronze plaque dominated the little square hallway. William Rust. Shame that he should have died so soon after the opening of the new building. It was over four years since she and Eddie had stood outside and cheered.

"Joe? There's a Margaret Houghton down here to see you . . . O.K."

The tubby man put back the receiver and turned to her.

"O.K.," he said, "you can go up. Know where it is?"

She shook her head and smiled at him, allowing herself the luxury of a five-second flirtation.

"Here, I'll show you."

He took her elbow and directed her to a lift and pressed the button.

She smiled at him again, thinking he's fat and fifty and knows there's nothing to it, but just that little smile and look between us and he's holding my elbow and feeling good. If I'd have been a man he's have said 'Take the lift' or even if I'd been old and ugly — or just ugly. What a lot they are.

The lift came down and the little man released her elbow, needing both hands to pull back the doors.

"Press that button. Fourth floor. Turn left when you get out, then left down the corridor, then second door on your left. Features Department."

There was an angry buzzing somewhere inside the lift. A number flicked on and off in a little dial. Two.

"Take no notice of that. Just press this button. O.K.?"

"O.K." Margaret smiled. He pulled the grey steel doors between them. The end of a perfect friendship. She pressed the button. Suddenly through the grille she heard him shouting. A last farewell?

"Not the first door. That's the gents."

She laughed.

The buzzing continued and the little figure two danced madly on the dial, screaming to be let out. The paint was scratched on the walls of the lift and there were marks where strips of sticky tape had fixed notices now torn down and forgotten. Workers of the world? Do not spit in the lift? Rally Trafalgar Square Three O'Clock ... tea will cost tuppence a cup as from Monday ...

The lift stopped. With an effort she pulled aside the gates and stepped out. The corridor was not well lit. A bulb was missing from the ceiling light. A grey smear ran along the wall by the corner where people had leaned against the wall and a crack like lightning ran down through the paint. As she passed the first door she heard an Irish voice singing above the running of water.

> That old triangle
> Goes jingle-jangle
> All on the banks
> Of the Royal Canal

With a gurgle the water stopped and the voice stopped too and Margaret had a momentary vision of a great red Irishman disappearing down the drain on the way to the Royal Canal.

She stopped outside the second door. Her hand went up to her hair but she stopped herself and knocked on the door instead. 'Hell,' she thought, 'why should I?' She turned the handle and opened the door. The room was surprisingly long and bare. Facing the door were metal filing cabinets and on a chair beside them a pile of newspapers. At first Margaret thought the room was empty until she heard a voice say "Come in, comrade."

She stepped into the room and there, down the far end, two desks were backed on to each other beneath a large window and facing each other across the papers sat a man and a girl.

"Come down this end," said the man, "it's warmer."

As she approached them he turned to the girl. "If you take those pictures back to Stan our comrade will have a chair to sit on." The girl sprang up and gathered a heap of photographs from a chair standing by the desks. With a smile at Margaret she indicated that she could sit down there.

"Will you be wanting me any more Joe," she asked, "or can I go when I've taken these back?"

"Sit down comrade, sit down." With one hand he waved Margaret into the chair and with the other picked up a photo and waved it at the girl. "Tell him I'm using this one, he looks nice and holy here."

"O.K. And can I go?"

"Sure, go."

She was at the other end of the room now, and hugging the photographs to her bosom with one arm she reached up for her coat with the other, unhooked it from the back of the door, flipped it over her arm and opened the door.

"Bye Joe. Bye comrade."

"So long Liz. And tell Stan I want one of Marilyn Monroe tomorrow."

"O.K. Bye."

Margaret turned and saw he had been looking at her.

"Marilyn Monroe and the Dean of Canterbury," she smiled, "a wonderful combination."

He held the photograph of the Dean of arms length and peered at it through half-closed eyes. "Marilyn Monroe and *anybody* would make a wonderful combination," he said. "There's an International Woman for you. Why don't you get her to your meeting? Wouldn't need any publicity."

"Wouldn't get any women either. The place would be packed with international men."

"Maybe. You're probably right."

He threw the photograph into a filing basket, pushed the papers on his desk together into a pile, transferred them to a drawer, picked up a steel rule and several pencils and laid them neatly on top of a layout pad on one side of the desk and leaned back in his chair and looked straight at her.

"Right," he said, "to business."

He was thin, beneath that shirt. She could see that when he leaned back. Hairy. The tie had been loosened and the top button undone and curly black hairs were visible at the base of his neck. His arms, too, were hairy beneath the rolled up sleeves. Inside his wrist a triangle of veins stood out on the white bare skin.

"I'm sorry about your meeting the other night, but, well, you understand."

"Of course. Is everything all right now?"

He shrugged, jerking his head forward as he did so, his bottom lip coming out into a sort of smile.

"All right? You get used to it I suppose. What is it, a week? Ten days. In ten days I've got used to it. In ten weeks perhaps, maybe ten months, my sisters will be used to it. My mother? Ten years maybe. Who knows? Anyway," he released his arms from the desk and fell forward, looking up at her, "how far have you gone?"

Margaret opened the file on her lap and took out a sheet of paper.

"Well" she said, "I told you on the phone about the general approach for this year's do, and, although everybody wanted to throw in everything but the kitchen sink we agreed in the end to concentrate on peace as the main theme."

He nodded and half to himself, half to her, said "The kitchen sink" with a smile.

Margaret stopped for a moment, querying with her eyebrows whether she should reply to this or carry on.

"Sorry," he said, noticing her look. "It just occurred to me that this was an occasion where the kitchen sink was probably the very thing that should have been thrown in."

Somehow he irritated her.

He was trying to be helpful, but she felt it was all a bit paternal. Giving a hand to the little women at their kitchen sinks.

"You really think so?" she said.

"No, no. Carry on. It was just an idea." He had reached for the steel rule again and was using it to push some of the papers tidily into heaps on the desk.

196

"I know that conditions in the home are important to most women," she pursued the matter, "just as conditions in the factory are important to most men ..." He stopped messing about with the ruler and looked at her. She went on. "But surely if the question of peace is the key one for men it is equally important for women?"

So now she's giving me a lecture. Ay, ay! Why the hell do all these characters who start off by asking for advice finish by giving you a lecture? Still, she's got something.

"Sure," he agreed, "you're right. Peace is the thing to plug."

That sounds like Sam. Get the product right.

"Good. Well, I wrote something out, as you suggested, and here it is." She put the sheets of paper on the desk.

"Fine," he said, reaching for the paper.

Hair on his knuckles too. Little patches of hair, but the fingers are long and almost pointed. Eddie's are shorter and Eddie's nails are bitten. Why did he turn over and look at the second page before he started reading, was it too long? He liked something there. His eyes are smiling but his mouth is frowning. His own articles are like that, always with a touch of humour, sarcasm maybe, satire. But deadly serious underneath. And power. That's what manages to get into his stuff that she hadn't got into this. Power. The article in today's paper, for example, on the way all the old Nazis are creeping back into positions of power in Western Germany. People who were directly responsible for the death of millions of Jews. Still, he was a Jew himself. That's not fair, everything he wrote had that power. Jews in the party were no more Jewish than ... than Eddie is Christian. No, that's not true either. They have their mannerisms still, ways of talking, ways of looking, sad laughs and eyes that look back over thousands of years.

He looked up at her.

"Fine," he said. "Did you do this?"

"Yes, you think it's all right?"

"Ever write any poetry?"

"No. My brother does."

"Really?"

"He's a miner."

"Sounds interesting. Got any of his stuff?"

"Not with me, but he writes me a letter now and then and puts a bit in. I think he's good."

"If it's good we could use some in the paper."

"I'll see if I can find some and let you read it."

"Good. But you've never written any?"

"No. Why do you ask?"

He turned back the page and looked through the type-written paragraphs again.

"Your use of images is good. This bit about the power of women if they really got together and decided there wouldn't be any war is very evocative. For me, anyway. You get the picture in your mind of a world without women. Bit like those Greek women in the play but better because all they did was to refuse to sleep with their men until they gave up war."

"Exactly."

She felt his praise flowing over her like warm water and relaxed back in her chair, feeling easy with him. He knew what she was getting at.

"People always talk about that play as progressive," she went on, "but I've always felt it reactionary, from the woman's point of view, that is. As if woman's only contribution to society was her body. I'm damn sure the capitalists would find a way round it if all the women stopped going to bed with them but they'd be in a hell of a fix if we all stopped working in their factories wouldn't they?"

Joe laughed.

"Pity we can't say that in here," he said, tapping the article with the steel rule. "But don't forget the period it was written in."

"Have things changed that much?"

"Surely they have."

"Well comrade . . ."

"Joe's the name."

Their eyes held each other in a moment of understanding.

"O.K. Joe. Do you really think things have changed?" she asked, "so far as men and women are concerned?"

"Well, they've got the vote, for one thing."

"Oh yes, they can go out and vote for one or other of two incompetent men every five years and between votes they're stuck in their little homes, chasing a few bits of dust from one corner to the other, bored stiff all day, waiting for their lord and master to come home and give them the benefit of his stimulating company for an hour or so before they go to bed."

"Ah Margaret, it's not all on one side though. Don't forget that in most cases the lord and master as you call him is as bored as she is, standing behind a lathe all day."

Margaret. It sounded funny coming from him like that. "Ah

Margaret . . ."

"But at least they're out all day, meeting people, doing something."

"Seeing the same people, doing the same thing, day after day. Out? Ever worked in a factory?"

She shook her head.

"It's killing Margaret. Day after day, hour after hour, the whine of the lathes, the same bloody thing all the time without end. And what about being down the pits all day? Christ, you should know all about that. No, the thing is, not to contrast one with the other, man against woman. It's workers against bosses, Margaret, men and women against the bosses. That's the issue. They're the lords and masters."

"Right comrade, that's me told off."

"No, but really . . ." he looked up at her, anxious not to be misunderstood, saw she was laughing and laughed with her.

"What do you do?"

"Do?"

"Apart from waiting for your lord and master to come home."

"I have no lord and master."

"But I thought . . ."

His eyes flashed to her hand, resting on her lap. No ring.

"Eddie? We're not married. He works, I work. Actually I'm a competitor of yours. I'm on the Express."

He looked interested.

"Oh? Doing what?"

"Very dull. In the library."

"Well, well. Know John Barlow?"

"The mighty Barlow? Who doesn't! Is he . . .?"

She left it unsaid.

He picked up the steel rule again and started tapping it along the wire mesh of a filing basket.

"Oh, we have a few friends on the Street." His eyebrows were thick and heavy and they were drawn together in thought now. "How'd you like to work here?" he said suddenly.

Her heart jumped.

"You mean in the library?" she asked.

"No, here, in Features."

"Wonderful! Doing what!"

"Writing. Subbing. Research. I was talking to Mick McKay this morning and he agreed I need somebody else. He told me to look around. So I'm looking."

His thick, rococo lips lengthened into a grin as he looked

straight at her, and then softened back into shape again. "What do you say?"

"I'd love it, but could I do it?"

"This stuff says you can." He tapped the steel rule on the sheets of paper in front of him. "I'll fix you up to have a word with Mick. If he thinks you're O.K. you're in. O.K.?"

She nodded. It had all happened so quickly. Why had he asked her? Her writing wasn't that good. Was there something else? He'd hardly looked at her all the time, not till just now when he'd grinned at her. Working at the D.W. . . . wonderful! But was she good enough? He was frowning now as he looked through the draft for the leaflet again.

"This stuff is O.K.," he said, wondering why he had suddenly asked her to work with him. She could write, yes, and Mick *had* agreed he needed somebody else, specially for the women's features. But he should have looked around. Had a word with the Journalists group. Sod the Journalists group. They never turn up with anybody unless they're too bloody useless to hold down a job on the capitalist press. She's working on the Express. Anyway, let Mick sort it out. If he thinks she's O.K. then she's O.K. She's got a mind of her own. Not a bloody yes-man. Yes-woman. The rest I can teach her. Take her out on interviews. Stand by her when she's subbing. Cut this out. Condense that. Scrub out that Party jargon, what do they think we are, a propaganda sheet? This is a National Newspaper. Under the light, her hair is more red than black. When she walked across the room towards him and stood there smiling while she waited for Liz to move those photos off the chair, that's when the idea had first come to him. Or was it way back when he had first met her in the cafe with Eddie? Mad! Didn't even know the girl. Must be all right if she's Eddie's . . . Eddie's what? She wasn't married, she didn't belong to Eddie. Don't start getting involved with that hair. Too late. Sod it. Leave it to Mick. He'll probably say she's no good. If he says yes? So it'll be yes.

"So," he said. "Let's get down to business on this leaflet."

"Which is what I really came for," said Margaret smiling, and, conscious now of the warmth of the room, her fingers began to undo the large round buttons of her coat.

"Which is what you really came for."

*   *   *   *

"Atha reetin to our Margret?"

200

"Nay, Ahv' doon that."

"Wha's tha reetin nah then?"

"Summat else."

She looked at her big son. The only one left to her now of all her children. He was big. So big it was hard to remember he had come out of her womb red and screaming and small as a plucked pigeon, and they wrapped him up and gave him to her to hold and she felt big in her heart with him instead of big in her belly as she had done all those months. He stopped screaming and she loved him because he had been so quick and easy. Easy come, easy go, but he had stayed and the others had gone. The first one had grown so like his father that sometimes she used to watch him walk across the room like a ghost of her youth, and she'd been glad when he got married and left because you can't live with your own ghost. Margaret, the baby, who might have grown up like her, had turned off down some side turning on the way where neither her father or mother had ever been or could ever follow, and she was away now in London.

But this one was big and easy and sat there night after night scribbling away and reading and puzzling things out in that big head of his in which she could still see the screaming red face of over thirty years ago.

She was tired.

She looked round to see that everything had been done. One side of the table was already laid for his breakfast. Cup, saucer, plate, knife, fork. Bread covered up. Butter. Enough sugar in the dish. Sausages in the pan ready with the fat. Teapot.

"Tha' milk's on t'stove," she said.

"Ah." He didn't look up.

"What's tha reetin?"

"Bout Margret."

"Our Margret?"

"Nay," he looked up at her now, smiled, and pushed a newspaper towards her. "T'other one. *Their* Margret. One wi' pictures in papers."

She picked up the paper but it was blurred before her eyes.

"What's in it? Ah can't see. Ah've not got me glasses."

"Princess, tha knows. One as coom dahn pit."

"Oh ah. Ah've heard tell. Dahn Denton?"

"Eee, th's forgotten quick. Ah told thee yesterday. She wor dahn pit yesterday arternoon. Ah spoke to 'er. Ah told thee."

She seemed to remember. But she was tired.

"Ah. Wa'she nice?"

"She's only a little 'un, tha knows. Big eyes though, and big 'ead. But she's bloody little. Only cooms oop to your belly button."

"Nay, did you have your shirt off?"

He laughed.

"Ah were working, tha' knows. Gaffers are all right for showing people round pit. Us lot 'ave got to get coal aht."

"But did she see yer, in . . . in pit mook like, wi'aht shirt?"

"Ah. Didn't seem to mind."

"Nay." She shook her head.

"Lookin' at soom of the chinless bloody woonders she knocks abaht wi' it's probably first time she's seen anything owt like a man." He pulled the paper back and gazed at the picture on the front page.

"Do her bloody good Ah reckon."

"What's tha doin' then, reetin to her atha?"

He smiled, and put the paper aside again. "Nay, moother, ah'm doin' summat for our Margret. For Worker tha' knows."

"Our Margret? Worker?" She shook her head again, not understanding, not remembering, and suddenly, feeling tired again, not caring.

"Go oop t'bed moother. Tha's tired."

"Ah."

She looked round at the things on the table again. They were all there. Cup, saucer, sugar, butter. Margret? Good girl. Edgar's wife, what did they call her then? Edgar's down pit, like his father. Still on neets. Bed's empty. But it used to be full of him. He filled the whole bed. He was so big he filled the whole room and filled her, too. He was all round her, all over her, all inside her. Ah. Bed's empty now. Room's empty.

"Goo'night loov."

Her hand patted his and he looked up and smiled.

Good lad. He's still here any road. Bed, empty bed. These stairs are harder to climb every day and the walls on either side get closer. There's no light up top and your shadows climbs the stairs before you, leaping up those top few and waiting for you on the landing.

> Dancing with my shadow,
> Feeling kind of blue,
> Dancing with my shadow,
> And making believe it's you.

That's all that was waiting. Shadow. But even the shadow disappears when you turn the light on in the room. Empty. Big bed empty too. Squeaks as you sit on it. That's better. Those china horses were looking at her. Boys won them at the fair. And he was looking at her out of the picture. Big he was then. What happened to him? What happened to me? What's *going* to happen? Cold in here and empty. Too cold to take off more than my dress. Look at them tits. Nothing. Nothing left there at all. Just skin hanging down over ribs. Ribs stick out more than the tits now. Nothing. Skin and bone. That's nice, that nightdress. Warm. But bed's cold. And dark now with the light out. Oh cold, cold. Still smells of him from this morning. The pit. Coal. Pit muck. Never get it off hissen now with those pithead baths. I used to get it off. All that hot water and him sitting there with great big shoulders all wet and white as marble and I'd rub the soap all over him. And when he felt like it, it'd be standing up like a lamppost, especially once when I managed to slide a bubble of soap over the tip. Bye, that were funny. He got up out of the bath all dripping and laughing too, and come over to me, stepping ever so careful so that the bubble wouldn't break, and it was like it was in a glass case and I ran away from him round the table pointing at the bubble and laughing and then he grabbed me and the bubble burst and he was all wet.

And now our Billy was what? Thirty? Ought to be married instead of writing away there every night. To Margaret did he say? Our Margaret. Who was that one in the paper then? Margaret worked on a paper now he said. Nice and warm now. That picture in the paper. Our Margaret. Good girl.

Billy looked at the picture in the paper again and then began to copy down part of the accompanying text.

'She arrived at the colliery in a mink coat and suede shoes.' Mink coat. Bloody hell, think she'd know better than that. Mink, pink, wink stink. Stink'd be good. Good contrast and mink has a feeling of stink about it. Stinking rich? Contrast? That's the way. Contrast her with the miner. Mink and pit muck. The old jacket.

He started to write.

He arrived in a blue serge suit
That was once his Sunday best

Best. Guest. Test. What about pest? Rest. All the rest? Vest. Dirty old vest. Sweaty vest.

Underneath, a flannel shirt
And a dirty sweaty vest.

No, that just sounds like he's a dirty bastard that can't be bothered to wash. Got to bring the pit in. Underneath? Underneath what?

That 'sweaty' is still not right. It's not sweaty. That means wet with sweat. This has been dried overnight in front of the stove. Sweat-dried? Pit-grimed, sweat-dried. Is that too much?

He arrived in a blue serge suit
That was once his Sunday best,
Beneath the jacket a flannel shirt
And a pit-grimed, sweat-dried vest.

Hm-mm. Mink coat and suede shoes. Those suede shoes are a laugh. Look at those bloody great boots. The bloody sound of 'em down the street in the morning's enough to wake the dead.

No suede, he wrote, just hobnails,
Each step exploding on the pavement
Like . . .

Like what? It's like you had caps in them. Those little red caps that kids put in guns and pulled the trigger and bang? But it was the emptiness, the blackness of the night that made the sound so loud. Coming home in the afternoon with the sun shining and people all round you hardly noticed. Black. The black of night, the black of the pit . . . that great heap of slag that makes even the blackness of the night go pale when you round the corner and come face to face with it. Slag. Crag? Not bad. Crags of slag. No. Slag-heap's crags. Jags, jagged. Rags. Flags, sags, tags . . . wags. What about flags instead of pavement . . . flagstones?

Each step exploding on the flags
something about the black of night
And the slagheaps something crags.

Creeping! Creeping crags! Yes, that says it. That's the image. The bloody thing is moving, alive, out to get you, creeping towards you in the black night, blacker than the night itself.

The black of night was blackened
By the slagheaps creeping crags?

Excited now, he tore off a fresh sheet of paper from the pad in front of him and wrote hurriedly

No suede. Hobnails,
Each step exploding on the flags
.Where the black of night was darkened
By the slagheaps creeping crags.

Now for the mink. The stinking mink. The lousy stinking pit and the dirt and the sweating and shoving and straining compared to the bloody mink. Going to work in the blue serge suit and the pit muck and the hobnail boots, round the corner, there's the pit.

He turned the bend, he saw the lights
He felt . . . no he smelt . . . what?
He smelt the something stink
. . . then finish up with mink . . .?

Breath? The pit's foul breath. It's been done before. Don't overdo the imagery. Keep it simple. What do you *feel*. What do you actually feel? You don't feel the bloody pit's an animal. You don't feel it's got B.O., it just stinks. It stinks of you and you stink of it. The same old bloody stink. So why not say so?

He smelt the same old stink

Mm-mm. That's all right for anybody who knows it. A miner. But anybody else? What same old stink?

The pit
Grit
Shit
Sweat
Spit
Vomit

He smelt the same old stink
Of pit and grit and spit and shit

Hm-mm. Not very poetic that. But true. Even princesses have to do it sometimes. In her mink coat? And suede shoes? 'I have great pleasure in declaring these bowels open . . .'

He laughed and wrote down the third verse under the others.

He turned the bend, he saw the light
He smelt the same old stink
Of pit and grit and spit and shit
But never, never mink.

Bit weak that, but sod it. Keep on now and come back to it later. What's the next bit?

He picked up the newspaper and read the rest of the story. 'At the pit offices she left her mink coat, put on a white overall, changed into brown brogues, wrapped a gay scarf round her head and topped it with a miner's white helmet . . .'

Bloody 'ell. Like a fookin white rabbit down bloody ole.

'She boarded the Paddy Mail — a Diesel hauled open train — by a step ladder which had been specially installed . . .'

The Paddy. First class passengers only. The rest of you bastards can walk. You just work here. This is for the tourists.

'. . . after a 1,000 yard journey she clambered among the pit props bent almost double . . .'

Bloody 'ell I'd like to catch her bent double. She'd get something more than a pit prop.

'. . . then all the dust began to fly as the coal cutter started. "It tastes delicious," shouted the Princess above the noise . . .'

Silly bitch. I suppose they've got to say summat but you'd think they'd have more fookin sense. Must be bloody coal from the neck up to say owt like that. Taste delicious. Cow.

'. . . grasping a clean white haft of a miner's pick — specially provided — she hacked out a piece of coal. "I'm going to have it mounted as a memento," said the Princess . . .'

Mounted! Why not eat the bloody stuff, if it tastes so delicious. Would you like some coal on your crumpet Your Highness? It tastes delicious in tea. Two lumps?

'. . . she emerged with only the faintest smudge of coal dust on one cheek. Her overalls had only one black mark and her shoes had only a film of dust . . .'

He looked at his pit clothes, hanging on the line in front of the stove, the sweat soaked coaldust drying in stiff folds. His mouth curled into a smile that had no humour in it and he pulled off a fresh sheet of paper and started to write again.

*   *   *   *

Joe put the poem into a folder with his other papers and went towards the door.

"It's not bad," he said, "I'll show it to Mick."

"Mick? What does he know about poetry?" Margaret felt uneasy. The poems had been personal things somehow between her and Billy. Every week a new one and through them she had seen it all again, the pit, the miners, their street, their home. And Billy, too. Especially Billy. Now, for the first time, she had shown one of the poems to somebody else and he was tucking it away in his folder as if it was just another article on nursery schools in Azerbaijan or somewhere.

He turned at the door and smiled at her. "Oh, Mick's a great man for poetry. Robert Burr-rr-ns and a' that."

"And you?"

He raised his eyebrows.

"Me? Depends. I go for the exotic stuff that nobody's ever heard of, like Pablo Neruda."

"Who's he?"

"Comes from Chile. 'Let the railsplitter awake?' Great stuff."

"Sounds awful. What about Eliot?"

He shook his head, wrinkling his nose in disgust. "'Orrible. Can't understand a word."

"What! 'I have measured out my life in coffee spoons . . .' Can't you understand that?"

"Don't like coffee. I prefer my life to be 'immense in passion, pulse and power', or, what's the other bit . . .?" He thought for a moment, repeating remembered lines over to himself. "Give me something or other," he went on, suddenly recalling the line, "'O such for me! O an intense life, full to repletion and varied!' That's more my cup of tea."

"Who is it?"

"Whitman."

"Oh."

"No good?"

"It hasn't got the depth, the imagery."

"Nor the bloody pessimism or misery. Or the obscure classical references measured out in soup spoons. This is living, comrade, living."

"Don't comrade me!"

He smiled. "Got to go. Be late for the meeting. Talk about it later."

He hurried along the corridor and down the stairs to the weekly editorial executive meeting, thinking about the list of next week's features that had been typed last night and sent down to Mick for discussion this morning, wondering if there would be any comments on Margaret's first two signed pieces which had appeared since the last meeting. The first one hadn't been too good but he'd put it in to give her confidence. The second one, yesterday's piece, had been good. Mick liked it. So that was O.K. Sod the rest of them.

The rest of them were already assembled. The Editor looked up at him as he came through the door and looked over to Walter Graham, the Assistant Editor, who was slumped in his usual position in the only easy chair in the room on the other side of the Editor's desk. On Graham's sharp bony skin lines on each side of his mouth ran like duelling scars down to his chin. A proletarianised intellectual, he fastidiously displayed his contempt for bourgeois society in every inch, from his uncombed hair and the soup stains lined up on his jacket like medals, to the wrinkled grey flannels that draped his long sprawling legs. Next to him, in complete contrast, sat Jim Davies, neat, almost dapper, looking no more like a miner from the Rhonda Valley, which he had been twenty years ago, than the Political Editor of a national newspaper, which he was now.

Graham was reading from a piece of paper torn from the tape

machine, and as he got to the end he whistled. "Kee-rist," he said, "looks as if the old man's gone off his rocker."

"Indeed," interjected Davies quickly, reaching over for the paper, "I would not be too sure of that myself."

"But he can't be serious?"

"Uncle Joe," replied Davies, "has the reputation of being a somewhat serious character."

Joe turned to his neighbour, a tubby little man with an almost completely bald head and short legs that hardly reached the floor as he sat, so that he was continually scraping the carpet with his outstretched toes neatly encased in highly polished shoes.

"What's all this?" Joe asked him.

The little man was sitting on his hands and swayed over towards Joe to give his answer.

"It appears that Uncle Joe has discovered a plot."

"Another one?" Joe lifted his eyebrows.

With the slightest flicker of a smile in his eyes the little man, who was the paper's Industrial correspondent, nodded his head.

"Who now?"

The high-pitched, bird-like voice of Walter Graham darted across the room in reply.

"It would appear," he said, "that while you have been sitting up there in that room of yours plotting to destroy the virginity of your newly-appointed colleague and help-mate, which," and here an expansive gesture of his long white fingers carved a wide arc in the air, "judging from the difference in quality between her first article last Tuesday and her second article yesterday, you appear to have achieved on Wednesday night; while you were plotting against this pure little woman, it appears that a dozen or so of your co-religionists, if a non-believer like yourself can be said to have co-religionists, were plotting against much higher personalities, all of them, unfortunately, friends, close associates, nay even colleagues of our august and revered leader and father, Joseph Vissarionarich Djugashvili!"

Closing his eyelids like dropping the curtain at the end of Act One, Graham inserted a long finger into his left nostril and moved it vigorously from side to side. Removing it, he opened one eye to study the tip of the finger, held a few inches from his face, wiped it on his lapel and turned to face the Editor.

"Shall we begin Michael?" he asked.

Michael Stuart McKay winced at the sound of his first name. Graham was the only one who ever used it. To everybody else, from the Political Editor to the tape-room messengers, he was

Mick. Mick McKay, Editor of the Daily Worker, Member of the Executive Committee of the Communist Party, founder member of the Party, twice imprisoned for his role in the leadership of the unemployed in the thirties, militant dockers' leader on the Clyde before the General Strike, magnificent orator in the old style with a mane of white hair flowing in the breeze and the rolling Scots 'r-r-rs' reverberating across the seas of upturned faces.

Mick McKay, a name to whitewash on the walls, a speaker who could fill any meeting; already, at just turned fifty, a legend and a father figure in a party that was younger than himself. Behind the big desk he looked shorter than he actually was, his big, docker's frame filling the brown suit, hands continually gripping the edge of the desk as if he would lift it bodily from the floor. At the age when most men begin to think of taking iteasy the Party had asked him to take on the toughest job in the movement. The most important job, some said, responsible for the day-to-day guidance, not only of the party, but of leading militant trade unionists, the key workers in industry, left-wing labourites and members of Parliament, fellow-travellers and sympathisers in thousands who constituted the readers of his paper over and above the Party members. Big job. Not only keeping the paper on to the line but *making* the line, every day, every minute, as the news breaks. And presenting the line in such a way that ordinary people would understand it. And getting the damn thing to press on time every day. Which was why he relied so heavily on Graham and put up with his arrogance and conceit, thinking 'we'd be in a right mess without him, and doesn't he know it. Loyal as they make 'em. Reliable politically, technically superb. But a sarcastic sod, cynical as hell. Can't make a simple statement without sticking in so many barbs that every rabbit becomes a hedgehog. All right if you understand him but these younger comrades haven't worked with him like I have. They either imitate him or hate his guts. Joe hates his guts. That's obvious. Better get started.'

"We-e-ell comrades," he started, gripping the desk as he drew out the introductory words, "after Wally's inimitable hor-r-rs d'oeuvr-res, we'll get down to the meat of the situation, shall we?" That'll take him down a peg!

"Or the meat and two veg, as our dear lady of the canteen says," sniffed Graham, poking the same finger up his right nostril this time.

"This story from Moscow," Mick went on, "has just come over the tape from Reuters."

Jim Davies leaned forward and quietly placed the paper on the desk in front of the Editor who glanced at it again as he continued. "We'll be checking with Bert in Moscow as soon as this meeting is over, but on the fact of it it looks authentic enough. It quotes a statement by Beria to the effect that twelve Jewish doctors have been arrested, all the top medical men in the Kremlin apparently, on charges of conspiring to poison a number of leaders of the higher command of the army." He paused, and there was silence in the room. "The statement goes on to say that this group of doctors was in fact responsible for poisoning Zhdanov in 1948 and Shcherbakov in 1941."

He paused again, and looked up.

"That's all there is from Reuter."

Nobody spoke.

Mick went on.

"Now the others are obviously going to lead on this today . . ."

"I'll say they are!" from Graham.

". . . and we'll have to say something although I wish we had more to go on. We'll get what we can from Bert but it looks a big thing. First because of the numbers involved. It's not a case of a couple of disgruntled individuals. Second because they're all Jews, or seem to be, and the press will fan this up to a case of state antisemitism, although the Russians have always been careful in the past to avoid mentioning Jews."

The hands were gripping so hard on the desk that he appeared to be going to tear it in pieces.

"We know they have been concerned over the recent period with the activities of the Zionists . . ."

"Cosmopolitans . . ." interjected Graham.

". . . ah . . . and the activities of the so-called 'Joint' International Organisation for Jewish charities. But this . . ."

He looked around the room.

Jesus! What do you say? How do you 'give a lead' when you don't know what's happening? Time . . . time to think. Time to sort it out with Jim. Time to phone Bert in Moscow and see what the hell is going on, if he knows. Time to have a word with Harry at King Street. Time. In a few hours we're going to need a front page. And a leading article. It's all so bloody complicated. An ordinary plot would be bad enough. But Jews! The party's touchy enough on the Jewish business in the Soviet Union already. We should discuss this. But how?

". . . this is different. I suggest comrades, that we can't do much about this until we've got a bit more information, and we postpone discussion till the 2.30 meeting. By then we'll have spoken to Bert and maybe have the official statement from Tass and we'll know where we are. Meanwhile, on the Home Front, the Tories are going ahead with their proposals to denationalise Iron and Steel, and Churchill . . ."

Joe looked at the Editor's hands, now confidently smoothing the wood along the edge of his desk as he leaned back and expounded on the wickedness of the Conservative Government.

What was he talking about? Is that all he was going to say about it? It can't be true. It's just some bloody story Reuters have cooked up. Yet Mick was taking it seriously enough. He could usually smell a fake. Was this it? Was the smell of antisemitism that had hung over the Soviet Union this last few months like the low early morning smoke of last night's fire, suddenly bursting into flame? Impossible. Look at them sitting around the room. Harry and Peter were Jews themselves. Arthur had been one of the leaders of the fight against Mosley in the thirties, Stan and Henry had fought the Fascists in Spain and Henry had lost his arm there. Walter's wife was Jewish and he had written a brilliant book on the whole question of racial discrimination. Jim? Out of the question. He had eyes on one thing only. A socialist Britain. Ruthless, hard as nails, absolutely determined, but a man whose practice will not deviate one shade from this theory. His theory had no room for antisemitism. But had his practice any room for doubt? Could Jim conceive of Stalin being wrong? Could Stalin *be* wrong? Well, he's not the bloody Pope is he? But why should he do it? Stalin. Who had spent his whole life working for a Party whose central principle was equality of all peoples, all races. Who had written theses on race and nationality that had become classics of Marxism. Doesn't make sense unless he's gone off his rocker. Or unless it's true. It could be. Doctors. They must be getting on in years to be top doctors in the Kremlin. Probably hangovers from before the Revolution. To become doctors in those days you had to have money. Middle class. Upper class. Bourgeois. Communist? Could have jumped on the band wagon. Knew which side their bread was buttered. Zionist? Could be emotionally tied up in some way. But hell, why should the Zionists want to kill Russian Army chiefs? Wasn't Russia the first country to recognise Israel? Then what? Some deal or other with America? After all, Israel was mostly financed by America. Could be some sort of deal like you get your boys to stir it up in the Kremlin and we'll make sure the Arabs keep quiet and leave you alone. 'Your boys'? Just because they were Jews does that

211

make them pro-Zionists? I'm not. Am I a Jew? The religion means nothing to me. I don't mix with Jews much, don't speak Yiddish, live any sort of Jewish life, not even married to a Jewess. Who decides? Hitler decides. A Jew is someone who gets sent to the gas chambers. And Stalin . . .?

Suddenly Joe realised that the discussion had stopped. They were all looking at him. What did they want?

Surely their eyes were saying 'Jew' . . . 'cosmopolitan' . . . 'saboteur' . . . Were they going to turn him out? Hypocritical bloody bastards. He could believe it of Graham. Even of Davies. One believes nothing, the other believes everything. But not Mick, surely. Yet Mick was staring at him now, his hands moving a pile of papers into position in the centre of the desk. He was frowning now. He was going to speak. This was it.

"Well Joe, next week's features list. What've you got for us?"

*   *   *   *

How he got through the discussion on the features list Joe never knew. But they discussed it and they discussed the drop in the paper's circulation and they discussed the arrangements for the paper's twenty-third anniversary and the meeting was over.

Back in his office, Joe remembered the poem.

"Did you show it to Mick?" Margaret asked.

He shook his head.

"No chance."

"Good meeting?"

He threw his papers on to the desk and sat down.

"What's all this about a doctor's plot?" she asked. "Stan told me something came over the tape. Did they mention it?"

Again. Like a great undigested lump, his belly rose and tried to push its way up past his heart.

He nodded.

"Reuter's," he replied. "Mick's getting on to Bert Fenton in Moscow to see what it's all about. We didn't discuss it."

"Didn't discuss it? It's important isn't it? Stan said they were all . . . Jewish . . ."

"Apparently so."

"How do they know?"

Joe smiled.

"How do you know I'm Jewish?"

"But this is capitalism. In Russia they did away with all these differences thirty-five years ago didn't they?"

"What differences?"

They looked at each other in silence until the telephone rang.

"Joe?"

It was the Editor.

"Yes Mick."

"Joe, it just occurred to me. Better look out what you can on the Zionists. We may need a bit of a background feature pretty quickly."

"Zionists?"

"You know. Israel and the Arabs. American finance. International connections. See what there is, eh?"

"O.K. Mick."

*   *   *   *

"Our Golden Boy not too happy?" Walter Graham eased himself out of the chair as the Editor put the phone down. He reached over and took up the Reuter's tape once again.

"Joe Gold's all right. I'm none too happy myself. What about you Jimmy?"

There were only the three of them left in the room now, waiting for the telephone to ring connecting them with the paper's Moscow correspondent.

"Won't do the Party any good," said Davies, standing with his back to the others, looking out of the window at the traffic below.

"That," said Walter Graham drily, "is the understatement of our twenty-third anniversary year. But is it genuine?" He held the tape up close to his eyes and screwed up his face as if looking for a watermark.

"Bert will tell us that," said the Editor.

"Oh it's genuine all right," said Davies. "I could see it coming when I was in Miscow last year for the Congress. Remember my report Mick?" The Editor nodded. "They were all expecting something then. The closing down of the Yiddish theatres and papers was an indication. Most of Bert's Jewish friends shut up like clams . . ."

"Even his best friends wouldn't tell him."

"Something like that."

"Political B.O. eh?" Graham put the Reuter tape back on the desk with a sniff. "Belsen Odour," he said.

"Oh Christ, Walter, don't be so bloody funny," Davies turned to him, the skin drawn tightly over the sharp bones of his cheek, so that the veins on either side of his head looked like cracks in his skull. He turned back to the window. "There was no antisemitism. I made that clear in my report."

"To which select group of our august comrades was this famous report delivered?" Graham asked.

"Political Committee," said the Editor.

"And why don't I get all this . . ." he paused and, removing a flake of dried mucus from his nostril, flicked it with his thumb across the room . . . "*invaluable* information?"

"Because you're not on the Political Committee," Davies snapped back.

Quickly, Graham sat upright and leaned across the desk. "No," he said, "I'm only the fucking Assistant Editor. I'm . . ."

The telephone rang.

McKay picked it up.

"Yes . . . all right . . ."

He put his hand over the mouthpiece and said to the other two "Moscow", then removed his hand.

"Hello . . . is that you Bert? Bert, we've just got Reuter's through on this Doctors case. Can you let us have something?"

The two men watched the Editor's face as he listened to the voice of his correspondent in Moscow three thousand miles away.

"Yuh . . . I see . . . Yuh . . . Bert, who are these doctors? Yuh . . . are they all Jewish? . . . aha . . . who? uh . . . all right Bert, good . . . but listen, three o'clock, eh? I must have it by then . . . good . . . good . . . fine Bert. Goodbye."

The click of the telephone falling into place dropped into the silence like the releasing of the safety catch on a revolver.

"It's official," said McKay, his hand still outstretched to the telephone, "Beria's in charge."

"Laughing boy himself," said Graham.

Davies said nothing, but looked at the Editor.

"The official statement," McKay went on, "describes them as Jewish."

Davies turned to the window again.

"Bert's clearing his story now. We'll get it before three. He . . ." McKay stopped for a moment, then appeared to be concentrating on rubbing a spot of dirt off the edge of the desk. "He couldn't say very much. But I got the impression that things are not too good."

Without turning his head Jim Davies replied.

"We'd better have a word with Harry."

*　　*　　*　　*

214

Zena's voice was worried over the telephone.

"Joe, I've just heard about these doctors on the one o'clock news. What's happening?"

What's happening! Christ, that's a good one. Who knows what's happening?

"I don't know yet, Zee. We've only had the bare announcement. We'll know more at the 2.30 conference."

"It can't be true Joe, can it?"

True? What in hell difference does it make. If it's true it's terrible. If it's a lie it's terrible.

"I just don't know Zee. I don't know."

"Phone me, will you? As soon as you know something . . .?"

Phone her . . . further to our telephone conversation this is to confirm that all my comrades and friends are a lot of antisemitic bastards . . . phone her.

"I'll try Zee, I'll try. But I'll be hellish busy."

"Try Joe, it's important. I can't just rely on the B.B.C."

Why not? Who then? McKay? Davies? Walter Graham? Himself? Joe looked at the file on his desk. It was marked "ZIONISM."

"All right love. I'll phone."

"Thanks Joe, Bye."

"Bye Zee."

He put the phone down and looked up to find Margaret looking at him.

"She worried?" she asked.

Joe gave a little sideways shrug, more with his face than with his shoulders.

"Just heard it on the one o'clock news," he replied.

"You worried?"

He shrugged again, looked down at the file on his desk then up at her again. "Aren't you?" he asked.

She shook her head and the black-red hair swung a little round her jaw, revealing the tip of her ear.

"No," she said, getting up, "not now." She came round and sat on the side of his desk. "I was at first." She stretched across him and opened the file on the desk. "But they know what they're doing."

He noticed, for the first time, that she used perfume and he was surprised. Her belly, as she reached across him, was flat, unlike Zee's. She had none of Zee's delicacy. She was strong. Confident.

"You're probably right," he said.

"I'm certain of it," she replied, looking through the cuttings in the file. "Shall I sort this lot out for you?"

"Good idea. But I've a better one."

"What's that?"

"Let's have lunch first."

* * * *

"What's up Joe, you look worried."

"You heard about this doctors' plot?"

"That what's worrying you?"

Joe nodded.

The cartoonist rubbed his nose with his finger and, as the lift stopped at the canteen floor, stood aside to let Margaret get out first.

"Imagine they're Armenian," he said.

"What?"

"Armenian. The doctors. 'Kremlin uncovers plot by Armenian doctors'. Would that worry you?"

"Not so much probably."

"It would if you were Armenian."

* * * *

"Joe Gold."

At the sound of the Editor's voice Joe looked up, the spoon poised above the apple tart and custard.

Standing by the wall telephone, plate in one hand, telephone receiver in the other, the Editor called across the table to him.

"Wanted on the phone."

Joe put down the spoon and went across to take the receiver.

"Hallo?"

"Joey?"

"Oh. Hullo Mum. How are you?"

"Joey. Are you all right?"

"Sure Mum. You?"

"You sure?"

"Of course. Why not?"

"I just heard on the wireless. About those doctors. Be careful Joey."

"Don't be daft Mum."

Joe looked round at the canteen, now filling up with people. He saw Margaret watching him. Next to her Mick McKay.

"Did you want anything Mum?"

"Only be careful. That's all."

"Don't worry."

"What then should I do?"

216

"Why don't you go and see Zee?"

"How is she?"

"Oh all right. Tired."

"I'll go over this afternoon."

"Good idea."

"I'll wait there till you come home."

Christ, that's all I'm short of. Not today. Not all those questions. Margaret was still watching him.

"I wouldn't wait Mum. I'm going to be late tonight."

"What's the matter?"

"Nothing. I've got a meeting. Tell Zee will you?"

"Sure Joey. But don't be too late."

"O.K. Mum. Must go now."

"All right. Goodbye."

"Bye Mum."

"Joe . . ."

"Yeh?"

"Be careful."

"Don't worry."

"Don't worry he says. Goodbye."

She was still looking at him as he put the phone down and walked back to the table.

McKay looked up.

"How's this Zionist stuff going?"

"Just looked at the files before we came up. Lot of stuff there."

"I'm going to need something tonight Joe."

"Margaret's working on it."

He looked up at her.

"I thought I might stay late tonight and get it sorted out," he said. "All right with you Margaret, or have you got something on?"

Margaret looked at him.

"No," she said, "I've got nothing on. I'll stay."

With a clatter of plates Walter Graham cleared a place for himself and sat down opposite Joe.

"Always keep something on when you stay late my dear," he said in a loud voice, looking first at Margaret, then at Joe. "Specially in his condition," he added.

Joe dug his spoon into the apple pie and started to eat.

The custard was cold.

*   *   *   *

"Joe?"

He closed the door and gave his usual whistle. Her voice had come from the bedroom across the hall. He took off his mac and threw it on to the chair, looked at the pad, no messages, then glanced at himself in the mirror before going in to her.

What the hell! Nothing happened anyway.

He opened the bedroom door and went in. The room was in darkness and the light from the hall made a path to the bed.

"Hullo Zee. Still awake?"

"It's late Joe."

"Yeh. Want a cuppa?"

"No . . . is everything allright?"

"Everything? That's a tall order?"

"Don't be silly Joe. This doctors business."

"Oh that. Sure, they know what they're doing."

He hadn't turned on the light. He sat on the edge of the bed, the light from the hall at his back. His eyes were in the dark. *They know what they're doing.*

"It sounds bad Joe."

"Sure, the press will blow it all up. They'll make the most of it as usual."

"But what's it all about Joe?"

"It's those bloody Yanks at the back of it."

"America? How?"

"Through Israel. The Zionists. And all these international Jewish charities. They've got their people inside. I've been working on it all day. I know. Believe me."

Believe me.

"What's going to happen Joe?"

God, why doesn't she leave it alone? How the hell do I know? Who am I, Joe Stalin? Who knows what's going to happen? She was beginning to wake up now.

"It'll be all right love," he said putting his hand on the roundness of her belly. "How't it going?"

"It'll be all right, love," she answered, and in the glow of the light from the hall he could not tell if her smile was happy or sad.

*   *   *   *

Eddie was still up when Margaret let herself in.

He looked up from his paper and said "Hullo girl, been out?"

"Working. I tried to get you at work but you'd left. Good meeting?"

He turned back to his paper.

"Useful," he said.

Useful. She looked at him sprawled full length in the armchair, his feet stretched out towards the dying fire, and thought he's getting fat. His fire is dying out, too. Not fat, perhaps but heavy. Round the chin. The jowls. The way he was sitting with his head bent forward, a roll of blonde-stubbled fat forced out over his collar.

"You look like a capitalist" she said.

"Eh?" he looked up.

"Sitting there reading The Times. You're getting fat."

"*You* can talk," he replied, not sure if she was joking or serious.

"Mine's in the right places at least."

"And mine?"

She went right up to him and, with a sudden impulse took the loose layer of fat between her finger and thumb. She wanted to pull it off. Pull till it hurt. Pull till he cried out. Fat. Fat. Fat.

"Look at this," she said in disgust, "anybody'd think you were fifty." She turned away from him and thought of Joe's chin. Sharp and pointed and with that slight chewing motion when he was thinking. Side to side, and his eyes moving too. Everything's always moving with him. Alive.

"What's up with you? You on heat again?"

She moved away from him.

"You make me sick."

"Come off it. You were the one who wanted it this way. Free and independent. If you want to live like a bitch you mustn't mind my calling you one."

"You *are* just like a capitalist."

"Just because I don't go around cocking my leg at every lamppost you want to string me up on one eh?"

"My, aren't we witty tonight! It must have been a useful meeting."

"It was actually."

"What was it?"

"Electrical Advisory."

"I never get these high-powered advisory committees. Who advises who?"

"Works both ways girl. We advise King Street about what's going on in the industry. They advise us what to do on certain things."

"Such as?"

"Oh, anything that comes up. Wages. Strikes, political issues."

"And tonight?"

"Tonight we talked about the elections. Executive elections are due in six months time."

"Union executive?"

"Yes. We decided I'm going on the Executive."

"That's handy. Suppose the members decide otherwise?"

"They won't. That's what the meeting was about."

"Long live democracy."

"Oh Christ, girl, don't start bringing your free and independent stuff into politics. It may be all right for sex but it won't wash in politics. Got a fag?"

She opened a bag and threw over a packet of cigarettes. Taking a lighter from his pocket he lit the cigarette and inhaled deeply, then he took the cigarette out of his mouth and offered it to her. She smiled and came over to him, kneeled down by the armchair and opened her mouth to receive the cigarette. As she inhaled the smoke she watched him light another.

The fat's deceptive. He's bloody tough underneath it. The fire may have gone out but it has left cold hard steel.

"Why won't it?" she asked.

He looked at her through a ring of smoke.

"In sex it gives you an advantage. In politics it's a disadvantage."

"Advantage? Over who?"

"In sex you have an advantage over the other woman. And the man as well. You're not playing according to the rules. You've got an advantage over the other woman in that you're not trying to tie the man down to anything, you don't want him to commit himself. You're offering, freely, what the other woman is haggling over and trying to use as a bargaining point. In this way you keep your dignity while the other woman turns herself into a prostitute. Right?"

"Right so far."

"You've got the advantage over the man in that, by refusing to make your body a battleground you make the battle unnecessary and he finds that when he's slept with you you still belong to yourself and not to him. By giving yourself so freely you give nothing."

"Nothing?" She pouted.

"Well a certain amount of pleasure, but nothing of yourself."

Even though she didn't want him she couldn't resist sitting on the floor in front of him with her knees tucked up so that her skirt fell away, and saying "Don't you feel I ever give *you* anything Eddie?"

He smiled but it was more to himself than to her. He sat up and leaned forward towards her.

"Making love to you," he said, "is like swimming into shore and being engulfed by those big waves. You're completely overcome, you battle with it, revel in it, lose yourself in it completely, and finish up by lying on the beach exhausted." He paused. "But the wave has gone. It took you, had you, pounded you to death, got what it wanted from you, and left you lying there."

He got up and, treading carefully over her feet, walked over to the fire and threw the remains of his cigigarette into the embers.

"Ashes to ashes," he said.

"Dust to dust."

"If the women don't get you, the Party must." He turned to her. "But the Party is not like sex, girl. Politics is a much tougher game. Anyone who thinks they can be free and independent in politics is just kidding themselves. If you're not on one side you're on the other. If you're sitting on the fence you're helping those who are in power. Nobody can opt out."

"I don't see why not."

"Don't you? Well, look girl, take this Mau Mau business. The Government cooked all this bloody stuff up and are busy shoving thousands of Africans into concentration camps all over Kenya. Now you can either agree with it or not, but if you sit still and don't say anything you're allowing the Government to get away with it, you're saying O.K., get on with it, I've no objection to concentration camps and you're just as bloody guilty as every bloody German was who knew about the concentration camps and did nothing about it. You can't opt out. You've *got* to accept responsibility."

"All right, all right, don't get excited. I'm on your side you know."

Eddie moved closer and, looking down on her sitting on the floor, put his hand to her hair, pulling it up at the back and letting it fall on to her neck.

"I sometimes wonder."

She looked up at him. "Wonder what?"

"Whose side you're on."

"Do you ever wonder whose side *you're* on?"

"What d'you mean?"

"Do you ever think about it? Have any doubts? Ever?"

"Doubts about what?"

"Well," she said, without looking at him, "take this doctors' plot they've just announced."

"Well, what about it?"

"Exactly. What about it?"

Eddie turned back to the fire and kicked it with the toe of his shoe, It was dead.

"They know what they're doing."

"Maybe. But do *you* know what they're doing?"

He raked around among the dead embers with his shoe for a moment before replying. Then he turned and faced her.

"Look girl," he said, "I may not know everything they're doing, but I know what I'm doing. I'm a Communist, see, same as them. Exactly the same. No different. I'm not in it for the money. I'm not in it for the power or the glory. There's bloody little prospect of power, glory or money in the Party in this country, you know that. But I'm in it for the same reason as you, because I want a better life for the ordinary working people. Right?"

She nodded. He went on.

"I don't want any medals. I don't want a peerage. If any of us wanted that sort of thing we could join the Labour Party. The only recognition I want is recognition by my mates on the job and in the union that the Party is working for them. The Party, not me. See? Well, in a way, we've got this recognition. In the unions and in the factories anyway. That's why our blokes keep getting elected. That's why we're strong out of all proportion in the E.T.U., the A.E.U., the miners, the docks. They trust us. And I expect that trust girl. I've got a right to it because I'm not in it for myself but for them. And if I do something they can't quite understand, or that I can't properly explain to them, or that might even look a bit funny sometimes, I still expect them to trust me, I've still got a right to it. My blokes say "You can trust old Eddie Sanders. He knows what he's doing." And I say "You can trust old Joe Stalin. He knows what he's doing.""

"But Eddie, suppose you're wrong?"

"Suppose my mates are wrong? Simple. Every time we let the workers down we put ourselves back a few years. Christ know we're wrong enough times, we make enough bloody mistakes. Sometimes we get some phoney individuals in the Party that get to the top. Sometimes even good people go bad. But if I were to discover tomorrow that Harry Pollitt is in the pay of the Tories that would make me change my opinion about Harry, not the Party. Because to me girl I'm the Party. I know myself. I know my motives. They have the same right to my confidence as I have to theirs. If they're fooling me that's *their* look-out. I'll carry on doing what I'm doing because I believe it's right, that's all."

She looked up at him, standing in front of the fireplace. He was not fat at all. His fire was still burning just as it had burned that first time she saw him speaking at the meeting in the square.

"Did you discuss this doctors' plot?"

"Doctors? Oh, no. We didn't."

"Not at all?"

"This was an Electrical Advisory meeting, not an International

Committee, you know."

"Yes, but before the meeting?"

"Oh. A bit."

"And?"

"And what? We'll have to see, won't we?"

"See? See what?"

"What's happened. I don't know what it's all in aid of."

"But the Russians say that these doctors — all Jews — have been plotting to kill a number of Party leaders. Right?"

"Apparently."

"Do you believe it?"

"Of course. If they say so, I believe it. Why should they make it up? Christ girl, the Party isn't taking up anti semitism. Our whole theory is against any sort of racial discrimination. You know that."

"Theory, yes . . ."

"And practice, too. Who are the people that fought Mosley and drove him off the streets? The Party, girl, remember that. Those people at the meeting tonight, not a Jew among them, but if there's any sort of anti semitism at the factories, those boys are out there fighting it, explaining why it's wrong."

"They'll have some explaining to do tomorrow morning."

"O.K. so they'll have some explaining to do. It won't be the first time."

"Or the last?"

"What's the matter with you any way?"

She was quiet.

Couldn't he see? Did she have to spell the thing right out for him? Or was he afraid to say it because he felt the same?

Finally, "I'm not happy about it Eddie."

"Happy? Who's happy?"

"Oh you know what I mean."

"What about the others?"

"At the Paper? Oh, mostly like you. Wait and see. Get the facts."

"So?"

"What facts Eddie? Where do you get them? Joe and I have been searching all day for the facts for an article. Facts. There aren't any."

"How does Joe feel about it?"

"He's worried, too."

"That's natural, I suppose."

She looked up sharply.

"Why?"

"Well . . . Joe. It's natural perhaps, that he should be a little less, objective, about it all."

223

"If they were Yorkshire miners instead of Jewish doctors, you mean, he'd be less worried and I'd be more worried?"

"If they were Yorkshire miners it'd be less likely to happen."

"Eddie! Why?"

"Yorkshire miners tend to have fewer connections in other countries. They don't have relatives and friends who are Zionists. They're not ..."

"Cosmopolitan?"

"That's one way of putting it."

"That's becoming a favourite work in the Party isn't it?"

"Is it?"

"Yes. I heard it three times today."

"So?"

"There's nothing in our theory against anti-cosmopolitanism, is there?"

*   *   *   *

Joe eased himself into the bed alongside Zena. She was nearly asleep again. "Night love," he said.

"Night Joe."

He lay for a while, side by her side, his hand on the softness of her nightdress. He felt the steep hill of her belly. The skin was taut and underneath it his kid was sleeping. Not long now.

"No Joe."

Out of her sleep she turned away from his hand and it slipped back on to his own thigh. He moved away from her and thought of Margaret suddenly.

Her closeness as they went through the files together. The sight of her breasts hanging down through the neck of her sweater as she leaned over towards him. His penis became big with thoughts of her and he cupped his hand round it, moving backwards and forwards gently so as not to wake Zena.

*   *   *   *

I'd better let him tonight or he might wonder, Margaret thought as Eddie moved on to her, his mouth sliding along her neck to where it joined her shoulders, his hands pulling the shoulder-straps down over her breasts. And I don't want him to wonder yet, when there might be nothing to wonder about. He's in a hurry tonight. Just as well. Get it over quickly. Oh, Joe, Joe. His hands on her, lips on her, tongue in her, all in her. Joe.

* * * *

"Who the hell do they think they are?"

"Don't get worked up David, it's not Joe's fault."

"Worked up? Why shouldn't I get worked up? What should I do? Wait till they've all been put in gas chambers?"

Joe interrupted.

"Nobody's putting anybody in gas chambers. Don't exaggerate."

"Exaggerate! Thousands of Jews are disappearing. This one who escaped writes in the Jewish Chronicle about the tortures they're going through, and you say exaggerate! What are you waiting for, a signal from your God in the Kremlin?"

"You don't want to believe everything you read in the Jewish Chronicle you know . . ."

"You mean *you* don't want to believe. That's the trouble with you. Good things about Russia you'll always believe. But bad things? They can't happen. You won't believe it. A nation of angels. Every man infallible. Be your own Pope!"

"I never said that."

"No but you believe it."

"You're mixing me up with yourself."

"Me?"

"You can't believe a Jew could ever do any wrong. You know bloody well that the Communists have always fought against antisemitism. You know that if it comes to a fight against Mosley it's the Communists that will lead it. But if they say that some Jews have been doing something wrong then suddenly the Communists have become anti semites! It couldn't be the Jews. Oh no! They'd never do such a thing."

For half an hour the argument had been developing. Joe knew it was going to happen as soon as Zena had told him they'd been invited round to Sadie's place for Friday night supper.

"*Lockshun* soup mit lectures," he grimaced.

"*You* can talk, replied Zena. "I seem to remember last time we were there you giving a brief three-hour analysis of Stalin's "Economic Problems of Socialism" that left nobody much time to say anything else but 'Goodnight, Joe, nice to have seen you.'"

"Ah, but that David, he exaggerates. He's always making such mountains out of molehills."

Zena looked down at her belly. "*You* can talk," she smiled.

"But you're such a beautiful mountain," he said marching his fingers along her thigh and up the round dome in a way that took her back to Lewis and an afternoon in the School of Art and the donkey stool going over.

"What're you thinking about?"

"Nothing."

"Nothing?"

That was the way it had been. Apart from Joe there'd been nothing. Nobody. Nobody had kissed her but Joe. No other hands, no other eyes, no other body. And now there was his child kicking and pushing around inside. In a week perhaps. Maybe more. Maybe less.

"You're crying."

She took his hand up to her mouth and bit hard on the flesh of the thumb.

A week later she recalled the incident as she lifted the leg of chicken to her mouth and heard the argument begin.

"Killed any good doctors lately?"

"David!"

"What's the matter Sadie? Joe doesn't mind. He's got an answer. Joe's always got an answer for everything. Right, Joe?"

Yes, he had the answer, but Zena could tell when he believed the answers and when he didn't. Tonight he was on the defensive. She could see he did not believe the individual answers he was putting up, but underneath it all he believed the truth of what he was defending. He knew there must be an answer and, until he knew what that answer was he was prepared to defend his position with anything that came to hand.

"The Joint Committee!" David snorted. "It is ludicrous to suggest that the Joint is organising sabotage against Russia. It's a charity committee. I'm a member of the Joint. I collect money for it. Do you think I'm a spy?"

"Look David. I'm a member of Communist Party which you are now accusing of anti semitism. Do you think I'm an anti semite?"

They looked at each other across the table, with knives and forks raised.

"Don't be silly the pair of you. Joe is not an anti semite and David is not a spy and I'm not a very good cook if that's all you think of my chicken."

Sadie's effort to ease the tension succeeded in bringing a smile to her husband's face and he looked down at his plate and speared a piece of chicken.

"You're right Sadie, he said. "And you're a wonderful cook. Right Joe?"

Without smiling Joe returned to his plate. "Sure," he said, "sure."

For a while they concentrated on the chicken in silence until Joe spoke again.

"The difference between us David is that you would be prepared to accept the necessity for Zionist organisations spying against, or fighting the Russians in some way, if it meant achieving the Zionist aims. There's nothing really against it in your theory or practice although you wouldn't publicly advocate it. On the other hand I would never be prepared to accept anti semitism in the Party because it's fundamentally opposed to our whole theory and practice."

"But Joe . . ." Zena, coming into the discussion for the first time, felt a sudden gush of fear as he turned towards her as if expecting a stab in the back. "Suppose . . . just suppose you became convinced that the Party, or the Party leaders . . . say, in Russia . . . were becoming anti semitic . . . no, I know you think it could never happen, but say it did. What would you do? Would you leave the Party?"

"Of course not. If the Party did ever support antisemitism, or declare in favour of higher dividends and lower wages, or support an Imperialist Government against an uprising of natives in a colony, or anything like that, then I'd fight inside the Party to reverse this policy and clear out the people who were doing it. I wouldn't just bugger off and leave the Party to the very people who were betraying it. Christ, Zee, I've fought for this Party. I get up at five o'clock in the bloody morning to sell Daily Workers, I shout my bloody guts out at street corners on Saturday afternoons, I work day and night at the Daily for a wage any unskilled labourer would laugh at . . ."

"You're mad!"

"All right David, I'm mad. But if I ever see you fighting and making sacrifices for your Zionists like that instead of drinking cocktails in comfortable drawing rooms in Hampstead Garden Suburb . . ."

"Joe!"

"Let him talk Sadie, let him talk."

"No, it's not right David, why should I? Sacrifices? Fighting? He doesn't know what sacrifices mean!"

"Who doesn't?"

"Look Joe," David put down his knife and fork and leaned across the table. "When you Communists start to fight for your country in the same way that we Jews have fought for ours then you can talk about sacrifices. We've *fought*. Not with petitions and meetings and marches but with guns and bombs and barricades. You get up at five o'clock to sell Daily Workers? Some sacrifice! You should be in a kibbutz surrounded by Arabs and you don't sleep all night. They don't pay you much at the Daily Worker? Sad. You should have joined some of our boys shipping refugees out of Europe through the

British blockade. They got nothing at all. Honestly Joe, I know you're trying boy but you're not getting anywhere. You're still bashing away at the British Goverment, *we beat 'em!*"

"We?"

"Yes, Joe, we. A Communist is a Communist and a Jew is a Jew. Just as you have to take responsibility for everything the Communists do in Russia so we have to take responsibility for everything the Jews do in Israel — and anywhere else for that matter. But it works both ways. Good and bad. If you want me to take responsibility for the activities of the 'Joint' that your friends accuse of spying then you must allow me to share the responsibility for driving the British out of Palestine. Right, Joe?"

"Fair enough."

"And more than that Joe."

"What, more?"

"Much more. You must allow me to share in the credit for doing the world's thinking."

"Thinking? How come?"

"All the really *big* thinking in the world has been done by us Joe. The world-shaking ideas. Religious ideas, scientific ideas, yes, even your Communist ideas. Look Joe . . ." He held up his hand and, one by one, unfolded his fingers as he went on. "Moses, Jesus Christ, Karl Marx, Freud, Einstein. In anybody's list of the ten greatest thinkers in world history these five must appear — and they're all Jews. Fifty percent. That's not a bad average for a nation that is less than one percent of the world's population! You think you're going to change the world. Fine. But that's nothing new boy. We've been changing the world ever since it began. We gave the world the idea of one god. Then we gave the world three gods in one. Then we gave the world the idea of no god at all. Then we looked inside man himself and came up with the idea of each man his own god. Then we turned the whole universe inside out and the whole thing became so big that the very idea of god was so small you couldn't see it. Boy, when God chose us he chose right. We've certainly given him a run for his money."

"David!"

"Ach, God won't mind Sadie. He's one of us."

They all smiled and Sadie turned to Zena. "Don't mind him Zena. He gets as worked up about Jews as Joe does about Communism."

"I feel, somehow, like a baby," Zena replied, groping for her meaning. "It's as if you've all been here for ages. For centuries, and I've just come in."

"Don't let it get you Zee," said Joe. "You're a member of the human race and humans have been here a lot longer than Jews. Unless there were Jewish monkeys?" He turned the question to David with a grin.

"Wouldn't be surprised."

"I bet the first monkey who said 'let's get down off these trees and walk' was a Jewish monkey!"

"And the first Jewish amoeba was the one who decided to split into two?"

"And the first Jewish amphibian was the one who decided to crawl up out of the slime!"

"And they've been trying to push us back ever since."

"Ah, but they'll never succeed while we can still make *Strudel* like this!"

"Coffee?"

"That's just it Joe. They'll never succeed. If the Egyptians couldn't do it, and the Romans, and the Spaniards and the Poles and the British and the Germans, how come the Russians?"

"The Russians aren't trying to Dave."

"I hope you're right Joe. I hope you're right."

"I hope so" added Sadie.

"Meanwhile," said Joe, changing the subject, and putting his hand on Zena's belly, "there's another one in here trying to get out."

"Another Einstein?" Zena asked.

"Another Moses," smiled Sadie.

"Another Freud," said David.

"Karl Marx, of course!"

Zena placed her hand alongside Joe's and allowed a little smile to grow in her eyes.

"It'll be funny," she said.

"What will?"

"If it's another Jesus Christ."

*   *   *   *

This is it. Must be.

In the dark Zena felt a sharp fist open and close inside her and knew.

Wait now. Count. Time it till the next one comes. What did they say, ten minutes? God I'm frightened. Perhaps it was nothing. A false alarm. Can't feel a thing now. No more kicking and pushing. He's sleeping as quietly as Joe. Nothing. Probably indigestion. Perhaps it wasn't a pain. Oh but I wish it was now, soon, tonight. So tired of waiting, waiting, waiting. Everything's ready. The flat is clean and tidy, the painting things are put away. Joe could manage nicely. Joe. Sleeping there. Like that first night we were married when he went to sleep so quickly after and left me alone by his side wondering what I'd done and his shoulders were so hairy and he looked so thin. He came into me so quickly and was trembling so much with excitement that I didn't know if it was a man or a baby I had in my arms. But his hardness was all around me. A hardness of muscle, bone and sinew, of thigh, penis, back and arms, around me, alongside me, up into me, right through me and then suddenly all over. No more. Finished. Joe going to sleep and me lying there alone in the world for the first time in my life with no father, no mother, nothing. Wonder what *they* are doing tonight? Dad looks so old now. Suddenly it's happened. Crumpled up like a bit of old paper. But he enjoyed the wedding. They both did. Standing there in the Registry Office with Reggie Smith from the Worker cracking jokes and Joe looking smarter than he'd ever been and my salmon pink dress and the flowers and none of Joe's relatives because I was a *shikser* and we were . . .

Ah! Again!

What is it, ten minutes? Quarter of an hour. Can't be. Definitely a pain this time. Shall I wake him? Wait till I'm sure. I've arranged about his dinner tomorrow, but what about the vegetables? Are there enough potatoes? Greens in plenty but he'll never eat them. Mrs. Weston will come in on Wednesdays and Fridays to clean the place up. Nice woman. It'll be good to be able to paint again. To stand up in front of a canvas and watch it coming to life. This is different. This happens to you, you don't feel you're doing anything about it except carrying it around and getting bigger and bigger. Now it's here. What will it be like? It's going to hurt. One, two, three. Like Joe's mother had said this morning. 'It should only be quick; one, two, three.' She was all right. She'll come over and look after Joe. Stuff him up with *lockshun* soup and cheesecake and all that. Wonder if Joe really misses all that sort of cooking? I should have got some porridge in otherwise he'll be going out in the mornings without any proper breakfast. He probably won't eat it anyway. Never bothers with food. That was funny when we went out for a meal in a chinese restaurant and . . .

Again!

Oh this time, yes, it stays long enough to feel that it really is pain. But *my* pain. Something I'm doing to myself, not inflicted on me from outside. A volcano must feel like this. Mother earth. How long? Ten minutes. He's a regular little so-and-so. Should I wake Joe? Leave him for a while till I'm absolutely sure.

The pain went and came back three times and the fourth time she

230

called Joe.

"Joe."

She touched him on the shoulder.

Without moving, he opened his eyes and was wide awake looking up at her.

"What's up?"

"I think it's here Joe."

He sat up quickly in the bed alongside her.

"You sure?"

"I think so."

"You all right?"

"I'm all right."

"Want anything?"

She smiled and shook her head.

"Does it . . . hurt?"

She smiled again.

"No, not really."

She put out her hand towards him and he took it up to his lips and kissed her fingers one by one, as if theywere some strange delicacy, looking up at her all the while.

"You sure?"

"Yes, I'm all right Joe. It sort of comes and goes. He's very efficient, our little one, does everything he should do."

"He'd better."

"I hope he's quick."

"One, two, three."

They smiled.

"One, two, three," she repeated.

On the three the pain came back.

She bit her lip and clenched his fingers in hers.

The pain, by myself, in the dark, is all right. It's me and I am doing it. But now, with the light on and Joe looking at me, it's different. It's a pain and it hurts.

"Joe."

"Zee, are you all right? Shall I get the doctor?"

"No it's going away now."

"Can I do anything?"

"No, it's all right now."

He is outside, helpless. It is nice to have him there, holding my hand, looking at me, but he is outside. Now it is all between me and that one inside. Joe, Joe, this is all your doing. You started all this, with your kissing and your feeling and your hands suddenly all over me and my legs suddenly opening and you coming right up inside me.

231

And now what you put in wants to come out and it hurts and all you can do is sit there with your big eyes and say is it all right. This is all your doing. Wonder what you'd say if I actually said all that to you instead of just thinking it? Do I even think it, anyway?

"What are you thinking about?"

"You."

"Me?"

"This is all your doing, you know."

His eyes were big as he looked into hers to see if she was joking. He held her hand up to his mouth again and turned it round slowly so that the open palm faced his lips and gently but deliberately bit into the soft flesh at the base of the thumb, still looking at her.

"You sorry?" he said.

She felt the little pain of his teeth in her flesh and smiled.

"Silly."

With an effort she heaved herself up and swung her feet round to the floor.

"Be careful."

"Don't be a *shmerel* Joe. I've been doing this every morning for months. Only just noticed? *Shmerel.*"

Somehow when she said anything in Yiddish it sounded more like Scottish and they always laughed.

"A *shmerel* means a dope, but with you it always sounds like a squirrel."

"So what's wrong with a squirrel?"

"Nothing at all. Squirrels are fine. Some of my best friends are squirrels."

"And some of my best friends are *schmerels.*"

"Including me?"

"Including you. Now go and phone the ambulance."

"O.K. I go ..." He waited at the door until she completed the catch phrase that half the nation had learned by heart from the wartime radio.

"... I come back!" She smiled, and he turned and went into the hall.

I go ... I come back. Signor So-so, and those other characters of Tommy Handley's that Mummy and Daddy and I used to listen to during the war. Can I do you now sir? That was Mrs. Mopp the charwoman. And then Mona Lot. It's being so cheerful that keeps me going. Who was it used to do all the voices? Whatever happened to all of them? Whatever happened to me? It was only yesterday that I was a little girl listening to the radio with them. Then I was a little girl playing at being married. Anyone can get married. There's

232

nothing to it. But this . . . this is where the game stops and life begins.
Down here inside me. There's two of us being born really. Him and
me. And will there be a new Joe, too, and will he carry on the same?
Already I feel older than Joe. What does he know about life? It's one
thing to write articles, interview people, go to meetings, but what
does he ever produce apart from a sheet of paper covered with
words? I'm producing life. Real life. Oh I'm so big.

Joe came back into the room.

"They're coming," he said.

"I'd better get dressed."

"Want anything?"

She stood up and, with an effort, pulled the nightdress up over her
head threw it on to the bed. She shook her hair over her shoulders and
said, "Take a good look Joe, next time you see me I'll be my old sylph-
like self . . . I hope."

I'm a great big fat ugly thing but I don't care. I'm going to have a
baby, a wonderful living child that I'm carrying and I'm bigger than
anybody, bigger than anything, great, huge, filling the room, filling
the whole house and it's all me and my baby and that's all that
matters.

He came over to her and held out his hands, looking not at her
belly but at her eyes. And as he stood next to her she felt the roughness of his pyjamas on her tight skin and then he was kneeling down
and his lips smoothed across her belly, all the way across from side to
side and up and down. He released his hands from hers and placed one
on each side of her belly the way he sometimes used to put them on
each side of her face when he kissed her, and then he kissed her belly
button and she heard him say, "I love you, love. Fat or thin, big or
little, ups and downs . . ."

"Ins and outs" she added.

"Round and round", He walked his fingers round her belly and
stood up.

"Mum and Dad?"

"Good and bad."

"Better or worse?"

"Cradle and hearse!"

"Don't be horrible. Sickness and health?"

"Poverty and wealth."

"So where's the wealth?"

"That's our wealth love, in your belly. We'll have it soon now,
eh?"

"One, two, three."

"One, two, three."

She dressed quickly lumbering about the room like a bear, making sure that everything was ready in her case, making sudden last minute notes of things for Joe tomorrow, looking at herself in the mirror, sending Joe into the other room to get a book when the next pain came, gripping the top of a chair, checking the time on her watch, hearing the ambulance stop outside, waiting for the ring of the bell.

"Joe, they're here!"

* * * *

In the Kremlin, too, that night lights were burning late as fifteen doctors, none Jewish, tried everything they knew to keep the world's leading communist from dying. At three o'clock in the morning they took off the leeches, swollen fat with the blood of the man who had spilt so much of his own countrymen's blood, and put them back in the jars.

It was over. Stalin was dead.

The end had been expected for some days by the group who waited for the news in an ante-room leading from Stalin's suite of rooms and they waited quietly and without excitement. Plans had been made. Announcements drafted. The succession cleared. All that remained was to press the button and a third of the world would go into mourning. Another third would rejoice and the rest would hold its breath and wonder what would happen next.

Among the latter were Russia's three million Jews who had been living in fear since the announcement of the "Doctors' plot" two months earlier. Would Stalin's death be blamed on the Jewish doctors and become the signal for a wave of pogroms? Or, now that Stalin was gone, would the whole thing be dropped? The photographs of Beria, head of Stalin's police and instigator of the "Doctors' plot" standing among the Guard of Honour by Stalin's embalmed body did not encourage confidence among Russia's frightened Jews. But in this they were wrong.

* * * *

"This can go back to the library now," said Joe, throwing the bulky blue file over to Margaret, as he came into the office.

She looked at it. It was marked "ZIONISM".

"Oh. Are we finished with it?"

"For the time being."

"What does that mean?"

234

"It means they're dropping the whole thing. That's official from Bert. Just come over the wire."

"That'll make a big story."

"Not with us it won't."

"Why not?"

He looked at her in surprise and leaned over and patted her cheek in a mock-fatherly manner.

"My dear comrade. How long have you been on the paper?"

"Three months . . . comrade." This last added in a warning tone.

"Three months. You should know by now, dear comrade, that there are some stories we make a big song and dance about and some which we prefer not to mention."

"And this is one of those?"

"This is. Oh, we'll mention it. Perhaps in an article on the benefits of the Soviet Judiciary, or the wonders of self-criticism where mistakes are brought out into the open, dusted off, and put back carefully for further use."

"Do I detect a note of un-Marxist cynicism . . . dear comrade?"

"Elementary my dear Watson. Aha . . ." they both looked up as their secretary came through the door balancing a tray with three cups of coffee, "just what I needed." They sipped the coffee quietly not speaking. Then he pulled some papers out of a folder on his desk. "Mick O.K.'d the International Women for Thursday."

"Just O.K.?"

"Well, he reckons the passion has gone out of La Pasionaria. He says the way he remembers her in Spain she would inspire the whole movement in one speech. Listening to her, even without knowing the language, was like drinking wine, making love . . ."

"Mick said that?"

"He did indeed."

"Well, well, one up for Comrade McKay."

"Right. But he also said he'd been told that making love to her was like listening to a speech."

"Only been told?"

"That's the way he put it."

"Aha. So what does he want us to do with the article, put in more sex, or more speech?"

"Neither. Just cut out the clichés, re-write the party jargon, the usual treatment."

"She won't mind?"

"She won't know."

"But she'll be at the meeting on Thursday."

"She's definitely coming? Visa O.K.? No problems?"

"Not so far. She arrives this afternoon. I wanted to ask if I can disappear for a couple of hours to join the welcome party."

"Sure, why not? Who else is speaking?"

"Oh it's quite a platform. Dame Sybil Thorndike, Simone Signoret and this girl from Indo-China."

"That should cover everything, La Pasionaria on the last big civil war, and your Indo-Chinese girl on the next one."

"The next one?"

"It looks like the French are nearly on their way out of Indo-China. Our guess is the Americans will take over and try to win back what they've lost in Korea. No men on the platform?"

"Who needs men?"

He looked up at her and moved his lips in the direction of a smile.

"Well comrade, the Americans are going to need them. The Indo-Chinese are going to need them. Even La Pasionaria needed them. Somebody has to do the dying."

"Oh they're good at that, certainly. Will you be coming to the meeting?"

"I don't know. I'll be going to see Zee and my big bouncing boy in the evening. I'll try and come in after that. About nine-ish." He hesitated. "Will Eddie be there?"

"Oh he's in the Midlands this week. Some E.T.U. course."

"Perhaps we'll have a meal after?"

Their eyes met over the coffee cups.

"Fine," she said.

*   *   *   *

"Well she was certain good, your Pasionaria, but not as good as the wine."

The bottle was finished. The elderly waiter gently held it up to the light, shrugged his shoulders and smiled, perhaps because it meant they would now have to go. Unless they wanted another bottle?

"No thank you. The bill please."

"Monsieur."

"Bad mark McKay. She was definitely not like wine."

"And making love?"

"Well, I've tried the wine ..."

"Monsieur." The bill, delicately face downwards on the plate.

"Fifty fifty, agreed?"

"After listening to all those high-powered international women I am fully convinced that you should pay the whole lot but as a gesture to the last remaining vestiges of my masculinity I agree to pay half."

"Tell you what. You pay the bill. I'll pay the taxi."

"A taxi already! Where to?"

"My place! O.K.?"

"O.K. But a taxi?"

"I'm in a hurry."

She certainly was. Leaving the money on the plate he followed her out past the waiter's inclined smile, into the Soho dark where she took his hand and ran, laughing and pulling him towards the lights of Cambridge Circus. Breathless into a taxi, still laughing, still holding his hand until, with the neon lights of Charing Cross Road striping their faces, they kissed savagely, open-eyed, open-mouthed as if this was not their first kiss but their last and everything, everything, had to be said in that one moment.

Released, they leaned back and took in deep breaths, she with her head back, he with his on one side, looking at her.

"Ayayay! La Pasionaria was never like this."

*   *   *   *

"God help us, I had the poor little bugger circumcised, what else does she want?"

Joe paced around the room as he did more and more these days. Angry. Caged. Chained.

"I don't know what you're getting so excited about. All she said was would I mind if he was given a Jewish up-bringing. What's so terrible about that? I don't mind. Do you?"

"A Jewish up-bringing! What the hell does that mean? Look, I had a Jewish up-bringing. What did it do for me? Bloody Hebrew classes every night except Friday. As soon as I'd done my homework down the road to the bloody *shool* where this silly bastard made us repeat after him the whole bloody five books of Moses, a different bit every bloody night. And translate it. I tell you, I started when I was five and went on till I was fifteen. I must have gone through that bloody bible, word for word, ten bloody times. Bloody barmy!"

"Well, you learned another language."

"Another language? You must be joking. I'll tell you what I learned. "*Vayedaber Adonai el Moshe laymor* . . . And the Lord spake unto Moses saying . . .' Like hell he did. The biggest con of all times. I tell you I must have repeated that phrase ten thousand times and by the time I came to ten thousand and one I didn't believe a word of it."

"But you said yourself Joe, get rid of all the mumbo-jumbo and the miracles and all that and it's the history of your people, right? So what's wrong with little Robbie knowing about that?

He stopped pacing up and down and sat down, facing Zee, at the kitchen table, moving their plates with the remains of their supper to one side, clearing a plastic battleground between them.

"Now look. I'm in favour of him knowing where he comes from, you know that. And part of that, only part of it mind you, is in that book. But the rest of it is pure unadulterated junk, and you know that too. I don't want him growing up thinking he's the chosen people, better than anyone else because God says so. I don't want him to think he has a right to somebody else's land because God promised it to him." With both hands he smoothed the tablecloth, sweeping it clear of all crumbs, and leaned over towards her. "We know there's no God, don't we? So why should we let them tell lies to our son?"

With a smile that was too tired to lift more than the corners of her mouth she stirred the dregs in her cup, the last barricade between them.

"We've been into all this Joe. What you know and what I know are two separate things. What you believe in and what I believe in are no longer the same."

After two years it still tore at her guts to say that to him. *What you believe in and what I believe in are no longer the same.* It had taken her a year to work up the courage to tell him. A year of anguish, a year of arguments, when each day she went to the edge of the precipice and stepped back. Because now there was Robbie. In a way it had all started with Robbie. The day they came home from hospital. Wasn't it good news about the Jewish doctors, Joe? Sure. What were they going to do now? Do? What do you mean? What is there to do? Well, I'd have thought . . . well, Beria for example, if the plot was a phoney he must have been responsible for cooking it up, right? Who knows? They'll sort it out. At the right time. The right time! When's that for God's sake? How can he be a Communist and cook up things like that? How can they be Communists and let him get away with it? Nobody's going to get away with anything. It takes time. The Americans would like nothing better than a big upheaval in Russia now, with Stalin just dead. They'd love that. Americans! Always Americans! *They* didn't cook up the whole phoney doctors' plot, the Russians did that . . . Beria, or Stalin, or whoever. Stalin? You must be mad. What's happened to you Zee? What's happened to *you*, Joe?

That was the beginning. Everything was different from then on. Thinking. No longer just agreeing, accepting. Questioning. Was that right? Why were they doing that? And then the family. Mother Gold, *booba* now, grandmother. Always coming over to see Robbie. A bottle of *lockshun* soup to heat up for him. There's enough for you and Joe too, if he should ever come home. Meetings, meetings. I've never known such a person for meetings. Just like his father *oleh basholem*. I made a *strudel*, too much for me, what does one old woman want with a whole *strudel*? *Nu*, and how's my little *Robbyle*? Such a big boy he's getting. He'll soon be going to *cheder*. Listen Zena, you don't mind do you, when he grows up, he should go to *cheder*, that's Hebrew classes. He should learn a bit of *Yiddishkeit*. After all, he should know he's a Jew, eh? Who's going to tell him, Joe? He should be so lucky even to see him once a week. Where is he tonight? Another meeting? I tell you he works so hard that boy. Without him there wouldn't be a Communist Party. Maybe that wouldn't be such a bad thing? And they laughed together like conspirators and that was when she realised it would be possible not to be a Communist any more. So when the time came round to re-register, at the end of the year, to get a bright new Party Card for next year, she said no. Sorry, Joe. And the world did not collapse. No big row. He must have seen it coming. All he said was 'You sure Zee?' I'm sure Joe. O.K. That's all. O.K. I'll give this to Stan he said. The old card. Fully stamped up for every week in the year, every week in my life, every beat in my heart. No more. Stan, the Branch Secretary, came round. That's just the trouble Stan. They *do* know what they're doing. If they didn't I could forgive them. He went away shaking his head. Nice man. He was sad to lose me. Was Joe? Did Joe know he was losing me? Did he care? It seemed like a weight off his mind almost. Something else moved to one side, the way he tidied his desk or the way he is doing now with the kitchen table.

"Come off it Zee", he said. "We're not that far apart."

Not far? I can't even reach her across the table. It's time, not distance. She's talking about ideas, integrity, good and bad. Me, I'm just talking about plain basic sex. Talking? How do you talk to her about that? Like that very first time, while she was still in hospital and I'd gone back to Margaret's laughing and running up the stairs to her flat, she disappearing into another room leaving me to 'make myself at home', looking at the prints on the walls, the records, the books, Eliot's slim volumes and the obligatory orange spines of Lenin's Selected Works. "Just like home" I'd said. "And is this just like home?" I turned and she was standing there naked just moving her body enough to make those big breasts swing gently from side to side as she crouched forward, her arms stretching out towards me, her fingers beckoning. And Christ! When I stepped towards her, the way she went down on her knees and started pulling off my clothes and the way she gasped when she held it in her hands and ah! when I felt the wetness of her lips all round it, her tongue licking, her teeth just nipping. Careful, I'm coming. Don't worry. Her face turned up to me, eyes glazed, her tongue licking the wet corners of her mouth. I've got you. And she had. Fingers of one hand round my balls, stroking them at the back and the other gripping the base of my penis, thumb pressing in to stop the up-flow of semen, she laughed and bent back and all I could see was that black-red hair and her shoulders and all I could feel was her sucking and licking and I knew she had me all right. Go talk to Zee about that. Zee whose loving was as gentle as a deer and whose ecstasy came on tip-toes, cautiously, almost fearfully until it burst upon us unawares, startled, trembling, a thing of amazing momentary beauty that was immediately gone, invisible, irretrievable. Sometimes. Other times it was like now. Miles away. The sheet, like the tablecloth, a battleground. And what was the battle of the day? Robbie? Why in hell hadn't the old girl asked me in the first place? Getting at me through Zee. That was funny. All these years she wouldn't even talk to her. Now she talks to her more than me. Great.

"What gets me," he said, "is the way she uses you to get at me. Why doesn't she ask me straight?"

"Because she never sees you. Whenever she comes round you're out."

"Well, you know where I am. You could tell her I was at a meeting."

"Why should I lie to her?"

The battle of the day.

He looked up sharply and his hands stopped in the middle of another sweeping movement.

"What the hell d'you mean by that? Who said anything about lying?"

"You said I should tell her you were at a meeting."

"So? What's wrong with that?"

"That would be a lie."

"What are you talking about? What would be a lie?"

With an effort she raised her eyes from the table, knowing that all she would see was the end of the film. The credits were already rolling. Directed by Joe Gold, starring Zena Gold and Joe Gold. Screenplay by Zuck from a story by Shmuck. Guest star Margaret Houghton? Be my guest! Pull up a bed. Rest your weary tits in my husband's hands. Do I have to go through the whole thing with him now? Why me and not her? Why any of us. After all, what are we talking about? That little bit of wrinkled skin that hangs between his legs? In Spain they sell the bull's scrotum to tourists as a purse. Olé! Why did I think there was more to it than that? There *was* more. Out of that little wrinkled bag came Robbie. And more than that. Like

240

when I made him find out the words we would have said in a synagogue, under an embroidered canopy, *Hurray at betubbas zu mekoodeshes li, keddas Moshe veyisroel.* Behond thou art sanctified to me with this ring by the laws of Moses and Israel. I should be so lucky. Sanctified I wasn't . . . and yet there were times when 'Behold!' was the only way to describe it. Behold I shall tell thee a mystery. Tell me the old old story. So tell me. Behold already!

"I'm talking about last Wednesday, Joe. District Propaganda meeting, you told me. I phoned up Steve's place to ask you something. There was no such meeting. Steve was home, yet later you told me in such great detail what he had said at the meeting! Wait, you asked me what I'm talking about. So listen. Friday night. Important editorial conference at Mick's. I phoned Mick. Oh, don't worry, when he told me that was no such meeting I made up some daft story about it must have been some other Mick. And don't think I did it to save your face. I just didn't want to look a fool, that's all."

Exhausted, she turned away from him. It was said. It was done. But not all. Wednesday, yes. And Friday. But not last night standing in the shadows and watching them come round the corner laughing, going up the steps to her front door and him holding the carrier bag while she found her key, opened the door, switched on the light. Oh what a light that was! As she stood by the open door waiting for him to pass he gave a little bow, his little bow, giving *her* part of *our* life. That was a game *we* used to play. Pray enter good Sir . . . Madame you are too kind . . . Strip her naked, leap on the bed, kiss her, suck her, feel her, love her, but not that little bow to her. The door closed and she ran to the tube station as if she had been raped, her arms crossed against her belly. That, she hadn't said.

"Look, I can explain . . ."

"I know you can explain. You can explain prison camps and you can explain doctors' plots, you can explain Stalin and you can explain Beria. For a man who can explain all that it shouldn't be hard to explain what you were doing at Margaret Houghton's place last night."

Explain, explain. That's where she was wrong. All the other stuff was easy. Everything came with its own explanation. It was the fault of the Americans, or the Zionists. Even the whole business of the purges and phoney trials had just been explained by Khrushchev. You wait long enough you'll get an explanation. Even a rehabilitation. Posthumous maybe but nevertheless a rehabilitation. But for this thing between him and her there was no more waiting and there was no explanation other than the over-simplification that he preferred to spend time with one rather than the other. Explain that.

241

Why should I have to explain anything? Am I owned by her, chained to her?

"Look Zee," he started.

"Forget it."

She pushed herself back from the table and, taking her empty cup walked over to the sink, her back to him.

"I think I'll take Robbie and we'll go away for a while." Still with her back to him, staring at the pattern of tea leaves in the cup. A dark stranger. A long journey.

"Are you sure Zee?" God! What that all? Was it no different from leaving the Party three years ago? What had she replied then?

"I'm sure Joe." She turned on the tap and washed the dark stranger out of her future.

* * * *

The appointment of Nikita Khrushchev as First Secretary of the Soviet Communist Party in 1954 brought a new and fascinating personality on to the world stage.

Short and fat with a shiny bald head and coarse peasant features, Khrushchev had grown up in the hard school of Russian communism, fought in the Red Army, worked his way up the ladder from position to position. Unlike the slow-speaking Stalin who had ruled Russia's two hundred million people with an iron hand for more than thirty years, dragging them through poverty and famine, Civil War and armed intervention, to a position where they could sit down with the mighty powers of the West on equal terms, Khrushchev bubbled over and amazed the wary world with the picture of a Soviet leader who could actually laugh and make jokes. They did not *like* his jokes but he was certainly different. Unlike Stalin, who had never set foot outside the U.S.S.R., Khrushchev travelled, carefully accompanied by Premier Bulgarin to avoid the new heresy of "the cult of the individual", going to India, Britain and even to Yugoslavia where he welcomed back into the Communist fold the ageing Marshall Tito who had been ostracised by Stalin for sticking to his own breed of Communism.

Khrushchev was everywhere. Pounding the table at the United Nations, cracking jokes with Frank Sinatra in Hollywood, jumping in with offers to build a mighty hydro-electric project in Egypt when the Americans blew hot and cold, and signing an agreement with the Egyptians which brought the U.S.S.R. for the first time into the Middle East arena.

But it was in Moscow, in February 1956, in the great Hall of

Columns, that Khrushchev rocked the whole Communist world. In his speech to the 20th Congress of the Soviet Communist Party Khrushchev described for the first time to the delegates how Stalin had hounded many of his own comrades to death, connived and plotted against many colleagues who opposed him, deliberately set up false "plots" like the Jewish Doctors, destroyed whole sections of the people in ruthless purges and built himself up as a God through a nationwide personality cult.

Khrushchev's speech, at first only revealed to the Soviet Party, then later to Communist Party leaders throughout the world, did more to change the Communist movement than anything since the Russian Revolution of 1917. It broke the chains that had tied all Communists to the Soviet Party. No longer was it possible to say "Stalin knows what he is doing . . . trust the Russians." No longer was it possible to wipe away all criticisms of the Soviet Union as simply anti-communist slanders. What the severest critics of the Soviet regime had been saying was now admitted to be true. Much of what the top Soviet leaders had been saying over the years to justify their activities had now been admitted to be lies.

That game was over and a new one was beginning.

Nowhere was it being played with more earnestness than in the countries of Eastern Europe whose Communist Party leaders, now acting as Prime Ministers, Defence Ministers, Chiefs of Police and Ministers of Trade and Industry, now felt immense pressures from below, from their own members who wanted to know if they too had been behaving like Stalin. In Hungary, Matyas Rakosi, the Communist Party Secretary announced the 'posthumous rehabilitation' of Laszlo Rajk, the former Party Secretary who had been executed by Rakosi three years earlier after a trial in which he had been condemned as a conspirator against the State.

But 'rehabilitation', posthumous or otherwise, was not enough. The pot was boiling and in June in the industrial town of Poznan, in Poland, it boiled over in four days of rioting in which sixty people were killed and over three hundred arrested as a result of what Polish Communists were later to describe as ten years of "accumulated resentment against the overbearing domination of the Soviet leadership."

And then Hungary.

* * * *

"How long is she going away for?"

They sat facing each other with two desks between them. Him

243

with tidy piles to left and right, a clear layout pad in front of him, laid, with ruler and pencils, as if for the next meal. Hers an untidy scatter of papers, articles, photos, proofs and headlines.

HUNGARIANS ASK SOVIET TROOPS TO GO.

100,000 DEMONSTRATE IN PARLIAMENT SQUARE.

"She didn't say."

"She didn't say. And what did you say?"

He moved one pencil until it was at right angles to the other making a corner at the bottom of the pad,

"Me? Nothing. What could I say?"

"How did she know about us?"

"I don't know."

"You didn't ask her?"

"What for?"

"What for? Well, I'd have thought it might be interesting to know."

"Interesting? Why? I couldn't care less, could you?"

"Care. Who said anything about caring?"

She was angry now, gathering the photos together and stuffing them into a folder. "I don't give a damn, I'm just bloody annoyed at the idea of being put into the position of 'the other woman.' Which I'm not."

"What are you?"

"I'm a person, that's all. What goes on between you and me is our business and nobody elses. You're not chained to her any more than I'm chained to Eddie. I'm not going to be labelled as just a bloody point in an eternal triangle."

"What does Eddie think about it?"

"Oh him!" She pushed her chair away from the desk and stood up, holding the file of photographs. "He's used to me by now. Any woman who had more than one man he thinks is a nymphomaniac. Typical bloody man. It's quite normal for *them* to go around sleeping with anybody they can but if a woman does the same thing she's some sort of sexual pervert."

"Which you're not, of course."

"If I am, what does that make you?"

The internal telephone buzzed and Joe reached to pick it up.

"O.K. Mick. Right away." He put the two pencils side by side on the pad and got up. "I'll be with Mick if you need me."

"Why should I need you?"

He picked up the steel ruler and threw it across the desk to her. "You can use this instead, till I get back."

"Boasting again" she called after him as he went through the door.

*　　*　　*　　*

As he entered Mick's office Joe was surprised to see that most members of the Editorial Executive were already there. "I didn't realise it was a meeting" he said, taking a seat next to the Industrial Correspondent.

"Are we all here?" McKay polished the edge of his desk as he looked across the room.

"The wheels of Parliament must be grinding to a halt," drawled Walter Graham, carefully studying an old soup stain on his trousers as if he had noticed it for the first time, "which may be why our illustrious Parliamentary Correspondent is not with us." He scratched at the stain with his finger nail. "On the other hand," he continued, giving up the stain, and looking round the room, "he's probably grinding away at our tea-lady as he seems unable to start the day without performing that service for which, I understand, he receives his ration of tea free, gratis and for nothing."

At that moment Frank Organ, the wavy-haired Parliamentary Correspondent appeared at the door, a mug of tea in his hand. "Sorry," he smiled, "hope I haven't held anything up."

"Aha! The mighty Wurlitzer!" Graham jumped up and with exaggerated politeness pushed a chair at the surprised correspondent. "Whatever you may have been holding up for the benefit of the tea-lady, dear boy, I can assure you that you have not held *us* up." Turning to McKay, he sat down. "Now we are all assembled Michael, perhaps you can tell us why you have taken us all from our labours."

McKay winced, smoothed his desk top and looked around the room.

"Your labours have been nothing compared with what they're going to be," he started. "This whole Hungarian thing seems to be getting out of hand. Imre Nagy has just made a statement in which he says he is abolishing the one-party system, and is taking Hungary out of the Warsaw Pact. From now on, he says, Hungary will be neutral."

"Phew!" Next to Joe, the feet of the Industrial Correspondent disentangled themselves from the legs of the chair he was perched on and sought the floor as he leaned forward. "What about Suslov and Mikoyan?"

"Rest assured," Graham interposed, "that our Soviet heavy brigade are engaged in comradely discussions with our Hungarian

245

comrades, although if the results are anything like their last efforts a week ago we will indeed be in trouble."

"This is no time for jokes. Nor for cynicism about our Soviet comrades." With a razor-sharp edge to his voice Jim Davies entered the discussion, his eyes glinting as he looked directly as Graham. "This is serious comrades. It's what we've expected for a long time and if Nagy really means what he says about pulling out of the Warsaw Pact it could be war. The Soviet Union could not stand aside while a great hole is made in its defences. We hear that Suslov and Mikoyan have flown back to Budapest and our guess," he gestured to include McKay, and looked pointedly at Graham, "and that means the Political Committee of the Party, is that if they can't persuade Nagy to change his mind those Russian tanks will be back there tomorrow."

"Any news from Danny?" Joe asked, thinking of the three unpublished reports lying on his desk from Danny Wade, the young reporter the paper had sent to Budapest a week ago when the first news came through of unrest in the Hungarian capital.

"Ah, Danny." McKay sighed and looked out of the window before replying. "I think we made a mistake with young comrade Wade. We should have sent somebody more experienced, more stable. Yes, yes, comrade," he lifted up his hand to stop Graham interrupting, "I know you're going to say you told me so. You were right comrade. I was wrong. Danny had a superb record with us, a first-class political mind, a first-class reporter, keen, young, enthusiastic. Let's face it comrades, who knew the way things were going this time last week? Anyway, what is done is done. Danny has sent us in four stories and Jimmy and I have spoken to him on the phone. So has Joe. We can't use his stuff."

"Why not?" Frank Organ took another sip of his tea as he asked the question. Joe thought of the way he had asked the same question of him two days ago after reading Wade's stories, his feet up on Joe's desk, the same mug of tea in his hand.

Davies replied to the question, still with the same sharpness of tongue. "Because comrade Danny Wade has got it wrong."

"But he's there." An unaccustomed sharpness was there now in Organ's voice too.

"You can be there comrade, on the spot, and still get it wrong. Trotsky was there, in the heart of things in the Soviet Union for years and he got it wrong."

Trotsky! Why bring him in? Anathema . . . throw salt over your shoulder, spit three times, drive a stake through the heart, an axe in the head. Joe felt a tingling in his spine.

"You think Trotskyists are behind it Jimmy?" It was the Industrial Correspondent who asked the question, sitting on his chair and swaying a little from side to side.

"We don't have enough information to answer that question. But we do know that so-called Communists, intellectuals, writers have been calling for Soviet troops to leave the country, blaming the very people who liberated them from Fascism for all the problems the country is suffering from. Now Wade's reports are full of this stuff. Panofi Group propaganda most of it. We can't use it."

"But isn't the Panofi Group mostly Communists? Didn't we specifically ask Danny to find out what they were asking?"

"There are Communists and Communists." McKay seemed to sweep them all away with his hand across the desk. "We didn't like the sound of it and it looks as if we were right." He looked at Graham and added, "For a change."

Graham snorted and brushed a drop of snot off his lapel. "Well, like Davey says, it looks mighty serious. Where do we go from here?"

"Fortunately we have one bit of good news." Davies picked up a piece of tele-tape from the desk. "It looks as if this Israeli invasion of Egypt is not an isolated incident. The British and French have just issued an ultimatum to Egypt telling them to stop fighting or be bombed. So they're going to have their hands full and will be in no position to go into Hungary."

"What about the Yanks?"

"That's the big question. They don't have enough troops or tanks to match the Russians quickly enough and they can't bomb Budapest without killing their own people. So there's a good chance it'll all be back to normal before they can do a thing."

There was silence in the room and nobody seemed to want to continue the discussion.

"Back to normal, Jim?" It was Organ who spoke, breaking the silence as he put his half-empty mug on the floor by his feet and leaned forward. "What is normal any more?"

The Welshman leaned forward towards him, their faces on a level. "Back to normal, comrade, is where Communists stand together to fight back any attack against the Soviet Union. Normal, for this paper, is not to publish anything that will damage the interests of the communist movement anywhere in the world, and in Hungary, as comrade Imre Nagy will find out, it is not for communist countries to be neutral but to stand four-square with the Soviet Union against the Americans. That's normal."

Imre Nagy, Prime Minister of Hungary, found that out pretty quickly. Soviet troops streamed back across the border on November 1st and Nagy was replaced by Kadar as Prime Minister. But the people of Hungary found it less easy to go 'back to normal'. As the Russian tanks rumbled through the streets of Budapest they were met with tears and stones and improvised bombs. Soon the Russians had to bring in artillery to stop the continuous street fighting. Encouraged by broadcasts from American sponsored 'freedom radio' other groups joined the original movement, and disillusioned Communists found themselves fighting side by side with supporters of the Fascist ex-dictator Horthy. Anti semitism, never far below the surface in Hungary, found ironic expression in attacks on 'Stalin's Jews' as many of the hard-line veteran Bolsheviks were called. But the promised help was not forthcoming. Communists who saw the way their original movement was being perverted fell away in disgust, the tanks and the guns stood at every street corner and everything was brought back to normal.

Except for the thirty thousand Hungarians who died in the uprising and the three hundred thousand who fled across the border.

And the thousands of Communists in every country of the world who had had enough, who had seen on film and television the Soviet tanks and the guns as if they were on their own streets and knew this was not why they had joined the Party.

In Britain ten thousand left the Party, one third of the entire membership. Among them were Margaret Houghton and Joe Gold. Nothing was ever normal for them again.

PART THREE

Nothing But Your Chains

1960 — Tomorrow

Oh when the saints
Go marching in
Oh when the saints
Go marching in
Oh Lord I want to be in that number
When the saints go marching in.

That number was around one hundred thousand by the time the 1960 Aldermaston March turned into Trafalgar Square. A great roar went up from the scores of thousands more who were there to greet them that Easter Monday, as after four days of marching from the Atomic Weapons Research Centre in Berkshire, the leaders of the march lifted their banner higher, forgot about their weary feet and waved and laughed to the cheering crowds.

Bands played, long-haired youngsters danced alongside elderly churchgoers, mums pushed prams, as spritely after their four days march as if they'd just been down to the supermarket to do the shopping. The big banner with the Campaign for Nuclear Disarmament symbol caught in the breeze coming up Whitehall and it was all they could do to hold it as, guided by the line of police, the march organisers made their way to the great stone platform at the base of Nelson's Column. Following were the banners of C.N.D. branches from all over Britain, Trade Union banners resplendent in gold braid and tassels, Labour Party and Communist Party, Anarchist and Trotskyist and thousands and thousands of just ordinary people, unattached, unorganised, uncommitted to anything except the need to ban the Bomb before the Bomb banned humanity.

Four days of hard marching, sleeping at night in church halls and village community centres along the route, eating at roadside canteens, sheltering from the rain, bandaging blisters, endlessly talking and singing together had worn away the edges of the "generation gap" and a very square-looking vicar remarked to his neighbour, a very hip-looking youngster, as they prepared to bed down on the hard floor of a church hall, how those long-haired bearded hippies reminded him of Jesus as they talked and sang so enthusiastically about peace and love. "Man," replied the youngster, "if the lion can lie down with the lamb, you can sure lie down with me and if we're not too bloody meek about it there's still a chance we will inherit the earth."

"Amen," said the vicar closing his eyes. And as he lay there in the dark he smiled to himself as he realised that he felt more contented than he had for many years.

"Friends . . ." As the voice of Canon Collins, one of the campaign organisers, reverberated through the loudspeakers, Joe looked at Margaret and said "Fancy a cuppa?"

"Mm-mm," she nodded, "what about them?" indicating a couple standing beside them who had been marching with them for the last two days. He a tall, blonde, farm-looking man. She, either a young gipsy trying to look posh or a college student trying to look like a gipsy. Whichever it was, neither quite came off.

"Sure," said Joe and leaned over towards them. "Dave'n Maeve" he said, "we're going to get a cuppa. Want to come?"

"What about this lot?" Dave pointed to the gathering of eminent speakers trying to make their bums more comfortable on the hard folding chairs, smiling at each other and at Canon Collins who was now in full flight, arms uplifted, like David amid Landseer's lions.

"I know what they're going to say," said Joe. "I've been hearing it for four days and I've been saying it myself for four years. I've collected nearly two hundred signatures on the petition, I've worn my shoes to paper and my nerves to shreds and what I need now is a cup of tea. You coming?"

Maeve giggled. "Let's go Dave, I'm starving."

As they pushed through the tightly-packed crowds towards the Strand, Joe greeted old faces that came to him out of old meetings, old committees, old campaigns, and wondered if they were still in the Party and if he would see Zee. He held out his hand to help Margaret through the crowd and felt a softer hand in his. He turned round and Maeve smiled at him. Behind them Dave was cutting a way through the people as if they were a field of wheat, and Margaret was with him.

"Popular bloke, your Joe," Dave came to a halt up against one of the fountains, looking for a way out.

"Used to be." Pushed up close to him by the press of the crowd she grabbed his arm and turned him round, pushing him on. "We won't be very popular if we lose them."

"Oh, I'm not so sure. Maeve wouldn't mind."

"Joe would."

"Would you?" he asked, over his shoulder.

Pushing him on, her hands on his back she could feel the great cage of ribs through his jacket.

Joe called to them. "Hi! Dave . . . Margaret, this way."

As they came together at the fringe of the crowd she noticed Maeve's hand still in his and took Dave's arm.

"Where we going?"

"The Corner House Joe?"

Margaret saw Joe drop Maeve's hand but she still kept her arm through Dave's. She slipped her other arm through Joe's and Maeve did the same on the other side and the four of them marched arm in arm up the Strand to the sound of the booming of the Canon.

*   *   *   *

"Shall I be mother?" Maeve giggled again, looking over the tray at Margaret.

"You'll very likely end up being just that, if you don't do your buttons up." The trouble with Dave was you could never tell if he was joking. The dead pan voice. The non-existent smile.

Maeve looked down at her gipsy blouse. There were in fact no buttons to do up. A loose cord laced through the embroidered edges, tied in a bow at the top. Or should have done. In throwing off her cape as she sat down, the bow had come undone. Maeve looked at Joe looking at her. Dave looked at Margaret looking at Maeve.

"Yes, you be mother. I think you'd be better at it than me."

"You seemed to know half the people in the square Joe."

"Only half?" Maeve asked, fiddling with the cord in her embroidery.

"I used to organise that sort of thing," Joe explained. "First in the C.P., then on the Worker. You get to know a few people."

"Bet you do. You said used to. No longer?"

"Not for four years."

"Hungary?"

"Among other things."

"There were other things?"

"There were. Poznan for example."

"The Jewish doctors," said Margaret.

"Sugar?" Maeve asked, cup in hand.

"Khrushchev's speech. Two please."

252

"Beria . . . Stalin . . ."

"Ah Stalin," Dave smiled, taking a cup that Maeve was passing to him, "I could have told you about him."

"Now he tells me," Joe looked across at Margaret but she wouldn't share the joke and sat stirring her tea.

"Not just now, Joe, but for years. It beats me how all you Party people were so surprised when Khrushchev told you Stalin had spent his life killing his own comrades."

"How could we know what was going on?"

"In Russia, maybe not. Specially when all those fancy delegations you sent over were blind, deaf and dumb. Mostly dumb. But what about Mexico eh?"

"Mexico?" Joe looked up, surprised.

"Right. Your lovely Mexico you were talking about all yesterday. Where they gave the walls to the artists to paint on, and all that beautiful revolutionary culture stuff. Right out in the open, under that great big Mexican sun, Stalin sent his Mafia to kill Trotsky and one of your big-deal wall painters was one of the gang. Siqueiros? It was done with an ice-pick wasn't it? Nice people. Great. Look my poor campesinos. Here is this great painting I've done for you on this great wall in Mexico City. If you ever get a day off in your life and have the money to come to Mexico City come and see it. And if you don't like it I'll chop your head off with my ice pick!"

Looking at Joe, Margaret saw for the first time some grey hairs curling round his ears. Well, well. Eliot wasn't so far wrong with his coffee spoons. Listen to them all, stirring their tea, munching their cucumber sandwiches and little cakes while out there a hundred thousand people think they're changing the world and in here I think I'm changing my man. He's a big one, this Dave. But they're all the same when you get your fingers round their balls. Whatever happened to Sally Marsden and Harry? And Charlie Wingate? Good old Charlie. He must be an old man by now. Over twenty years ago. Bet he's . . .

Joe's voice interrupted her thoughts. "You're right about Stalin, Dave. And you're probably near enough right about most of us in the Party all that time, lapping up the reports of delegations just back from Russia as though they were mother's milk. You're right that Siqueiros was involved in an attempt on Trotsky's life, but that was earlier, before the assassination. Still, your point is valid, but you're wrong about his paintings. They're great. And they'll last. Longer than Stalin probably and longer than Trotsky. Listen, can you tell me the name of the Pope in Michaelangelo's time? Or anything about him? Bet he was top dog too in his day. Bigger than Stalin or Trotsky or any of them. But nobody remembers him today except through Michaelangelo. As for Trotsky, there's nothing in what he's written to lead you to suppose he'd have done things differently if he'd been in power. The dictatorship of the proletariat would just have been the dictatorship of Trotsky rather than the dictatorship of Stalin, right?"

"Well right now we're going to have the dictatorship of Maeve and you're going to stop talking politics all the time. Four days of it is enough. Have a pastry."

They looked at her, a Noel Coward gipsy with a plateful of pastries.

Silly bitch, thought Margaret, that 'simple little girl who doesn't understand politics' game won't get you anywhere with these two. And yet it must work with Dave. They've been together for a couple of years and from the odd bits of conversation she'd picked up on the march they seemed pretty fond of each other. He was a teacher of mathematics at a secondary school in North London and she an art student at Hornsey. They lived together in a commune they had helped to set up themselves in North London.

"So when are you coming up to look at our place?" Dave was asking. "You'll see some real painting on walls there. Just like the Mexican Government, we decided to give the walls to Maeve . . ."

"Stop it Dave . . ."

". . . the only trouble with it she's a bit one-track, like all these other artists of yours, only with her it's not politics it's . . ."

"Dave! Shut up. They can see when they come, if they want to."

Dave lifted an eyebrow and reached out for a jam tart.

"Sounds great Maeve, we'll certainly come and see." Joe looked at Margaret for confirmation. She nodded and took a cake. "You said 'we decided to give the walls to Maeve' . . . who's 'we' Dave?"

"All of us. We have a house meeting once a week when we all have to be there and we sort out any problems. Of course we meet for supper most evenings anyway and anyone can bring up anything there too but that tends to be more informal."

"How many is 'all of us'?"

"Twelve. Twelve adults that is. Six couples. And there's three kids. And one more on the way."

"How does that work out? I mean like for rooms, eating, sleeping, sitting around?"

"Well, it's one of those big old Victorian houses. Five bedrooms and an attic. Each couple has their own room, five on the first floor and we," nodding to include Maeve, "have a room on the ground floor. The kids all share the attic. They love it. Downstairs we have

254

this fantastic great kitchen. We all eat in there. You know. Big table, great big kitchen stove, cupboards all round. It's fantastic. Then there's a sort of common room where we sit around and talk, play music, see our visitors. That's where Maeve has painted the walls. And a smaller room for reading and quiet. That's about it, right Maeve?"

"There's the cellar."

"Oh yes we've got this terrific cellar going right under the house. When we get real flush we're going to stock it up with Chateau Lafitte and a few cases of genuine 1959 Coke, but till then we're not sure what to do with it. Maeve wants to turn it into a cave so she can do some contemporary cave paintings."

"Where do you get the money? Who owns the house?"

"Well actually I do. I came into a bit of dough when my old lady died last year and I put down the deposit and I'm responsible for the mortgage. On day-to-day running expenses, heat, light, food and general maintenance, we all chip in."

"On what basis?"

"Oh you'll like this Joe. From each according to his ability . . . to each . . ."

"According to *her* need," Margaret finished off the slogan in her own way.

"Right" said Dave.

But Joe wanted it spelled out.

"That's fine, but who decides ability, who assesses need?"

"We all do Joe. Together. That's what the whole commune thing is about. I told you about the house meetings each week, right?" Joe nodded. "Well, every month we have a council meeting. Obligatory. Everybody must attend. That's for big policy decisions. Finance. Work. Expulsions when necessary. New people, all that. Things that everybody must have a say in."

"Expulsions," Margaret asked. "On what grounds do you expel people?"

"Anything that might harm the commune. We don't have rules, as such. We take it as it comes and sort it out between us. Majority vote. Very democratic."

"But what sort of things?" Margaret persisted.

"Well, give you an example. Six months ago we had a guy come in. Nice guy. Engineer in fact. Nine to five man. All the right ideas, long-time friend of one of our founder couples. Seemed perfect. Well, after a while we found he was spending most of his spare time in the attic with the kids. We didn't twig straight away. Thought it was great for the kids to have more contact with the adults, until one of the kids told us what was going on. So we all talked about it and talked to him too and he was O.K. for a while but then it all started again and he had to go. So," Dave shrugged, "we don't have any rules about people exposing themselves in front of kids but it could have fucked up the whole thing so he had to go. We're not judges, or policemen or doctors, although one of our blokes is a psychiatrist, we just have to sort things out as they arise. O.K.?"

"Sure. And the finances. According to ability. How does that work?"

"Well there are twelve of us. Six couples right? One of those couples is homosexual, so we've got five women, seven men. One woman is this one," putting his arm round Maeve's neck "and doesn't believe in working for a living so she contributes in kind rather than cash."

"Like painting the wall?"

"Right. Two of the women have jobs, one up West, one locally, and they put their salaries in the kitty. The other two more or less run the house. Of the seven men four are working full time and just put their money in the kitty every week. One of the others is a plumber and decorator and he's responsible for all the maintenance. He does outside jobs too and what he earns like that goes into the kitty too. The two who live together are in the theatre and when they're working they chip in. When they're not, and that's been for a couple of months now, they don't. They help out though, everybody mucks in."

"Sounds great doesn't it Joe?"

"Very interesting."

"Oh good," Maeve smiled all round, missing nobody out. "Then you'll come and have a look?"

"Only to see your murals," Joe smiled back.

"Oh them. I'll paint them over before you come."

*   *   *   *

But she didn't.

Two weeks later when Joe and Margaret rang the front door bell of the Lucky Dragon Commune they had forgotten the paintings. The stained glass windows of the double door spoke of more prosperous days and a general air of benevolent neglect hung over the whole street. Dustbins stood by the back doors with drunken lids askew, and memories of paint clung wearily to window frames preparing to give up the struggle. Although it was almost noon, milk bottles waited patiently on the doorsteps. It was, after all, Sunday

256

morning, and the landlord of the corner pub was doing better than the Lord of the gothic monstrosity on the opposite corner.

"Joe! Margaret! Come in. Dave, they're here!" Maeve greeted them with an enthusiasm that spoke her age more accurately than the kohl-rimmed eyes that showed gipsies were out and Indians were in this week. But farmers were always farmers even when they taught mathematics and Dave took them warmly by the shoulders and guided them through an open pair of panelled doors into a large airy room.

"Like I said, this is where we see our visitors, and just to smack 'em in the eye as soon as they arrive we show 'em Maeve's picture."

And there it was, covering the whole of one wall, a huge landscape, a mountain range of penis tips set against a blue sky flecked with distant clouds. Seven penises, each about two foot wide delicately painted in Dali-esque detail extended across the room, only the tips visible above a shroud of mountain mist.

"How's that for Socialist realism, Joe?"

Joe shook his head, laughing. "Realism, maybe, but Socialist, I don't think so."

"Don't Socialists have pricks then?" asked Margaret going close up to the painting. "But they're certainly realistic" she added, turning to Maeve. "Are they portraits?"

"Of course," Maeve replied, strangely defensive.

"You did say seven men and five women here?" Margaret asked Dave.

"Right," said Dave, enjoying the situation, "and no prizes are offered for guessing who is who."

"I don't need to guess. I'd recognise my Bert anywhere." A tall blonde-haired woman had entered the room while they were talking and went up to the painting and patted one of the penises fondly.

"Margaret, Joe, this is Edna," Dave made the introductions.

"Hallo. And Margaret, Joe, this is Bert, my old man." She pointed to the painting. "He looks a bit droopy, but it's difficult keeping your end up for all that time, specially with me there. He might have looked a bit different if I'd gone out and left you two alone, eh Maeve?"

"Oh be quiet Edna, you know that wasn't the idea at all."

"What was the idea?" Joe asked.

"Oh I just got so fed up seeing all these naked ladies all over the museums. 'Déjeuner sur l'Herbe' and all that. It seems that in the last hundred years every nude that's been painted has been a woman. The National Gallery, and the Tate, is full of beautiful boobs but there's not a penis to be seen. I just thought I'd rectify the situation."

"You certainly did that love," said Edna going over to her and putting an arm round her waist, "and nobody's more pleased than Bert. Fame at last he says. Why don't you folks sit down?"

As the others sat themselves down on the assortment of armchairs and settees that were scattered around the room, Margaret stepped back from the painting and pointing to the central penis, looked at Dave.

"Is that you?"

Dave smiled. "I told you. No prizes for guessing who's who."

"But is it?"

"No, it's not." It was Maeve who replied.

Dave looked at Maeve sharply. "Come on," he said. "I think we've spent enough time looking at Maeve's pricture, as we call it, let's all sit down, eh?"

"You know Maeve, you've got an interesting point there," said Joe.

"Seven in fact," said Margaret, sitting next to Edna on the settee.

"No, seriously. I'd never thought about it before. The nude in this century certainly, perhaps with one or two exceptions like Rodin, has been almost hundred percent female. Is that because all the great artists have been men?"

"Have they?"

"Well, name a great woman painter of the last hundred years. Well, wait a minute, not just the last hundred years, name me one great woman artist."

"Well, apart from Maeve ..."

"Oh, don't be silly Dave, this is serious. What about Suzanne Valadon? Kathe Kollewitz?"

"O.K. I give you those, and a few more besides, but they are not among the greats, are they?"

"That's because women have been kept down," Margaret said. "The little woman. Good for bed and breakfast and keeping the house tidy for hubby to come home to. Want to be an artist? Good God, whatever next?"

"But there have been great women writers. The Brontës, Georges Sand. Great actresses. Composers? Can't think of any."

"Yes, but look at the problems they had getting recognition. It's a rotten man's rotten world."

"Not here it isn't!" A short squareish man appeared at the door wiping his hands on a grubby white apron that was tied around his waist. His wispy red hair gave the appearance of floating round his head. His whole face collapsed into lines as he smiled at them.

"It's all right for you lot," he said, "sitting here having those high powered intellectual discussions, but we poor men have got to keep working in the kitchen or there'll be nothing to eat."

"Alfredo!" Maeve jumped up and went over to him, giving him a hug. "I bet it's something terrific." She turned to the others. "This is Alfredo, Fred for short, our Cordon Bleu chef. Fred, this is Margaret, this is Joe."

"Cordon bloody blue is right," he grinned offering his wiped hand. "The only bloody cordon I've been involved with is a bloody police cordon and some of them were a bit blue when I'd finished I can tell you."

"Ah, now we get his childhood reminiscenses. Must we inflict these on our guests Alfred?" Edna turned to Margaret. "I ought to explain that you're in for a bit of a treat today, being Sunday. Normally I'm cook here and if you'd have come during the week you'd have had plain beef and two veg. But at weekends Fred and Stan take over the kitchen. We think it's because it's the only opportunity they've got to cook up their foul anarchist plots and God knows what else, but anyway who's complaining? Not me!"

"And not any of us" Maeve gave Alfred a squeeze. "And what have you made for us today Alfredo?"

"Well that's what I came in to tell you." said Fred returning her squeeze, "not my childhood reminiscences. The bombs are about to explode any minute. If you want anything to eat you'd better come quick."

The 'bombs' were a new kind of dumpling that Fred and Stan had cooked up with raisins and chiles, Mexican style, in honour, so they said as they brought the steaming dish to the table, of Joe's interest in Mexican paintings which Maeve had told them about. "We call it a Zapata Platter and suggest you keep a full glass of water handy. It's a little bit hot". It was, more than a little, but it spiced the conversation around the big table. One couple and their daughter were away for the weekend and the two actors were away, one of them auditioning for a provincial repertory company and the other had gone with him. But that left ten adults and two children and the Mexican bombs were soon finished and replaced with a large board of cheeses and hunks of home-made bread as they talked about Aldermaston. "We need more direct action. If we really want to stop the Bomb all this peaceful parading up and down once a year has got to develop into something that really hurts. It's no good just assembling outside an Aldermaston and walking away. We've got to pull the place to pieces. So some of us will get arrested. So? Isn't that a sign of how much they don't give a damn about our marches when no one is arrested?" ... "O.K., so thousands joined the march,

259

Members of Parliament, churchmen, intellectuals, trade unions, you name 'em we've got 'em, but we've still got the bloody Bomb. So the Unions will vote against the Bomb at the next Labour Party Conference. Is that going to change the Labour Party with Gaitskell and his mob in power?"... "Look, Castro did it the right way last year in Cuba, with guns. That's the only way you get things done . . . and the way they're building up this man Kennedy as the next American president. A man of the people! They must be joking. Haven't they seen his family?"... "There's no point in relying on any of them to change the world. It's *their* world, why should they change it?"... "To change the world you have to start with yourself. Change yourself. That's what communes are all about. Make your own world. Choose your own environment. Do your own thing."... "Sure they operate within the outside environment. But as the movement grows, as it has done in the States, then more and more communes will become self-supporting and independent. Communes will trade with communes, food for clothes, spare parts for services of all kinds. Maybe we'll have to go back, if you call it back, to small manageable units working with animals rather than machines. But who said big is beautiful except Mr. Big? We've got to break those chains of tradition that say this way and only this way is the way. There are other ways. Look at what they're doing in China, creating small steel works in their back yards."... "We could have a steel works in our bloody basement!"... "That's going to be my living exhibition!"... "What? I thought that was ear-marked for our bomb factory?"... "Ah well, there go my dreams of Chateau Lafitte!"

*   *   *   *

"What d'you think, Joe?"

Later that night as they lay, once again, on an undisturbed bed looking at the ceiling, Margaret turned and lifted herself up on one elbow.

"About what?"

"You know about what. The commune."

"What about it?"

Exasperated, she turned and took a cigarette from the pack on the bedside table.

"Will they accept us, that's what."

"Did we ask them to accept us?"

She inhaled deeply. It was going to be one of those nights.

"Well, not in so many words, but when they said those two actors might not be staying on if they got those jobs in Leeds it was sort of

260

hinted we might like to take their room and we didn't say no thanks, did we?"

"We didn't say yes please, either."

"True, but when they said they'd put it to the House Meeting next week we said O.K. *You* said O.K., right?"

"Maybe." He affected a cough as the cigarette smoke drifted over his head. "Why don't we wait till then eh?"

"All right. I'm not asking for any high-powered decision Joe. I only asked what you think."

"About what?"

"Oh Christ!" She jumped off the bed and walked to the window. It was a warm night, a reminder of summers gone and summer coming and the intermittent neon sign lit up her body through the nightdress. Our own private strip club he'd called it. They'd wanted Soho from the first and when the chance came for this room right on Cambridge Circus they took it without thinking that the lights would keep them awake. But there were things to do when they were awake and then they slept knowing that they, at least, would dream in colour.

Soho was where it all started and where it was going to finish. They both knew that. He turned to look at his own private strip club and felt nothing. Again.

He sat up. The breeze from the open window blew the cigarette smoke back into his face. He grimaced but didn't cough.

"Look," he struggled his arms into his dressing gown, "you want to talk?"

"That *was* the idea."

"O.K., but not just the commune?"

"There's something else?"

"You know there is."

"Aha. Now it's your turn."

"Want a cup of coffee?"

"With spoons?"

He looked at her and smiled.

"With spoons."

While he was at the stove making the coffee she stood for a few minutes at the window and then looked around absent-mindedly for something to put over her shoulders, decided on a shawl and went out to join him. They sat in two armchairs facing each other holding the hot mugs between their hands. He had nothing in front of him to move, tidy up or clear away. Only her.

"Look Mag. If you're looking at the commune as a way out of your problem, or our problem, you're making a mistake."

"Our problem? Which one?

"There's only one problem with us . . . us."

"A very penetrating analysis . . . comrade. And having arrived at that clear Marxist viewpoint, are you now going to place it in its wider perspective, like . . . er . . . 'us' in the peace movement, 'us' and trade unions, 'us' and . . ."

"Oh turn it up Mag. If we're going to talk let's talk sense."

"Well, that's what I was trying to say to you. 'The problem with us is us.' What sort of sense does that make?"

"All right." He put the mug of coffee on the floor by the side of the chair. "I just meant that everything about us is a problem. Is that going too far?"

"Everything?"

"Well, let's see. Number one, sex . . ."

"I see you keep your priorities right, anyway."

". . . number two, politics. Number three, work. Number four . . ." he searched in his mind for a category for the next one "well, us. Our future, if any. That's about it I suppose."

"Well, it'll do for a start." She took a sip of coffee. "Sex is certainly a problem, but don't you think it might arise from our arguments over the other things?"

"It might but I don't think so. Not if we're honest."

"Oh let's be honest by all means."

"Now don't get sarcastic just because I question your approach to sex."

"Is that what you're doing? Sorry, I hadn't realised. What *is* my approach to sex? . . . comrade . . . I'd like to know."

He really needed something in front of him that he could move around but in the absence of this he picked up his coffee and took a sip and, thinking, put it down on the other side of the armchair.

"I've thought about this . . ."

"Oh good, I am pleased!"

"Now, now. Take it easy. You use sex. Sometimes you use it as a bargaining . . . weapon, maybe. Sometimes you use it to show, or to establish, some sort of superiority. Not just physical superiority, but a real sexual, the female sex over the male sex, type of superiority. That seems to be very important to you."

"And to you it's not?"

"How do you mean?"

"How do I mean! Honestly, you men, you're so bloody innocent. For bloody generations you've been literally top dog when it comes to sex. You're there on top. You play around till you're good and ready then up you get. 'Mounting' d'you call it? Like the bloody Lone

Ranger. Hey ho Silver! Talk about ride a cock horse. And when you've worked yourself into a lather and can't control yourself you piss yourself into us like we're some sort of bed-pan, then lie there, flaked out, dead to the bloody world while the poor woman, who nine times out of ten hasn't felt a bloody thing except her nipples being twisted off and that futile bloody fumbling till he gets it in the right place like a drunk with the door-key . . . oh, no, Joe. That's not for me."

"Did I ever say it should be?"

"Joe, you never had a chance. And nobody ever will. I've had it that way in the past and never again."

"Mag. There is another way."

"Yes, I read about it in the *Kama Sutra* but I'm not a contortionist and if anybody really thinks I'd get any pleasure out of lying there with this guy's left big toe stuck up me, while he sticks his right toe up somebody else, his index fingers up two more women and his doings up some other lucky lady they must be out of their tiny Hindu mind."

Joe laughed and shook his head.

"Ay, Maggie, Maggie, we'll never get anywhere with this one, will we? We know bloody well I'm not talking about the position of your body, but the position you take with your mind. Nobody has to be top dog. Neither one of us has to do all the taking or all the giving. It could be give and take. I don't like those words anyway. There needn't be either giving or taking, just . . ." he spread his hands in an effort to explain ". . . loving?"

They were both quiet for a while, then she sighed and said "You're a nice guy, Joe. I know you believe it. Maybe with somebody else you could 'just love.' I don't know. It's a pity. You liked it enough, my way, at first didn't you?"

"At first!" He leaned back in his chair and stretched his arms and legs, looking at the ceiling. "At first it was a new world. It was like being used to a fortnight's holiday in Southend every year and suddenly going on a trip up the Congo or the Zambezi or somewhere like that . . ." he leaned forward, his eyes shining, "with great flocks of flamingos suddenly taking flight, and lions coming down to the water holes at dusk, and crocodiles flopping into the river as you go by in your canoe, and great curtains of fireflies in the clearings of the jungles that would make these fucking neon lights look like candles, and humming birds, and papayas and the juice of mangoes . . ."

"Hey, get your country right!"

He left his armchair and knelt by her, holding her legs and looking up into her eyes. "It wasn't just one country Mag, it was a world, a world of countries, a world of love."

She stroked his hair and remembered how the other day she had noticed the first grey hairs and had meant to tell him and had forgotten.

"So what happened?"

He turned round and picked up his mug of coffee and took a drink before returning to his armchair.

"I couldn't stand the mosquitos."

"Mosquitos?"

"And the snakes, and the scorpions, and all the other things they don't mention in the brochures . . . including the tourists."

She looked up at him.

"Joe, we've been through all that. You know we agreed that I don't belong to you or anybody else. You know you don't believe in private property."

"Property, no. But a few years lease maybe?"

"That's really what it's all about itsn't it Joe?"

He nodded, without looking at her.

"Well Joe, your lease has expired. All the other things you mentioned, politics, work, the future, are really unimportant aren't they? So that's it. The fireflies have gone out and we're left with the stinking Coca Cola sign going on and off all night."

He sipped his coffee, looking at her, saying nothing.

"Which leaves the commune. I know it's not the answer to our problem if we look at it simply as you and me joining them and trying to make a go of it. But I was thinking of it in a different way."

"You and Dave?"

"And you and Maeve?"

"Thanks very much. I'll make my own arrangements thank you."

"But she fancies you."

"Oh I know that. That became clear when she took me down to show me her ideas for the cellar."

"Oh?"

"Oh yes. A great subterranean cavern of 'living art' with, guess what, huge erect stalagmites rising from a floor covered with real pubic hair. Me? I was to be the central stalagmite, seven foot high, made of glass and illuminated from within, no less."

"Oh Christ, what did you say?"

"I told her the way I felt these days I would be better as a stalactite than a stalagmite and then told her that I first met Zee through her painting and what sort of things she painted, and about Robbie and all that."

"That must have encouraged her I'm sure."

"Well, I'll give her that. She said she'd like to meet Zee and see some of her work and it all finished up very matey, with me feeling like some sort of uncle."

"And will you?"

"Will I what?"

"Take her to see Zee?"

"I don't know. I said I would. But I'll have to ask Zee first. Anyway that's something else. But so far as the commune is concerned it's not on, not for me, anyway."

"I can see that and I'm sorry. I think I'll go, if they'll have me. What will you do, stay on here?"

"Might as well. Here, at least, my lease has not expired."

With a sigh she lifted herself out of the armchair, bent down to pick Joe's empty cup off the floor and looked down at him.

"Sad?"

He looked up at her and smiled.

"Sort of."

She smiled back and took the cups to the sink and washed them up. Then she walked through to the bedroom leaving him sitting in his chair.

"Hey!" she called to him from the bedroom.

"What?"

"That bloody Coca-Cola sign has gone out!"

"Oh Christ. Now we'll never get to sleep."

* * * *

"Joe! Joe Gold! What are you doing here?"

The stillness of the National Gallery's air-conditioned room especially built to house Leonardo da Vinci's 'Madonna of the Rocks' was broken by this sudden exclamation.

Heads were turned in hushed disapproval, eyebrows raised in shocked alarm, and Joe looked up to see Maeve, standing before him with arms outstretched in greeting, radiant with pleasure. He looked around at the other people frozen into attitudes of air-conditioned annoyance, put a finger to his lips to hush any further outburst and patted the leather seat beside him.

She giggled (still, after all this time!) and sat down. He bent his head to her ear and whispered, pointing to the infant Jesus in the painting, "You're quite right, it's the only prick in the Gallery. Ayayay!" He looked around the room. "What's such a nice young Jewish boychik doing in a place like this?"

"That's what I wanted to know," she whispered back noticing

how grey his hair was, curling round his ear.

"Let's go," he said.

On exaggerated tip-toes they went through the double doors and ran down the stairs two, three at a time until they burst out into the sunshine, holding their sides with laughter.

"Shall I be mother?" she asked when they had recovered, leaning against the stone balustrade.

"You put it so nicely," he replied, with a little bow, "how can I refuse?"

As they made their way across the great square towards the restaurant where she had asked that question three years ago Joe bought an evening newspaper. Taking up most of the front page was a photograph of a Buddhist monk sitting, in flames, on a pavement in Saigon, protesting the conduct of the war in Vietnam by turning himself into a living human sacrifice.

Subdued, their laughter soured by the smell of burning, they ordered tea and pastries and waited in silence until Maeve said "It's no good Joe. Life has got to go on even if it's only so that those of us who are still here can fight it. Isn't that right?"

"You're right Maeve," he smiled. "Somebody has to fight. It's like dear old Arnold Wesker says, 'You've got to care.' And every time I've carefully got myself into a state of not caring I see something like this poor bastard and I know I can't do it."

"You, not caring? I don't believe it. Where did you disappear to? What happened to you in all this time? What is it, nearly three years?"

"Just over, I imagine. It was Easter, or a couple of weeks after wasn't it, when you showed me your proposed subterranean palace of heavenly delights with me as the number one attraction, or should I say erection? Boy, did you have me wrong!"

"I had myself wrong too Joe." He noticed she was no longer a Noel Coward gipsy but was dressed in a roll-neck sweater with her hair tied behind in a pony tail.

"And now?"

"Now I'm O.K. I'm teaching now, and painting and going to exhibitions ..." She reached across the table to hold his hand, "... and meeting old friends."

The tea came, with the cakes. Here at least there was no change. The same pallid pastry, the same obscene eclairs, and tarts so tired they could not contain themselves.

They looked at each other and burst out laughing again.

"Yes, yes!" he said, "don't ask. Be mother. Pour already!"

"Sugar?"

"Please. Two." As he stirred he looked down into his cup and asked, "Are you still . . . at the . . ."

"Commune? No chance. When your Margaret came I went. Oh, some of them wanted to make a thing of it at the House Meeting but honestly, what was the point? In the first place it was Dave's house, nobody'd ever done anything about turning it into a co-op so what Dave said, went. And anyway I didn't fancy staying under those conditions so I went, too. Best thing that ever happened to me."

"That was quite a painting."

She burst into another fit of laughter, spilling her tea. When she recovered she explained.

"That painting. I had my own back. On the last night, before I left, I crept in to the common room when they were all asleep and repainted our Dave."

"Re-painted? You mean . . . ?"

She was now laughing so much she had to get up and walk around, holding her sides. "Yes, I did."

"But how did you know what . . . I mean . . ."

Wiping the tears from her eyes she sat down again and leaned over to whisper.

"I've been around you know."

"I'm sure you have, but . . ."

"Oh Joe . . ." the laughing tears were turning to real tears now as she began to cry.

"What is it?"

"I've just had a horrible thought."

"What?"

"I do hope you don't have any birthmarks, or moles or what have you, or any sort of distinguishing mark. I did so want Margaret to think . . . have you?"

He signalled the waiter for the bill.

"I don't think so," he said, "why don't we go and see?"

*   *   *   *

"Not a mark, not a mole. Beautiful. Obviously the work of an expert . . . what do you call 'em, circumciser?"

"A mole."

"A what? You're kidding. Seriously." She sat up and let it drop back on his thigh. It had been good. After all this time. True she was enough to make anybody good. But the timing had been right, the tenderness had been there, the loving.

She levered her body up alongside his and her nose on his, her great

267

eyes wide, asked again.

"Seriously. A mole?"

"Spelt more like mohel . . . m-o-h-e-l . . . but you don't pronounce the 'h'. So it's mole, right?"

She bent down again over his body and held it up to examine more closely.

"You know," she said, "it *looks* like a mole."

"Thanks for nothing."

"Well, *now* it does. You look."

He lifted his head, saw the poor little thing, limp in her hands as she pointed it now this way, now that, like a mole. He laughed. Nice not to have to try to look like a giraffe when you're only a mole.

"A definite mole," he said.

"From now on," she said, "I'll call him Moley."

From now on. That sounded like a long time.

"I am a mole and I live in a hole." Like a child with a new toy. He looked at her and tried to stop feeling like an uncle. He must be nearly twice her age. So?

She put down her toy and snuggled up to him. "Is that what you were doing these last three years?"

"What?" he asked, surprised.

"Being a mole in a hole."

He thought about it. "A little, maybe," he replied.

"Did you miss her?"

"Margaret?"

She nodded.

"At first."

"What did you do?"

"Oh I drifted a bit." A bit? Like drifting to the North Pole. The waves, the waves. And the bloody cold.

"And?"

"I ended up in the North, near Durham. A couple of my old mates from the Worker were up there bringing out a local paper. I joined them for a while but it didn't work. They had left the Party but couldn't shake the jargon. One day I heard myself say "let's not kid ourselves, comrades" and decided it was time I left. Then I met another of my old mates and did some work with him on the New Left Review . . ."

"What is that?"

"What an ignorant child you are. Some of my dear old comrades who left about the same time as I did decided to fight back and started a paper called the New Reasoner. That became the New Left Review and I wrote one or two things for it but it was a dream.

268

Change the Party! It's easier to change the world. In fact that's what's happening. The whole world is changing but the Party carries on in the same way as if nothing ever happened. Khrushchev told them they'd been lying and cheating and murdering for years and still they didn't change."

"You've changed." She had the sort of breasts that bobbed up and down when she changed her position, as if they were at the end of a string.

"How?"

She ran her hand all down the side of his body, right down to his feet. "Your feet are nicer," she said.

"Eh?"

"That's the first thing I remember about you. One evening after marching from Reading was it? — you sat down and took your socks off and your poor feet were all red and blistered. They're much nicer now."

He sat up and looked at his feet next to hers. "That's what I like about you," he said.

"What?"

"Here we are in the middle of this high-powered discussion on the fallibility of the Communist Movement and you tell me I've got nice feet."

"It wasn't that high-powered."

"True," he smiled, ruefully.

"And your feet are nice."

"True again."

"Did she like them?"

"Margaret? I don't know. She never said."

"Do you ever see her?"

"Not since she went to Dave. You ever hear from Dave?"

"Not for some time. I heard the commune broke up and Dave and Margaret went off with Fred and Stan and set up some Anarchist place in South London."

"Anarchist? I thought Dave was a Trotskyist."

"Was he? I could never tell. Every time he joined one group they seemed to split up and form another half a dozen, all fighting each other."

"And Margaret. Well, well. I'd never have believed it."

"Oh she was a tough cookie your Margaret."

"True again."

"But she'd better watch out with that Fred. And Stan, too. I know you thought they were joking when they talked about using that cellar for a bomb factory, but they weren't joking. They're really serious guys."

"But bombs?"

"Why not?"

"Hell, you don't change anything with bombs. Not here anyway."

"So what do you change with marches and demonstrations? All you get is red feet."

"Funny girl. We have a Labour Movement here. We can do things through the Trade Unions . . ."

"Like what? Remember the way we talked about the Ban the Bomb Resolution that the Transport & General Union passed that was going to change the policy of the Labour Party? Nothing changed did it? Fred said that was the trouble with the Labour Movement, it's all chained to its tradition. The C.P., the Unions, the Labour Party, they're all links in the chain that preserves the status quo and keeps the workers happy thinking they've got some sort of voice somewhere."

"And all you need is one big bomb to blow the whole lot up, workers and all!"

"Something like that."

"Well, that would change things all right, I'll give you that!"

"Not me silly, Fred. I'm happy with things as they are." She stretched out alongside him her fingers reaching along his thighs. Surprised, he felt himself getting hard again. "You know the trouble with you?"

"Trouble? Not my feet again."

She sat up quickly, bobbing away. He was definitely hardening up. Again!

"No silly. I'll tell you. All this time you've been hibernating up North or wherever, the world has been changing and you haven't even noticed it. It's all very well you talking about the Party, but you're just as bad. I bet you've never even heard of Charlie Parker?"

"He plays centre forward for Arsenal, doesn't he?"

"What an ignorant man you are," she mimicked. "He's the greatest Jazz musician of all time."

"That's a contradiction in terms."

"What is?"

"Jazz and musician. It's a common misconception however. Because Jazz is often performed on musical instruments people have jumped to the conclusion it's music. It's like making love."

"How?"

"The fact that it is often performed on a bed might lead you to the conclusion it's the same as sleeping, but we know better."

Kneeling astride his chest she could not see what was happening behind her but as she leaned back it became clear to her.

"I am a mole and I live in a hole."

"Come home Moley, all is forgiven."

*　　*　　*　　*

Two weeks later an unexpected phone call from Sam, his sister Hetty's husband, took Joe up to Mayfair. As he sat in the smart reception office of the advertising agency now partly owned by Sam he wondered what the reason was for the sudden call and the mysterious way Sam had parried his questions on the telephone, saying that there were no personal problems involved but he'd rather not talk about it on the phone.

"Joe. Thanks for coming."

Sam was fatter than he remembered, well dressed, almost well groomed. His dark, striped suit had wide lapels and the silk tie was colourful but not loud. His hair was longer, both at the back and sides, than when he and Joe had last met maybe five years ago but there was still a genuine warmth in his handshake and in the way he guided Joe through the thick glass doors on to the street.

"I see you got your name on the door." Joe pretended to polish the metal name-plate by breathing on it and rubbing it with the elbow of his jacket. "Stainless steel. That should last a while."

"Aluminium actually, and it'll only last till I can get rid of all the other names."

"They look impressive."

"They impress everybody but the client. But enough about them. How've you been keeping Joe?"

"Fair. It's a tough world outside you know."

"It's tougher inside. Believe it or not. Let's go in here." Sam turned down a flight of tiled stairs into a dimly lit club where he was clearly well known and, after signing a book, led the way to a corner table where a pin-striped head waiter held chairs out for them and enquired if they wanted a drink.

"Punt e Mes," said Sam, "You, Joe?"

"What's that?"

"Italian drink. Tastes rather like Campari, only worse."

"Then why?"

"I feel I am doing myself good. Try it? Two Punt e Mes. Look Joe let's get the big decision over first, like what we're going to eat and drink, then we can get down to business."

The big decisions taken, and the waiter despstched, Sam got down to business.

"Mosley's back."

"Yes, I heard something about it last year. Didn't he try to have a big rally in Trafalgar Square and got sent off with a flea in his ear?"

"Something like that. Were you there?"

"No. I was up North at the time but I heard about it."

"Aha. I thought I might have seen you there."

"You mean to say you were there?"

"Sure. He doesn't belong just to you, Joe."

"You can have him. What actually happened?"

"I'll come to that in a minute. You know the same thing happened to Colin Jordan a few weeks earlier?"

"The neo-nazi?"

"Why neo? He's a Nazi. Wears Nazi uniform, gives the Nazi salute, picture of Hitler in his office, runs an outfit called the National Socialist Movement. What more do you want? Anyway, the same thing happened to him. Meeting broken up. A lot of his bully-boys found reception committees waiting for them on their way home. They won't be in any great hurry to attend any more rallies in the near future."

"Glad to hear it Sam. What's all this to do with me, or you for that matter?"

Sam waited for the waiter to serve the hors d'oeuvres before replying.

"When we heard these two meetings were being organised the Jewish community was amazed. Here we were, just finished a war against Fascism and Nazism in which millions of people were killed and suddenly our Government was allowing old friends of Hitler and Mussolini and people who openly say 'Hitler was right' to hold meetings attempting to start the whole Nazi thing going again. It was crazy. Of course the Community leaders protested, the Board of Deputies of British Jews, the Association of Jewish Ex-service Men, the Chief Rabbi, they all protested but got nowhere. Apparently we were no longer in the business of fighting Fascism, and it was now O.K. for those bastards to start up in business again."

"Surprise, surprise."

"O.K., we should have known. But after those years of listening to politicians talking about destroying the evils of Nazism, and all those lives that had been sacrificed doing just that, we believed it was true. It seems we were wrong. So some of us got together and decided that if the Government wouldn't stop it we would."

"Who's 'us'?"

"A few friends. Twenty or thirty. All Jewish boys. Ex-service mostly. A few tough nuts. A few professional people. Lawyers and so on. A few with special skills. And a lot of contacts. We can rustle up three or four hundred boys at twenty-four hours notice for special occasions."

"Like Trafalgar Square meetings?"

"Right."

"Sounds interesting. What d'you want with me?"

"We need special skills. Special contacts. Above all we need people we can trust."

"In what way?"

"Well, like I said, the law says it's O.K. for mass murderers to set up shop once again. We say it's not O.K. So occasionally we may have to come in conflict with the law, right?"

"Understood."

"So we have to be able to vouch for everybody who comes in with us." Sam paused for a moment and then, as the waiter approached, he said, "And I vouched for you, Joe."

There was silence as the plates were cleared, the main dish served and the wine poured. Then Joe exploded.

"Vouched for me!" he exclaimed. "You've got a nerve. What do you want from me?"

"Take it easy Joe. This wine has a very delicate bouquet, it can't stand too highly charged an atmosphere." He sipped it lovingly and continued. "All I said was I vouched for you. That means I think you're one hundred percent with us in our cause, right?" He looked at Joe.

"Carry on."

"And you won't go running to the police to tell them what we're doing, right?"

"And that is?"

"One moment. The third reason for coming to you is that I believe you are the person best qualified to help us get what we want. Now here is what it's all about." Sam looked around and lowered his voice so that Joe had to bend his head towards him to hear.

"We have people inside all these organisations. Mosley's, Jordan's, all of them. Some of them are our people that we trained to go in, worked out a proper cover for, sometimes to the extent of providing duplicate jobs, homes and completely documented lives. It's been professionally done, believe me." Joe nodded and said nothing. "Others are their own people who are prepared to give us information if we pay for it. Some are reliable, some not, but on the whole we have a pretty good picture of what is being discussed and what is being planned in all these organisations. Now we act on this information in different ways. If they're doing anything blatantly illegal we tip off the police. If the police move in, fine, if they don't, we do. Either by tipping off the press or by taking remedial action ourselves."

"Remedial action. What's that?"

"Whatever we decide is necessary."

"And now?"

"Now we're on to something quite exciting. Our information is that some of the Nazis here are setting up an illegal para-military organisation, guns, bombs, uniforms, the lot. Money is coming to them, and this may be no surprise to you, Joe, from South Africa and Rhodesia, and they're setting up arms caches in five different parts of the country and have instructed their members to join the Territorial Army and get their weapons training free of charge by courtesy of Her Majesty's Government. Now the big thing is that we have learned that some time this year they're going to have a big camp at a country estate that's owned by one of their friends out in the country, and some of the European Nazis have been invited and, what is really interesting, one of the old-time top Nazis who's been hiding in the Argentine since the end of the war."

"Who?"

"We don't know yet except he was a top man in the SS and the talk among the British Nazis is that he's got things set up nicely in South America and has been in touch with Europe waiting till he thought the time was right to establish contact here."

"And now the time is right?"

"Well apparently he is greatly encouraged by the fact that the British Government has allowed some Nazis to set up legally here and gave them permission to have a meeting in Trafalgar Square. The fact that the meeting was broken up he doesn't regard as a problem. That's only a question of money and organisation they think. The money seems to be there. The purpose of this camp is to start building the organisation."

"Fascinating." Joe took a sip of his wine. "The bouquet seems fine to me," he said, "what do you want me to do?"

"Well this is one of those occasions when we put the police in the picture and we don't think they're going to do anything about it."

"Bastards."

"Well, not necessarily Joe. Bear in mind they've got their own people in these organisations. Quite often they'd rather just sit tight and watch what's going on, building up their files, maybe thinking they'll act when the time is right from their point of view. The trouble is it might be too late. From our point of view. Governments can change. Policies can change. Crises can develop. Before we know it we could find a strong, well-organised and financed Nazi movement in action in Britain, putting up candidates in elections, cashing in on unrest, perhaps over coloured immigration or unemployment, or both, and then it becomes more difficult. Not impossible, just more difficult. Better to smash them early. So . . ." he finished his glass of wine and signalled to the waiter to re-fill the glasses. "So we want to do two things. First we want to get the full story of this camp splashed all over the press, pictures, the inside story, everything. Secondly we want to get hold of this SS man and put him out of action. Permanently."

"Permanently?" Joe looked up, surprised. Sam nodded and looked around again, dropping his voice still lower. "One of two ways. The Israelis could be interested in him. Ever since the Eichmann trial the top Nazi brass have been lying low and this might be an opportunity for them. On the other hand they wouldn't be keen to be involved in any snatching on British territory. I imagine they'd prefer to catch him on the way here or on the way out but not here. Our problem is we don't know, and are not likely to know, how and where and when he's actually arriving. And if we did find out and we let the Israelis know about it they might want to jump in beforehand and that could bugger up the whole thing."

"You said there were two ways. What's the other way?"

Sam looked at him and Joe saw this was no advertising meeting with clients. This was serious. "He'll just have to disappear Joe. That's not your department. Coffee?"

"Please. So what's my department?"

"Well I was talking to Zee a little while ago . . ." he held up his hand to stop Joe's question, ". . . don't worry, she knows nothing about this. Nobody does. She doesn't even know I'm seeing you. But she did mention, in passing, that you had, or used to have, some very good contacts at top level in Fleet Street. Now we have one or two friends there as well, but in this case we think it'd be better for it not to come through us. Specially if we're involved in operation number two. We need somebody in between, a first class cut-off that is professional enough to set the thing up based on our information and carry the thing through and yet know nothing, and I mean nothing Joe, about what happens to this bastard if any questions are asked."

"Will questions be asked?"

"Could be. Kidnapping is still highly illegal in this country. O.K., so officially nobody's going to even admit the guy was here but they're going to be a bit cross if he just disappears off the face of the earth. It's untidy. It won't look good in their reports. So there could be questions and who better to question than the guy who exposed the whole thing to the press? He must know something, they'll figure."

"And when they find out he doesn't?"

"They'll be disappointed Joe. Very disappointed. Ever been involved with the Special Branch?"

Joe smiled and waited till the waiter had poured their coffee.

"Curiously enough, never. You see, believe it or not, the Party is always very careful to keep well within the law. Oh, people get arrested now and then for getting a big stroppy at demonstrations, but apart from that it's all very legal and above board. I don't think any C.P. leader has been arrested since the General Strike. Maybe that's the trouble."

They were both silent for a while, drinking their coffee from delicate cups.

"You say you saw Zee?" Joe asked.

"About two weeks ago. With your little Robbie. They were round at your Ma's place when Hetty and I popped in."

"How was she?"

"Fine, fine. Getting older, like all of us. Your boy is growing up. He must be what, getting on for thirteen?"

"Right. He's a bright kid. Wants to be a lawyer already."

"What else? D'you see him much?"

"Oh, every month or so. I go over there and Zee makes a meal. All very civilised. Sometimes I take him out."

"Do you ever think . . . well, it's none of my business really . . . but would you . . .?"

"Get together again? What's the point? I fucked that up properly a long time ago and Zee has her own life now. She's doing well as a designer, makes good money, has a nice place, is more Jewish than the Chief Rabbi . . . who needs me there? No, I still have a drawing she did of herself when we first met and it's up on my wall and I look at it and know it was good and we were both lucky to have had it like it was for a while. But that's all in the past. How's the old girl?"

Sam laughed and signalled for the bill.

"Your mother never changes. When we were there that time we saw Zee she insisted on giving us practically a whole *strudel* she'd made that morning. I ask you, who needs it? Hetty wanted Zee to take it but she already had a whole bottle of chicken soup! How she was going to get it home I don't know. Why don't you go over and see her some time Joe?"

"Me? You must be joking. She hasn't forgiven me because I told her I won't go to Robbie's *Barmitzvah*. I told her I went to the circumcision and that was enough for me. *Barmitzvahs* already!"

Sam shook his head. "Ayay. You're an obstinate lot you Golds. What would it cost you to go to your own son's *Barmitzvah*? Anyway," he looked at his watch, "that's your business, but if there's anything I can do to help at any time, you know, with Zee, or the old girl, let me know eh?"

"Sure Sam. Thanks. Actually what we talked about is already a big help. It's good to know you can bloody do something positive that's actually going to be worth while for a change. Know what I mean?"

Sam signed the bill that was discreetly put before him. "Joe, at four o'clock this afternoon I shall be making a presentation to one of our top clients. It's good stuff and it will help to put him right in the leading position in the market and make him another fortune. I happen to know he is a confirmed life-long anti semite and hates my guts but comes to us because we give him the best advertising he's ever had. So I know what you mean Joe. I take it from what you just said that you'll be prepared to come in on this little . . . venture . . . with us, right?"

Joe nodded.

"Good. I'll report back and we'll fix a meeting, probably in somewhat less glamorous but more suitable surroundings in a week or so and we'll take it from there. Shall we go?"

*   *   *   *

The black Rover stopped at the wrought iron gateway as two men came out of the Lodge and walked towards the gates. At a signal from the man next to the driver they swung the gates open and allowed the car through as, simultaneously, four men appeared from behind trees on the opposite side of the road and walked towards the gates. After talking to the driver of the Rover for a minute they looked down the road at the sound of another approaching car. This one, a white Mercedes, also swung into the drive and stopped only momentarily at the open gates for two of the four men to get in, one in the front, one in the back. The Mercedes then proceeded up the drive following the Rover and the gates were closed. The four remaining men returned to the Lodge house.

All along the top of the ten-foot high brick wall, which extended right round the estate, the autumn leaves of the huge oaks continued the mellow tones of the bricks into the deep greens of the firs that lined the gravel road until they gave way to the rhododendrons and azaleas of the shrubbery that bordered the circular driveway in front of the house. A big ugly house as only the Victorians knew how to build, intended to impress with its solidness if not its beauty.

As the Rover came into view at the approach to the house Joe turned and whispered "Here they come." His companion, looking as if he had spent all his life in the branches of trees and not just the last six hours, lifted the camera to his weather-wrinkled face and checked the adjustment of the telephoto lens. "Which one?" he asked.

"Don't know" Joe replied, studying the second car through his binoculars. "Better get both. No, wait." He watched the Rover go past the stone steps that led to the front porch. As it stopped all its doors opened and four men jumped out and ran back to the Mercedes. "He's in the Merc. Might have known." His companion was already clicking away as the Mercedes drew up slowly and two figures came out of the house and ran down the steps. The men from the Rover were now on all sides of the Mercedes, one opening the back door, the others looking around in all directions.

"Quite an operation," muttered the photographer. "Reminds me of Nuremberg."

"That's him" whispered Joe excitedly as a short figure got out of the Mercedes and was warmly greeted by both the two men who had come down the steps.

"Got him?" Joe asked.

"Providing I remembered to put some film in the camera." He was still clicking away. Joe grinned. Good old Herbie. Best bloody photographer in the Street. If anybody could get this photo he could. All night they had sat silently together in the undergrowth, having selected this vantage point before nightfall. They had been let in through a side gate just before dawn on the day before. When Herbie saw the uniformed, jackbooted 'storm trooper' beckoning them in from behind the gate he nearly had a fit, and automatically reached for his camera.

"No photos," said Joe, "he's one of ours."

The 'storm-trooper' led them to a copse of larch trees at the edge of a clearing and pointed to the group of tents arranged in a semi-circle around a raised platform. To the side of the platform was a flag pole from which a red flag with a white circle was hanging. A breeze fluttered the flag and they saw the Nazi swastika black in the white circle.

"Fucking bastards" muttered Herbie.

"I'm going to leave you here," said their guide. "They'll be getting up soon. Reveille, trumpets, ablutions and all that. Then there'll be a bit of marching around and after that some weapon practice."

"That's what we want," said Joe. "What weapons. Where?"

"Rifles, light machine guns, grenades. That'll all be over there." He pointed to a space beyond the tents where the first rays of sun picked out a number of targets set up in a row. A trumpet sounded and suddenly there were signs of activity around the tents.

"Must go. The house is right back there." He pointed directly behind them through the copse. "About half a mile. There's plenty of cover but watch out just before dark and just after dawn. That's patrol practice. They may come through here. The rest of the time they're too busy marching up and down playing soldiers. But they've got some nasty specimens among them so watch out. If they catch you there's nothing I can do."

He was gone, his jackboots glistening in the early dew.

"Brave fellow," said Herbie.

"Takes all sorts."

"It certainly does," sighed Herbie, carefully taking his equipment from a haversack that was slung round his shoulder and focussing first on the tents and then swinging round to the target area. "The parade ground and the tents are O.K. but we're going to have to get a bit nearer to that firing range or whatever it is if we want any decent pictures."

Joe had taken out a pair of binoculars from his rucksack and surveyed the area at the same time as Herbie, agreeing with his comments. "Why don't we get what we can from here when things start happening, then move over there and see how close we can get before they start shooting. Then we'll move back nearer the house and find a good spot before night falls so that we'll be all ready for the big boy first thing in the morning?"

"Sounds fine to me," said Herbie. "You're writing this piece Joe, just tell me exactly what you want and I'll get what I can. Right?"

"Fine Herbie."

When Joe had taken the proposition to his contacts in Fleet Street that was the way he had wanted it. He would do the story and Herbie would do the pictures. The full picture-story would be an exclusive for one of the top circulation Sunday papers and a general follow-up would go out nationally through the News Agency. None of them knew anything about the SS man except Herbie and he'd only been told by Joe as they drove out from London. No details. Just 'some important Nazi from abroad.' There'd be a special deal on that one with the negatives going to Joe and no talking to the press about it until Joe was ready. Herbie raised his eyebrows but grunted his agreement. He'd been on odd assignments like that before and it was none of his business who did what with the photos so long as the money was right. And it was.

Now sharp little sounds of command could be heard from the tents and about forty men and youths, all dressed in brown uniforms with black boots and Nazi armbands formed up and stood to attention in front of the platform as a jeep emerged from the direction of the house. "Well, well, well, don't they look smart!" said Joe, watching the jeep through his binoculars as it slowed down to a halt before the platform. "Get as much as you can of this lot Herb, they're Her Majesty's Herrenvolk. They have a photo of the Queen on one wall and one of Hitler on the other."

"She'll be pleased," said Herbie, starting to click as the three men climbed out of the jeep and on to the platform.

At another bark of command the men and boys threw their arms up in the Nazi salute and the three men on the platform did the same. Click! Then 'the leader' stepped forward, resplendent in a khaki safari jacket, Sam Browne belt, breeches tucked into jackboots and a red, white and black Nazi armband, and started to address the group. Click! Neither Joe nor Herbie could hear what was being said. But it seemed to hold everybody's attention except the other two men on the platform, who had probably heard it all before, and were looking around impatiently. Click! "That's a good one," said Herbie. "I've just got the fat one picking his nose. D'you really rate these guys Joe? I mean are they a danger to anybody or just a bunch of layabouts who like dressing up in uniform?"

"Hard to say Herb. You couldn't have found a bigger bunch of scruffs and perverts than Hitler, Goering, Goebbels, Himmler and all the rest. But they got the financial backing from the big money boys in Germany and they were able to put on a show. Uniforms. rallies, banners, pogroms . . . there's no business like show business Herbie. You should know. You took some of the best pix of Nuremberg ever published. So, if they get the financial backing these boys could make it if the economic situation were to change. My guess is this is what all this is about. They're putting on a show for the big guy tomorrow. If he approves the money will be there."

"You reckon there's enough money available?"

"Who knows Herbie? A lot of money disappeared after the war mate. Switzerland . . . Argentina . . . your guess is as good as mine. But let's face it, it's not only old Nazi money we're talking about. There's plenty of brand new lolly waiting to be poured into any set-up that can crush the Communists and the unions. Money talks, Herbie. If there's enough of it, it can do anything."

"Even buy negatives," Herbie cracked.

For an hour they stayed in position and then moved back into the copse and made their way through the trees towards the target area. As they improved their position the full extent of the preparations became visible and it seemed clear that some sort of a show was going to be put on. After a while the three men left in the jeep and the group was split up under the command of a few with obvious military experience who went through exercises in the use of machine guns and grenades while Herbie clicked away, cursing and blaspheming all the while, and Joe made notes after peering through his binoculars. Towards evening they moved further back into the woods towards the house and found a spot where they could eat some of the food they had brought with them. Then they made their way towards the house and found a perfect vantage point in some low branches of a tree which Herb judged would enable him to get the best photos of people coming and going. Satisfied with their day's work they moved back into the woods a little and, dividing the night into watches, settled down till the morning.

As the sun rose behind the house a thin wisp of smoke curling up from one of the chimneys warned them that somebody was up early. Cautiously they climbed into their perch and ate their breakfast. Joe looked at his watch. "He should be here around ten," he said.

"You seem to have pretty good information about all these bastards Joe, how come?"

"Weren't you ever a boy scout Herb?"

"Eh?"

"Be prepared, right?"

"So?"

"So get your camera ready. I could be wrong."

But he wasn't. His information was good and just before ten the two cars turned into the drive and Herbie started clicking.

"Ten pictures, right?" Joe looked across at Herbie after the party had gone into the house.

"Who's counting?" Herbie grinned.

"I am," Joe grinned back.

Later they moved back into the woods and took up their position again just in time to see two jeeps arrive at the target area. The first with the British Nazi leader, the SS man and another man in flannels and a sports jacket who Joe could not identify. In the second jeep were crowded the men Joe had called Laughing Boy and Fatso and three other men in uniforms of different colours and with different insignia on their armbands. "Foreigners," Joe commented. "I think France, Belgium, Italy." Click! Click! The visitors were given seats and the show commenced, as on the previous day, but this time with more precision, more barked commands, everything at the double.

"They're working hard for their money," Herbie said, "reckon they'll get it?"

"He's the one that who decide that."

"You know Joe, these guys look nothing without their uniforms. This one looks like a middle-aged bank clerk waiting for retirement."

Joe peered at the face through his binoculars trying to recognise the features but there was nothing he could fix on. Anyway it was twenty years since this one was last in uniform strutting around the world. Now he looked an old man. Maybe over sixty, with a healthy, bronzed, but wrinkled face. Gold-rimmed spectacles. Walked with a slight limp. Neat grey suit more or less in current fashion. How the hell were they going to grab him? And where? Here? Too dangerous. Too many of those bastards around. And guns. No, it'd have to be outside, on the way back, perhaps when the Nazis were a bit over-confident after their successful operation.

Which was exactly the way it was done, as Sam described it to Joe two days later.

"I wasn't there myself but it all seems to have gone like a dream. What helped most was that, for some reason or other, they had decided that they shouldn't be in the Mercedes with the Colonel. Security maybe, in case they were intercepted by the police. After all their guest is still," ... he hesitated, "or was, a war criminal wanted by five countries. So they put their strong arm men in the Rover and drove ahead in front, not behind, to show the Colonel's driver the way. Which was their second big mistake. We knew we had to do this quickly and as soon as possible after he left the estate, before they got into any traffic. We went over every possible route back and reckoned that only one was likely. Then we discovered the ideal spot. There is a little hill after you go through the village and we experimented and found out that when one car went over the brow of the hill there would be a few minutes when he wouldn't be able to see a car behind him till it reached the crest of the hill. A gate in a field just before the top of the hill provided a place to hide and we had two cars waiting in that field. The first a quick get-away car and the second a white Mercedes. Don't ask how we knew Joe, we just knew. You did your job properly. We did ours. O.K.? Anyway when their Rover passed the gate and went over the hill our first car drove out and turned down the hill blocking the Colonel's car. At the same time our Mercedes drove out and over the hill and kept on steadily following the Rover till they got to the next village and then smartly turned off and kept going like mad. God knows what those toe-rags in the Rover thought but there was no chance they could catch the Merc. Don't even know if they tried. Meanwhile our boys in the get-away car pulled out their home-made 'interpol' badges and, in perfect German, told that Nazi bastard they were arresting him for killing five hundred Jews in 1944, showing him the Extradition Warrent and explaining that he would have the benefit of being tried in an English court! The facts were so genuine and the bastard knew he was guilty, and everything looked so bona fide, that he went quietly without any trouble. I imagine the idea of getting the benefit of British justice may have appealed to him as well. Anyway it was all over in five minutes and there he was, with his driver, handcuffed, in the back of the car, while one of our boys followed behind in their Merc."

"Fantastic," said Joe. "What a story that'll make."

"Afraid not my friend. So far as anybody else knows that guy was never in England. In fact nobody even knows what happened to him after the war. There are stories that he turned up in Argentina but nobody really knows. He just disappeared. That was *his* story. Now it's true. O.K.?"

Joe shook his head. "And these pictures?" He looked at Herbie's photographs spread out before him. Beautiful. The SS Colonel being greeted at the steps of the house, shaking hands with the British Nazis, going up the steps, turning to look at the grand setting, looking directly at the camera, arriving at the target area, watching the machine gun practice, recoiling a little from a grenade explosion, laughing with the man in the sports jacket, congratulating the British Nazis, talking earnestly with the British and foreign Nazi chiefs, getting back in the jeep. Great photos.

Sam gathered them together and carefully checked them with the negatives. "You sure this is the lot Joe?"

"I'm sure. I counted them."

"Good. We'll put them in the files."

"Not going to use any of them? What shall I tell Herbie?"

"Tell him he's expensive. But if we ever want to use them we'll pay him double. Fair?"

Joe shrugged. "Seems fair enough to me Sam. But it's not just the money. Herbie hates Nazis as much as you do, you know. It's not only Jews that are concerned with this fight Sam."

Sam sighed. "I know that Joe. But we have a vested interest in it. For us it's a question of survival. And let's face it, politics change, like I said before. People always used to say what a perfect English gentleman Neville Chamberlain was. You used to say what a great fighter against Fascism Stalin was. But for their own reasons they both did a deal with Hitler. We can't do deals. And we can't rely on people who might do deals. There's plenty of opportunities for everybody to join in. The blacks will have to get organised here soon. And the left. Don't worry Joe, this little adventure is not the end of the struggle. It's going to hot up we reckon, and we're not always going to have it as easy as the last few days."

*   *   *   *

"Man, you're like a Chelsea Pensioner still fighting the Crimean War."

Joe looked at the young man who had made the comment, lying back on the cushions, holding the reefer up in the air at arm's length as he inhaled. His long blonde hair fell back over the shoulders of his embroidered shirt and one blue-jeaned leg was curled under the other, the edges of the jeans fraying over a bare foot.

"Oh I dig those Pensioners." The girl in the T-shirt walked over and took the cigarette from the outstretched hand. She inhaled deeply wandering round the room, stopping before a poster on the wall. *Che lives!* "Those red coats. That red." She wheeled round gracefully as if practising a ballet step and offered the cigarette to Joe.

"No thanks Maeve. I've got to go."

She smiled sadly. "Will I see you tomorrow?"

"Warhol at the Tate," he reminded her.

"Arsehole at the tit," sung the young man.

"He could be right," Joe smiled at her.

"He couldn't be right if he tried," Maeve shook her head.

"I can't even try." The young man looked up at his hand in faint surprise to see the cigarette was no longer there.

"*Tant pis!*"

"Oh yes I can." He waved his hand at Joe. "Ciao man. Keep socking it to them."

Joe closed the door and went down the stairs.

"It's all balls!"
As they stood in front of the new Warhol Joe exploded.
"Joe you don't understand."
"Understand? I understand that this thing is a silk-screen printed
reproduction of the same bloody stock photograph of Chairman Mao
that appears on the front of his Little Red Book! And if you call that
art you're mad."
"But Joe there are four of them in the painting. All different.
Don't you see how they show different aspects of Mao's thought?"
"What d'you mean 'painting'? They're four different coloured
prints, that's all. Any tuppenny ha'penny printer could do that. As
for different aspects of Mao's thought I defy you to tell me one single
thought you can identify. The only thought I see is that con-artist
Warhol thinking how much he can screw out of the nit-wits who run
this gallery. Your friend was right. Arsehole at the Tit. I'm going."
Maeve grabbed him by the arm as he turned to go. "O.K. O.K.
But I want to see the Lichtenstein painting before I go."
"Oh come on. I'll buy you a Beano Comic at the station. You'll get
fifty Lichtensteins in there."

"I must say these drawings have a certain . . . panache." As the
Tube train rushed them through the tunnels of London's
underground Maeve flipped through the pages of 'Beano'.
"Panache my eye," replied Joe. "Bed-panache more likely.
Honestly you're so up to the eyebrows in dope that you wouldn't
even recognise the Emperor let alone his new clothes. And you kid
yourselves you're casting off the shackles of the old world, liberating
your minds, or your ego or whatever. None of you realise that you're
being taken for the biggest load of suckers by the commercial boys."
"Oh come off it Joe, people like Warhol and Lichtenstein, the
whole modern movement, is taking the piss out of the commercial
world. Even at your valuation, which I don't accept, they are
producing crap and the commercial world is lapping it up."
"I once heard Tommy Jackson, an old time Marxist intellectual,
say the same thing about Picasso. Comrade Picasso, he explained,
fooled the whole bourgeois culture world by producing this artistic
rubbish and forcing the capitalist art world to accept it as the work of
genius. Picasso, he explained, was laughing all the way to the bank.
The truth was of course, just the opposite. Here was this great

painter, who was also a Communist, turning out mountains of junk and every bit of junk he painted was snapped up at ridiculous prices so that, after Guernica, the great man said absolutely nothing about Fascism, about the Bomb, about Korea, or exploitation and poverty, and particularly about Communism. It was like Karl Marx spending his life writing porno paper-backs. If ever a man was totally, one hundred percent corrupted by the big money that was Comrade Picasso. Yuch!"

"And you're saying that Warhol and the others are corrupted too?"

"I wouldn't give 'em that much credit. Picasso at least had been a great artist. The guy could paint. And he had shown some sort of social conscience by becoming a Communist. But these guys? They were born corrupt. They grew up a part of the whole dirty system. None of them have ever said anything worth while listening to. Look, in the last few years the Americans have started a major war in Vietnam. There have been big race riots all over the States, little Red Guards are running all over China waving their Little Red Books and the Israelies have been waving *their* book saying it gives them the right to take over the Middle East. Look who's been asassinated . . ." He ticked them off on his fingers. "Kennedy, Verwoerd, Che Guevara, Martin Luther King . . . to say nothing of the thousands who die of starvation every day in India while bloody Allen Ginsberg chants his Hari Khrishnas to a lot of middle-class drop-outs who think the world is changing just because they're not conscious enough to see straight." He paused for a moment in his tirade as the train slowed down. He jumped up and made his way to the door.

"You coming? We're here."

She looked up from her comic and smiled at him.

"*You're* here," she said. "I'm staying. I haven't finished my Beano yet."

*   *   *   *

1968 was the year when 'The Peace People' went to war.

After collecting millions of signatures on petitions, sitting down with Gandhian non-violence in all the main thoroughfares of the world, relying on peaceful persuasion and docile demonstration, they had had enough.

The bombs were getting bigger. Everyone was getting in on the act. A bearded poet who had been a chef in a Parisian restaurant had thrown the French out of Indo-China and turned it into Vietnam. Now the Americans had moved in and the Peace Movement — and others — were determined to move them out.

Sitting in a café with some of the 'others' after the demonstration in Grosvenor Square, Joe listened to them and wondered at their openness and almost childish naiveté. Did they really think revolution was round the corner, just because of a couple of confrontations with the police? Had they not learned from the 'events' in Paris that you've got to have the workers, the organised workers, with you? It had been a bloody good demonstration, I'll give 'em that.

And it had brought Margaret back to him.

"She hasn't changed," thought Joe as he sat with Margaret and the three men around the table in the bookshop basement that had become the favourite eating place of Britain's burgeoning Anarchist movement. Two of them had long hair and wore the regulation jeans. The other was almost entirely bald and he was doing the talking as the others ate hungrily. There was nothing like a good punch-up to make you hungry. And tonight at the Square had been a good one. Railings torn down, Police Riot Squads in action, running battles around the Embassy in Grosvenor Square and down Park Lane, helmets knocked off, police horses brought down and a new type of viciousness on both sides unknown in British politics for many years. Nearly one hundred people arrested, over a hundred injured including many police.

It was one of the incidents with a horse that had, literally, pushed Margaret back into Joe's arms. Coming up Grosvenor Street, as the organisers had agreed with the police, the crowd of demonstrators found itself blocked along the south side of Grosvenor Square and a group of Anarchists had turned into the entrance of the neat grassy square, followed by hundreds more like a dam bursting its banks, and headed, shouting, right across the square towards the American Embassy, only a tidily cut laurel hedge between them and the Embassy steps. A group of mounted police quickly clop-clopped across the pavement to plug the gap. But too many were pushing forward and soon the hedges were trampled down and a quick command brought more horses into action. Sensing the weakening of the police strength the main section of the marchers pressed forward sending up a great swelling sound. "Ho-Ho-Ho-Chi-Minh ... Yankees out — people in," a cry that had been heard earlier that year in immense student revolts in Paris that brought De Gaulle scurrying back from Rumania, and in Chicago where Mayor Daley brought in the National Guard. But this was London where the un-armed British police felt quite capable of handling a few unruly students.

Until the breakthrough into the square.

Then the police panicked and truncheons beat on unprotected heads, horses reared and in the side streets alongside the Embassy van loads of riot police adjusted their helmets and checked their tear gas guns.

One horse, driven too hard into the crowd emerging through the laurel hedge, tripped on the wire that supported the hedge and hurtled sideways into the crowd, its rider thrown high in the air and landing on the grass verge. Demonstrators near the frightened, kicking horse pushed backwards and Joe suddenly found Margaret alongside him trying to get out of reach of those kicking hooves.

"You hurt?" he asked, as he put his arm round her and lifted her bodily out of range.

She shook her head, still holding his arm tightly. "Don't think so." She looked down at her leg where the stocking was torn, bent over and felt it and came up with blood on her hands. She smiled in disbelief.

"Don't worry," she said, "I've got another leg."

He pushed a way through the crowd for both of them and sat her down on a park bench, while all around them people were yelling and screaming, horses were whinnying and the sound of fifty thousand feet stamping, marching, pushing, and running across the roads and paths flowed around them.

He knelt down to look at her leg.

"Looks like you cut it. The stocking's all torn. Better take it off." He reached up under her skirt, remembered, and withdrew his hands. "Sorry."

"For what?"

She stood up and, lifting her skirt, wriggled the tights down to her knees. "You do the rest, eh?" she told him, and, kneeling in front of her he started to pull the torn tights gently over the bloody knee.

"A right bloody time you picked to take her pants down. Don't you know there's a war on?" A group of students, three boys and a girl, stopped in front of them in amused curiosity.

Joe looked at them, embarrassed, and then he looked up at Margaret. She pulled his head towards her and laughed back.

"There always is, comrade," she shouted above the noise of the demonstration, "there always is."

After the demonstration, after what seemed hours of excited discussion and analysis at the restaurant, after they made love to the accompaniment of the same old neon lights, they agreed on coffee without spoons and talked together in the same old armchairs.

"Who's the bald guy?" Joe wanted to know.

"Pete? Comes from Bristol or somewhere. We met him at the last Grosvenor Square do. Good bloke."

"Did you check him out?"

"What d'you mean, check him out?"

Security. That's one thing he'd learned from Sam's outfit. Check everybody out.

"How long does he say he's been in London?"

"Only since that last demo. What's that, about six months I guess."

"Six months. Remember that little exchange between him and me about the Fascists?"

"Yes. I thought you were being a bit cagey about all that. What's the mystery?"

"Damn right I was cagey. Remember what he said?"

What's your particular involvement in all this Joe, he'd asked, haven't seen you in the Blue Goose before. Well, I told him, I've been concerned with fighting the bloody Fascists in this country more than the Fascists in Vietman, and he looked at me a bit funny and I knew I'd seen him before and couldn't place where. Christ he'd said are you one of that lot? What lot? I've seen some of your boys in action at Kerbella Street when the Fascists were speaking, or trying to, and he turned to the others and got all enthusiastic. You should see them go to work on a police cordon, he says, cut through it like a piece of cake. In and out, platform down, speaker rendered speechless, loudspeaker equipment ruined and they're away. Then I remembered. Kerbella Street a year ago. I was just on a watching brief there and suddenly I saw this guy watching me. He had his hand up to his face. Could have been holding a miniature camera or maybe he was just picking his nose. But when baldy mentioned Kerbella Street it all fitted into place.

"Are you sure it was the same one?" asked Margaret.

"Who knows? Better check him out."

"How? We're not the secret service you know Joe. We don't work like that. Somebody comes in, he wants to help, he's prepared to do something himself, he's in. He's one of us. You know that."

"Not when you're making bombs he's not. Or you'll all end up in jail."

She sat up quickly and looked at him.

"Who said anything about bombs?"

Joe sipped his coffee.

"I didn't. If you're not doing anything you don't mind the police knowing about, you needn't worry. Otherwise check him out." He put his cup on the floor and leaned forward, "Margaret, check everybody out. Your free and easy, no organisation, no leaders, Anarchist set-up is wide open to police infiltration. That means everything you do is known beforehand. And if you don't do anything they'll suggest things for you to do. Useless and harmless bloody things like a bomb outside somebody's door that blows up while they're away, bullets sprayed through an office window when they've all gone home. Nothing really but it looks like something and you can all get arrested and after a big trial all the top brass get a pat on the back and everybody's happy. Vive la Révolution!"

"All right, all right, James Bond the Second, but how do we check him out?"

"Next time you're all sitting around wait for a while and then say how interested you were in his description of the way the Group, well this outfit he was talking about, broke up meetings, and get him to expand on it. Then just drop in a question like when was this or when did he see it happen and see what he says. You see there hasn't been a meeting in Kerbella Street for over a year. That punch-up he was referring to put the bastards out of action and they've never been back. And if he tells you the truth about when he was there then you can challenge him about only coming up to London six months ago. Of course he might have come up for the weekend. But you'll see him swimming around a bit in his eyes if he's in trouble. Watch his eyes."

"And if we find out he's been kidding us?"

"Depends how serious you are and how much you think he knows. If he doesn't know much you can just tell him to piss off.'

"And if he does know something?"

"That's your problem, love. What does Kropotkin say?"

*　　*　　*　　*

"I see your old girl friend has got herself arrested."

"Margaret?" Joe looked up at Zena as she came back into the room and put the tray down on the low coffee table. He thought once again, as he always did, how strange it was for him to be here in this quiet haven of middle-class comfort and respectability that was his wife's, and his son's, home.

Coffee here was not served in mugs but in delicate little china cups on a small round tray with a lace tray-cloth and matching sugar bowl. Coffee was not boiled up on the stove in the corner but came with some sense of ceremony through a door that swung back on its hinges when the coffee had passed through. Coffee came with biscuits on a small plate. It came after a dinner served on a white table cloth with whiter than white napkins and knives, forks and spoons arranged in anticipation of soup, meat and dessert.

They had talked of Zena's mother and how she was getting on by herself three years after the old man had died. Of the Lowry exhibition and how they could have bought that factory landscape ten years ago when they had seen it together for, what was it, four hundred pounds? And now they were asking four thousand.

And they talked about Robbie and how he was getting on at school and what he was going to do when he left and they looked at each other as the boy talked excitedly about the student revolts in Mexico where three hundred people had been shot down by the army.

Now with dinner over and Robbie gone out, now came coffee.

"Of course Margaret," said Zena as she poured his coffee, "how many other girl friends have you got who have been arrested?"

"She's a silly cow. I bumped into her at that big Vietnam demo at Grosvenor Square last year and met some of her pals. I didn't fancy them very much and I told her to be careful."

"Careful of what?"

"Oh, some of the things they were doing. Some of the people they were involved with."

"Did she want you to get involved?"

Joe smiled at the protective note that had crept into that question.

"No chance. Anyway Maggie lost interest in me four years ago."

"Lucky you."

He watched the way she sat down with her delicate coffee cup and saucer delicately held in one hand, her other hand smoothing her skirt over her knees. Beneath those well-cut expensive clothes was there still the body of the young girl in the drawing he had pinned to the wall of his room? Why should there be? After all, who was he to talk? Sometimes when he caught sight of himself in the bathroom mirror he wondered about the biological process that, quietly and imperceptibly every year, lowered the chest down into the stomach and folded the shoulders forward to hide the loss. Breathe in man! That's better! One, two. One, two. You're not bloody ninety yet.

But *she* still looked so young. Still looked as if she would look the same, underneath.

"What are you looking at?" she asked.

"I was just looking . . ."

Was this the time? The right moment?

". . . and thinking."

"About what?"

Hell, why not? What can I lose?

291

"About you."

A step. A scout sent out to spy out the land and scuttle back quickly to hide, if necessary, behind a quick smile, a flip remark.

"What about me?"

"I am always amazed at how you can look so young and beautiful while I get old and grey and fat and flabby." There it was. Wrapped up a little in cocktail party verbosity but there, definitely there, waiting to be picked up. Would she? He felt his fingers tensing and put the coffee cup down on a side table.

"It's that decadent life you lead." Was she serious? "Anyway you're not fat. It's just the way you hold yourself. You've just let yourself go."

Don't let's get trapped into discussing him. It was *her* he wanted to talk about. But it was too late. She was away.

"The trouble with you Joe is that you like an easy life. You like sitting around talking to people and if you can you'll do it all day and all night and that means you're eating and drinking all day and all night too."

"But that's how I earn my living Zee. I'm not just a journalist. I'm a specialist. I talk to people, I research, I dig, I find out. It's taken me bloody years Zee, as you know, to get where I am. First it was all those little magazines, underground, fringe, whatever you want to call them. Then the big boys started to get interested. Now it's the National Press. They come to me because they know I can get to the right people. And they know I won't let go, won't give up till I've got the story. But it takes time Zee, getting the truth out of people who don't know what the truth is. I can't write about these people and what they're doing and what they're thinking unless I talk to them. Sometimes it takes all day and sometimes it goes on late into the night because I have to get 'em when I can, and if I do manage to get 'em talking I don't want to stop them. It can take two hours chat before I get them round to what I want to know."

"And what is it you want to know?"

"How the world is run. Who runs it. What they're going to do next week."

"And you think they're going to tell you, all these people you interview? You think they even know?"

"Not everything Zee. You're right. Individually they don't know that much and what they do know they're not going to tell. But it's like a jigsaw puzzle. You pick up a piece here, a piece there. Then you remember a piece you had before that didn't fit in anywhere and suddenly it fits. That gives you a lead and you go and see somebody you'd never thought of, and maybe, if you're lucky it begins to come clear and you can formulate the right question and put it to the right chap and bingo, while his lips say 'no comment', his eyes tell you you've hit the bullseye and there's your next article."

"And now?"

"What d'you mean?"

"Now you know how the world is run, what now?"

"Ayayay . . ." He gulped down the remains of his coffee, levered himself up out of the chair and stood by the imitation log fire. "Why do you always have to take the mickey Zee? You have your life. I have mine."

"You were the one that was complaining about being fat and flabby, not me."

"Actually what I was saying was not so much that I was fat and flabby and old and grey but that you are still so young and beautiful."

"Now he tells me." Flustered, realising perhaps that however she diverted him he was going to keep coming back, wanting to hear it but somehow, after all this time, not sure, or not ready, to deal with it, she started to gather up the coffee things and walked across to get Joe's cup from the side table. As she leaned forward, her back to him, she felt his hands on her hips.

"Stop it Joe, I'll break the cup."

"No you won't." One hand reached round to take the coffee cup from her and place it on the mantlepiece, the other hand remained on her hip, pulling her gently towards him. He had not been this close to her for maybe fifteen years. It couldn't be the same and yet . . . Years ago, on his way up North he had stopped overnight in the town where he had first met Zee, looked for the shop he had gone into with Smudger to look at the local art exhibition and seen Zee sitting there. Nothing there was the same. The shop had been pulled down and a new parade built up. The street had changed beyond recognition and it was not until he walked out of the town along the canal bank where he had walked with Zee that a feeling of the past in the present entered into him. Over beyond the far bank, beyond the little bridge, were the same hills, the same fields, even the same sheep. And here, beneath the new perfume, the expensive silk blouse, the tailored bra was the same Zee who had walked with him over the hills and closed her eyes tight the first time he kissed her.

"Joe, what do you think you're doing?"

As if she didn't know.

"Remember that painting you gave me the first day we met?"

"Oh. That one. Well?"

"Well I want to see if you've changed and I can't with all this on."

Buttons. Zip. Hooks and eyes.

"Joe you *know* I've changed." She pulled herself away and turned to face him. Unbuttoned. Unzipped. Unhooked. Her face flushed. "You're a fool Joe. Don't you remember we had a baby? *I* had a baby. And I fed him and brought him up and made a living for both of us all these years while you ..." she was doing up her buttons, and hooks and zip angrily as she spoke, "... you were busy with other people all the time ... seeing how the world was run. Did it ever occur to you when you were sitting talking to one of these pieces of jigsaw late into the night that I was sitting here all by myself? All right, all right. I know. We've been into all this before. Ages ago. We agreed. You have your life, I have mine. So I'm glad to see you Joe, and it's nice for Robbie. He's glad to see you too. And it's nice to sit down, all three of us, and have a meal and a talk once a month or whatever, and it's all very civilised and very adult and all that and that's O.K. But that's all Joe, that's all. Don't start upsetting me. Don't try to start something you can't cope with."

She was finished. Composed now.

"What can't I cope with?"

She came up to him and lifted her hand to his shoulder. "Love," she said, and taking the cup from the mantlepiece turned and put it on the tray.

"Love! But I just ..."

She interrupted. "You just! You just wanted a quick poke before Robbie gets back and away you go, thanks for having me, see you next month! Well that's not for me Joe, you should know that's not for me." Quickly, holding back the tears, she picked up the tray and went into the kitchen.

Not thinking now of what he should do, or what he should say, or how he should say it, Joe followed her, disturbed somewhere at the bottom of his stomach by her tears. She was standing by the sink, the tray on the draining board, her shoulders bent forward in a way Joe knew was nothing like that drawing on his wall. He put his hands on her shoulders, gently, just to hold her and leaned his head against hers.

"I'm sorry love," he said. "You're quite right. I'm a bloody fool. I just ... well you're right, I just wanted you. But Zee, wait," he touched her lips with his fingers to stop her interrupting, "listen, it's not just tonight. I've been wanting you for years, every time we met. It's taken me all this time to pluck up courage to do something. And then I made a mess of everything."

He turned her round and she smiled ruefully through her tears.

"Silly boy."

"So what's new?"

She sighed. "Nothing. Nothing's new, I suppose." She put a hand up to the rough stubble on his cheek, "That's new," she said.

"What?"

"You're going grey. Just there."

"Silver threads among the Gold?"

She laughed. A little silent laugh.

"Were you really afraid?"

"Still am."

"Why? We *are* married. Aren't we?"

"Is that what they call it?"

"Oh Joe . . ."

Married. That was what they called it. The one link they had never broken. Why not? They had asked themselves the question many times over the years. Robbie probably. Like Joe's mother said, 'The boy needs a father.' And Zee seemed to be in no hurry to get him a new one, just as Joe seemed in no hurry to get another wife. Margaret? She wanted a man not a husband. And Maeve? Her mural had been prophetic in a way. One man was much the same as any other to her. She could take them or leave them. Or take one of her girl friends instead. 'Not so messy' she used to say. Wasn't that what he wanted, too? No mess. No ties. So what was it that kept bringing him back to Zee?

Watching her undress now, for the first time in years, he sensed, rather than understood, the thing that was happening to him.

The movement of her hand over to her hip to unzip her skirt pushed her breasts together above the lace of her slip.

"Why are you smiling?" she asked, her arms above her head, the lace engangled with her hair.

"I was remembering the last time I watched you undress."

"And?"

"It was suspender belt and stockings. Now it's tights."

"That dates you."

"And you."

"And me. And which do you prefer?"

"Neither. As you are now."

Throwing the tights on the floor she walked towards him and, as he caught a glimpse of her sideways in the mirror, he recognised the girl in the drawing on his wall.

Now he knew that it was. A sense of wonder. Even though it hadn't worked and he hadn't been able to control himself and it seemed to be all over before it had even begun, there was still, as they lay there together, a feeling of wonder.

Is that what she thought he couldn't cope with? After all this time? Could he?

The telephone rang.

"Leave it," he said.

"It might be Robbie."

"So?"

"So I'll answer it."

Relaxed now she slipped out of bed, opened the wardrobe, put on a dressing gown and went through the door to the hall. Funny girl. She'd even been pleased that he had come so quickly, that he had not been able to control his excitement. "You'll be better next time" she'd said. Next time.

Through the open door he heard her answer the phone. She was silent for a while as what sounded like an excited woman's voice, loud enough to be heard in the bedroom, talked at her until she said, "Oh no! When did it happen?"

Robbie! He jumped out of bed and ran quickly into the hall. She held out a hand to him.

"It's Sadie," she said. "She's at your mother's. Wait a minute Sadie," she said into the phone, "Joe's here. Let me tell him. Your Uncle Chayim. You know he was on his way here from Israel?" Joe nodded. "Well his plane has been hijacked. It was on the radio. Will you talk to her?"

"Sure." He took the phone.

"Sadie? This is Joe. What's happening?"

As Joe, squatting naked on the floor, listened to his sister talking, Zee couldn't help smiling at the sight and went to get a blanket which she draped round his shoulders.

"How's the old girl taking it?" he asked. As his sister's voice went on he held his hand over the mouthpiece. "Can we go round there?" he asked. Zee nodded. "In your car?" She nodded again. "What about Robbie?" "He's got a key."

"Sadie, listen. Listen a minute. We're coming over straight away. Sure. And Zee. Who knows what can be done about it? Anyway, we'll see, O.K.? See you."

He put down the phone and sat, huddled in his blanket, looking into the distance, remembering his meeting only a month ago with a young Maoist who had just returned from a four-week "training course" run by the Arabs in Jordan. 'Funny lot' was the way he had described them and cocked an eyebrow when Joe had asked "Who? Them or you?" He grinned beneath his Zapata moustache, "Both, I guess," he replied, "specially when we found out that two of our lot were somewhat dubious politically, more interested in getting Arab support to fight the Jews. We soon got rid of them. The trouble with our Palestinian friends is they can't tell Jews from Zionists."

"Can your Chinese friends?"

"They can't tell Jews from Americans. So far as they're concerned the Zionists are just the representatives of Capitalism in the Middle East."

"And Arafat?"

"He represents the victorious struggle of the oppressed peoples."

"All paid for by that well-known champion of oppressed peoples, King Faisal of Saudi Arabia!"

"Ah, that's one of the contradictions of Capitalism."

Perhaps he could do something through the Maoists? They'd certainly liked his article when it appeared, even phoned and thanked him for 'the best explanation of their philosophy that had appeared in the capitalist press'! How much pull did they have with the Arabs? Depends which particular group had pulled off this job.

"So?"

He looked up at Zee standing in the bedroom doorway. All dressed and neat and tidy. It wasn't just that she used Jewish expressions such a lot now. That's understandable, seeing the old girl so much. But her intonation was Jewish, the way she put her head ever so slightly to one side as she looked at him and said "So?" He stood up, like an Indian chief with the blanket draped round him, and went over to her.

"I love you Zee," he said, dropping the blanket as he held her.

"Now he tells me," she laughed, pushing him away. "Go and get dressed while I do a note for Robbie."

As the car drove through the streets of North London Joe watched the competent, efficient manner of Zee's driving and wondered where the wonder had gone. For it had certainly gone. Had it just been sex? No, with Margaret it was sex. With Maeve it was fun. With Zee it was ... well, love. And she was probably right that he couldn't cope with it. Could she? The edge of a smile on the corner of her lips as she pulled up at the traffic lights seemed to show that she could.

"What are you smiling at?"

She darted a look at him and, as the lights changed, took her foot off the brake and edged forward to the centre of the road preparing to turn. A little green light clicked on and off on the dashboard.

"I was thinking how lucky we are they haven't invented telephones with TV screens."

"Eh?"

"Sadie might have had a surprise."

"Oh," he smiled at the thought. "She sounded pretty cut up. What's she like these days?"

"What's she like? Oh yes, I keep forgetting you haven't seen her for years. I still think of you as one of the family,"

"Thanks a lot. Coming from a *shikser* the dear family wouldn't even talk to for five years that's great. Anyway, answer the question."

"The question. Oh yes, Sadie. Well, she's a nice fat prosperous housewife, mother and businesswoman. She still has an interest in the old restaurant down in the East End but, as I'm sure you know, the East End is not what it used to be. As Sadie says, all the better class of people have moved out ..."

"By which she means Sadie!"

"Naturally, and now the whole place is full of Pakistanis."

"Pakistanis! What are they?"

"Oh they're funny people with beards who wear long coats and fur hats."

"You mean like these?"

They were passing through the North London suburb of Stamford Hill which had, in recent years become a centre for Chassidic Jews, an ultra-orthodox sect still retaining many of the clothes and customs of the medieval *shtetel* Jews of Eastern Europe. Standing on the curb, immersed in discussion, were four of these Jews from another world, another time, dressed in long black coats and fur-brimmed hats. They talked passionately, fingering their beards and their long black *pays*, curly locks of hair that hung from their temples.

"What d'you think they're getting all worked up about, the Torah?" asked Zee.

"More likely the results of the three-thirty at Sandown Park. You know they never change, these guys. Uncle Chayim, poor bugger, at least moved with the times."

"Perhaps he'd have been better off not to."

"Couldn't help himself. He had to clear out of Russia when he was a kid because of the pogroms and made the fatal mistake of staying put when he got as far as Germany. If he'd have gone on to England like my mother he'd have been all right but after losing an arm for the Kaiser in 1918 he found himself being called a dirty Jew again when Hitler arrived and had to clear out once again. When he got to Israel he said he'd stopped running."

"I remember him saying that when he came over for Robbie's *Barmitzvah*. 'From now on', he said, 'we don't run no more. We fight.'"

"I suppose that's how they all feel over there."

"But you don't agree with them, do you Joe?"

"I think Jews have stopped running everywhere, not just in Israel. What I don't agree with is when they stop on other people's land."

"So where is their land? Where can they stop?"

Joe didn't answer for a while, watching the little semi-detached houses go by as they drove through the suburban back streets, here a laburnum, there a lilac, even an adventurous monkey-puzzle tree, behind the close-clipped privet. Then, without looking at Zena he repeated his last phrase, "Other people's land ... You know Zee, you get so bloody used to certain accepted ideas and ways of looking at things that you just repeat them like bloody parrots without even thinking whether they're right or not. It's not just the Party that has its jargon. This business of land. Look at all these little houses and gardens. Thousands of them all over the country. They've all got their own piece of land. They cut the grass, prune the roses, clip the hedge. A good proportion of these houses round here are owned by Jews. And it's theirs until somebody comes along with enough guns and police and stormtroopers to take it away from them. Like they did with poor old Chayim. Twice. And nobody really gives a damn. Until you stop running and start fighting."

The houses were getting bigger now. More imposing, detached, bigger front gardens, driveways. "The best," Joe said to himself, thinking of the old man as the car pulled up at the curb. Zee put on the hand brake and took the key out, turning to Joe.

"It's like Chayim said."

"Wait a minute Zee," said Joe, a note of excitement in his voice, "I want to work out something before I go in there. Look, it's not only like *he* said, it's also like *they* say."

"Who?"

"The Arabs. I didn't tell you this, and I don't want to tell them," he nodded towards the house, "but last week I met one of their top men. It's part of a series of articles I'm doing. Now he was saying the same thing. He was justifying all these hijackings by saying they can no longer just sit down quietly in their refugee camps waiting for the world to do something. They've got to kick the world in the arse and say 'Do something now!'"

"But what about all the innocent people who get hijacked? The women and children?"

"They say they're at war."

"But if they're at war with the Israelis why don't they fight the Israelis?"

"Ah, that's another question. He ducked that one, but Zee that's not what I'm getting at. I've got another appointment with him next week and . . . I think . . . I've got . . . an idea . . ."

"Joe, you don't think you can get him to do something about the plane?"

"No. But there may be another way. Will Sam be here tonight?"

"Yes. Sadie said Hetty and Sam were on the way over."

"Good. Look Zee, I'm not saying anything about this tonight. O.K.?"

Mystified, Zee nodded.

"O.K. What's there to say? You know the man who hijacked your uncle? The less you say about that the better!"

"Right. Let's go in."

Nothing changes. The same *lockshun* soup smell, the same carpet, a little frayed by the door and the edges of the stairs, the same gold embossed wallpaper, rubbed bare just by the light switch and near the hall table where the telephone was. Without going up the stairs Joe could feel the concealed join in the banister rail and was certain that the fifth stair rod would still be loose.

She was changed though. She looked at them both as they went into the lounge and without getting up, reached up to kiss Zee on the cheek and then offered a cheek to Joe. A polished cheek, the skin drawn tight across the bones and wrinkling down into her neck, a pair of black National Health spectacles magnifying the lines round her eyes, and what might have been a tear that had escaped despite all her efforts.

"It must be serious," she said without vindictiveness, "Joe's here."

But there was a closeness, too, that Joe could only remember as something associated with his childhood. The family. A strange assortment of people with nothing in common except their blood, coming together in concern for somebody they hadn't seen for years, hardly even knew. David, fat now and silver-haired, busy speaking over the telephone in anxious tones to somebody at the Embassy. Sadie, even fatter if truth were known, but it never would be known, at least not in public, busy making tea and suggestions. Hetty and Sam arrived.

"Long time no see," said Sam.

"Long time," Joe agreed. Then quietly, as they stood together with tea cups in their hands, "I need five minutes with you, alone, before we go. O.K.?"

"Can't it wait till tomorrow?"

"It can't wait."

"O.K. Let things settle down here first."

"Have some *strudel*." Hetty came up with a plate in her hands an enquiring look in her eyes. "Are you two" she nodded towards Zee, "together again?"

"We were when Sadie phoned."

"And?"

Joe looked round for a place to put his cup, found a side table by an armchair and turned to face the rest of the family. "Look," he said in a loud voice so that everybody stopped talking and looked at him, "I've got an idea."

He sat down on a chair next to his mother, and Zena noticed that he made no attempt to move the tea things on the small table in front of him.

"I don't know if it will work," he said, "but I think it's worth trying. I think I can get out there."

"Where? Damascus?"

"Yes. Wherever the plane is. I was asked a few weeks ago by one of the magazines I work for if I would like to do an on-the-spot account of the guerrillas in the refugee camps . . ."

"Terrorists you mean."

"Terrorists, guerrillas, doesn't matter what you call them . . ."

"Oh but it does, you call them guerrillas and you turn them into nice responsible people already."

"Leave it David," Sadie interrupted "let's hear Joe's idea."

"But . . ."

"Leave it."

They looked at each across the room. David shrugged and left it.

"The thing is, this magazine can get me there. At least I think so."

"Why should they talk to you?"

"They'll talk to the magazine because it's on their side, and they need all the publicity they can get. That's what these hijacks are all about."

"And whose side are you on Joey?"

Joey! He hadn't been called that for God knows how many years. And hearing it in that little old voice took him back a hundred years and a thousand miles to another world of freshly baked bread and heavy lace curtains where questions could be answered with a saucy grin. But not this one. Not now. No good talking to them about history and treaties and refugees. They'd cap each one with their own history, their own treaties, their own refugees. Whose side *was* he on?

"Right now Mum," he turned to her and put his hand on hers, which was resting on the arm of her chair, "I'm only concerned to see if I can help Uncle Chayim. This side, that side . . . we can talk about that later, right?"

"Joey doesn't change, does he?" She addressed the question to nobody in particular looking round the room. "He's always ready with an answer."

"Even if it's not an answer to the question you asked." This time it was Hetty, still holding the plate of *strudel* in her hand.

"Don't knock it Hetty," said Sam. "Joe's right. We're not here tonight to talk politics, we're here to help that old boy sitting there in the desert. Right Ma?"

Sam always called her Ma. He was the only one to do that. Joe and Zena called her Mum, the girls called her Mother. David? He couldn't remember what David called her. Maybe nothing. But right now he could feel her fingers gripping his hand as she answered Sam.

"Did I say he was wrong? Of course he's right. But Joey," he felt her fingers gripping tight, "you have to be careful with these people Joey. They're not nice people. Anti S'mits."

Anti S'mits. Funny the way she always pronounced that. Like the old man. A hang-over from Russia maybe. Anti S'mit. Much worse than anti semite, which was somehow a word for sociological discussion. Anti S'mit was a word for pogroms.

Go tell her they are not anti semite but anti Zionist. Not now. "Sure Mum, I'll be careful. Look . . ." he turned to the rest of them, "I don't know if I can get there but it's worth a try. It's something. And if I get there I don't know if I can get to the right people, but I think I can. I've got a better chance than most. And if I do I have no idea what I'm going to say that's going to make any difference. Maybe I'll think of something. At least it's better than sitting round here worrying because there's nothing you can do. If you think it's worth a try I'll have a go. Only make up your minds now because I've got a lot of phoning to do."

"I think it's worth a try."

"What can we lose?"

"I don't trust those Arabs. Better to shoot them than talk to them."

"I don't know. What do you think Mother?"

The old lady shrugged her shoulders and looked quizzically round at her family, releasing Joe's hand as she did so.

"Joey is right. First get my brother out of there. Later on we can talk about shooting them."

Later on, after more talk and more tea and more *strudel*, Joe and Sam sat in the kitchen.

"So, what do you want from me?"

"Mahrbash is in town."

"The terrorist?"

Joe smiled and nodded.

"I did an interview with him last week. I've got another appointment with him on Wednesday."

"And?"

"If he could be . . . lifted . . . I'd have a strong bargaining point when I'm talking out there."

"You must be joking. His security must be tighter than Buckingham Palace."

"On the contrary. These boys trust nobody. Not even their own people. Specially not their people over here. I can tell you where he will be and when. I can't guarantee there won't be somebody nearby keeping an eye on him who may be prepared to shoot if he thinks he can get away with it. It's risky. But it's possible. And it could save a hundred lives."

"Only a hundred?"

"My guess is they'll let all the non-Jews go . . ."

"Non-Jews? Not non-Israelis?"

"It's only my guess. Then they'll make a big deal concession and free the women and children. The rest they'll bargain for. Maybe fifty. Maybe a hundred."

"And you reckon they'll be prepared to swap them for Mahrbash?"

"Who knows? At least he's something we'll have to swap."

Sam got up and walked round the kitchen. The baking pan in which the *strudel* had been cooked was on the draining board. He took a corner piece which had been left in the pan and put it into his mouth, licking his fingers clean afterwards.

"Two things, Joe. First, we don't get involved in anything to do with Israel. And they don't get involved with us. We could overcome that one I think. It's a British plane that's been hijacked, and if, like you say, they're holding Jews, and not Israelis, and probably a number of British Jews, then we might regard it as our business. The second thing is more difficult." He sat down again, facing Joe over the table.

"And that is?" Joe asked.

"Why should we trust you?"

"I'll get my brother-in-law to vouch for me. He did it before you know."

"Touché." Sam smiled. "But that was more straight forward. A Nazi is a Nazi. No discussion needed. But here the politics are, shall we say, more debatable. When is a terrorist not a terrorist? The answer seems to vary the further left you get."

"Or the further right. Depends which side you're on in any given political struggle. Look at what's happening in Ireland now."

"True. Why did you drop out of the Group Joe?"

"It was full of Jews."

"Some of them, I take it, not your best friends?"

"Right. Seriously, I'm off all these exclusive groups fighting for their own sectional interests. Women's Liberation, Gay Liberation, Palestine Liberation. If we're going to beat the Fascists I can think of a lot better ways of doing it than by bashing them over the head. And if we're going to bash them over the head I can think of a lot better people to do that than your boys. No offence meant."

"None taken. But why don't they do it? We're not stopping them."

"It always takes longer to build up a mass movement than to pick up a phone and call out a couple of dozen boys. It's beginning to happen. But to answer your question I can't think of any reason why you should trust me more than I trust you. If we do this thing we'll be in it together. We both run certain risks, right? But at least your boys are on their home ground. They have lawyers, friends, even the dear old British police force. Christ knows what the reaction to my proposal will be out there."

"And your proposal will be?"

"They release the hostages. We release Mahrbash. No publicity. Nobody knows. The world will think what nice reasonable people they are, responding to the appeals of the Red Cross and all that jazz. Good for their image, too."

"They should pay you a fee!"

"That's what I'm afraid of."

The two men sat and looked at each other across the table.

"Good *strudel* that," said Sam, standing up and going over to the draining board. "There's a bit left. Want it?"

"No thanks, I'm slimming."

"Wise man. Look Joe," Sam carefully put the remaining crumbs into his mouth, "I can't decide this one by myself. You'd better come with me."

"Where?"

"Lou's place. You met Lou when we were working on that . . . holiday camp. O.K.?"

304

Tall man. Very thin. Permanent stubble on his chin and scrawny neck, black hairs growing out of his ears. Thought about every word you said. Not just the meaning of the words and what you were saying but carefully considering why you had chosen each of those words. And his answer would always wait until he had made up his mind about those words and then checked the words he was going to use in reply. A thoughtful man, Sam had called him. He could say that again.

"When?"

"Tonight, if he's in. I'll phone him now. Can Zee take Hetty home in her car?"

"Why not? I'll ask her while you're phoning." As he was going through the kitchen door he stopped and turned to his brother-in-law. "One thing Sam."

"Yes?"

"Are you with me on this?"

Sam turned on the kitchen tap, held his fingers in the water and dried them on a teacloth. "I'm with you, my friend. All the way." He took Joe's shoulder as they went out into the hall together, and as he stopped by the phone he looked at Joe.

"Much good may it do you," he said.

On the following Wednesday afternoon the telephone rang on Sam's desk and his secretary, who was taking dictation, picked up the phone.

"There's a Mr. Gold on the telephone. He says it's personal."

Sam took the phone from her.

"Joe?"

"I'm at the airport. My plane leaves in half an hour. Everything O.K.?"

"Everything went perfectly my friend."

"No problems?"

"No problems."

"Good. See you."

"When do you think that might be?"

"Who knows? Maybe the weekend. Watch the TV."

"I'll do that. Have a good trip."

"I'll try."

"Bye bye."

"Oh Sam . . ."

"Yes?"

"Give my love to Lou."

* * * *

Although the sun had been set for more than an hour the heat
enveloped him like a blanket as he left the plane and he could feel the
perspiration running down his side as he walked across the tarmac
towards the lights of the airport buildings.

What now? A taxi to the hotel, a long cool drink and a few hours
sleep before he phoned them in the morning? Or would they phone
him first?

Neither. One of two men standing by the International Arrivals
door who were scrutinising every passenger, looked at him,
compared his face to a photograph he held and said, "Mr. Gold?"

"That's right."

"Will you come with us please."

"Who are you?"

They hesitated and one spoke in Arabic to the other who shrugged
his shoulders and he replied.

"We are from Abdul Gadawi. We have a car outside. You have
luggage?"

Gadawi. Number One. The last Joe had heard of him he had been
in North Korea. It looked like the message had certainly got through
from the magazine.

"Good," he said. "No luggage. Only this." He held up his attaché
case and camera with one hand. In the other he had his passport,
ready for Immigration. "Passport?" he asked.

"Is not necessary. Come."

They led the way around the airport building to a battered grey
Peugeot that was standing by a high wire gate. One of the men
opened the door to the back of the car. "Please," he said. Joe got in.
The two men got in the front of the car and the one in the driver's
seat switched on the engine and the lights and gave a light hoot on the
horn. A uniformed soldier came out of the hut by the gate and swung
it open without a word, watched the car edge slowly though the gap
and closed the gate after them.

As the car gathered speed, its headlights reflecting the white paint
at the base of the palm trees that lined the road, the man next to the
driver turned to Joe and smiled.

"You are hungry?" he asked.

"Thank you, no. I had a good meal on the plane."

"Air France." The man's smile widened. "Always good food,
yes?"

"Certainly was. Look, what's your name?"

"My name is Ben. This is Ahmed."

"Ben. O.K. Look Ben, are we going to see Gadawi now? Or my hotel? Where?"

"No." Ben picked his words carefully, translating to himself as he went. "Gadawi tomorrow. Not here now. Now we go . . . are going . . . to plane. Long way."

"The plane! Which plane? The hijacked plane?"

"Sure thing." This Ben was certainly a big smiler. Although he had turned now with his back to him Joe could see that smile reflected in the windscreen, illuminated by the dashboard lights. "We go to the hijack plane. Gadawi says you will see the plane. Also the people there. Hostages. Then come back and talk to him . . . interview, yes?" He looked over his shoulder and Joe nodded. "Interview for English newspapers. Tomorrow. Maybe around two o'clock. O.K.?"

"Whatever you say Ben. Pity I wanted to talk to Gadawi straight away. I have some important news for him."

"Good news?" The smile faltered a little as it fought with a question mark.

"Maybe. It'll keep till tomorrow."

The smile was back. "Good. If you hungry we must eat soon before we leave the city. Otherwise no food till we get to plane. Long way."

"Where is the plane?"

"Long way."

"Sure, I know. But . . ." Forget it Joe. They're not going to tell you. Perhaps I'll see a road sign. They seem friendly enough. It'll be good to see the hostages before I meet Gadawi. There would certainly be no chance after!

"You not hungry?"

"Oh! No. No thanks Ben. Really. But I'm certainly tired. Have I got time for a sleep? How long before we get there?"

"Plenty time for sleep." Ben smiled again. "Maybe four, five hours. Long way. You comfortable?"

Joe glanced at the speedometer. They were doing eighty now and picking up speed as they left the town. A long straight road ahead fixed by their headlights. Eighty. That's kilometres. About fifty miles per hour. They'll probably move up to seventy and hold that for five hours. Three hundred and fifty miles. Judging from the moon they're heading due East. Maybe a little South-East. Towards the Jordanian border. That's odd, the news was that the Palestinians were still fighting Hussein's troops in Amman. There's one thing to be said for those Palestinians. They may not kill many Israelis but they certainly kill a lot of Arabs.

"Ben ..."

"M'sieur?"

Funny. The old French dies hard. Sykes-Picot. Who the hell was Picot? You have this bit of Palestine, we'll have this bit of Syria. Vive la France, Vive l'Angleterre, Merde les Arabes.

"What's new from Amman?"

The smile disappeared.

"Butchers. Murderers." He half-turned to Joe. "Gadawi will talk to you about this."

"Sure Ben, I'm sure he will. I just wondered if the fighting had stopped yet?"

"The fighting will never stop."

That means Hussein has won. This time. So we won't be going there. Better get some sleep so I can be awake before we get to the plane.

"You're right Ben. Fighting never stops. I'm going to have a little sleep. Give me a shout when we get there, right?"

As Joe settled himself down in the back seat, Ben turned round, all smiles again. You comfortable?"

"Fine Ben, fine."

Rising on one elbow to arrange himself comfortably Joe glimpsed for one moment the eyes of the driver looking at him in the mirror. He was no smiler that one. David's words came back to him "I don't trust those Arabs. Better to shoot them than talk to them." Fat slob. It's fine for him. I can just see him shooting this pair. Or talking to them either. Ayayay. Ahead of them a man in long white robes was caught momentarily in the headlights. White clay walls flicked by as they sped through a village. A white dome. Black holes in the walls. The shadows of trees fanned quickly across the buildings. Two black-robed women shielding their eyes from the headlights and once again the long straight road hypnotising him to sleep.

He woke several times during the long night, and each time, as he moved to make himself more comfortable he saw the driver's eyes glance at him, unsmilingly, in the mirror, the speedometer at a steady one hundred kilometers, the headlamps climbing bare hills ahead for mile after miles.

Now, straight ahead, there was a rim of yellow outlining the uneven horizon. Joe lifted himself up and yawned causing Ben's smile to turn on him.

"Awake?"

"Mm. More or less. Is that dawn up there?"

"Yes. It is the dawn."

Joe looked at his watch. Five thirty.

"How long now Ben?"

"Not long. Maybe half hour. Are you thirsty? I have coffee."

"Great."

Carefully Ben poured coffee out of a thermos into a plastic cup and handed it back to Joe who drank it gratefully, feeling the warmth flow through his body.

"That's good," he said, passing back the empty cup.

"More?" Ben asked.

"No thanks. But I'll tell you what I would like."

"What is that?"

"A quick pee."

"A pee. What is that?"

"Oh. Piss. You know." Joe put his hand between his legs and mimed.

Ben watched him, puzzled, and then laughed.

"Pee! Of course. Me too." He spoke to the driver in Arabic and as the car slowed down and stopped all three men got out. Joe walked to the side of the road, shivering a little in the sudden cold and turned his back on the others as he fumbled for his penis, hoping they would interpret his action as natural modesty rather than the need to avoid the suspicion that circumcision might arouse. He presumed that Gadawi had checked him out and knew who he was and what he was but these characters might not have the same understanding and here, in the middle of the desert, was no place to start explaining.

"Cold," he remarked to the others as he tucked himself back and zipped his fly.

"It will soon be warm. When the sun comes up," smiled Ben, pointing to where the yellow rim had widened and lengthened into a barrage of orange rays which, as they watched, spread right across the horizon and in the increasing light picked out a pattern of sleepy cirrus clouds, not yet fully awake, and sent them bleeding across the sky. Although no sun was yet visible the tips of barren hills suddenly blossomed on both sides as though switches were being turned on all over the place turning it into a shallow rock-strewn valley surrounded by hills of bright gold where deep blue shadows quickly slipped away to hide among the boulders.

And there below them in the valley was the plane, emerging from the shadows like a Disney dinosaur eager for extinction.

"That it?" Joe asked.

"Yes. It is the hijack plane."

"Where are the people?" Joe asked, trying to make out if there were any huts or buildings in the area.

"The hostages are all in the plane."

309

"Four hundred of them?"

"No. About a hundred. The rest have gone."

"What rest? Where have they gone?"

"All the non-Israelis were taken off yesterday and today they will be flown home. Come, we must move now."

Back in the car as it chased the last of the shadows down into the valley Joe wondered what he was going to say to these people. Could he offer them any sort of hope? They would certainly recognise him as a Jew. Whose side would they think he was on? Could they possibly understand? What would *they* ask *him*?

As if to answer his questions Ben turned round to him.

"Gadawi has said you will see ten hostages. Outside the plane. You can talk to them. Ask questions. Half an hour maybe. One hour most. No more. After that you look inside plane if you want. No talking. No questions. Just quick look, for magazine, then we go back. O.K.?"

"Ten hostages," Joe exclaimed. "Who picks them?"

"The Commander," Ben replied. "He is in charge at the plane. He is the boss. Whatever he decides, that's it."

"Are there other newspapermen or only me?"

"In the city yes. At the plane no. You the only one. Tomorrow film people coming. Television maybe. But they won't talk to hostages. Only you. That's Gadawi's orders. He must think you good guy, eh?"

He should only know, thought Joe.

"I guess so," he said, as they bumped along the road which was now running across the valley.

"Why did the plane land here?" he asked. "There's nothing here. No airport. No runway. Bit dangerous wasn't it?"

"Not dangerous. This was old French airfield. For military. Runway not bad. Anyway, plane landed. See?"

Now, as they approached the plane the sun was tipping one wing and the top of the tail and glittering in the glass of the pilots' cabin. It seemed to be waking up. A figure appeared in the open doorway high up above the ground and an improvised staircase was being moved up to the door by a group of men dressed in European style clothes and Arab headdresses, some white, some black. The car stopped about two hundred yards from the plane and two men carrying sub-machine guns came towards them. One of the men had a moustache. The other a week-old growth of stubble. The one with the moustache spoke rapidly with Ben, looking at Joe from time to time. Then he motioned to Joe with the barrel of his gun.

"He says you go with him. Ahmed, that's the Commander, has got

310

everything ready. He is over there by the plane. I come with you."

"O.K. that's fine," said Joe, looking towards the plane where three men were standing at the bottom of the stairway watching a group of people who were coming out of the plane and making their way down to the ground backwards as if it was a ladder.

Joe walked towards the plane with Ben on one side of him and the man with the moustache on the other side. The other man walked behind them. Ben hitched up his trousers as he walked and Joe noticed for the first time that he had a gun in his belt. He also saw that he was no longer smiling.

At a shout from one of the men at the foot of the ladder the man with the moustache stopped and they waited as the man who had shouted the command came towards them. He was tall and heavily built with a greyish safari-type jacket over a pair of baggy arab-style trousers tucked into his boots. He wore a black and white checkered head-dress with a black cord round it. A pair of dark glasses hid his eyes and his age, but Joe thought he must have been quite young as there were no signs of grey hair in his thick black moustache and beard.

But he was tired. A week in charge of all this, the huge plane, the hostages, food, water, shit and piss, his own men, the explosives, all this weighed heavily on his shoulders and pulled at his feet as he made his way towards them, but he pushed back his dark glasses and smiled at Ben, shaking his hand and talking to him in Arabic. He was clearly not in agreement with something Ben was saying and the weariness left him as his voice rose excitedly but as Ben replied with frequent mentions of Gadawi he shrugged his shoulders. Ben turned to Joe.

"Here is Ahmed Salim, Commander of Operations here at the plane. He speaks no English and asks me to welcome you here. He has arranged, as Gadawi has ordered, that you will meet ten of the hostages," he gestured to the group which had now completed the journey down and were standing by the immense wheels of the plane looking at him curiously, "and you can talk to them for half an hour. He is not happy for you to go into the plane but as Gadawi has authorised this you may go inside for just a few minutes if this is essential for your magazine. But he will accompany you and you will not speak to anybody. O.K.?"

Joe nodded and smiled at Salim. "Please tell the Commander that I appreciate the excellent arrangements he had made, at the . . . request . . . of Gadawi and assure him that I will do whatever he wishes. Except that I understood you to say that, if necessary, I could spend a maximum of one hour talking to the hostages? After all that is only six minutes with each. Also it is essential I go into the plane, even if it is only for a few minutes. Please explain to Salim that I am here to tell the world about the way your people are treating the hostages and that I am a man of truth. That is why Gadawi has allowed me to come."

Ben looked at Joe for a few seconds before turning to Salim and translating the message. Joe kept his eyes on the Commander as he listened to Ben apparently with no reaction apart from a slight tightening of the lips. At the end he said a few words to Ben, replaced his dark glasses, turned and walked back to the plane.

"So?" Joe asked.

"He says it is O.K. You must wait here. The hostages will be brought here and you will talk to them. For one hour."

The smile returned momentarily. "Here they come."

There is something about the way Jews walk to their death that is almost banal. Joe had this feeling of commonplace, the totally expected, we-have-seen-it-all before expression in the way they came towards him, shepherded by four men with machine guns. The whole world was talking about them. Debates at the United Nations, Presidents and Prime Ministers telephoning each other. "So what else is new?" they seemed to be saying. Every year for three thousand years they remembered how the Egyptians had enslaved them and they celebrated their liberation with *matzos*, the unleavened bread of the Bible. Every year they commemorated the story of Haman the Babylonian and celebrated his defeat by eating *"Hamantoshen"* or "Haman's ears" the triangular cakes filled with poppy seeds. "Why don't we celebrate the fall of the Roman Empire?" Joe asked once at Hebrew classes, before his *Barmitzvah*, "after all they destroyed our temple and look what happened to them." "Ah," sighed his teacher, a little man with a grey trilby hat and rimless spectacles, "if we had a celebration of the downfall of everybody who had persecuted our people we would spend our whole life celebrating."

He looked a little like his old teacher, this one standing in front of him now. He wore a trilby hat and similar, steel-rimmed glasses. But he wore no jacket. His white shirt sleeves were rolled up above the elbow and a pair of black braces held up his crumped trousers. They were all men, some young, some old. One was a rabbi, or something, Joe thought, by his beard and black coat and the little *yamalka* on his head. Most were coatless and tieless, and their shirts were beginning to look grubby and their chins stubbly. And they all think they are going to die, maybe today, Joe thought, and they're wondering who the hell I am and what this is all about. Joe looked at his watch.

"Please listen everybody," he started. "My name is Gold. Joe Gold. I'm a journalist and I've been given permission by . . ." If he called them terrorists Ben would stop him, if he called them guerillas the hostages would not trust him. "I've been given permission to meet you and talk to you for one hour only. It's now seven fifteen."

The little man in the trilby hat looked at him quizzically for a moment and then turned to the others and held up his hands in a gesture of query. One of two of them shrugged their shoulders. The others kept their eyes on Joe. There is a way to shrug your shoulders without moving your shoulders. A Jewish way. You do it with your mouth and your eyes only. That's what the little man did as he turned back to Joe.

"*Nu*," he said, "so talk."

For one panicky second Joe realised he was going to have to find a way to tell them. Without letting Ben know. So he was going to have to wait till Ben was off guard, not paying too much attention, or thinking of something else.

"Ben," he asked, "can we sit down?"

Ben thought about it, looked to where the Commander was talking to his men at the other side of the plane and decided to take the decision himself.

"O.K."

That will let them know that Ben can speak English.

Joe sat on the ground, cross legged, and the others followed, making a half circle round him.

"Now I know you will want me to contact your relatives when I get back to let them know, well, to let them know I've seen you, and we don't want to waste too much valuable time discussing that, so, with permission," Joe turned to Ben, "I'm going to pass round this paper and pencil," he tore a blank sheet from his notebook and passed it to Ben with a pencil, "and get you all to write your name and a phone number on it. Nothing else. No messages. No addresses. Just your name and a phone number I can call. When the list is finished this . . . gentleman will want to see it. So don't waste time putting anything else on the paper. O.K. Ben?"

Ben looked at the blank sheet of paper, turned it over and looked at the other side then shouted out to one of the four guards still standing by the group who came over, took the paper and pencil and gave it to one of the hostages, a young man with a newly acquired suntan who was probably on his way home after a fortnight's holiday in the sun.

"We thought . . ." It was the little man, obviously spokesman for the group, "when they asked for ten men that they wanted a *minyan*." He studied Joe's eyes as he said the Hebrew word for the group of ten men required by Jewish law before prayers can be read in synagogue. Getting the recognition he expected he continued. "We thought they wanted us to pray for them."

"Better we should pray for ourselves." A voice from the back Joe could not place.

"That shouldn't be necessary," Joe smiled. "They're all praying for you out there. The Pope, the Archbishop of Canterbury . . ." he watched the paper being passed round.

"You think God will listen to them better than our little *minyan*?" The little man smiled back at Joe, noticing the way he was watching the paper going round.

"What else are they doing apart from praying?" The suntanned young man asked this one and it gave Joe a chance to tell them about world reaction to the hijack and the efforts that were being made to get them released. The sun was now above the tops of the hills and although they were in the shadow of the plane Joe was sweating and thinking of the hundred and fifty people sitting in the heat of that plane all day. Yes there were around a hundred and fifty they reported in reply to his question. To be exact forty-seven women, eighty-six men and twelve children. Four of the men and two women were sick and needed treatment. The children were O.K. but who knows, with precious little food and water, no toilet facilities, the plane toilets having packed up after the first day, and this terrible sun all day, who knows what today will bring? When they'd taken all the non-Jews off . . .

"Non-Jews?" Joe asked. "I thought it was all the non-Israelis that had been taken away?"

"I'm not Israeli," said the young man. "I'm British. Born in Manchester, like my parents before me."

"But how did they . . . well, make the selection?"

"They looked at passports," said the man with the trilby hat. "I'm also not Israeli. But in my passport, my British passport, my name is Cohen. They can't tell the difference. To tell you the truth neither can I any more. It took a Hitler to make a lot of us realise we were Jews. Maybe it will take the Arabs to teach us we're all Israelis. Aha . . ." He took the paper and pencil which were passed to him and wrote his name and a phone number at the bottom of the list. "All present and correct. Now I'll pass this over to your . . . Mr. Ben," he leaned forward across Joe to hand the pencil and paper to Ben and as he did so whispered "*Shpricht Yiddish?*" Joe started. Yiddish? It has to be now, while Ben is studying the list.

"*A bissel*" he nodded, finding himself making a sign with his forefinger and thumb to indicate "a little". And in a pidgin-yiddish that he had not spoken for years he went on.

"*Ich glaub . . . as sey werden . . . lossen alle frei . . .* maybe today . . . *efsher morgen. Aber sey mussen . . .*"

"*Mussen?*" The little man asked, startled.

"Must," Joe nodded, and both their eyes were on Ben who had turned over the sheet and notes puzzling his way through the list on the back.

"*Wir haben einer von seyer . . .* top men . . . as hostage."

At the word "hostage" and a sense of the electric current that ran through the group as they heard the news, Ben looked up, smiling. "Everybody looks happy," he said.

"We appreciate, Mr. Ben," interjected the little man, "your arrangements for this gentleman to give a message to our families. At least they won't be so worried and we . . ."

His words were cut off by the return of the Commander who pointed to his watch and ordered the group back into the plane. As they rose to their feet Joe whispered to the little man. "*Zug goor nicht. Sey wissen noch nicht.*"

As the men climbed up the stairway Ben handed the paper and pencil to Joe. "Good idea that," he smiled, "it make them all happy."

"Right," said Joe, returning his smile.

Then it was Joe's turn to mount the steps. Never a head for heights, he grasped the rails tightly as he neared the top wondering how the women and children managed when they needed to go to the holes in the sand they had been given as toilets. Inside the plane there were no smiling hostesses, no "good evening sir" from smart uniforms, no soothing music, no message from the captain. The lights were turned off and the shafts of sun coming through the portholes fell on those same pale upturned faces he had seen in magazine articles on the Holocaust, and the Jumbo cabin became a cave full of people with the smell and the feel of the gas chamber. It was just another place for keeping Jews before you killed them.

Sick, Joe turned to go. A voice called out to him. It was the little man. "The thing about Jewish prayers, Mr. Gold, is that most of them are not asking for anything, but simply saying thank you." He turned to the rabbi who was standing beside him. "So pray already," he said, "pray!"

It was not until he was back in the car climbing out of the valley in a cloud of dust that Joe realised he had not seen his uncle.

He had certainly not been one of the ten hostages he had interviewed, and by the time he had climbed up into the plane he was in such a turmoil that he had forgotten to look for his face in the Economy Class ghetto.

Even if I had seen him, Joe reasoned to himself, there was nothing I could have done, no way I could have shown my recognition or acknowledged a greeting from him. Let's hope it works, that's all. Then it won't matter. Let's hope they keep their mouths shut too. I'd hate to have that Commander radio the news to Gadawi before I get to him. Ayayay. That's a risk I'll have to take. Bloody daft. Why in hell did I tell them? It just came out. In Yiddish, too!

Now the sun was behind and above them as they drove steadily down from the plateau. Another four or five hours, Joe calculated, looking at his watch, would make it about mid-day when they got back to the city.

"Will we be going straight to Gadawi?" Joe asked, "or will I have time to go to my hotel and get something to eat?"

The smile was back. "You hungry?"

"Not now but I will be by the time we get back."

"I must bring you to Gadawi at two o'clock. O.K.? We get back to city maybe twelve-thirty. Plenty time. Want more coffee?" He held up the thermos flask.

"Please," said Joe.

As he sipped the coffee from the plastic cup Joe knew that somewhere, sometime in the last few days he had changed sides. It had started with him sitting naked on the carpet of Zee's flat, holding the phone and hearing his sister's voice. "It's Uncle Chayim. He's on the plane that's just been hijacked." Chayim. Funny name to give a child. It means 'life' in Hebrew. He'd only seen him once in his whole life and then only spoken to him for, maybe, half an hour. But when the family had all been together in his mother's house it seemed that their only concern was for this old man. But now, down there by the plane his concern for the old man had disappeared like a river that flows into the ocean and it had all become much bigger than Chayim, bigger even than the hostages in the plane. What was getting into him? The Wandering Jew, let my people go, *shema yisroel* and all that crap?

"Thanks Ben." Joe handed the cup back over Ben's shoulder.

"More?"

"No thanks. I think I'll get a bit of sleep." He put his feet up on to the seat and settled back, catching the driver's eyes in the mirror again as he did so.

"Fuck you, too," he thought and went to sleep.

*   *   *   *

"Wherever they're taking me it's still in the city," Joe thought as, six hours later, he sat, blindfolded, in the back of a car between two men armed with machine guns, bumping over cobbled roads. He could recognise the city sounds all round him still, although they must have been driving for a quarter of an hour. Probably going round and round. Same bloody donkeys, same car horns, same market cries and same police whistles. Stopping, starting, turning, now smooth surface, now cobbles. Lucky, Joe thought, I had time to get a meal and phone London. At least they'll know what to put on their front page if I don't phone them back in three hours.

The car stopped and Joe was helped out and, still blindfolded, taken across what he felt was a courtyard. The traffic noises were muffled and mixed with the clucking of chickens. Into a ground floor room where he was backed on to a chair and his blindfold removed.

"You O.K.?" Good old smiler.

"Sure Ben. Fine. We here?"

"Yes. You wait with these men. I tell Gadawi you're here. O.K.?" He turned and went off through an open doorway facing him that seemed to be an office of some sort, with typewriter noises and people talking.

Wait with these men. He looked at the sub-machine guns resting on their laps. I have a choice? Well, he still had some sort of choice. Whether to go ahead with the kidnap scheme and try for a hostage swap or forget the whole thing and just get a good story. That's a choice? Anyone can get a good story. How many people can change the world? Arrogant bastard, he argued with himself, what are you changing? A few people's lives maybe, so what? So go and ask those poor sods on the plane, that's what. But the world, Joe, change the world? Admitted you're helping those hostages but how are you changing the world? Well, the Arabs are going to find out that two can play at that game aren't they? There must be hundreds of sheiks and sheikesses walking round in London, Paris and Rome just ripe to be picked up. They want to play games with innocent peoples' lives. O.K. we'll play games. That could change things. Ay, Joe, you're as bad as them, you'll never . . .

His argument with himself was interrupted by Ben's return. That was quick. Good or bad? No smile but that could be his headquarters image. Stern. Tough.

"O.K." No question this, more like an order. The machine gun boys got up and so did Joe as Ben turned and they followed him

317

through a different door this time, the cracks in the grey cement walls emphasised by the yellow light on a bare bulb plugged into a holder on the low ceiling. So low Joe had to duck.

At the end of the corridor Ben knocked on a wooden door, waited for the word from within and then pushed open the door and signalled Joe to go through.

Facing him, along the wall was a bare trestle table and seated behind the table looking at him were five men. The one in the middle, the only face he recognised, was Abdul Gadawi, Secretary of the Palestine Arab Liberation Movement, known all over the world as PALM. It was a face made remarkable by a pair of blue eyes that were extraordinarily out of place between those shaggy black eyebrows and moustache. He rose and held out his hand to Joe.

"Mr. Gold. Good to see you at last. I have read your articles with great interest. Please sit down."

A tough handshake. But friendly. Phew! That was a relief. At least he still had the initiative. Introductions, smiles all round. Looked as if they had assembled half the High Command. Coffee? What a privilege it was for him, what a pleasure it was for them, what a lot of balls all this chit chat was. Right. Let him have it.

"Look, Mr. Gadawi. Before we start talking I have been asked to pass on to you some very important and confidential information. My sources specifically asked me to give this information to you alone and I would suggest that you ask your colleagues to leave us alone for a few moments. You may of course wish to search me before we are alone together and this I quite understand. But I do assure you this information is of the greatest importance to you . . . and to the whole Arab Liberation Movement."

Although he had rehearsed the speech backwards and forwards many times in the car on the way back from the plane, as he heard himself talking, and watched those blue eyes narrow beneath the black brows, Joe knew now that he had taken the step that could cost him his life, and that there was no going back.

The five men behind the table conferred quickly in Arabic and all except Gadawi rose and left the room.

"It is not necessary to search you, Mr. Gold." The mouth beneath the moustache curled up a little at the ends but the smile did not reach into those blue eyes. "We believe you are a friend. Otherwise you would not be here. Please say what you have to say."

On the whitewashed wall behind the Arab leader Joe saw the pictures of Lenin and Marx and the poster of Che Guevara with Arabic lettering. Che lives? What would old Vladimir Ilytch have said about hijacking Joe wondered. What would Marx have said to

Uncle Chayim and who the hell cares anyway? What matters was what Gadawi would say after he heard the news.

"On the morning that I left London I received a telephone call from a man representing an organisation called the Friends of Israel. They had heard from some of their contacts in Fleet Street that I was coming to interview the hostages and asked me to get a message to you personally. I told the man that I could not guarantee that I would be able to see you but if I felt the message was worth passing on I would try to do so. When I heard the message I knew it was essential. I asked your people to take me to you as soon as I got off the plane last night but they told me you were away and I could only see you today. The message concerns Salem Mahrbash . . ." Only the slightest ripple of the blue eyes betrayed the surprise at the mention of the name. "He has been . . . captured . . . by this Group and I was asked to tell you that unless all the hostages are released and on a British plane bound for London through Zurich by midnight tomorrow Mahrbash will be killed."

The Arab leaned back in his chair until his head rested on the Che Guevara poster behind him and reached down into the pocket of the jacket which was hanging on the back of his chair, taking out a pack of cigarettes and a lighter. He lit a cigarette and inhaled deeply before replying.

"Is that all the message?"

"No. There are two other points. One, they say they are prepared to make the exchange at Zurich and I am to phone my paper at nine o'clock this evening to let the Editor know if it is yes or no. They will be phoning my Editor at nine-thirty." Gadawi looked at his wristwatch. Two thirty. "Point two," Joe went on, "they are prepared to do everything without publicity. You make whatever announcement you like about why you are doing it. Nobody will know that Mahrbash has been captured, or released. They say their only interest is the lives of the hostages. All of them. And that's it."

There were only three small windows on one side of the room and these were high up near the ceiling. The afternoon sun was just coming through the window, striping the wall and folding across the bare trestle like a tablecloth. Joe put his hand on the table and felt the warmth of the sun.

"That's it, eh?" Gadawi jerked forward, stubbing his cigarette out in a full ashtray in front of him and leaned across the table to Joe. "And you, Mr. Gold. How do you fit in with all this?"

Joe withdrew his hand from the sun. It was getting hot.

"I don't," he shrugged. "I'm just the messenger boy. What I'm here for is my interview with the hostages, which you very kindly

319

organised for me, and then to get your side of it for the British Press. When I left London yesterday you were not getting a very good press." He paused and then continued.

"Of course I well understand that, after getting that message you may not feel inclined to go ahead with the interview, or perhaps put it off until some other time. But I thought I ought to give it to you straight away so that you can make up your mind how you want to play it. You'll probably want to check with your people in London anyway to see if the story is true. After all, it may just be a hoax."

"It is no hoax Mr. Gold." Gadawi lit another cigarette. "I telephoned Mahrbash this morning at a time previously agreed with him. He was not there. His hotel says he has not been there for twenty four hours. I was . . . well, a little puzzled. He had previously told me of your first interview with him and your plans to meet him again yesterday . . . that is why I was . . ." he hesitated ". . . interested to hear you were coming here. Even you, Mr. Gold could not be in two places at once. It seems somebody else may have taken your place?"

Maybe it was the brightness of the sun, now flooding the room, but Joe, looking into those eyes a few feet away from him across the table, felt rather than saw a subtle change of colour, a greenish tinge entering, a greyish shadow retreating, a golden glint reflecting the window. He was suspicious. He didn't like the whole thing. He was looking for something he could do, something he could say, some way out. Take it easy Joe. Just play the innocent messenger boy. He'd got the point about your Editor waiting to hear from you.

"Not possible," Joe replied. "Only Mahrbash knew about our appointment. Unless . . ."

"Unless?" The cigarette held between finger and thumb, the smoke curling white in the rays of the sun.

"Unless Mahrbash told some of your people in London . . ."

"Ah, London is a curious place Mr. Gold. I would not like to go there. Anything can happen in London." In a sudden change of mood the Arab leader smiled at Joe, stubbed out his half smoked cigarette, and rose to his feet. "As you say, I must talk things over and decide what to do. Now is not a good time for an interview, but perhaps later this evening we will meet again and I will tell you what to say to your Editor . . . before nine-thirty . . . and then maybe you will have an interesting story for your papers that will do us more good even than your interview. Who knows?"

He held out his hand, smiling, but the hand held no warmth this time. A quick command in Arabic brought the machine-gun boys back with a frowning Ben and they were back in the corridor, Joe ducking his head again to avoid the naked bulb.

The last thing he saw before they put the blindfold on him again were Gadawi's four colleagues, looking very puzzled as they filed back into the room.

*   *   *   *

It certainly was a good story. Two days later, as Zee drove him out of London Airport, he flipped through the pile of newspapers on his lap, throwing them, one after the other, on to the back seat of the car as he finished with them. 'HOSTAGES FREE!' 'ARABS RELEASE HOSTAGES!' 'GUERRILLAS AGREE TO RED CROSS REQUEST!' 'DESERT TERROR ENDS IN SMILES!'

All good stuff, he thought, turning to Zee.

"Thanks for coming to meet me."

She gave him a quick smile.

"Not at all. I want to hear all about it."

"It's all in these."

"Is it?"

"Well, not all of it maybe."

She said nothing for a while, concentrating on the signs ahead, her stockinged feet moving from clutch to accelerator, her shoes lying on the floor of the car, her skirt just above her knees. As they moved on to the motorway back to London she relaxed a bit, after looking over her shoulder.

"Did you see your uncle?" she asked.

"No." He shook his head.

"He saw you."

Joe looked up in surprise. "You've spoken to him?"

"Oh yes. There was a big party last night. Everybody was there, except you. As usual." She took one hand off the wheel and put it on his thigh, smiling. "No offence."

"None taken. He said he saw me?"

"Yes. He said you had this meeting with representatives of the hostages and said they were going to be set free. Then you came into the plane and he recognised you. Funny."

"What's funny?"

"Well . . . he said when you left they all prayed for you."

Joe looked out of the window. Why on earth should something daft like that make him want to cry? "Much good that'll do me," he said, putting his hand on Zee's. "So where are we going now, to join the party?"

"No," Zee replied. moving her hand further up his thigh, "I thought we'd go back to my place and carry on where we left off before Sadie telephoned."

*　　*　　*　　*

It was a week before he managed to get together with Sam.

"Why all the mystery?" Sam asked him, looking round with some curiosity at the occupants of the three other tables in the tiny Greek restaurant in Soho where Joe had arranged to meet him.

"I'm being followed," Joe replied, signalling to the waiter.

"Well you're safe here," said Sam. "Nobody in their right mind would follow you into this place. Seriously, who's following you?"

"PALM, I imagine. I've spotted this guy a couple of times as I left home and managed to lose him without making it too obvious. I think. But I didn't want to take a chance."

Sam looked round again, more carefully. "Did they . . .?"

"No chance," said Joe. "I don't mind them following me. Sooner or later they'll realise I'm not involved with any Israeli group and then they'll pack it in. I just didn't want them to connect me with you. What are you eating?"

Sam studied the greasy card with its handwritten list of Greek dishes.

"I used to like stuffed vine leaves until I read Lady Chatterley's Lover. Since then they seem somewhat obscene."

"I thought it was forget-me-nots and wild flowers," said Joe looking through the list. "Moussaka," he said to the waiter.

"Make it two."

"Two moussaka. Any wine gentlemen?"

"Retsina," said Joe.

Sam winced. Joe was moving his knife and fork about, tidying up the glass salt and pepper cruet. "Your people did a good job," he said.

"Chalk it up Joe. One day I'll tell you about all the jobs that didn't come off. You didn't do too badly either."

"Funny what you can do when you try."

"So keep trying."

"I intend to. But first I have a message for you."

"From?"

"Gadawi."

"For me?"

"For the Friends of Israel, whoever they are."

"Who are they?"

322

"That's the name I gave Gadawi for the group that snatched Mahrbash."

"I see. And the message is?"

The waiter returned with two wine glasses and a carafe of white wine. Joe poured two glasses and as they both lifted their glasses to their lips Joe said "Be careful what you say. This is very delicate stuff. It takes umbrage."

Sam sipped the wine. "Umbrage," he said. "Hmm. I think you're right Joe. I would say it has already taken a goodly amount of umbrage. *Lechayim.*" He raised the glass in a toast.

"You should be so lucky," Joe responded.

The waiter returned with two plates. On each of them was an earthenware dish which appeared to be full of custard. The waiter carefully emptied each dish on to its plate, trying to keep the custard whole and uppermost. But not succeeding in either case. Beneath the top layer was an evil looking mixture of minced meat and aubergine and onions and potatoes and tomatoes. Joe forked a helping of mince into his mouth. "Shepherd's pie," he remarked.

Sam did the same. "Right," he said, "and if I'm not mistaken, made with real Greek shepherds."

Between the retsina and the moussaka, and a salad that arrived when they were half-way through the meal, Joe reported on the trip, the ride to the plane, the meeting with the hostages, the look inside the plane, the journey back and the first interview with Gadawi.

"You think he suspected you?" Sam asked.

"Who knows? I thought so at the time but there was nothing he could do. Mahrbash was more important to him than any number of hostages. But then when I saw him later that day he was all sweetness and light. We had a meal together and he gave me the interview I wanted, answered all my questions and talked about his plans. He couldn't have been nicer."

"I'm sure your Uncle Chayim would appreciate that."

"I was thinking of that while he was talking. It's strange really. I've talked to Gadawi and, since I got back I've talked to Uncle Chayim and let's face it I've got more in common with Gadawi than the old boy. I agree with most of what Gadawi says about freedom and liberation and socialism and land. Chayim, on the other hand, is a Capitalist. Oh, I don't mean the cigar-smoking, money-grabbing caricature. He's not bad politically, but he runs a business, employs people, owns property and . . . he's not my sort of person. He doesn't want the sort of world I want. Gadawi does. And yet . . ."

"And yet?"

"I went out there, took sides with the old man against Gadawi and pulled it off. Why?"

Sam held his glass up to the light and turned the captured reflection this way and that.

"Blood is thicker than Retsina, and all that?" he suggested.

"Maybe," Joe replied. "I thought about that too." He paused for a moment. "I remember what somebody once said to me at the time of the Jewish doctors' plot. Would you be so worried, he asked me, if they were Armenians."

"Good question. Would you?"

"I don't know. But if they'd hijacked a plane load of Armenians I doubt if I'd have flown out there and risked my neck to save them."

"There's your answer Joe, To each his own."

"But it's not as simple as that Sam. You know that. You're prepared to have a go at those National Front bastards when they say send the blacks back."

"That's because I know they're only practising. A Nazi is a Nazi and we all know that they're using the anti-immigrant thing simply to win popular support and when they're ready, and strong enough, they'll start on the Jews, then the Trade Unions, the other political parties the lot. It's all in *Mein Kampf*. It's there for anybody to read."

"So you're fighting the National Front not because they're anti-black, but because you think you're next on the list."

"I suppose that's right Joe."

"That's the difference between you and me Sam. I'm against racialists even if they're not anti semitic, even if they're Jewish. And I'll fight black anti semites too."

"And Russian anti semites?"

Joe nodded.

"Right," he said.

"And your Arab friends?"

"Ah that's it. Coffee?" Sam nodded. Joe went on. "I talked to Gadawi on this and he was trying to draw a distinction between Jews and Zionists, or between Jews and Israelis. Unfortunately for him I'd seen the hostages first and I was able to point out that many of the hostages were not Israeli but were separated from the others and kept behind because they were Jews. He was a bit put out at that and swore that was against instructions but that was a lot of balls. You could see that from the way he said it. Then I tackled him on the Arab boycott and quoted the terms of the questionnaire which specifically talks about Jews, not Zionists. Of course he says he is not responsible for the boycott but I pointed out the whole purpose of it was to help the Palestinians."

"He must have liked you."

"Oh I was just interviewing him and telling him some of the questions that are giving him a bad image. He didn't mind. The thing that bugged him most was the business with Mahrbash. You see that was a new development. Somebody playing his own game. He could see how vulnerable his people are if anybody starts an anti-Arab terrorist organisation. Something he said after that makes me think we're in for a new type of activity, and I think it'll be political rather than terrorist. And this is the message I was telling you about. 'Tell your friends ...' I protested at that of course and he smiled and changed his way of putting it, 'Tell those people who contacted you about Mahrbash that they are too late. The time for this sort of activity is coming to an end. The Israelis used terrorism to fight the British and now their top terrorist Menahem Begin who was the leader of the Irgun is now a respectable member of the Israeli Parliament. We are using terror to fight the Israelis and maybe soon we will be sitting in our own Parliament, and in the United Nations, and everybody will think how respectable we are'."

"The United Nations? He said that?"

"Right. I tried to draw him on that but he wasn't having any. He just went on about the 'Arab Nation' whatever that means, specially after the Palestinians and the Jordanians had just been tearing each other to pieces. I think this is some new line that's coming out of Saudi Arabia. Remember they pay all the bills and Gadawi had apparently just come back from there."

"You mean the Arabs will be all pals together? I don't believe it. They hate each other more than they hate the Israelis, and who can blame them?"

"If they do get together it won't be just against Israel but against the West. They know they can't get anywhere against Israel by military means. They feel embarrassed at being the only Liberation Movement in the world that has not yet liberated one square inch of territory. No that's not the direction, as I see it, but some big push against the West, particularly America, which they see as Israel's main supporter. Again, not military but more diplomatic, maybe economic."

"What can they do to influence the West? What have they got that we haven't got?"

"How about oil?"

"Oil! But if the sheiks don't sell us their oil how are they going to run their Cadillacs? Seriously, that's all they've got. If they don't sell it they'll go broke. And if they don't sell it to *us* we'll go broke. I would have thought the last thing in the world that Saudi Arabia wants is for the capitalist system to go under."

"O.K. But it depends how far they push it. They might just try it on for size. Give everybody a fright. Force some of the weaker ones to recognise Gadawi possibly, maybe even get him into the United Nations . . ."

"The United Nations. I see."

"I wish I did. It's only guesswork really. But it's a possibility. Only I wouldn't like to be in Faisal's shoes when they do it."

"Why not?"

"Well the Americans don't like being pushed around, specially by people they regard as second-rate nations."

"What could they do?"

"Ever heard of the CIA? I wouldn't give Faisal more than a couple of years if he pulls a stunt like that on the Yanks."

"But you reckon they'll do something?"

"That's just the way I interpret what Gadawi told me. Where, when, how . . . your guess is as good as mine. But I think they'll need some pretty good excuse to start something like an oil boycott. It'd have to be something big. So big perhaps that the West would maybe accept the boycott almost with relief as the lesser of the two evils."

"And what could that be Joe?"

"War."

When the war came, and the accompaying Arab oil boycott that rocked the already weakening economies of the industrialised nations of the West, it was Yaser Arafat and not Abdul Gadawi who took the stage at the United Nations.

An unprepossessing man who seemed no more able to control his permanent untidy stubble than he could the more militant terrorist groups in his Palestine Liberation Organisation, Arafat rode to the UN on the crest of an oil wave which his Saudi paymasters had organised to drown Israel and also, coincidentally, to double the price of oil. He spoke of coming to the UN with an olive branch in one hand and a machine gun in the other, and if the olive branch was not immediately apparent to the Israelis the gun was certainly clear to terrorists throughout the world who aspired, if not to the lofty heights of the United Nations, at least to power in their own countries.

In South America, in Canada, in Northern Ireland, in West Germany and Africa bombing, assassination, kidnapping and other forms of terror opened a new door to nationhood. The Third World was invented as the prize in the contest waged by the other two worlds.

The contest was fought with machine guns here, with ideology there, with corruption and bribery, blackmail and intimidation, idealism and self-seeking, with hatred . . . and with love. Above all it was fought by the Intelligence Organisations of the opposing powers, using the vast resources at their disposal to wage a war that must never develop into nuclear war, a tightrope war where nations were won and lost, governments overthrown, new governments established while the main protagonists sat at conference tables, agreed on armament limitations, worked out formulas for "détente", gave each other medals, paid official visits and photographed each other's rocket installations from satellites each of them sent strangling round the globe.

*   *   *   *

The satellite photographs joined the telephoto shots and miniature camera negatives and the tapes and the reports and the file that piled upon file in the intelligence sections and the analysis departments until one morning a bright young man whose job it ws to look at these things all day and every day came into his superior's office on the twelfth floor of a new block that dominated the centre of a market town in the Home Counties and put a green file on his desk.

"The fellow Gold is becoming quite interesting," he said, standing respectfully on the other side of the desk and noting the single rose that stood in the delicate glass vase in the centre of the desk. It was still early in the day and the rose, no doubt grown in his superior's three-acre garden and picked this morning, had not yet fully opened.

"Which fellow Gold?" His boss picked up the file and opened it. "Oh, him. What's he up to now?"

"Going to the United Nations apparently."

"So?"

"Well, as you know sir, we've been watching him for some while and he always seems to pop up in different parts of the world when there's trouble."

"That's his job isn't it?"

"As we agreed sir, when this chap was first brought to our attention, it's more likely that his job is his cover. It certainly was that first time."

"When was that?" His boss flicked the pages of the file through his fingers. "I'm sure it's all in here somewhere, but refresh my memory Turner. And sit down."

"Thank you sir. As you say, it's all in there, but you may recall that

327

the first occasion this man was brought to our attention was at the time of the BOAC hijack in Syria. We had previously had him in Section twenty-five as a fairly small time political, ex CP, played with Trots, friends among the Anarchists, ex-girl friend with the Bomb Brigade and all that. Then he got involved with the Jews. He is a Jew himself sir, and got mixed up with that funny business with the SS Colonel who, er, disappeared. He doesn't appear to have got on too well with his Jewish friends . . ."

"Not surprised."

Turner smiled and continued.

"Well, then he seemed to find his feet, professionally that is, and became rather in demand as a freelance political journalist specialising in what used to be called "Liberation Movements" in different parts of the world. Worked for some of the best papers, sir. The full list is in the file. That's where it started. At least to the best of our knowledge, sir."

"Hmm. Whenever I hear people say that I get the feeling that they mean they've got no bloody idea."

"Not exactly sir. There could have been incidents before. You can never be sure, as you know yourself, but in the overall picture it's not of any consequence. Our information on this particular occasion was specific and first rate."

"Who was it?"

"A533 sir, Ben something or other. If I may." Turner rose slightly and, bending over the desk quickly turned the pages of the file back until he could read, upside down, at the top of the page, BOAC HIJACK/SYRIA/Page Three from Two.

"Just there sir," his finger pointed to the middle of the page. His boss started to read aloud the section he had indicated.

"In the course of his dicussions with the hostages, at the time when he might have assumed that I was occupied with reading the list of addresses, Gold spoke to the hostages in Yiddish, a language which he probably guessed, and correctly, that I do not understand. However, this language, used by Jews all over the world, derives largely from German in which I am fluent. He told the hostages '*Ich glaub as sey werden lossen alle frei* . . . (something) *morgen. Aber sey mussen.*' Translation: 'I believe they will set everybody free (something) tomorrow. But they must.'

"This last word was heavily emphasised and queried by one of the hostages. Gold then confirmed this, going on to say '*Wir haben einer von seyer* (top men . . . as hostage.)' Translation: 'We have one of their top men . . . as hostage.' The last four words were spoken in English, possibly because Gold, who did not appear too fluent in this

328

language, did not know the Yiddish words."

He stopped reading and leaned back in his chair.

"Yes, I remember that now. Good report."

"Good man sir. One of the best of our Arabs. Christian actually. Very good type. Most unfortunate."

"Eh?"

"Killed last year sir. You may remember."

"Oh, that was him was it?"

"Yes sir. Good man." They were both quiet for a moment, and Turner noticed the perfume of the rose. "On that occasion sir, as you may recall, we suspected Gold's collusion with Jewish friends but were unable to confirm this. Since then we suspect his involvement in five other incidents and have definite proof of two more."

"Where?"

"Oh, Uganda, Argentina, Germany twice, Switzerland, France, South Africa."

"Always abroad eh?"

"Precisely."

"He's a busy little bee."

"And getting busier, sir. Three of the incidents have occurred in the last year, two the year before and one in each of the previous years."

"Any pattern?"

"Possibly sir. The German incidents and the one in Argentina all concerned ex-Nazi top brass."

"Any connection with that chap in Austraia?"

"Simon Wiesenthal, sir? None at all ... to the best of our knowledge." They exchanged glances across the desk and Turner continued. "The Uganda one you know about sir, the Swiss was the one about the gold bullion that disappeared, allegedly on its way to fund various European right-wing groups including two over here. The French one sir concerned a British citizen but as it was not in our territory ..."

"Who was that?"

"Sir Oswald Mosley, sir."

"Proof?"

"Not that one sir. Unfortunately."

"Pity. Not nice, that."

"Quite agree sir."

"What happened to that Swiss gold? Did it ever turn up?"

"No sir. Sunk without trace, to the best ..." He looked up, shrugged his shoulders and allowed himself a small smile.

"He wasn't in Egypt at the time of ... ?"

Turner looked up sharply. "The Sadat assassination? No sir, we checked on that at the time. He was in England."

"Hm-m. Funny business that."

"But not wholly unexpected sir, surely. After all, Sadat had stepped out of line so far as the Arabs were concerned. They wanted his blood. Said so publicly at the Tripoli Conference."

"Yes, yes ... " A certain weariness crept into his voice as he turned the pages of the file. "Pity though. They seemed to be so near a peaceful solution at the time. That's probably why."

"Indeed sir. Quite agree."

"I take it he had been abroad on occasions when *nothing* has happened? I mean things do happen *without* Gold sometimes I trust?"

"Indeed sir."

"I mean to say, we can't go issuing warnings to all and sundry every time this chap gets on an airplane can we?"

"Point taken sir. I just thought I should draw it to your attention sir."

"Quite right Turner. Glad to see you're keeping a watch on the fellow. Married is he?"

"Yes sir. One son. Lives apart. Has his own flat but they seem . . . very friendly sir. Visits her a lot, go out together, quite often stays overnight . . ."

"Seems like a good arrangement to me. Have to ask him how he does it, eh?" Turner smiled. "Anyway keep watching. All these things, Germans, Nazis, Blacks and that, don't really do us any harm. All abroad. Interesting that. I didn't like that Mosley business but even he . . ."

"Sir?"

"Well, he was a bit of an odd chap. Know what I mean? Hitler at his wedding and all that. Married one of the Mitford girls. Now *they* were a funny lot." He looked into the past for a moment then closed the file and handed it back to Turner. "Thank you Turner. Good work. Keep it up."

"Thank you sir." He rose and as he turned to go he looked at the rose.

"Peace, sir?" he asked.

"Eh?" The older man looked at him for a moment puzzled, then, realising he was talking about the rose, he laughed heartily and replied, "Peace, yes. Picked it this morning."

*   *   *   *

"Married! You must be joking!" Joe exclaimed when Zee told him

330

their son was thinking of getting married. "He can't be more than twenty."

"Fine father you are, he's nearer thirty."

"Christ Zee, I'd better warn him."

"You what?"

"Well, I'd be failing in my fatherly duty if I didn't point out to him the pitfalls in the path he is considering."

"You didn't do too badly." She smiled, fondling his hair, still thick and wiry but now completely grey. And that little silver moustache that he had grown two years ago. Most distinguished. Definitely elder statesman. And husband. That's how she thought of him now. Husband, as if he'd never gone away. As if he was there all the time. He's away on a job, she'd say to the family. And to herself.

"Badly I should do, *noch*? That's what my old man used to say when Mum told him he wasn't doing too badly. 'Badly I should do *noch*?' He meant it too. Nothing should be done badly. Everything had to be 'the best'. Ayayay. She had a tough time with him."

"But you told me it wasn't his fault. He was sick."

"Sure but when the old guy starts shouting at you and losing his temper who knows it's because he's sick? He's just a bad-tempered bastard."

"She knew at the end."

"Ah, the end," he sighed. "Everything comes out all right at the end. When it's too bloody late." He put his hand up to her, sitting on the arm of his chair, and she took it in hers. "It should be better for people Zee. It should be better. Not at the end, but all the time."

"It's better with us now, isn't it? And we're not at the end."

He looked up at her and she bent down to kiss him.

"No love, we're at the beginning," he said.

"I don't feel like a beginner."

"You certainly don't," he grinned, releasing his hand and putting it on her breast.

"And you don't act like one," she replied. "So will you talk to Robbie?"

He nodded. "Better I should talk to his girl friend. What's her name?"

"Better you shouldn't," she removed his hand and went to sit in the chair facing him. "I wish you weren't going away tomorrow. They're both coming round to dinner. Is it so important?"

"Afraid so. It's the big United Nations debate on Israel. 1948 in reverse. This time they want to un-make a state instead of making one."

"They can't do that can they?"

331

"On paper they can do anything. 1948: 'We declare this is now a State'. Tomorrow, 'we declare this is not a State'. The Arabs can blackmail enough people to go with them by now."

"But the Americans won't agree surely."

"I'm not so sure. The oil is one problem but a bigger problem than this is their own Blacks. More than one in ten of the population is black. Over the last few years the Blacks have been building up this "Black Nation" thing, working very closely with the African States. It's not beyond the realms of possibility that there could be a black separatist movement, backed by the Africans, the Arabs and the Communists in the UN and that would really throw the black cat among the pigeons."

"But how could that affect this Israel situation now?"

"They could be doing a deal. I smell a deal, love, a deal between the Yanks, the Arabs and the Africans."

"But what would the Russians say to that?"

"Ah! Now that could be really fascinating. If the deal includes a break with the Russians by the Arabs and the Africans, and that's what America has been working for, then the Russians will move over to support for Israel. Not at the UN, and not straight away, but arms to begin with, then a word here and there. Resumption of diplomatic relations, trade missions, cultural exchanges. Then a Russian base in Haifa maybe and missiles all round. Musical chairs."

"But the Israelis won't want the Russians in."

"They want to survive. Russians, Americans, what does it matter so long as you've got your health and strength."

"Oh Joe, it makes me so sick, the way they push everybody around. Sometimes I wish somebody would blow the whole lot of them up."

*   *   *   *

When Joe got off the plane at Kennedy Airport next day he took a taxi straight to his hotel and made two phone calls.

The first one was very short.

"Hullo, I'm here."

"Good. Everything O.K.?"

"Fine. You?"

"Absolutely. Five o'clock O.K.?"

"Fine. See you then."

"See you."

The second took longer and was with the New York correspondent of the London newspaper that had commissioned Joe to write a series of interviews with the leading figures who would be participating in the big UN debate.

"Hullo, may I speak with Mr. Gerry Rushton please."

"One moment" . . . a pause . . . "who is that calling?"

"Tell him it's Joe Gold, from London. He's expecting my call."

After a few moments and various clickings and snippets of conversation, a very fruity, very English voice poured into Joe's ear.

"Hullo, my boy. You finally made it."

"Hullo Gerry. Yes, I just got in. How are things?"

"Things? Things, old boy, are boiling up beautifully. It certainly looks as if you've come just at the right moment. The debate starts tomorrow as you know and I've laid on all your interviews, two a day for the next three days, as you suggested."

"First class Gerry, first class. All the people I asked to see have agreed to talk to me?"

"Every one, Joe. The only problem I had was with the Israelis but when I told them who else you were seeing they had to fall in line although between you and me old boy, I don't reckon much to their chances of still being in the club by the time all this is over."

"Like that is it?"

"Looks very much like it old boy."

"Well, that'll make it just like that golf club of yours Gerry."

"Eh?" The fruit went a little sour. "Oh, I see. You're right."

"Anyway Gerry, it looks as if we've got a lot to talk about, can you join me for dinner tonight?"

"Love to old boy. Shall I pick you up about seven?"

"Make it eight will you Gerry. I've got a date for five o'clock at the Twentytwo Club. I could be an hour or so then I have to get back here and wash up. No, seven-thirty. O.K.?"

"Good old Joe. You don't waste much time. Give her my love. I'll pick you up at 7.30. Ciao."

"Ciao Gerry."

Joe put down the receiver, patted it gently and said, "Now off you go to the Twentytwo Club my friend, and the best of luck to you."

An hour later as he left his hotel he hailed a cab and loudly asked the driver to take him to the Twentytwo Club. After the cab had driven a few blocks he knocked on the glass that separated him from the driver and said he had changed his mind and gave him an address in the opposite direction. Checking through the back window he was confident that his cab was not being followed and leaned back, smiling, in his seat. After nearly half-an-hour the cab stopped outside a bar in a side street that looked as if the weight of the buildings on each side had, over the years, pushed them down below the level of the road. Everything seemed to be sagging, especially the metal stairway that led to the basement bar. As he held on to the metal rail he felt he was boarding a ship. A sinking ship. His impression was strengthened by the rolling gait of the man who came out as he went into the dimly lit interior. A man whose eyes had grown accustomed to the dark gave him a rodent glance, twitched his nostrils and turned away. I am a mole and I live in a hole. Joe smiled to himself and sat down at a table facing the door.

The table was wiped and a scotch brought at Joe's request, the yellow liquid eddying round the rocks as he waited and wondered how the hell it had all started.

Sam's lot and the Nazi Colonel? No, it was way before that. The Peace Movement? The Party? Maybe even Cable Street. Watching all the forces of Law and Order mobilised to protect the same Blackshirts who bashed me up a few weeks before. If the police don't defend you then you defend yourself. That's all there is to it. And they never bloody learn, never . . . Forty years later here it is all being repeated, with National Front marches through the predominantly black areas. *Shmerels*.

Why keep on fighting? Why go on? Survival. That's what it's all about. Simple survival. Which is why I was so ready for Sam's little adventure. It was something that could be done. That *I* could do. Not just sitting and waiting to see if some bloody politician would have the guts to stamp on the Nazis as soon as they started coming back. They used me, Sam's lot. And I was glad to be of use. But it felt good to be able to use *them* in the hijack rescue. And so bloody good to see how Gadawi and his merry men were forced to play it my way, while prime ministers and presidents where shitting themselves all round the world, ready to give in, release the terrorists in prison, give them a few million dollars donation to their funds and sit back and wait for the next lot. Little men, little men. You think you run the world. You couldn't run a . . .

"Hi Joe." The voice came from behind his shoulder. Surprised, Joe looked up at the tall Black in a dark blue T-shirt who had spoken to him. It was Wilf Strawn, an American he had met in London a year ago in a Charing Cross Road bookshop. He had been stretching out his hand to reach for a book on terrorism that had just been published when a black hand grasped the same book just ahead of him. After apologising to each other they had started talking, and Joe had discovered that Wilf knew friends of his. They arranged to meet for a drink in a few days. Checking with his friends, Joe learned that the young man had been associated with the Weathermen and various black liberation groups in Chicago and New York. They met and talked and rang the right bells with each other. But it was only on the night that Wilf described the Black Nation movement as "black chauvinist pigs" that the idea first came to Joe.

"Every time I hear the word 'nation' I spit blood," Wilf had said. "Black Nation. That's a laugh. Is that going to solve the problems of the Blacks in the States? Unemployment, that's our problem. And that means poverty and bloody misery. Stinking lousy housing, an environment soaked in crime and violence of every kind. Man, the only way you change that is by changing the whole rotten society not just changing its colour."

In the weeks that followed, getting more and more excited as every check he made on both sides of the Atlantic confirmed Wilf's story right back to his childhood in a Chicago ghetto, Joe realised that this could be it, the opportunity for him to change the world, to stop the whole gruesome game for a few days and show people where it had all gone wrong and open up new doors for them, new thoughts, new worlds. That side of it he could do. What he needed was the technical know-how.

It took a little while to work it out but Wilf had already told Joe about his work with the Weathermen. He was the technical man, the one who knew how to put wires together and connect them with the timing mechanism so that the big bang occurred in the right place at the right time. Hopefully.

An electrician by trade, a bomb-maker by inclination, he had got out of the Weathermen before the FBI got in and started playing around with fuses and blew themselves up. "Organisations are death," Wilf said. "Specially when there are bombs around. Me and you could do it Joe. Just the two of us."

"Do what?" Joe asked, knowing in his mind what *he* wanted to do.

"Blow the whole fucking lot up. All those bastards who reckon they're running the world. One after the other. Bang! Bang! Bang!"

Joe hesitated for a moment before taking the step that could set the whole operation in motion.

"Why one after the other?" he asked. "Why not all together?"

"Hell, man, where you going to get them all together? What you going to do, invite them all to a party?"

"Would you believe the United Nations?"

Wilf looked at him, his eyes opening wide, and gradually a great grin spread across his face. He started laughing and rolled back in his seat, roaring such such delight that Joe suddenly found himself laughing too, laughing so much that his sides hurt, so that he had to get up and walk about, holding his sides as tears streamed down his cheeks and, bumping into Wilf, clasping him in his arms and giving him little punches in the ribs.

So that whenever they met after that they would remember the laughing and hugging and smile at each other at the memory of it.

Like now, in the bar, as Joe looked up at him with his Afro haircut he smiled and returned his greeting with an upraised hand.

"Hi, I didn't see you come in."

"No man, you wouldn't. You was looking the wrong way. I came in that back way, and that's the way we going out."

"Good. You want a drink?"

"No way. Not in this place. You finish lickin' that yellow stuff off those lumps of ice and we'll go back to my place. O.K.?"

"Sure Wilf. I've finished. Let's go."

Joe signalled to the waiter that he was leaving his money on the table and followed the black man out of the back door into an even smaller and seedier side street and along an alleyway that seemed to be designed as an obstacle course with dustbins and packing cases, through a doorway and up two flighrs of stairs lit by a skylight at the top of the stairwell. On the landing Wilf stopped and took a key out of his pocket and unlocked a door. Joe followed him through and was surprised by the size of the room and the windows that ran the whole length of one wall. The furnishings were minimal. Two mattresses on the bare floor covered with Indian style rugs and a pile of cushions, a low table with unwashed crockery, three tourist posters pinned alongside each other on the wall opposite the windows showing demure Japanese ladies in bright silk kimonos standing by rustic wooden bridges crossing carp-filled streams. Japanese Air Lines. At the far end of the room a partition wall with a door in the centre. On the floor at one side of the mattress with cushions, was an expensive looking record player and tape deck and on the other side a telephone.

"Not bad eh?" Wilf waved Joe to a seat on the mattress and went up to the door at the far end of the room. "Sit down man, make yourself comfortable, I'll get the stuff." He disappeared through the door and Joe sat on the mattress, reclining Buddha-style on the cushions. Comfortable? He pulled himself up and tried to sit crosslegged, looking up to see Wilf standing in the doorway, smiling at him with a box in his arms.

"Now I know why those Yogis prefer to lie on a bed of nails."

Wilf laughed. "Man your trouble is you are so used to sitting on chairs that you've forgotten how to be comfortable. Don't forget Joe," he came and sat down beside him, "we are going to change the world, man. Ain't going to be no more chairs."

"I thought you had some concealed intention. Me, I want to inaugurate the new workers' republic of the world. You, you want to get rid of chairs."

"Like the man says Joe, the end justifies the means."

"So let's have a look at the means already."

The means were very simple, very ingenious. Very dangerous.

"This here little travelling clock is the timing mechanism. It's the smallest I can get it. It's in a normal clock that you can buy in any of the stores. It looks just like a travelling clock when it's folded up and it looks like a travelling clock when you open it out. But there's another fold out here," he demonstrated, folding the clock out flat, "that reveals this little socket. In there you just plug this." He held up a fountain pen. "Just a pen, man, just a pen. But you unscrew the bottom, not the top and you see this little plug, right?" Joe held out his hand but Wilf held the pen away from him. "Not so fast man, this is no ordinary fountain pen. This pen is not only mightier than the sword, it's mightier than a whole army. This pen is dangerous."

He held the end of the pen close to Joe's face so that he could see the two tiny metal prongs of the plug and gently, very gently, showed Joe how the plug fitted into the socket.

"That's it," he said.

"What's the other socket for?" Joe asked.

"Another pen," said Wilf. "You'll have to use your own judgement on that. One should be enough to blow that whole press booth to pieces, glass front and all. But if you really want to blow the whole Council Chamber to bits, use the second one as well."

He took another pen from the box, unscrewed the bottom, and plugged it into the second socket.

"Great," said Joe, holding out his hands, "now let me practice."

Wilf took the two 'pens' out of their sockets, screwed back the bottoms and laid them gently on the mattress. Then he folded up the travelling clock and placed it alongside the pens.

"It's all yours Joe," he said. "Oh, one point I forgot." He picked up one of the pens and unscrewed the top this time. "This end, it's just a pen." He held it up and turned it round, showing its shiny nib. "It's even got enough ink in it to write a few lines if anybody wants to check it."

"Fantastic." Joe picked up the clock, unfolded it out and gently plugged the pens in and took them out. Then he put everything back and repeated the operation twice.

"You're learning Joe," Wilf commented approvingly. "Now look at these." He reached into the box and took out another, identical, travelling clock and two more identical fountain pens.

"Like we agreed," he said. "Days one and two you go in with this clock in your briefcase and these pens in your top pocket. The two days will give us time to sort out any problems we haven't anticipated, and let the security people get used to you. If there's a security check tell those guys you broke your wristwatch and bought this in Macy's to tide you over till you got home. Thirty seven dollars fifty if they want to know. Make a big joke about it so they remember the clock. Day three you take in the real clock. This one. And the real pens. You set the alarm like this for the time you want, say a couple of hours after they've all gone home, plug in the pens and tape the whole thing to the underneath of your table. It's better than leaving it in your briefcase. Somebody could notice it and come running after you. The taping. That's the part you'll really need to practice. I got a little dummy here for you to try with." He took out of the box a third clock, this one with two pens already plugged in and taped to the case of the folded out travelling clock. "The secret is to get them all plugged in and taped together in the john or somewhere. Then it's easy with this stuff to tape them on to the underneath of a table or whatever you have there. Look."

In the palm of his hand he held a length of material from which he peeled off a muslin cover and then laid the back of the clock on the exposed surface. It stuck fast, leaving an area of material each side. Putting his hand under the low table he pressed each side upwards and, when he removed his hand the clock was firmly attached to the under-side of the table.

"Quick enough?" he asked.

"Fine," Joe replied.

For the next half hour Joe practiced, fitting the pens to the clock, sticking the clock to the table, timing himself, seeing how possible it was to plug the pens in and fix the tape on inside a briefcase which Wilf produced so that all he had to do was take his hand out of the briefcase which was on his lap and slip it under the table.

"There's only thing you've forgotten," said Joe.

"What's that?"

"In the Security Council they don't sit around on the floor. They have chairs."

The United Nations.

As the taxi stopped outside the great glass fronted building on the East River, with a gentle breeze rustling the flags of one hundred and fifty nations, Joe saw Gerry Rushton standing at the top of the steps waiting for him. He paid off the cab and turned to meet him coming down the steps.

He was a fat man, and although tall enough to compensate for it, each step seemed taken with some difficulty and a covering smile. A sporty trilby seemed over-casual for the immaculate lounge suit and the expensive brogues.

"Morning Gerry. Lovely day."

"Good morning old boy. Dead on time. The debate starts in half an hour and I've got everything arranged for you."

"Good man."

Rushton guided Joe through the swing doors and led him up to the Reception Desk.

"Mike," he said to the red faced, chubby man in uniform sitting behind the desk, "this is my colleague, the famous Mr. Joe Gold. You remember I was telling you about him just before. If you'd like to let the Press Office know he's here, they'll send your favourite girl friend down here to look after him and see he comes to no harm."

"Ah now Mr. Gold, do I believe everything this Englishman has been telling me about you?" It was said with a smile and a pair of blue-grey eyes that could be used as bullets when the ammunition ran out.

"Don't believe anything anybody tells you about me, especially an Englishman," Joe replied with an answering smile.

"Oh it's been only good he's been telling me about you."

"Then definitely don't believe it."

The banter over, the call made to the Press Office, they waited, Gerry pointing out the geography of the building, and some of the politicians and statesmen who were arriving and hurrying through the lobby, followed by anxious aides and eager abettors.

"Mr. Gold?"

Joe swung round to meet the dark brown eyes of a tall woman with jet black hair swept back from her face and gathered in a bun at the back of her head. Suntanned, as if back from a long holiday.

"Ah, Lupita." Rushton greeted her warmly and turned to Joe. "Joe this is Lupe Fernandez who will open all doors for you. This charming lady will now whisk you away to her mountain fastness where she will provide you with a magic piece of paper which all and sundry will look at in wonder and bow down to you and make obeisance. Is that not so, my dear?"

The dark brown eyes had been smiling into Joe's while all this was going on, widening a little with something that might have been an answer if Joe had only known the question. But now was not the time.

"I'm not so sure about the obeisance, but if you'll come up to the Press Office Mr. Gold we've got your Day Pass already made out for you and that will certainly open the door to the Security Council debate which, I understand, is what you want to hear."

Most people don't open their mouth when they smile. Lupe did and it made Joe feel good, walking alongside her into the lift. While they walked she explained how the pass system worked and how, because he was not a full-time UN correspondent he would require a new pass every day. However, it was just a formality. As his official accreditations had come through a week ago' both from his Editor and the British Embassy, it would just be a question of picking up the pass each day. She would have it ready for him. It was for three days wasn't it? Joe, in turn, explained how he would be meeting the six statesmen, two each day, for his interviews, and watching their public performances in the Security Council as the debate went on. And how he would be leaving on the third evening, probably before the vote was taken, in order to catch the plane back to London and complete his story in time for the big splash in Sunday's paper.

"What a pity you will be going back so soon," she said as she handed him the Press Pass, "I had hoped to have time to talk to you. I read your article on the Mexican painters and I would have liked to talk to you about it. Not many people know, or care as you do, about my country Mr. Gold."

"You are Mexican then?"

The eyes became impossibly wide.

"But of course. What then?"

"I thought, foolish of me . . . Fernandez . . . I thought Spanish."

"A bit Spanish, yes," she made a pendulum movement with her fingers, "but mostly Indian." Indian. Not suntanned. "But you should hurry now. Shall I take you upstairs?"

"Upstairs? Sure!"

"To the Security Council Press Gallery," she laughed, and led the way out of the Press Room, pointing out the door to the Members' Lounge and the Press Bar, accepting with a smile Joe's invitation to meet him there for a drink later, and introduced him to the Security Officers at the entrance to the Press Gallery of the Security Council Chamber. It was as they had anticipated. Polite. Informal. No briefcase check. Joe wondered momentarily if he should joke about the ticking in his briefcase and show them the travelling clock, but thought better of it. They're not fools. Just play the whole thing very cool. Don't draw attention to yourself unduly. Just smile at the gentleman and walk through the door, along the corridor, past the television booths, everybody fussing about with their bloody great cameras, who would notice a couple of fountain pens? There was Gerry at a desk, waving, making room for him. And there, down below through the glass windows that enclosed the Press Rooms were the faces he knew, sitting round the big horse shoe-shaped table, looking at their papers, leaning back to consult their experts, their white faces and fluttering papers like a wreath preparing itself for a funeral. The Council of the Gods. Making and breaking. The way *they* wanted it. All wearing their neat colourless uniform lounge suits. Except the Chinese who were still wearing their neat colourless Mao uniform, and the Arabs who were wearing token white head-dresses with their neat colourless lounge suits. Is this the way nations were united?

"Here comes the chairman," whispered Rushton, and the debate commenced.

On the morning of the third day Joe woke early in his hotel bed. No song of birds woke him. No sunlight penetrated the high walls of the courtyard outside his window. The only sign of life was the steady hum of the air-conditioner.

Lupe. Why the hell hadn't he asked her? She could be there beside him now, sleeping, lying on her back with all that black hair round her shoulders and those big balloons floating gently up and down on the tide of her breathing. Ayayay! You're slipping, boy. Ten years ago you'd have asked her on the first day and not thought about whether she'd say yes or no. Now you think what the hell would a young girl like that want with an *alte kvatchka* like me? And why can't I accept her for what she is, a charming intelligent person, and just spend a pleasant couple of hours talking to her? Do you have to sleep with every good looking girl? You should be so lucky! *Schmerel*, it's because of what she is that I want to love her. Every girl I don't think of that way. Just ninety percent of them. Get up Gold, you've got a big day ahead of you. Look out of the window at that great New York landscape. The backs of buildings crawling with fire escapes. Look in the mirror and see what she would have seen if she'd have come. Now you know you did the right thing. That bony nose rising from the jungle of a tarnished moustache and encroaching stubble, just like one of her ruined pyramids. *Yuch!* Lupe, my lovely, you don't know what you missed. That's what you missed. Down there hanging between my legs, soft and floppy as a day-old chick falling out of its nest. Ah, but it's wonderful what a bit of soap and water will do. And like the sailor said, it's better than fucking because you meet a much nicer class of people! Which is more than you can say about the waiters in this place. Everything slung on to the tray. Paper bags of sugar, plastic jars of Shmuckers famous jams, paper napkins and yesterday's tray-cloth. It must be yesterday's. There was a stain there already and he hadn't even poured his coffee. But there was a little paper flag stuck in the middle of his grapefruit. *Oh say can you see by the dawn's early light* ... And the papers. Stained, too, with yesterday's news. 'ISRAEL SAYS NO!' How big that little man looks dressed in two-inch deep headlines. When I spoke to him yesterday he showed me the concentration camp number tattooed on his arm, but that was no longer news. For years, he told me, Hitler and his maniacs tried to find a perfect way to kill and dispose of millions of bodies. Gas ovens, lime pits, mobile death trains. Now they've found a way. He smiled with that two thousand-year-old Jewish smile. They will just drive us into the sea. After him came the Russian delegate, demanding freedom in a voice so loud it could be heard all over the world except in the Lubianka prison. Today it would be the French and the Americans. And then the vote. Which was already known. The West would abstain. There would be no veto. Israel would be out. The question was what happens next? Among all the big talkers nobody was talking about this. Except the packs of pencil-licking predators with hungry columns to fill, and advertisers to satisfy. With the scent of blood in their inflamed nostrils they scurried each day to their phone booths, each with their tasty morsels, like you Joe, with your big splash for Sunday.

During the next hour Joe went through the morning's papers and checked his notes for the remaining two interviews. He planned to arrive deliberately late at the UN hoping to increase his chances of getting through quickly without a check. Before he left the hotel he checked the false 'travelling clock' and pens and locked them, with the tapes, in his case in the bottom of the wardrobe. He set the real clock, wound it up and put it on the table, piled the newspapers on to the waste-paper basket, stuck the paper flagon top and walked out.

Thank God for these interviews, he thought as the taxi sidled into the traffic. They'll take up every minute of my time today. No chance to think. To change my mind. To regret. To calculate. Like the vote this afternoon, it's all decided. It's as good as done.

No going back.

Not that the interviews gave him any inclination to go back. At the Saudi Embassy spirits were high. Big smiles and little cups of coffee. Much oil would be poured on troubled waters, and at all those dollars a barrel that was a good reason for smiling. No, they were not afraid of Jewish terrorism. The United Nations would now pass the necessary resolutions and take the necessary actions on an international scale to prevent any more terrorism. Why hadn't they done it before? Ah, before, Mr. Gold, there were no terrorists, only guerrillas, as you know very well. The British, too, when he met them for lunch in a small private room at the back of a very expensive restaurant off Madison Avenue, were in a good mood. After all, Mr. Gold, you will remember that the people who are now in power in Israel were the very people who were busy killing British soldiers at the time of the Mandate. Patience, Mr. Gold, patience. That's what one needs in politics. It's all coming right in the end. Now the Americans have ditched the Jews, sorry, Israelis, that whole Middle East situation will roll back on the Russians. Oh, yes. The Americans will announce that this afternoon. Mark my words. It's all agreed. Poor old Gromyko. I'm sorry for him in a way. Nice chap really. Now he was a man with patience Mr. Gold. Twenty years work down the drain. Ah well, here's to the next twenty years. Cheers! I say old man, look at the time. Must get back for the debate. Got all you want? Anything else you need, just give me a tinkle. Glad to help. Look forward to reading all about it eh? Good man.

Joe wondered about these people on the way back to his hotel. They know I am a Jew, of sorts. They know I'm not a Zionist from my articles. They know my politics. And yet they see me, talk to me, even explain their philosophy to me. They love to see themselves in print. Even the biggest of them can't resist talking to the big splash on Sunday.

Back in his hotel room Joe moved quickly. The watch in the briefcase. The pens in his top pocket. Wrist watch off. Tape in the briefcase already cut to size, with lots of paper, notes, press cuttings. Tools of the trade. Down in the lift, one hand raised to touch the clips of the pens. Don't be daft. Smile at the Bell Captain. What a glorious title. *Oh captain, my captain, my fearful trip is done.* Well, almost done. What could be more fearful than this ride in a New York taxi? The driver's name next to his little photo is Abe Steig and if it hadn't been for the bloody Romans he and I would be sunning ourselves on Tel

Aviv beach right now. *Ayayay*.

Up the steps and into that great entrance lobby once more, across the marble chessboard to the desk. Hi Mike! Hallo there Mr. Gold. You're late today. Indeed I am Mike, my last day, so much to do, can you . . . Already done Mr. Gold as soon as I saw you come in. She's on her way down. Sorry to see you go Mr. Gold. Will you be coming back? Who knows, Mike, who knows? Maybe some day but I'm sure I can leave the United Nations in your capable hands. Ah here she is, thank you Mike, bye now.

Lupe, Lupita. Why can't I say something to you now, before it's too late, before the wheel turns, the clock goes off, the world stops? You're coming towards me smiling like the Indian girl Malinche came to the Spaniard Cortes. And I'm going to fuck up your people like Cortes fucked up Montezama. But he at least had your beautiful Malinche. And he raped Mexico too. All I've got is your smile.

"Joe, I was worried, you're late."

"I know, I know. That last interview took longer than I thought and I had to go back to the hotel. Have they started?"

"Just. But it's the French first. Then the Americans. You haven't missed much. I've got your pass ready."

They talked as they walked. His hand on her arm.

"I didn't upset you last night did I?" She looked at him anxiously as she spoke.

"Upset me? Of course not. Why?"

"Oh I thought you looked a bit down. And you went off . . . well, a bit abruptly . . . I thought perhaps you were annoyed with me because of what I said about the Jews . . . and the Mexicans."

"Annoyed? Christ no. You were absolutely right . . ."

She had been right. The Jews were massacred in their millions by the Germans. But the Jews aren't the only ones. Her own people had been slaughtered, enslaved and tortured by Spanish conquistadors with the blessings of the church. They had been robbed of their lands, their cities had been destroyed, alien cathedrals built on the ruins of their great temples just as mosques and churches now stood on the ruins of the Jewish temple in Jerusalem. The whole history of mankind is the story of man's inhumanity to man, whole nations had been wiped out, people sacrificed on the altar of this or that religion. The Aztecs had been doing it to others for years before the Spaniards ever got there. That's what the United Nations was all about wasn't it?

". . . no I wasn't down. Well, yes, I was. Look Lupita I can't tell you now. There isn't time. And when I come out I've got to rush for the plane as you know. I want to talk, and talk. Last night was only a

344

beginning. I'll come back soon . . ."

Liar. You know bloody well you won't be back. And she knows I won't be back from the way she's looking at me. Why don't you tell her? You've got time. It's only the bloody French and nothing they say is going to make any difference. Nothing any of them say is going to change anything now. Why not just go in, tape the clock under the desk and then take her back to the hotel. Take her! What are you talking about? Who says she's interested in you? So she's smiling at you. She works in the Press Office. She smiles at everybody. Last night? Gold, stop kidding yourself. You're a famous correspondent, an interesting man maybe, but be your age, put your geriatric gerry back in its truss and carry on with your job. You've got a whole world to destroy!

The lift stopped and they walked quickly along to the entrance to the Press Gallery, and up to the Security Desk. Would they just pass him through the way they had every day so far? The Security Officer looked up in surprise as they approached him. Joe put his briefcase down on the desk and took one of the 'pens' out of his top pocket.

"Look Lupita," he said, taking out a pad from the briefcase, "you never know, you may come to London one day, here's my address and phone number. Look me up, eh?"

Let's hope that bloody pen works. Enough ink for a couple of lines Wilf had said. It worked. He tore the top sheet off the pad and gave it to her, leaving the pad on the open briefcase.

"Thanks Joe," she gave him that big sun-burned smile, and held out a hand for him to shake. All pals together. He smiled and shook her hand.

"Have a good trip back."

"Thanks. And thanks for all your help. Don't forget to look me up."

"I won't." She turned and walked away.

Joe turned back to the Security man and winked at him.

"Nice girl," he said.

"Sure is Mr. Gold. You're a bit late today."

"Ah well, it's my last day and I wanted to say goodbye properly didn't I?" He clipped the 'pen' back in his pocket and put the pad back in his briefcase. "I can always read what *they* say in the papers can't I?"

"You sure can Mr. Gold. Your pass?"

Christ! She didn't take it back with her did she? A frantic fumble in his pocket produced the magic piece of paper. O.K., Mr. Gold, have a good trip back, and he was through, into the Press Gallery, past all those expensive pieces of television equipment that would soon be in ten thousand tiny pieces, to Gerry's anxious face. Joe, I wondered what had happened as you're late and all that. Never mind Gerry, old boy, it'll soon be over.

Down there, through the glass, the rulers of the world were busy ruling, aware that everybody was going to be reading their prepared speeches, which outlined their prepared positions on the situation they had been so carefully preparing ... yet unaware that every decision they took prepared the ground for somebody, somewhere to say no. No more. No longer. And those voices would be heard, not in this handsome chamber with its great mural painting and everybody sitting round with ear-phones listening to translations and television cameras peering through glass walls like anxious sharks.

Their voices will be heard, Joe thought, in quiet whispers and concealed messages, through silent machines and empty dockyards, through trains rusting in the sidings and planes folding their wings in hangars. Through hands raised to vote and fists raised to fight. There are people hiding in the mountains somewhere with something to say, people in caves in the desert, people drawing aside curtains in upstairs rooms to look down into city streets, people waiting their turn, people fitting fountain pens into travelling clocks and taping them to the underneath of desks.

He had already set the clock for midnight. It was now five o'clock and the American delegate, the last to speak, had just risen. He would take about an hour the press had been informed and then the translations would follow and then it was expected that the vote would be taken about seven. Allowing for interruptions, last-minute excitements, it should all be over by seven-thirty, eight o'clock latest. By nine o'clock the Council Chamber would be deserted. By that time he would be on his plane and way out over the Atlantic. The cleaners don't come in until early in the morning so there was no chance of anybody being around when it went off. It would have to be both pens. He had told Wilf about the plate glass booths and he estimated that one pen would have completely destroyed the Press Gallery and a small area of the Council Chamber in its immediate vicinity but that would have made it clear that the explosive had been planted in the Press booths and would have pointed the finger at him too clearly. Both pens together would destroy the whole Chamber and probably bring a great deal of structure down. It was possible an investigation would locate the approximate centre of the explosion, but that would take time, and so much more of the evidence would be destroyed that it would be more difficult to establish anything with certainty. It was a chance, but it had to be taken, and carefully, one after the other, Joe took the pens out of his top pocket and put them into his briefcase which was resting on his lap and, each in turn, unscrewed the bottom caps and plugged the delicate prongs into their sockets. Appearing to be searching the papers in his briefcase, he slid the muslin off the tape and stuck the clock to the tape. Then he sat back with one hand still in the briefcase, the other on the desk. Leaning forward slowly so that the briefcase on his knees went right under the desk and his body pressed close to the desk hiding the movement of his hand, he quickly moved the taped clock out of the case and pressed the tape to the underside of the desk. He knew it would stick because he had tried it yesterday in a 'dry run' with the ordinary clock. Yet he was afraid to remove his hand. Don't be mad Gold, leave it. It'll be O.K. Closing his eyes, he removed his hand and laid it on top of the desk for a moment. He looked around. Gerry and the other pressmen were engrossed in the words of the American delegate expressing for the first time his country's decision to support the Arab resolution.

A drop of liquid fell on to the desk and Joe realised that his brow was covered with sweat. He pulled out a handkerchief and wiped the perspiration away. Gerry looked at him and looked back at the Chamber. Joe took the pad out of his briefcase, put the case beside him on the floor and started to make notes. Got to show interest, play the game. Irresistibly his hand sought the tape again. It was sticking firm. No problem. Make notes, listen to the speech ... "and so, distinguished delegates will understand ..." Yes, they understand. A new alignment was taking place in the Middle East, born out of the Kissinger mission in the mid-seventies when Egypt was bribed out of the Soviet orbit and the West realised that the price of Arab support for the destruction of the Soviet spearhead into Africa was the destruction of Israel. It also meant the destruction of the Arab militant left but this was something that both the West and the Saudis were equally happy about. They had served their purpose. Now they would be crushed and, in a short sharp war of annihilation the Jews would be pushed into the sea. Without American military support they would not last a week. With a UN resolution against them nobody would come to their aid and it would all happen too quickly for the Russians to jump in. They could see the way things were going but this time they would be caught on the hop. A cease-fire could be arranged before they had a chance to intervene and after the Arabs had achieved their objectives. Official protests, regrets and resolutions would be forthcoming but a *fait accompli* had never yet been reversed by the United Nations. Hungary, Chile, Angola, Uganda ... What's done is done. That's one thing the nations were united about as the distinguished delegates simply wiped the blood off their hands and went on to consider the next item on the Agenda. Oh, the distinguished delegates understood well what they were doing. But did the rest of the world? It was odd, Joe thought, the way people thought of the United Nations as an almost independent body, a forum of world opinion that was somehow above power politics, in which the nations of the world were in some mysterious way busily working away for world peace. Whereas, in fact, it was a vehicle which the super powers and other power blocs were using to impose their will on other less powerful peoples. They would do this anyway, but here, by making speeches and passing resolutions they covered their actions with a cloak of legality. Joe saw his article taking shape, the facts assembling themselves on the other side of the glass, and he was sickened by the nation he knew to be responsible for the murder of thousands in Chile now uttering the same platitudes about peace and international morality as had been voiced the previous day by the nation responsible for the murders of thousands in Hungary. It was macabre.

Maybe he would be able to express something of his feeling in the paper on Sunday.

If the Editor would wear it.

But editor or no editor, delegates or no delegates, nations or no nations, the world would hear his voice at midnight.

He felt underneath the table again and the tape was firm and smooth against the desk. It was done. He had finished what he came to do and now he could go.

He sat back and closed his eyes. He was empty. Exhausted. The American voice went on and on and suddenly it stopped. He had finished. Now there would be translations into the other official languages and the vote would be taken. He had already explained to Gerry that this was the time he would leave so that he could catch his plane to London, and had arranged to talk to him over the phone next day to pick up any other bits and pieces that might occur after he left. Gerry would be sending over his own coverage of the debate which would be the page one story. His "splash" would be inside, right across the middle pages, giving the interpretation of the events and looking into their meaning for the future.

The future. He smiled as he shook Gerry's hand and thought how the event just a few hours in the future was going to affect Gerry's page one story.

Waving to the other correspondents he had come to know in the last three days Joe made his way along the corridor, past the television booths and the security desk, down to the great lobby and out into the plaza. He thought for a moment of Lupe as he walked through the lobby and took a last look at the mural painting. That girl up there in the painting had her hair done in the same style as Lupe, jet black and drawn back tightly into a bun. Her shoulders were bare and he wondered about Lupe's shoulders and whether the painting would be damaged.

It was late afternoon and the rush hour traffic was building up. He had allowed for that, too, and now he sat back in the taxi, relaxed and easy, with a feeling of accomplishment and superiority as he watched the cars and taxis jostling each other to cross the junction as the lights changed. *Walk. Don't walk.* The peremptory instructions to pedestrians amused Joe. Typical. Walk. Don't walk. Live. Don't live.

In his room all was as he had left it except the bed was made and the wastepaper basket emptied. He packed his few things quickly and looked around, a sudden chill in his stomach. He sat down on the bed, feeling faint, and went through everything in his mind. The real travelling clock was in his case now, the real pens in his pocket, his watch back on his wrist.

The phone rang.

It was Wilf.

"Everything O.K.?"

"Fine."

"Time as agreed?'

"Right."

"You off now?"

"In a few minutes."

"Have a good trip."

"Thanks. See you."

"See you man."

The traffic on the way to the Airport was even more crowded but at least it had the advantage of keeping the taxi driver busy and after nearly an hour of hearing solid cursing in Polish and Bronx, Joe stood at the check-out desk with his ticket and passport and that same chill in his stomach. Something *could* have gone wrong. This is where they would be waiting for him. But they weren't. Picking up copies of *Time* and *Newsweek* Joe looked up to see, across the other side of the bookshop, a woman who reminded him of Zee, with her neat woollen suit and silk blouse. He went into the Duty Free Shop and looked for *Je Reviens*. It was years since he had bought her any perfume and the big bulge in his briefcase made him feel better. It was a connection maybe with another world. With people who got up in the morning and had their breakfast and read their newspapers and went to work. People who drank cups of tea, watched the telly frequently and made love occasionally.

The plane was being called.

He walked with others along endless corridors, remembering those far-off days when you didn't have to walk half-way to your destination before you reached the plane. Progress. As he took his seat he looked at his watch and thought that they would have taken the vote by now. Yes, he'd have a whiskey. Mad. He didn't even like whiskey but it might calm him down, get rid of that heavy weight on his stomach. That wouldn't help, plastic chicken garnished by little green plastic balls and warm brown finger-lickin' grease. No thanks, no earphones. But a film. A new John Wayne looking so like a very old John Wayne that you looked for the face of Richard Nixon among the bunch of crooks that propped up the bar of the seedy Mexican saloon. Ah, Lupe should be here now, alongside me instead of this fat slob snoring his way across the Atlantic.

Ten-thirty. Another whiskey please miss. He was feeling better now. Sleepy. It had been a long day. Outside there in the darkness the world was carrying on with whatever it thought was important. Up here the lights were dimmed and John Wayne had been put back in his can. A uniformed girl walked quietly up the gangway looking with a motherly smile at the slumped bodies arranged in rows, heads awkwardly bent, ties undone, shoes kicked off, the cellular edges of airline blankets trailing on the floor. Joe's fingers relaxed and *Time* magazine fell into the gangway. The girl in the uniform bent down to pick it up, looked at Joe's sleeping face, and smiled to herself. She put the magazine on the open tray in front of Joe, taking away the empty whiskey glass.

It was five minutes to eleven.

Sleeping soundly for the first time in a week Joe did not hear the captain's voice over the intercom. If he heard anything through his sleep his subconscious told him not to bother. It was only one of those routine announcements about thousands of feet, hundreds of miles, slight turbulences and fastening seatbelts.

But it wasn't.

"Ladies and gentlemen," the voice said. "This is Captain Webster speaking. I am sorry to disturb you at this hour but we have just had some very important news over the radio which we felt you would want to hear. An Atomic Bomb has been exploded in Saudi Arabia. It is not clear yet who is responsible but reports coming in indicate that the Saudi Arabian oil fields have been completely destroyed. This follows a vote in the Security Council this evening giving overwhelming support for a Saudi Arabian resolution condemning the State of Israel and it is feared that the bomb may be a pre-emptive

350

strike by Israel setting off another Middle East conflict. The Security Council, which had just broken up after its three day debate has been recalled and is now in session. If we get further news ladies and gentlemen we will come back to you. We apologise once again if we have disturbed you but we felt you would want to have this important news. Thank you."

An hour later Joe woke up and looked at his watch. It was just gone twelve o'clock. It's all over, he thought, and went back to sleep.

He woke again to see a red line across the window and realised that it was dawn. He looked at his watch. One-thirty. He struggled back into the world through an aching back and a taste of stale whiskey, twisting his neck from side to side. It must be about half past six English time. Heathrow in about an hour. Lights were going on. Dishevelled passengers were beginning to queue outside the toilets. A child was crying down the other end. The fat slob had stopped snoring and was looking at him with red eyes.

"Did you hear the news?" he asked.

"What news?"

"Somebody dropped an Atomic Bomb on Saudi Arabia. About time I say." The red eyes closed again.

Joe pulled himself upright and leaned across to him. The chill was back in his stomach.

"When? How do you know?"

One red eye opened and looked at him through a morning mist.

"A few hours ago I suppose. The captain announced it. He got it off the radio. Good job too. Getting too big for their boots . . ."

A gentle chime interrupted him, followed by the voice of the captain.

"Good morning ladies and gentlemen, this is Captain Webster speaking. We are now making our approach to London Airport and I would ask you to fasten your seatbelts. We should be arriving on time at seven-fifteen local time and the weather is cloudy with slight drizzle. If you would like to adjust your watches it is now exactly six-forty-five local time. There has been a serious development in the United Nations where a bomb exploded in the Security Council Chamber while the Council was in session, especially recalled to discuss the Saudi Arabian crisis. We don't have any information about the damage done by this explosion but it is feared that a number of people, including members of the Security Council were killed and many more injured." There was a pause and the voice continued hesitantly. "The . . . er . . . temperature in London is ten degrees centigrade, that is fifty degrees fahrenheit. Thank you."

Joe closed his eyes so that he didn't have to talk to his neighbour.

He saw the huge mural painting with a great lightning crack through the naked shoulders of the girl with her black hair in a bun. Lupe. Gerry. The glass. The television cameras, and there below the well-known faces, the distinguished delegates in their indistinguishable suits. Mike, Lupe, Lupita. She must have been there. The press. Gerry, the poor silly bastard. Going down. Down. No good. No way. Wheels bumping, brakes screaming. Announcements in a girl's voice about London and passengers going on and immigration and thanks for flying with us and Lupe with that big sun-burned smile. "Have a good trip back." Maybe she hadn't been there. Gone home. Perhaps they hadn't been able to contact her. But Gerry, poor bastard, would have been there. Right there on that same desk, his big fat body bent over the desk, listening, writing, enjoying the whole bloody thing, knowing it was going to be the big page one story. Our United Nations correspondent . . . Gerry.

He opened his eyes to see them all crowding in the gangways, cameras round their necks, hanging cases over their shoulders, coats over their arms, tourists, travellers, people of the Bomb. Must go. Lupe. Perhaps I can phone. Nothing wrong with that. Only natural.

Bloody corridors. Overseas passports this way, UK and EEC that way. UK here. No questions. No waiting. Everything normal. Downstairs for baggage. Messages? G for Gold. Nothing. Aha, here it is coming along the ramp, round the corner, into his hand.

"Excuse me sir. Mr. Gold?"

Joe looked up at the two men dressed in grey raincoats. He had seen them upstairs as he waited in line with his passport.

"Yes. That's right." he said.

One of the men took a hand out of his raincoat and showed him a card with his photograph on it. Alongside were the words SPECIAL BRANCH and some other printed words.

"We'd like you to come with us please. We have a car waiting outside. I'll take your bag."

He felt a hand grasp the handle of his case and he released it. The briefcase, too, was slipped quietly out of his grasp.

"Your hand please sir."

"Eh?" He felt a cold metallic ring around his wrist.

"This way."

The first man moved off and he felt a sharp tugging at his wrist. He looked down at the chain that bound him to the man in front. He felt a push from behind.

"Come along. Get moving."

As they went through the gate marked 'Nothing to declare' he thought of Zee's perfume in his briefcase and smiled.